CROOKED WINGS

Crooked Wings

ISBN: 978-1-7363082-2-6 (hardcover)
           978-1-7363082-0-2 (paperback)
           978-1-7363082-1-9 (ebook)

Printed in the United States of America

CROOKED WINGS

A Novel

PART ONE
OF A TRILOGY

by

ALASTAIR SHARP

OTHER NOVELS

Spreading Wings (part two of the trilogy)
There's a Way
Devil Whisperer
Up from the Bottom
The Book of Consequences
Taking Care
Alone

For Khadija and for Lorie,
from
whose inspirational lives
this trilogy took flight.

Homage to the Conference of the Birds*

So full of hope the company
As we took flight.
So sure of the goal.
So long the journey.

Valleys crossed, innumerable,
Named and unnamed,
Known and unknowable.

The cynical crows, barking from barren cliffs
Derisive witnesses to our travail,
Crying «Why?»

Those of us with mighty wings, high on the wind,
Effortless and regal,
While we, the sparrows and the wrens
Desperate to keep up,
Furiously flapping till we founder in fatigue.
So many birds dropped from the sky
Along the way.

How inspiring the eagle,
How tenacious the martins
How wise the Hoopoe, spurring us on.

And at last we few, the remnants of our flock,
Ragged and deplete
Entering the realm of the King of the Birds
Only to hear, as if on the dying breath of the wind,
«There is no King of the Birds.
It is a myth.
Only this can you know:
That for which you have flown so far
Is and was
Always
And only
Inside you.»

* *Conference of the Birds* is a Persion poem by Farid al-din Attar, written in the twelfth century. This poem is my own and is not based on any particular translation.

BOOK ONE
DIASPORA

SHAAFIA

In Morocco, on Fridays, the markets in Casablanca are always packed. Dust and diesel fumes rise in the haze amid the shouts of vendors, the thin imperious bleats of motor scooter horns and the acrimonious complaints of rooftop crows. Donkeys bemoan their fate, harried women yell at their children from shadowed doorways and decrepit trucks with blue exhausts inch through the congestion. The little monkey jumps in a neat somersault when a dirham lands in the cup, then retires to sit in nervous anticipation, in his little red hat. Always in his cup just a single coin. His handler, with his white beard and white cap, appears to doze against the wall of the tea merchant's shop, but one eye is always open. Across the market the spice tables flaunt their little mountains of coloured granules and powders. The old narrow pedestrian bridge, crossing the railway line to the port, funnels the throngs into and out of the market in an endless flow. The ascent and the descent are packed with bodies going both ways, a moving mass of intent-laden humanity.

The girl, tiny for her age, clutched the hand of the dark-skinned woman and stayed close to her. Every Friday they would set out to buy the *ras al hanout* before evening prayers. A single dirham would buy a small handful and the little girl held the coin with great care in her other hand.

As they descended from the bridge, they passed the wide arched front of the mosque. People sat gossiping on the steps and others passed in and out, leaving and collecting their shoes. Suddenly out of the crowd spilling from the bridge, swept a very tall man in a simple long white robe. White wisps of hair blew back from the crown of his head and his dark skin was deeply lined, He wore no shoes and his wide feet dwarfed those of the little girl as he stood before her, blocking her way. He laid his hand on her head, his long fingers covering her scalp. She stood still as the crowd pushed and swelled around them. The weight of his hand seemed to hold her in its grip and she dared not look up at him. There was a scent in the air of something delicate, was it jasmine?

"In the nest, in the air", he said, speaking to her in the Berber of the south, "so many birds. Find the little bird with crooked wings. *Ham de lila*", and then the hand was lifted and she felt weightless and floating.

When she looked up, he was gone. "Dada", she whispered to her companion, "who was that man?"

The older woman squinted into the dusty throng and shook her head. "I cannot say. Perhaps he is a sharif", she said, with her thick sub-Saharan accent.

"Yes", said the girl. "That's what he was." She strained to see if she could still see him, but the crowd was too thick. The scent was still there.

"It is a holy thing he has told you." said the older woman. "He has given you *baraka*. It is a blessing".

Diving into the throng of the market to purchase the little mound of pungent spice, the little girl could not forget the weight of the hand on her head. She looked and looked, hoping he would reappear in the swirling crowd. A sea of faces and bodies ebbed and swelled around her but he had gone.

When they reached the spice seller's stall, he greeted them as he did each Friday. "Ha! My best customer is here! What magic can I sell you today?" knowing of course that the single dirham would buy what it always bought. The girl shyly passed over her coin and watched the brown powder being poured into a cone of newspaper. She sang softly to herself "Crooked wings, crooked wings".

On their way back, carefully protecting her package from the pushing crowd, she repeated exactly what the holy man had said, not wanting to forget a single word. "So many birds. Find the little bird with crooked wings." She walked to the rhythm of it, the cone in one hand, Dada's wide calloused hand in the other.

When they reached the shade of the huge old fig tree, near their house, the older woman stopped to catch her breath. The little girl sat patiently, sitting on the gnarled roots. She looked high up into the branches and saw several swallows flitting from branch to branch. "Dada", she said. "What does it mean, crooked wings?" "Ah, Shaafia", sighed the older woman. "What do I know of such things? I am just a slave. You must ask your father. He will know."

In the courtyard of the house Shaafia found her mother sweeping the terrace with a straw broom. "*M'ui!*" she called, at last letting go of the dark-skinned woman's hand and running to her mother. "We saw a sharif and he put his hand on my head."

The woman rested her straw broom. "For you, I am happy", she said. "Every blessing adds to your treasure house."

At that moment one of her older sisters, Nayla, came out of the house. "Where is the *ras-al hanout?*" she demanded. "You get blessings but you don't do your duty!" The little girl held out the preciously guarded little package wrapped in its newspaper cone and said nothing.

Their mother turned on the older girl. "Shaafia knows her duty", she said. "More than some others in this family." The older girl snatched the little package and turned to go inside. Their mother shook her head and went back to sweeping.

Shaafia watched her sister and the words of the sharif sang in her head. "So many birds", and she shivered.

Then she shook her head and went into the house where another of her other older sisters, Afifa, was looking after Habib, the fourteenth child of the family and doted on by all of them. "Where is *Ba?*" she asked and felt the stab of disappointment when she heard that her father had already left with his older sons for the mosque and the beginning of evening prayers.

She wandered into the kitchen where her other sisters were cooking. It was her habit to retrieve the little pieces of newspaper that the spices were wrapped in so she could read whatever was printed on it. As a large and poor family, books were not a luxury they could afford and she adored reading. Nayla glared at her. "Nothing to read for you, you have had your blessing already", and she ostentatiously threw the scrap of paper into the cooking fire. Shaafia stared at her sister and felt her resentment rise but then from inside her, she heard the voice, "Find the little bird with crooked wings", and she smiled and turned away.

That evening when her father returned with his sons from the mosque, she waited for the moment when she could talk to him on her own. Finally as he took his glass of mint tea out onto the terrace, she came and sat by him.

"*Ba*", she said quietly.

He looked down at her with his quiet eyes. "Yes, my pigeon?"

"Today I was with Dada in the market. We saw a sharif. He put his hand on my head. There was the scent of jasmine. He spoke about birds. He told me I should find the bird with the crooked wings." She paused and watched his face. He looked off into the gathering evening, sipped his tea and nodded his head. "What is crooked wings?" she finally ventured.

His eyes came back to rest on her face. "Such a one as that will speak in mysteries. He has given you a quest", he said. "It is for you to find out." It was not often that she spoke with her father, but when she did, she paid close attention. There was no disappointment in receiving his answer but rather a little inner shudder of excitement. "Yes *Ba*", she said, "I will find it".

II

Long after the family had gone to bed, all the girls on their mats sleeping together in one room, Shaafia had a dream. She was in the middle of the ocean, and far off she could see an angular figure in silhouette and she knew it must be the bird with the crooked wings. She could not see it clearly and she strained and struggled to reach it. It did not seem like a bird; more like a…more like a…but she could not tell exactly what it was. The more she tried to reach it, the more she seemed to sink into the ocean and she began to drown. She called out to the bird "*Aat quoni, aat quoni*, save me, save me", and in so doing she awoke, with all her sisters sitting up on their mats in alarm around her.

Suddenly she felt her mouth fill with a foul taste and a grey oily mucous oozed from her lips. One of her sisters had lit a lamp and the others were calling frantically for their mother. When she saw what was happening, she took up a large terracotta jar and began pulling the mucous from her daughter's mouth with her fingers, muttering Koranic verses under her breath. The other girls shrank back as handful after handful of the foul liquid filled the jar. Her father stood in the doorway watching impassively.

Finally it eased and her mother washed Shaafia's face with fresh water and made her rinse out her mouth. "It is gone", she said and laid her daughter back on the mat. "Do not be afraid, my daughter, I will give you something."

While she was gone, the other sisters all moved their mats as far from Shaafia's as they could and Nayla sneered at her, saying, "You are cursed and God is punishing you".

Her mother came back into the room with some mint leaves and an old metal door key with a long shaft and a square end. "Chew the leaves and hold this key in your right hand", she said. "It will protect you from demons." For the rest of the night as the wad of mint cooled her mouth, Shaafia lay open-eyed clutching the key to her heart, terrified.

When the dawn came and the roosters called out their shrill *kok au yu*, all the girls rolled up their mats and kept well away from her. Shaafia stayed still on her mat when they had gone, holding the key against her forehead and praying to God for protection.

Finally she gathered her courage and went out into the morning sun. She saw Dada washing clothes and went up to squat beside her in the dirt. "Dada, I think that I am cursed", she whispered.

The older woman looked down at the tiny earnest face. "Do you think so?" she said. Tears ran down the child's face and the woman used the cloth she was washing to clear them. "You cannot think that you are cursed", she said. "You will see."

Shaafia showed her the key and the old slave found some string to tie the key round the child's neck. "There. You will see", she repeated. "You will see."

Shaafia spent the rest of the day by herself, as none of her older siblings would come near her. The younger ones played as always but even they sensed that there was something strange in the air.

When it came time for all the women to go to the *hamam* for their bath, she hung close to her mother while holding the hand of Adila, the sister just a year younger. Adila, named for her beauty at birth, was by far the most placid of all the sisters and was, of all them, the one Shaafia felt closest to. But even Adila, influenced by the others, had avoided Shaafia all day. Now as they walked to the bathhouse, she held Shaafia's hand and seemed at peace. She felt comforted by her sister's presence and protected by the key bumping gently against her chest with each step.

At the *hamam*, groups of women greeted each other with their girls in tow. Shaafia saw her friend Rachi, who waved to her, but the events of the past day had unnerved her and Shaafia stayed close to her mother. Once inside the entrance, her mother had the older girls collect the younger girls' clothes and wrap them in bundles that they would then hand to the attendant. Shaafia took off her clothes but held onto the key. Staying very close to her mother, she whispered, "Can I keep this with me?"

Her mother frowned for a moment, stroking her daughter's hair. "Yes, my child, keep it." Luckily, there was very little light inside the *hamam* so no one else noticed.

Her mother paid the attendant and they each received their portions of liquid soap and their wooden buckets, before moving to their habitual place in the coolest of the three rooms. The older girls filled the buckets with hot water, cleaned the area where they would all sit, and began to bathe, the older ones soaping the little ones. Little Habib was the only male present and Afifa was getting upset with him not sitting still enough to be properly soaped. Usually Shaafia would soap herself but her mother came over to her and gently bathed her daughter, lifting the key to lather her chest then laying it back. Nayla saw all this and said to her sisters, "Some girls can't even put on their own soap". But no one took much notice.

As her mother ran her soapy hands over her daughter's body she felt lumps on her daughter's skin and she bent down to look closely. Shaafia ran her hands over her arms and legs and felt the lumps.

"What is it?" she whispered.

"It is nothing", her mother said. When it came time for the scrubbing, the family shared the one rough glove, the older girls scrubbing themselves and then the little ones. Once again Shaafia's mother took care of her, using the glove unusually softly over the lumps of her skin. Normally the glove is used harshly and rolls of black dead skin peel off even the youngest child. "Go and rinse", her mother said and let her go.

Shaafia went over to the hottest of the rooms with her wooden bucket and dipped it into the hottest of the pools. Then taking a breath, she poured the scalding water over herself. The pain of it was immediate and terrifying, but somehow she knew that she had to do this and she bore it without making a sound. Finally, the water drained from her naked body and she stood very still, the key hot against her sternum.

When she opened her eyes, Nayla was standing in front of her. Although it was very dark and full of steam, Shaafia caught the look of hatred in her sister's eyes and shrank back. Nayla turned and was gone. A tremor of fear shook Shaafia's naked wet body. She ran her hands over her body, normally so soft and smooth, and felt the lumps. "It is a curse", she whispered. She closed her eyes and for a moment she could see the tall man who had placed his long fingers across her head near the mosque. Once again she felt the weight of the hand and its breadth covering her scalp. "Help me", she prayed.

Outside she dressed herself quickly so that no one would notice, but she saw Nayla talking nastily to her sisters and knew what was being said. They walked apart from her, even Adila, and Shaafia felt alone.

III

For the rest of the day, Shaafia kept to herself. When night came, she put down her mat in a corner before the other girls came in and turned her face to the wall. She lay still but slept little, holding the key to herself and praying, sometimes to God, sometimes to the sharif.

The next morning although she dreaded the thought of what her siblings would say to their friends, she prepared for school. She, more than any one else in her family, loved school. All the others in her family of school age attended school. This was unusual for a family like hers, as in most poor families the girls were kept at home and received no formal education. What had happened in her family was that at the birth of the first child, Shaafia's eldest sister, a holy man had been invited to perform the naming ceremony He had looked at the child and said that she should be called Zarifa, the intelligent one, and that she and all her sisters should go to school. In that way, he said, they would each be always independent and able to care for themselves. This holy man had been the spiritual advisor to Shaafia's father since he was young, as the holy man's father had been to Shaafia's father's father. Although Shaafia's father had no education himself, nor had his wife, and neither could read or write, they were devout and followed the master's commands exactly.

Although it was a financial burden for the family, every child had been sent to school. The girls had proved to be the most adept and, of them all, it was Shaafia who had shone. She had a thirst for learning and a speed of comprehension that allowed her to take in whatever she was taught. In Moroccan schools the subjects are taught in Arabic in the morning and in French in the afternoon, and so she became tri-lingual, still speaking her native Berber at home. It was words and language that delighted her the most. She read whatever she could get her hands on and she would recite tracts of the French poems they were learning, having heard them only once. *"J'ai cueilli cette fleur pour toi sur la colline. . . Que l'aigle connait seule et seule peut approcher…"*.

But now, while the others went off to school, each in their hand-me-down patched-up uniforms, her mother told her that she should not go.

Though Shaafia's heart was torn, secretly she was relieved and for the next week she hid away in the shadows until the last of her brothers and sisters had left for school. Only when the last straggler had said goodbye to their mother would Shaafia appear.

When they were all gone, each day she would seek out Dada and stay with her. They would speak in whispers about the sharif and Shaafia would wonder if she would ever see him again. She had so many questions, which Dada she knew could not answer.

Dada had come to stay with the family just as Shaafia was born. The local midwives had found her wandering outside in the streets barely covered in rags and with no home. One of them had taken pity on her and suggested that the family could take her in to help with so many children. Dada had meekly accepted the offer, which came along with one simple but decent dress offered by one of the midwives to clothe her. The family had no way to pay her but she was given a corner of the kitchen to sleep in and she made herself indispensible to the running of the household.

At first she would not speak, lowering her eyes when anyone approached her and doing obediently whatever she was asked. However, as Shaafia grew and began to talk, little by little, Dada came out of herself, especially with the children, and very much so with Shaafia, who had been her companion all along. It was to her that Dada revealed where she had come from.

She was from a dark-skinned race of people from the Upper Niger. All she could remember was that her family had been victims of a long drought and that she and her younger brother had been sold as slaves when she was very young, maybe no more than four or five years old. She was not sure of the names of her parents or exactly where they were from, and she had no real memory of them. She didn't know if they had sold her or someone else had taken her. She spoke little about what her life was like as a slave but said that in her teens, she and her brother had escaped and had somehow managed to make their way across the Sahara to Morocco.

Dada would not say much of what she had suffered in that journey but as Shaafia grew older, she began to understand something of the terrible life Dada must have endured. Other than her sisters, Dada was the most important person in Shaafia's world.

Once Shaafia could read, she began to read aloud to Dada, especially when she was lucky enough to have a book from the school library. Dada spoke no French but she loved to hear Shaafia read in Arabic. They would sit in the shade of the fig tree when Dada's duties were done, often in the heat of the afternoon when everyone else was asleep. Dada would close her eyes, tip her head back against the thick, knotted trunk and rest her hands in her lap to listen.

Several days after she had been touched by the sharif, the lumps on Shaafia's arms and chest began to suppurate, breaking open and weeping white puss. Her siblings were even more horrified, and Nayla led them in pouring scorn on Shaafia for her misfortune. Her belief that she was cursed, that she was full of poison kept her in a state of continuous terror, but her mother patiently bathed her sores every day.

Then one day Shaafia awoke with such a swollen tongue that she could not speak or eat. When she tried to say something, her sisters and brothers hooted with laughter but they also stayed well away from her, taunting her that she had become crazy. Her mother's response was to take her to a healer. The family had much more faith in traditional healing than Western medicine, which they couldn't afford anyway.

The healer was a scrawny bent-over woman with wrinkled hands and a thin faraway voice. She lived in a windowless hut behind the halal butcher and her visitors sat on the earthen floor, all listening to what each one received. Her method was very simple and the same for each person. She kept a coal fire burning continually, over which sat a large skillet that would otherwise be used to fry *bachrir*, the fluffy pancakes enjoyed during Ramadan. In this frying pan was boiling water into which she would drop shavings of candle wax. As the wax melted, the person who needed healing would come forward so that the healer could hold up a candle to see their reflection in the water. Then she would read the shapes that appeared in the melting wax. Finally she would scoop out the wax and give it to the patient to take home and burn.

When it was Shaafia's turn, her mother pushed her forward as the old woman scooped out the wax for her previous client with a wooden ladle. The healer squinted up at Shaafia and told her to come close to the fire.

Shaafia could feel the heat of the coal and was painfully aware of other people sitting in the room behind her. While the water came back to the boil, the old woman ran her right hand down Shaafia's arms, where most of the lumps were, making a clucking sound. Then she threw in a handful of the wax shavings and ordered Shaafia even closer to the fire. For several minutes the healer seemed to have gone to sleep, then she tilted her head to one side.

Without resorting to the candle, she muttered "*Ham de lila*", praise be to God, and beckoned Shaafia's mother to come close. The old woman whispered into her mother's ear, so that no one else in the room would overhear. "From the inside comes the poison. It comes out. Beneficial. Beneficial. She heals herself."

Shaafia's mother was relieved to hear this but she asked, also in a whisper "What poison?"

The old woman began to sing softly to herself and to sway over the fire. "Inside", she said. "The poison of before, becomes the poison of today. It must come out."

Shaafia's terror, always close to the surface and threatening to make her cry out at any moment, seemed to reach out around her as if she were about to be swallowed up. She held her mother's key and called inside herself, *I am cursed. I am poisoned.*

"What is the remedy?" asked Shaafia's mother.

"I will give", the woman said. She went to a side table where wooden racks held rows of small bottles. She pulled some dry leaves from a bottle and then some brown chips that looked like bark. With a mortar and pestle, she ground these together and poured the powder into a cone of newspaper. The woman said "Make soup. She must drink this at sunrise and at sunset. It will fix everything."

She looked at Shaafia for a long moment, her sharp eyes seeming to push into the girl's soul, forcing her to lower her eyes and shiver. Surely this old woman could see her terror.

Finally the woman spoke. "I see there is something more." She straightened up her bent back and looked at the other people in the room: several old men, another woman with a baby in her arms and a boy with a withered arm. "No more today. Come tomorrow", she told them. "Out now. All out." She shooed them towards the door. She held her hand up to Shaafia and her mother. "Not you. You stay." They waited and watched as she scooped out the wax from the skillet and went into the back of her kitchen.

She came back with a small piece of lead about the size of a dirham. "She has a future to see", the healer said and dropped the lead into the boiling skillet.

"It will take time." Only once did she look directly at Shaafia. "Do not be frightened. We will drink tea", she said. She lifted a black kettle from the same fire and made a pot of mint tea. They waited in silence, the old woman occasionally speaking to the fire as if they were old friends. When the tea was made, she poured it into little rose-tinted glasses for her guests. With her swollen tongue Shaafia had trouble with the hot liquid. The old woman noticed and took the glass from her, pouring the tea from high up into another glass, to cool the hot liquid. This she did several times before she handed it back to the child.

They sat again in silence, drinking tea, while the fire spat and crackled. The old woman peered into the skillet every now and then to check if the lead was melting. Finally she pronounced her satisfaction and commanded Shaafia to come very close to the fire. The heat was intense and burned her legs, but she stood as close to the fire as she could. Then the old woman bent down and wafted Shaafia's dress up and down to make a breeze that fanned the fire and rippled the boiling water in the skillet. At last the healer bent very close to the skillet and peered into the steam.

"*Aaaah*", she said. "*Mmm*. That which is, it is not so easy. Difficult. That which will come, she must be strong. The poison within, it comes from the long past. It must come out. It is not so easy. Though now you have no tongue to speak, in the future you will speak. You will be the tongue for others to speak. But I tell you this my child, you will be strong. You are the one who can heal. You are Shaafia, the one who heals."

When she moved back to her side table, she picked up a battered leather-bound copy of the Koran. She looked at the child. "You read, do you not?" When Shaafia nodded, the woman held the book in her right hand and opened it by inserting her finger toward the beginning. She took up the candle and held it close to the book as she read, then smiled and nodded with satisfaction. She showed Shaafia the verse, the *Surath*. "You will read this verse every day at the time of evening prayers." Shaafia carefully read the verse and made sure she knew how to find it in her own family Koran.

Meanwhile the old woman had moved away from the fire to clear away the tea glasses, signalling that it was the end of her consultation. When her mother asked if she would say more about the poison—what was it, who would do that, why did it happen?— the old woman simply shook her head.

Her mother pulled several dirhams from the pocket of her long dress but the old woman held up her hand. "Not now", she said. "There will come a day when this child will have many dirhams. Then she will remember and she will go to the mosque for Eid il Fitr and she will give *zakat* and many will benefit. That is the way. This girl will not forget. I know her."

As they walked back to the house, Shaafia longed to ask her mother to explain what she had understood from the healer, but her mother seemed to be far away, withdrawn into herself.

Only for one moment did her mother stop and look down at her. "It is good that you read", she said, and that was all.

IV

When they arrived home, Shaafia hid herself away behind the fig tree and began to think of the verse that the healer had given her. The verse is from the section of the Koran called "The Heifer" and speaks of guarding against a time when souls will not be able to protect each other. It says that those who live in faith and perform righteous actions will be called Companions of the Garden. The verse was deeply mysterious to Shaafia but somehow it also seemed to be speaking to her innermost self. She loved to imagine herself in God's garden; there would be birds in the garden and among those birds she felt she would find the bird with crooked wings.

By the evening her tongue began to subside and she drank the healer's soup that her mother prepared and she found she could speak. At sunset, she sat with Dada by the well in the garden and whispered what had happened. Dada listened carefully and then, in the gesture of deep respect, she reached for the top of Shaafia's hand and kissed it.

"You will be a great person one day. A blessed person. One day." Shaafia looked up into the lined dark face of the old slave and saw that she had tears in her eyes.

Each day, when it was the time for evening prayers and her father had taken her brothers to the mosque, Shaafia sat quietly by herself by the well in the garden and read the verse. And every day she thought of the tall man, the sharif, and she thought of the bird with crooked wings. Often she thought she could smell the jasmine, as she read the verse, and often she imagined that hidden in its words she would find the secret to the bird with the crooked wings.

As the days went by, while her siblings kept their distance, Shaafia learned to recite the verse by heart and it began to repeat itself in her head on its own. It was as if the words had become her intimate friends and her guide. The lumps on her body gradually subsided and her tongue slowly went back to its normal size. Finally her mother told her she could go back to school and in most ways everything seemed to be as it had been before.

And then one of her sisters died.

There was no warning, no symptoms. In the kitchen one day, as she was helping with the food preparation, Adila cried out and fell to the floor unconscious. Shaafia was beside her, crouching by her head, as the other sisters screamed and their mother came running. She sent Zarifa for the healing woman, but Shaafia instantly knew that her beloved Adila was already gone.

Her face was pale and still, her breath a tiny trace of air that would not move a feather and Shaafia knew that the soul had already left the body. She looked up, while all around her the sisters panicked and shouted at each other, the healing woman arrived and her mother began to wail, and above all the terrible noise Shaafia heard the verse of the Koran being recited. It seemed to be Adila's voice.

She could hear it as if only she and Adila were present, as if they were protected from everything else that was screaming and whirling around them. In the midst of the turmoil, she saw the healing woman suddenly look at her and nod, then gesture for her to leave. Shaafia took herself out to the well and sat quietly on a stone. There, the verse began repeating itself inside her, sometimes as her own voice, sometimes as Adila's. There was a sweetness to it, a cadence of at once sadness and yet also harmony and beauty. She let herself melt into its embrace and was lost to everything else.

In the evening, when so many neighbours had come and so many people had been involved in making endless mint tea and organising the preparations for the burial, with the dust of the courtyard stirred by so many urgent feet coming and going and the air quivering with the voices of women weeping and wailing, Shaafia spoke to Adila inside herself. *I will not forget you*, she said and in that moment she knew that she had begun to become a new kind of person.

She felt herself to be apart, not so much cut off from her family but now discovering that she had a place inside herself where no one else could touch her. In this place she felt a great confidence that God was watching her, that Allah was her constant companion, and that her observation of everything else around her was like being at a circus, like seeing the man with the little monkey in the market place. She could look at it or not look. She could laugh or not laugh. She could choose to be afraid or not to be afraid. She could give a dirham or not. There was always a choice. And in this way, the death of her sister was the beginning of her new life.

In the years that followed, Shaafia never forgot the verse from the Koran and she never forgot her beloved Adila. In her deepest inner secret world, where she remembered the sharif and the image of the bird with the crooked wings, they were alive and they seemed like pillars in a sacred shrine that only she knew. In this way she moved steadily forward.

Her family seemed to experience one difficulty after another. Her oldest brother Ayman lost the job he had finally found. Another brother, Ihab was arrested for having drugs and it looked like he might go to prison. Yet another brother Samit was caught drinking alcohol. Her mother gave birth to no more children and seemed to slowly shrink down into herself. Sometimes Shaafia would see her praying in a corner and always she would hear her muttered words "Why is my family cursed?"

Shaafia went on to high school, and more and more of her focus went into her studies. There she was free from the heavy constraints of the family and there she could begin to revel in her delight at learning. She and her friend Rachi were good students and they challenged each other. When one discovered something new, the other would strive to know it too. They were thirsty to know about everything and their enthusiasm had their teachers pushing them along. More and more Shaafia delighted in her prowess, the facility of her mind as it grappled with challenging ideas and the excitement she felt as she explored the unknown.

At the same time she was diligent in her spiritual practices. She prayed every day. She would pray for Adila and she would recite the verse. And despite whatever may have been swirling around her, she had an inner quiet place that was her oasis, her haven, and no one could touch her there.

V

As Shaafia's two oldest sisters, Zarifa and Afifa, married, they left the family home but none of her brothers had done so. They seemed to be a lethargic group of young men, clinging to the family house and showing no ambition or desire to find work or begin a career. Her father never slackened in his religious duty, going to the mosque every evening for prayer, but his sons no longer went with him. Instead they would sit around, some of them now openly smoking in front of their parents and going off into the neighbourhood and returning, agitated and bleary-eyed.

Nayla, the third sister, found a good job in a bank and, as soon as she could, rented a separate apartment for herself. She had sneered at the males in her family and accused them of being without any male pride. They glowered at her but had no way to counter what she said. It was not usual for a young woman to rent an apartment by herself until she was married, but Nayla was a force unto herself and went her own way. Nayla had a power to her that no one was prepared to push against. Her mother had protested mildly but did not prevent her headstrong daughter either from tormenting her brothers or from moving from the family home. It was almost a relief when she was gone, but the family had been deeply troubled by the stir she caused. And always it seemed that Nayla kept her bitterest scorn for Shaafia.

Their mother had become quite ill, having experienced so many pregnancies and given birth to many children of whom thirteen had survived. She became more and more indrawn and depressed, now openly grieving in her belief that her family had been cursed. The death of Adila had been the beginning, and their mother kept asking "Where is the benevolent angel who should be guarding my family?"

Their father said nothing, but continued with his business and his focus on God with stoic persistence.

Nayla would return to the family home every Friday and supervise the preparation of the evening meal. Since she had left, she had become even more forceful, yelling at her younger sisters and abusing her brothers. Fridays became a nightmare for them all, but otherwise she was not around the family at all. This was a relief for Shaafia, who continued to be the most frequent target for her older sister's unending vitriol.

Although their father was unwavering in his faith and utterly dedicated to his religious discipline, his tea business struggled to make enough to support such a large family. The family went through a period of real anguish and desperation. Often there was little for them all to eat and the husbands of the two married sisters did not look kindly on providing help. The head of the family steadfastly continued with his devotion and his business, but he became thinner and more frail as he carried the burden of his family's misfortunes.

Despite her family's troubles, as she matured into a young woman, Shaafia discovered the joys of languages and her own facility with them. As well as Arabic and the French that was used for all subjects at school, she also began to learn English. Of everyone in her family, she was the most adept student and was always top in her language classes. Although their home was chaotic and in turmoil, Shaafia buried herself in her studies and in that way kept herself, if not happy, at least focused. It deeply troubled her that her family seemed to be always beset by misfortune, but she sensed that the only way she could help was by being the best student she could be.

Her favourite teacher, her French teacher, was Madame Clae who had come from France as a young woman and had married a Moroccan businessman much older than herself. She had converted to Islam but was not able to have children. Her husband divorced her, but by then she loved Casablanca so much she had stayed and eked out a humble existence as a teacher. Shaafia and Rachi were her pet students and Madame Clae encouraged them to think about going on to study after high school. No one in Shaafia's family had ever done that, not even Nayla.

Sometimes Madame Clae would invite Shaafia and Rachi to tea in her shabby little apartment down a narrow alley full of chickens and laundry, not far from the high school. Sad though she found the humble home of her teacher, Shaafia was delighted by her shelves of books in French, Arabic and English. She would hold a treasured book in her hand and enjoy the feel, the weight, the scent of it. Madame Clae would tell the girls stories of her youth in France, her student days in Bordeaux, showing them the now well-fingered photos in her album.

As Shaafia and Rachi neared the end of their final year of high school, Madame Clae helped them submit applications for study abroad. The two girls spent hours talking about their futures. The idea of going to school in France was terrifying for Shaafia, but at the same time she felt that perhaps she had to go far away from her troubled family. And, secretly, always there was the desire to find the bird with the crooked wings. She had never forgotten that. Perhaps France was where the sharif's prophecy for her would happen. In any event, Madame Clae's unbridled enthusiasm carried the girls along. There were people the teacher still had contact with in Bordeaux, and she spent quite some time and effort contacting people she knew, clearing the way for her protegés.

In all this, Shaafia felt the need to keep her dreams to herself. She had told no one in her family about her hopes for more education. Rachi's family were as traditional as Shaafia's, and she too told no one what she was aspiring for. They both gave Madame Clae's address as their own in their applications. When the two letters from Bordeaux University arrived on the same day, it was Madame Clae who received them. The two letters sat on the shelf where Madame Clae kept all her precious little treasures and when the girls came to see her, Madame Clae could not contain her excitement.

"*Oh mes cheries*", she exclaimed. She always spoke French with Shaafia. "Such good news for you, *toutes les deux, j'en suis sûr*".

Shaafia's fingers were trembling as she opened the envelope. Rachi held hers nervously unopened as if she dared not think of what it may contain. She watched Shaafia carefully read the letter and then wordlessly pass it to her teacher. She had not only been accepted but was being offered a scholarship with a small stipend. The enormity of it struck her as she watched her teacher reading, and they both saw tears in each other's eyes. "It will be wonderful for you", said Madame Clae and she impulsively pulled the shy girl into her arms and hugged her. "I give you all my blessings. May Allah protect you and guide you."

Shaafia struggled to find some way of thanking her teacher but words seemed completely inadequate. She let herself be held in the embrace but eventually gently pulled herself back. "*Merci Madame, merci infiniment.*"

And then Rachi finally found the courage to open hers and it was the same. They hugged each other and began to imagine how their lives would be, studying together in a new country.

For several days the girls met secretly and talked over and over about their news. The most challenging for both would be telling their families. They agreed they would do it on the same day.

It was with trepidation and great excitement that Shaafia carried the letter home on the day she would announce her news. She first approached her father and solemnly told him what she had been offered. He looked at her earnestly for a long moment. "To this family you bring great honour", he said and he hugged her. He had never been a demonstrative man and to find herself held in his arms was for Shaafia to be cradled in a way she had always yearned for. It touched her deeply and she promised him to be a good student and to always make him proud of her. When she told him that Rachi had been accepted too, he was pleased. "You will both go to France. You will be great students. You will be a great student."

Most of the family were very proud of her too and shared in her joy. She sensed, however, that not all of them did. Several of her brothers were obviously resentful and envious and, of course, Nayla was not pleased at all and accused her of running away from the family when they needed everyone to help. Nonetheless, Shaafia knew that she had to go.

At the end of the day she and Rachi met by the fig tree. Rachi was distraught. Her family had not been happy at all, and her father had been furious that she had not consulted him before she applied. She was forbidden to go. Even worse, her father threatened to have her married as soon as possible. She was to have no choice. The girls cried together as their plans dissolved. Shaafia wondered if perhaps her own father could speak to Rachi's, but Rachi knew her case was beyond hope.

For Shaafia the idea of going alone, without Rachi, was terrifying and she began to wonder if she could dare do this. Rachi made her promise that she must. At least one of them should succeed, she said.

As Shaafia contemplated the challenges that faced her, she felt another sadness. Dada, who had always believed in her, had not lived long enough to see her triumph. When it was apparent that Shaafia's mother would no longer bear children, Dada had left the family and reunited with her brother, her only relative. He had found work in a small chemical factory outside Casablanca and so he could take her in.

Shaafia wept as she parted with Dada but was also happy to know that she would now have a home of her own, as she was growing noticeably less robust as she aged. Not long after Dada left, however, the family heard that her brother had taken a wife and thrown his sister out of his little house. Homeless, Dada had died in the street.

Shaafia grieved privately for her gentle guardian, and like her sister Adila, she vowed not to forget her. In her daily prayers, she always invoked the memory of her beloved servant. "One day", she promised Dada, "I will find the bird with the crooked wings. I will find it for you and for me. Then you will be at peace."

Grudgingly Rachi accepted the inevitable future but was full of encouragement for her friend. She talked of Shaafia's plans as if they were still her own and this gave Shaafia confidence.

When it came time to apply for Shaafia's passport, she went to the office with her father and her paternal uncle Samad. Neither of the men was comfortable in such surroundings and Shaafia did all the talking, and as neither of the men was literate, it was also she who filled in all the forms. The most difficult question was the matter of her birth date, of which there was no record at all. The government of Morocco did not keep birth records, and with such a large family and almost annual births, it was hard enough for parents, who didn't write, to keep track of each child's year of birth, much less the day. So they guessed at Shaafia's birthdate, using the day they applied for the passport and a random year that seemed vaguely right. It did not appear to be all that important and the official behind the desk was happy to have filled in the empty box. A few extra dirhams had helped him to feel at ease about it.

To pay for her airfare, she borrowed money from Zarifa's husband, Ahmed, who worked in a bank. Zarifa had had to fight hard to make this happen and the money was not given with much grace. It was only enough for the trip and Shaafia had no other money to establish herself in France. She would only receive her scholarship allowance once the academic year began. Still, she was grateful for the help, and she promised one day she would pay Ahmed back.

VI

On the morning she was to travel, Shaafia lay on her mat for the last time. She gazed around this room in which she had spent her entire life, her two younger sisters still asleep, and thanked it. The first rays of the sun painted a pink arc across the wall above her head. It is a sign of God's blessing she thought to herself.

The idea of getting on a plane for the first time in her life and travelling alone to a different country filled her with terror. She ate a little of the special breakfast her mother had prepared. Her younger sisters and little Habib watched as she did her best to honour the fresh bread her mother had baked, spread thickly with Amloh paste, crushed almonds with Argon oil, mixed with the rare luxury of honey.

Although tremors of foreboding threatened to ruin her breakfast, there was also a deep inner certainty that she had to do this. She willed herself to chew, to swallow and to smile. She drank her last mint tea in the house of her birth and passed the unused portions of her breakfast to her siblings.

Rachi had given her the name of a cousin who lived in Bordeaux, and Madame Clae had given her the names and addresses of some of her old friends. Shaafia made sure she had all the precious details in a tiny leather notebook given by Madame Clae. These would be her only contacts until she started her studies. To get the cheapest airfare, she had arranged to arrive several days before the student housing was available. At least, she told herself, with the contacts she had, she would not be completely alone.

When she walked from the house for the last time, carrying her small bag, held together with an orange scarf, the whole family was there. She embraced her brothers and her sisters, even Nayla, who hugged her and dropped a little bag of herbs into her pocket, saying it would help her to be safe. Her mother held her for a long time, praying that she would be in God's hands. The key that she had given Shaafia as child was in her hand, now hanging from a simple chain. "May God always keep you safe", she whispered and placed the chain around Shaafia's neck, now tied with a white ribbon.

Rachi was there, full of tears, and she held Shaafia as if perhaps she thought she would never see her again. "Write to me", she begged, "and tell me everything."

It was to her *Ba* that she came last. Her father embraced her and told her softly that he would pray for her every day in the mosque. He also gave her a small wallet of dirhams, what little he could manage. He told her that although it was not much, she could be certain that she would prosper, because every single dirham had been honestly earned. "You will come back to us and you will bring a good name to our family."

Ahmed was to drive Shaafia to the airport and as she turned towards his car, she paused by the fig tree. She closed her eyes and for a moment she stood very still. She spoke inwardly to Adila, to Dada and to the sharif "Now I will go to find the bird with the crooked wings. I know you are with me."

At the Casablanca airport, where burqa-clad women huddled in groups and dusty taxi drivers with anxious eyes held battered signs over their heads looking for lost passengers, Shaafia felt the sharp claws of fear tighten in her belly. She got through the crowd to the ticket counter with Zarifa pushing her. Shaafia held on tight to her small bag with its tatty corners and her ticket, reciting silently the verse from the Koran. She dreaded the moment when she would have go to the plane on her own. Her bag disappeared on a conveyer belt, Zarifa kissed her hands and blessed her and then came the moment when Shaafia stepped through the gate, showing her ticket and her new passport and walking across the hot apron to the waiting plane.

Sealed inside the plane's metal skin, she shrank down into the seat and closed her eyes. Here once again she called to those who inhabited her inner world: the sharif, Dada and Adila. "I am going to find the bird with the crooked wings. Please stay with me." The instructions from the flight attendants simply amplified her terror and she understood none of what was said. She pulled on her seatbelt as tight as she could and mostly kept her eyes closed. Nonetheless when the engines began to roar, she stared around her, certain that something terrible was happening. From her window she saw the men walk away from below the plane and it began to move. She heard the pilot announce they were cleared to take off and her heart pounded. The huge metal tube in which she sat shuddered and then raced across the ground and suddenly tilted up and away. When finally Shaafia had the courage to look out of the scratched round porthole once again, she caught a glimpse of the grey brown filthy air of the city of her birth, far below her, obscuring everything she used to know. "Goodbye!" she called silently inside herself. "Goodbye." Soon all there was, was the sea, remote, featureless and uncommunicative.

By the time the plane entered French airspace, in less than two hours, she had accepted a tepid cup of tea and a packet of salted peanuts and become a little more accustomed to the constant roar and the confined space. Beside her slept a sweaty businessman who had ostentatiously ignored her from the moment he strapped himself in. She had shyly said *"Bonjour"*, but she couldn't even tell whether or not he was a French speaker. He had taken possession of the central armrest and closed his eyes. The acrid masculine smell of him pushed her hard against the window.

When she felt the plane begin to descend, her stomach momentarily rising to her throat, the pilot announced first in Arabic then in French that they were approaching Bordeaux. She peered out of the window to catch her first glimpse of France. The plane banked sharply, forcing her against the window and she saw the clouds thinning out to reveal a countryside that was green and lush, where chateaux and vineyards, neat little villages and winding rivers promised a life very different from what she had known. She felt the frisson of anticipation in the pit of her stomach as the plane cruised low, west of the city of Bordeaux, and she saw the half-moon curve of the river Garonne. The plane dropped suddenly and hit the ground with a bump that took her breath away.

The hostess welcomed them all to France and Shaafia breathed out, realising that in some way she had held her breath ever since the plane had taken off. She waited till the businessman had gathered his laptop and moved down the aisle before she dared to begin her exit. She felt her mother's key against her chest, she fervently repeated her verse and she prayed that all would be well in her new country, then she filed out of the metal tube onto another continent.

Somehow she put one tremulous foot in front of the other as she followed the arriving passengers in search of their baggage. Her heart thumped in her chest and she put her hand up to the key again and again.

While she waited for her suitcase to appear on the carousel, she watched the bags of all different sizes and shapes, colours and styles that preceded it. Each one, as it bounced through the trapdoor, was like a book, she thought; the book of a person's life, it contained the stuff of their existence. She thought about what was in her own bag and she knew that it wasn't really her. If the bag didn't come…Well, it would not be the end of her life, would it! She owned nothing of value really. It made her feel less afraid to think like that, but when her bag finally did appear, she was pleased to see it. Shaafia lifted her humble suitcase, held together with its bright orange scarf, like she was greeting an old friend and she turned to begin her new life in France.

VII

Passing out into the high-ceilinged lobby, Shaafia saw various people waiting to greet the new arrivals. She wished someone would be there to greet her, but she knew she was on her own. In that moment she missed Rachi terribly.

She exchanged her dirhams and saw how few euros she received in return. She found the counter for the airport bus and was horrified to learn how much the fare was. It would take so much of what her father had given her. Was there another way to get to Centre Ville? The French woman at the information desk made little effort to disguise her contempt but gave Shaafia a local bus map and pointed vaguely in the direction of the bus stop.

She waited alone for more than half an hour, sitting nervously with her bag between her feet, before a bus appeared. The air was unnaturally cold and she pulled her thin Moroccan coat around her shoulders. With her hands deep in her pockets, she found the little package of herbs that Nayla had given her. She pulled it out and was about to inhale their scent when the bus drove up. She put the packet down beside her on the bus shelter seat.

The bus was empty and the driver immediately got out and locked the door. She nervously approached him and asked in French if this was the bus to downtown. At first the driver shook his head and began to walk away.

Then something made him stop and he turned back. "Where have you come from?" he said in Arabic. She was surprised and shyly told him. Then he smiled at her. "First time in France?" She nodded. "You wait in the bus." he said. "I will take care of you." He went back and unlocked the door.

She sat in the front behind the driver's seat with her bag beside her and repeated her Koranic verse. It was certainly warmer in the bus. Finally the driver came back and started the bus. "You have a ticket?" he asked. She shook her head. *"Ce n'est pas grave"*, he said, as the bus rounded the curve beyond the airport terminal. "First time is free." And he grinned at her looking up into the big mirror above his head. He seemed to be a good man. He was balding, with a round face and nice eyes. Somewhere in his forties perhaps.

After a while he said "Me, I am from Tunisia. I have been in France fifteen years. I have three children. Thanks be to God." He negotiated his way round a tiny slow-moving mini car and looked up at Shaafia again. "You will study here, in Bordeaux?"

She nodded shyly. She had to speak loudly over the noise of the bus. "I am going to learn to be a translator."

He nodded. "You will make your family proud."

The bus passed through various suburban streets and soon other passengers had appeared. To her horror Shaafia realised that she had left the little package of herbs from Nayla back at the bus shelter. "I am sorry, my sister", she said inwardly but recognised that it was not so important. «*Ce n'est pas grave*» she told herself.

The bus only went part of the way to the centre of Bordeaux, but the driver gave her clear instructions about how to catch the next bus and he also gave her a ticket. "May God take care of you, my daughter." he said before his bus drove away.

She waited with several other passengers to catch the connection and in another half an hour, she found herself in the large open tree-lined space called Quinconce. She stepped from the bus with her suitcase and looked up. In front of her towered a tall stone column on top of which a winged female figure, in weathered blue-green bronze seemed to be flying through the air carrying a broken chain in one hand and an olive branch in the other. Did she have crooked wings? Shaafia gazed up at the figure. There was nothing crooked about it all. It was huge and powerful, flying high above the stately buildings that surrounded it. On both sides of the marble surrounds at its foot were massive blue metal sculptures of what looked like seahorses or sea dragons leaping away from the base of the column with water fountains spewing from their nostrils into ponds. There were chubby sculpted babies and naked full-breasted women, giant fish and men with horns, all in the greeny-blue hues of the metal. She stared at it all for a while and wondered what it meant. There was nothing like it in Casablanca.

She went to a phone booth and dialled the number of Rachi's cousin but the phone rang on unanswered. She felt a moment of fear and aloneness. Then she took a breath and looked up the numbers that Madame Clae had given her. After each one went unanswered her panic mounted. Finally one of the calls was answered. Hesitantly Shaafia told the person who she was and that she had just arrived in Bordeaux. The person was very short with her, saying there had been a death in the family and they could not help her.

She had run out of numbers.

Shaafia sat on a bench watching the long grey and blue Bordeaux articulated trams glide in and out of the Quinconce interchange. Everyone had somewhere to go. She told herself that she had expected to be able to stay with Rachi's cousin, based on what Rachi had said, but then she wondered if Rachi had actually checked with her cousin. She tried the number again, but without getting any response. « *Ce n'est pas grave.* » she told herself but it was hard to believe.

It was beginning to get dark and Shaafia shivered, unaccustomed to the colder climate, even though it was not so cold a day. Wrapped as tightly as she could in her thin coat, and to keep herself from crying, she began to repeat the verse from the Koran. Without realising it, she closed her eyes and began to repeat it softly but aloud. She felt its comfort, she felt a presence and her fear softened.

She became aware of someone close to her on the bench and was suddenly very frightened. She opened her eyes and checked that her suitcase was still there. It was. And next to it were two small black sockless feet in white American sneakers. She looked up from the sneakers, past brightly coloured cotton, to see the wizened black face of an African woman, her hair covered in a bright yellow scarf, and her head tilted to one side. The woman was looking intently at Shaafia.

"God will take care of those who pray to him", she said in French, with a voice that rasped and cracked. "You pray to Jesus, he will save you."

Shaafia smiled nervously. "*Bonsoir.*"

"You seek a place for your head to rest, isn't it so?"

Shaafia nodded hesitantly.

"I could see it", said the woman. "God shows me what I need to see. I will take you to Serenité." She stood as if there was no question that Shaafia would not follow her. She had a pronounced lean as she walked, favouring her left side. Shaafia watched her, uncertain. Then with a resignation that held equal fear and hope, she picked up her suitcase and followed.

They boarded a tram. The woman ignored the ticket validation machine and motioned for Shaafia to sit next to her. After a moment the doors slid closed and the sleek tram moved silently away through the tall trees of Quinconce. She welcomed the warmth in the enclosed space. Next to her, the woman was quietly humming and looking out of the window. Shaafia followed her gaze. On her left, as the tram turned onto the boulevard, the rippling grey expanse of the river Garonne surged, wide and muddy, beneath the stone bridge, Pont de Pierre. On her right, stood the stately stone edifices of the Bourse, uniform and solid, testament to the commercial power of the region's vineyards. Fountains played and small children jumped and ran through the water. Late afternoon coffee drinkers sat outside under brightly lit awnings. Obviously they didn't feel the cold as she did.

The tram emptied outside the huge train station Gare St. Jean, and when it moved on, they had space around them. The woman continued to hum and seemed to have no need to make conversation. Since they were sitting side by side, Shaafia could not study her face but as she looked at the woman's hands resting in her lap, she noticed the small winged figurine on a silver chain at her wrist. It was an angel, its wing upturned and wide. Shaafia stared at it. She was seeing creatures with wings. Not crooked wings but at least she felt they were signs, positive signs, hopeful signs.

When the tram reached the end of the line, the woman beckoned her to follow and Shaafia hefted her suitcase and walked behind her. They sat side by side at a bus shelter and Shaafia began to feel the need to say something to this woman.

"You are very kind to me", she said timidly.

"Do you think so?" The woman looked at her inscrutably and Shaafia felt confused. She was unsure how she could answer, when the woman put her hand over Shaafia's. The tiny silver figurine touched her wrist. "Kindness", the woman said. "It is a virtue to be cultivated."

"I would wish to thank you, at least."

"Maybe one day you will do the same for another and that will be thanks enough."

They sat again in silence until a bus came and the woman got up. "We take this", she said and, following several other passengers, she climbed the steps, again ignoring the validation machine for tickets. Shaafia had seen all the other passengers validate their tickets and she was frightened. The woman seemed supremely confident, however, so Shaafia pulled her suitcase in close to her feet and prayed that all would be well. It was now fully dark outside and she had no idea where the bus was going.

To keep her rising panic at bay, she silently invoked her Koranic verse. Suddenly the woman turned to her and said "Your prayer is good", and humming to herself looked back out the window.

Stop by stop, the bus emptied until they were the last two. Finally it arrived in the square of a small village and turned around. The driver turned the engine off.

"Now we walk, not so far", the woman said and led her off the bus. It was a relief to Shaafia, to have travelled without trouble, but there was also the deep trepidation of not knowing where she was or where they were going. She had no choice but to grip her suitcase and follow the woman, who limped determinedly away from the square and down a narrow dark street with small shuttered houses on both sides.

The houses soon gave way to wooded land, unlit and encroaching on the narrow road. There were sounds of rustling and movement in the bushes and Shaafia shivered both with cold and fright. Finally, they arrived at a pair of high iron gates, fixed open. To one side was a stone wall with a niche holding a small white statue of the Virgin, draped in a blue cape. Above it shone a small white lamp and below it was a brass plate that said Le Nid Des Oiseaux Serènes.

Suddenly Shaafia's heart leapt. "The Nest of the Serene Birds." Whatever fear had been coursing through her as she walked in the darkness now vanished. It was as if the tiny illumined statue had spoken to her and she felt a rush of relief, a certainty that she would be safe.

She turned to the woman. "You cannot know how grateful I am."

The woman stood still and looked at Shaafia with deep eyes reflected in the small light above the Virgin.

"It is not for me to know.", she said and turned to walk up the driveway.

VIII

The long curved gravel driveway with tall plane trees on either side was lit by a row of small blue solar powered lights under each tree. The pale blue illumination made the overhanging branches look like translucent blue beams in a ceiling. The woman had said nothing more as they walked, but she was beginning to breathe heavily and Shaafia realised that she was not young and she was tiring. A spontaneous feeling of love welled up for this generous soul. She prayed inwardly that this woman be taken care of, that her sweet charity would be rewarded. Her little suitcase felt as light as air.

At the end of the drive, a circular turn-around with a lily pond and a fountain in the centre prefaced a large white building, not a château but certainly a substantial piece of solid nineteenth-century architecture, with a columned entrance and high white shutters on all the windows. An elegant row of dormer windows graced the slate roof. Off to one side was a white-stone chapel with a small cross on the top and a gabled slate roof.

The African woman limped purposefully up to the wide front door of the main building and pressed the bell. As they waited, Shaafia turned back to look at the fountain. Around its perimeter were little statues of sparrows, as if they had been frozen in the moment of drinking. In the pale blue glow of the solar lights they did seem to have unusual shapes. She was tempted to put down her suitcase to see if one of them perhaps had a crooked wing, but at that moment the door opened.

A nun stood before her, dressed in grey, with a simple headdress, loose enough to show a crop of short grey hair. She was very large, both tall and wide, taking up much of the space of the stately door she had opened.

"M'bella", she said, smiling. "*Quelle surprise.*" Her voice was soft and warm.

The African woman gestured at Shaafia. "Here is a little bird in need of a nest."

Shaafia smiled shyly and said "*Bonsoir*".

"Then you must come inside", said the nun and stood back from the door. The African woman put her arm behind Shaafia to motion her forward and they entered the building. As the nun closed the door behind them, she said "I am sister Geneviève."

Shaafia saw that the nun was expecting to shake her hand, so she hastily put down her suitcase. "I am Shaafia", she said and they shook hands.

"Have you come far today?" asked the nun as she led the way down a wide tiled hallway.

"From Casablanca."

The nun stopped and looked at her. "You have flown from Morocco today?"

Shaafia nodded, feeling embarrassed to be under such scrutiny.

"And is this your first time in France?"

Again she nodded.

"Then we must take good care of you indeed." Sister Geneviève opened a solid oak door at the end of the corridor. It was a formal dining room with a massive refectory table in the centre, around which sat a dozen nuns and some other women, all with bowls of soup before them.

"A pilgrim has come to join us, all the way from Africa, just today." announced Sister Geneviève. There were noises of welcome from the table and several of the nuns got up to organise chairs for Shaafia and for her rescuer. The African woman seemed to know everyone and went around table kissing them all on both cheeks. Sister Geneviève put Shaafia's suitcase by the door and drew her into the room.

"Sit here my child." She drew out a chair for her as another nun brought a spoon and a bowl of soup.

"We were just about to say our blessing", said Sister Geneviève, as she took her place at the end of the table. Another nun then stood to lead the blessing. Shaafia sat very still. Inside, her stomach was responding to the savour of the soup, but her mind was a turmoil of confusion. She stared at the nuns as the blessing was spoken, wondering if they knew she was not a Christian. Somehow up to that point she had not thought that her religion needed to be mentioned but now as the nuns intoned their amen, she felt afraid. They all bent to their soup. She tentatively took up her own and was about to put the first spoonful in her mouth, when Sister Geneviève spoke sharply: "Shaafia!"

Shaafia looked up, her spoon poised. "I think we have not served you well." Sister Geneviève pushed back her chair and stood up to come round the table. Bending over Shaafia's shoulder, she took the spoon, emptied its contents back into the bowl of soup, and took the bowl from the table. Shaafia was petrified. The whole room was staring at her as Sister Geneviève disappeared out a side door with the bowl of soup. Shaafia stared down at the empty place in front of her. Into the silence, one of the other nuns spoke. She was an old lady with a nacreous complexion and not so many teeth.

"You are of Islam, my child?" she said, her thin voice carrying no rancour or accusation. Shaafia nodded.

"Our soup would not be suitable. Our sister will bring you something else."

Shaafia felt terrified but also knew that she should say something. "I do not understand", she said without lifting her eyes.

"In Islam, you do not eat the meat of the pig, is that not so?"

Shaafia nodded.

"In our soup there is the fat of the pig, *lardon*. It would not be suitable."

A warmth arose in Shaafia's chest and she realised that she might begin to cry.

"Thank you", she managed to say, almost in a whisper. "You are very kind."

The African woman who had guided her to the house, began to laugh. She had a full, generous laugh that made her body roll from side to side.

"*Ooh la*", she said laughing, "*Ooh la*. This girl sees kindness in the trees. She sees kindness in the birds. *Ooh la la!*"

The rest of the room smiled with her, relieving the embarrassed silence and several felt the infectiousness of her laugh and began to chuckle. Shaafia allowed a shy smile to cross her own face. The side door opened and Sister Geneviève reappeared with an electric jug and empty bowl.

"Bouillon", she said. "It is chicken." In her hand she had a cube wrapped in foil. She undid the foil and then broke up the cube into the empty bowl, before pouring boiling water over the stock. "Stir it with your spoon", she said, handing Shaafia a clean spoon. "It will serve you well." Shaafia dared to dart a look of thanks and began diligently stirring the mix. As Sister Geneviève went back to her place, she said to no one in particular, "O Lord, may I be more mindful in my old age."

"Amen!" added several of the other nuns and the African woman began

laughing again. "Oh you sisters, so pious, don't be so hard on yourselves."

"M'bella", Sister Geneviève said with a smile, tucking her serviette under her chin. "You are quite right of course."

Everyone bent to their soup and Shaafia continued with her stirring. After a few moments, the nun sitting to her left leaned over and said very quietly, "I think it is ready now."

The bouillon was hot and she felt its warmth course into her as she took her first spoonful. She realised that she had eaten nothing since the plane in the middle of the day. The flavour of the soup was exquisite. It felt like the first moment of breaking the fast at Ramadan. Inwardly she thanked Allah for his grace in bringing her this nourishment and then she looked up to see M'bella looking at her with her laughing eyes. Shaafia managed a smile and the old woman simply nodded.

After the soup they had a giant homemade *pain de campagne*, fresh crusty bread that was still warm, and the copious cheese plate did the rounds from hand to hand. When it reached Shaafia, the nun to her left turned to offer it to her.

"Do you like cheese?"

"In Morrocco we do not have cheese."

"Ah, but now you are in France and so we must introduce you to the innocent pleasures of good cheese. I suggest you start with something very simple and step by step you will discover which cheeses fill you with delight. To enjoy cheese is no sin. This is *brebis*, the cheese from the sheep. It is simple and generous. It has a flavour of the gentle lamb and asks no great effort on your part to enjoy her. Will you have a portion?"

Shaafia was entranced by this almost passionate invocation and had no way to refuse. "Thank you", she said, as the nun cut her a wedge.

"With this bread", smiled the nun leaning in close to Shaafia, "you have a perfect companion for the *brebis*." Then she tore a chunk from the big loaf and laid it on her plate. As Shaafia took her first bites of both cheese and bread, the nun studied her face. It was true, she had never tasted cheese and she let the texture and the scent of it rest in her mouth. She nodded at the nun, who seemed very pleased.

"Tomorrow", said the nun, "St. Nectaire."

Following the cheese was a compote of fruit. This too, she was told, the nuns had made themselves from the fruit of their own orchard. Shaafia was feeling well fed and suddenly very sleepy. The events of the day had taken all her strength and concentration, and she was beginning to fade away.

Sister Geneviève noticed her pallor and drooping eyes from the end of the table and when the compote had been finished, she announced "Our international traveller must be weary. Come, I shall show you where to sleep."

She came round to Shaafia's chair and led her to her suitcase. Shaafia turned and faced the room. To speak to a group of people all at once was a test for her but she felt compelled to acknowledge what she had received.

"*Merci infiniment de fond du coeur*", thank you from the bottom of my heart, she said to them all.

The room echoed with their responses and wishes for her repose. M'Bella also stood. "I leave you in good hands." she said.

Shaafia followed the nun along a corridor and then up two flights of stairs, by which time they were both breathing heavily. At the topmost landing a series of doors opened on all sides around the stair head. Sister Geneviève opened one of these doors, which revealed a small room with a sloping ceiling. A single bed lay against one wall, with a simple wooden chair beside it and opposite a hand basin. Otherwise the room was bare. Above the bed hung a small unadorned wooden cross.

"Put your case under the bed" the nun said, "and I will bring you some blankets. No doubt you will feel the cold after the climate of your country." And before Shaafia could say anything, she was gone. Shaafia stared at the room. She had never slept by herself in her life. It was a wonderful room, luxurious compared to what she had known, and yet she was terrified. How would she be able to sleep here all by herself?

She heard the nun returning and obediently slid her suitcase under the bed.

"Voilà", said Sister Geneviève as she bustled back in. "These will keep you in good company."

Despite her inner turmoil, Shaafia had to smile. She would not be alone; she would have friendly blankets. The nun explained where the toilet was and the showers, gave her a towel and told her that she should take no notice of the sounds she would hear in the early morning. The nuns, she explained, had their strict routine and she would be very welcome to sleep as long as she wished. She should come downstairs for breakfast whenever she was ready. Wishing her sweet dreams, Sister Geneviève closed the door.

Shaafia made up the bed, using all the blankets, aware of how silent the big building was. She washed up in the cold water of the basin and brushed her teeth, then climbed onto the bed. It was alarmingly soft, so unlike her old sleeping mat. She sat there, with the light still on, remembering that only that morning she had said goodbye to her mother and to her father. She had left Rachi and come alone. She had walked past the fig tree and the well, and she had flown away from Morocco. When would she come back?

With a full heart, she repeated her Koranic verse. She remembered Adila, she remembered Dada and she remembered the sharif. As she repeated her verse, she closed her eyes and she saw the different images of beings with wings that she had seen that day, the statue in Quinconce, M'bella's bracelet, the little stone birds in the fountain. And she also remembered where she was, the nest of the serene birds. Surely now she would find the bird with the crooked wings.

At last she arranged all the blankets on the bed and turned off the light. In the sudden darkness, she fearfully felt her way to the bed and crawled under the blankets. She lay there in the dark, listening to the silence of the house, missing the breathing of her sisters and the warmth of their bodies close to hers.

She curled up into a ball and prayed, "I am alone but I know that I am not alone. I am afraid even though I know that I am not alone. I pray to have courage. I pray to have strength. I offer my gratitude for all the blessings that have come to me on this day." And Shaafia faced her first night alone on this new continent.

IX

How much she actually slept, Shaafia couldn't tell, but it was totally dark when she began to hear the nuns moving on the lower floors. She tried to sleep again but she was cold and lonely. She got up, shivering, groping for the light switch near the door. She dressed in nearly every piece of clothing she had and went looking for the shower. In Morocco they had no hot water in their own house, and so the possibility of hot water did not occur to her. There were two taps, so she turned one of them on. Initially it ran cold and she undressed and got under it. Suddenly it got hotter and hotter and she fled in terror. She managed to turn it off and then tried the other tap. This ran cold and she let it run for a long time to be certain, before she went under it. It was incredibly cold and she washed rapidly and jumped out as quickly as she could.

Now shivering terribly, she again put on all the clothes she had. She prayed to have courage for her second day in France. Then she faced the challenge to go down the stairs. At the first landing one of the nuns was coming up.

"Good morning my child", she said very softly. "You have risen early. Did you sleep well?"

"Thank you, yes", whispered Shaafia.

"We have just finished our mornings prayers, so you are just in time for tea." The nun looked at her closely. "You are cold?"

Shaafia nodded with embarrassment.

« You must take a hot shower. That will warm you. »

Shaafia thought about this for moment and the nun caught her hesitation. « You know where the bathroom is? »

« Oh yes. »

« But something is bothering you? »

Shaafia hung her head, not wishing to complain, but she knew something must be said. « It was too hot and it burned me. »

« Ah. Come.»

The nun gave her a quick demonstration of how to mix hot and cold. « You know, » she said, « I take many things for granted. Thank you for reminding me that it is by God's grace that we can enjoy the small things. »

« Thank you » whispered Shaafia

"Now, we will have nettle tea", said the nun. "It will warm you. Come." And she turned back down the stairs, taking Shaafia's arm. As they descended, the warmth of the woman's hand on her arm was most welcome.

In an enormous kitchen with a large central table dominated by a big urn, various nuns were pouring themselves tea into big mugs. Along one wall was a long rail with many hooks on it and an array of different coloured mugs. The nun took two of these and drew Shaafia to the table. It was while the nun was pouring the tea that Shaafia realised that no nuns were speaking. Several smiled at her in greeting as they sipped their tea.

When the nun brought her the tea, Shaafia looked at her and brought her fingers to her lips asking if she should remain silent. The nun smiled and nodded.

The tea was very mild in its flavour but wonderfully warm. Shaafia felt it course through her and her shivering subsided.

After the tea, the nuns went to the chapel and Shaafia followed. It was only as she went in and watched as each nun genuflected at the door, that she felt the significance of entering a Christian church. She had been in several before in Casablanca, but only as a casual visitor, a tourist, with a Christian school friend. Now she was entering with practicing Christians and she wondered what would be expected of her. She need not have worried. Sister Geneviève greeted her and softly said "We are going to chant to God. If you would like, you can sit here with us and listen."

"Thank you", Shaafia whispered. She sat on a wooden chair by herself, behind the nuns. Several other women were there too. There was a small organ to one side and the nun who had greeted her on the stairs seated herself at the keyboard. As she waited, Shaafia felt a tremour of guilt, a subtle throb of betrayal of her own path, the prophet and her father's faith. However as the organ began to play, her guilt vanished. What followed was perhaps one of the most beautiful sounds Shaafia had ever heard. The nuns sang like angels and it made her want to cry.

Her Koranic verse rose up naturally inside her and seemed to find its cadence with the music and the soaring harmonies of the nuns. Shaafia closed her eyes and swayed with it, lost in a sweet embrace of protection and grace.

When the chanting finally concluded, they sat in silence for quite a while. She opened her eyes to make sure that she was doing the right thing. The chapel was darkly still, smelling of wax and incense, and the few flickering candles made the shadows undulate on the white walls. In the front, hung a pale wooden sculpted crucifix, with the agonised body twisted in suspension from the cruel nails. It was lit from the sides, accentuating the contortions of the chest and hips, over which the sculpted scrap of cloth hung like a rag. She stared at this aweful image and tried to imagine how Christians could feel love for this. Coming from a religion that doesn't have any human images at all, Shaafia found it impossible to grasp how such a sight could give them support or confidence. Islam acknowledges that Jesus was an important prophet of God and so, in himself, she had no doubt that he was worthy of their respect and devotion, but to see him in such pain. . . It was beyond her understanding.

Finally, one by one, the nuns came to the front of the chapel, knelt for a moment and then turned and left. As Sister Geneviève passed her, she smiled down at Shaafia who got up to join her and they walked out together.

"You like the way we chant?" Sister Geneviève asked as they passed beyond the chapel door.

"It is very beautiful, yes", Shaafia responded shyly

"Good." The nun was striding and Shaafia quickened her pace to keep up. "Now we will have breakfast. Come."

Over the bowls of milky coffee and chunks of baguette, the nuns chattered amongst themselves. Shaafia looked around to find her friendly guide from the night before. "Where is M'Bella?" she asked one of the nuns.

"Oh", said the nun, "she went home last night to her children and her grandchildren."

"Does she live close?"

"Oh no, she lives in one of those big housing towers near the Pont D'Aquitaine."

Shaafia thought about that for a moment. It meant that her guide had left her own family to go out of her way to find shelter for Shaafia and had not gone back until late in the night. The nun was watching her, nodding.

"M'Bella has a soul that radiates generosity. You are not the first little bird with a broken wing that she brought to us."

The bird with the broken wing. The unexpected shock of the phrase took Shaafia's breath away. Perhaps she herself was the bird with crooked wings?

X

"You may stay as long as you need", Sister Geneviève had said. She had snorted when Shaafia asked if she could pay something towards her "*pension*".

"You grace us with your sweet and innocent youth." the nun had said with a finality that invited no further discussion. There were several days before she was required to register at the university, and so Shaafia said that she was most grateful and that she would be happy to help out in any way she could.

"Maybe you can see if Hortensia has something you can do."

So Shaafia went to the kitchen and helped to peel potatoes and cut leeks. One day Sister Hortensia, who was clearly queen of the cuisine, asked her to clear some old containers from the big walk-in refrigerator. "Anything that smells off, throw in the garbage." Shaafia dutifully sorted through the containers and jars and found several that smelled suspicious. At first she double-checked with the nun and each time the item went into the bin. Sister Hortensia went out to the herb garden at one point and Shaafia went on sniffing out what needed to be eliminated. The last section of the fridge had cheeses, and here everything seemed to smell. In particular, one large round cardboard container of white cheese was truly offensive to her nose, so she had no doubt and threw it in the bin.

When Sister Hortensia came back, carrying a bunch of fresh basil, Shaafia told her that she thought she had finished. The nun was very pleased and thanked her. Shaafia was just about to leave when the nun happened to glance into the refuse bin and let out a shriek. Shaafia jumped. Pperhaps there was a rodent loose in the kitchen! Instead she saw Sister Hortensia dive into the bin and retrieve the big round of white cheese. "*Non, non, mais non, pas le Camembert!*" Shaafia stood very still, shocked. When Sister Hortensia saw her stricken face, she broke into a smile. "Ah my child", she said soothingly, "I must apologise. In your country they do not have Camembert, is it not so?" Shaafia nodded. "Once you have spent sometime in France, then I am sure your nose will become accustomed to such exotic sensations as this. This is perfume in the nose of the connoisseur."

At lunch that day Sister Hortensia regaled the table with the story of the discarded Camembert and the nuns laughed delightedly. Shaafia felt embarrassed and flushed under the gaze of the assembled nuns. The nun who had introduced her to the delights of cheese on her first night leaned over to her. "My dear", she said, "the mysteries of cheese will take some time to master. I will be your guide, but do not throw away anything until you check with me, *d'accord?*"

"*Merci*", whispered Shaafia. From then on Sister Catherine introduced a new cheese each day. One day she told Shaafia her own story. "You know," she said, "I am like you. I am a *pied-noir.*"

When Shaafia looked puzzled, she grinned. "As you, I was born in Africa. We are called the "black feet", the many French people who were born in Algeria and other countries of the French colonial times. When the war in Algeria was lost, my family had to leave Algiers and our African life and we could never go back."

"Do you miss it?" Shaafia felt shy talking to this nun, but she loved the discovery of someone in the convent who had the same roots as her own.

"I do. I had many friends there, many of them Muslim, as you are. We were very happy together."

When there was not so much to do, Shaafia went outside and walked in the grounds. Her favourite place was the fountain in the centre of the driveway with the little statues of the birds drinking and fanning their wings in the water. She would sit on one of the stone benches built into the rockery around the fountain and imagine all the little birds coming to life. Some of them did have wings that perhaps were a little crooked. Sister Agnès, who played the organ, came to sit with her one afternoon and told her the story of how the fountain came to be there.

She said "Just after the war. . . the first war, 1914 to 1918. There was a man who had fought in the north. You know about that war?"

Shaafia nodded. She had studied it at school.

"So this man, his name was Artur, he had been poisoned by gas. The Germans used a terrible gas to poison the air. His lungs were very bad. At that time this building was used as a hospital for the soldiers who were injured. The nuns were called upon to be nurses. He was sent here.

He had been a sculptor who worked in cemeteries before the war. He used to make angels and saints. So he decided that he would remember all his comrades who had been killed along the Marne where he was fighting. And so you see each of these little birds is a fallen soldier. Each one is a young Frenchman who did not come back from the war to his family or to his wife or to his children. Each one is a little bird. Before Artur finished the work, his lungs became so bad, he could not go on. But one of the nuns found a woman who could also do that work and she finished it for him. If you look at the birds, they are all the same. She was very faithful to Artur's vision. So that is the story of our fountain.»

She showed Shaafia the plaque with his name on it, giving it a polish with her handkerchief as she did.

From then on Shaafia studied each little bird and imagined it as the soul of a dead soldier. She offered them her prayers.

As she became more comfortable in the company of the convent, Shaafia began to share a little of herself. She told the nuns that she was going to study to become a translator and they were universally enthusiastic. It didn't seem to bother them at all that she was not a Christian. In fact they seemed to be rather proud of having her with them. Every morning she attended their chanting, joining them for tea, and every day, as she sat in the chapel, her own spiritual inclination took her to her own practices without feeling at all out of step with where she found herself.

She shared a little of this with Sister Catherine, who she felt of all the nuns would understand her best. The sister smiled when she hesitantly told her how she would do her own practices in the chapel. "You are concerned that we may be offended?" she asked.

"I was not sure if you would be upset with me." Shaafia admitted.

The thin white-skinned face of the older women crinkled into a hundred little creases as she laughed. "My child", she said, "you can be sure that God is never upset when any one of us prays to him."

On the day of registration at the Domaine Universitaire, Shaafia set out with the bus and tram map supplied by Sister Geneviève. Ceaselessly repeating her verse from the Koran, she found her way to the university and went through the tortuous business of enrolment. There seemed to be endless papers to sign and documents to read. The offices were packed with new students, many as lost as Shaafia was. Within minutes she had a pounding headache and felt that everyone was talking to her very loudly.

At last she completed all the forms and deposits and schedules and set out to find her room. It was along a dimly lit tunnel of a corridor, on the third floor of a dingy concrete building that had brightly coloured shutters on the outside, as an obvious but pathetic attempt to liven up the grey cement. With the key she had just paid a deposit on, she opened the door. Her room was a double and she saw that her roommate had already arrived and had installed herself over much more than half of the room. According to the slot for the names on the door, her roommate's name was Nicolette.

Shaafia added her name to the door and closed it against the noises outside. She moved some of Nicolette's possessions off what she assumed would be her bed and sat on it. It was not as soft as the bed at the convent but still much softer than her old sleeping mat.

Other students were moving in and there were shouts and laughter in the echoing corridor. *This is where I will live for the next four years,* Shaafia thought. *I will be strong.*

She was still sitting there when the door burst open and a girl shunted in backwards dragging a young man with her. Their lips were locked and she was pawing at him as she drew him to her bed. With one hand she pushed whatever was on the bed to the floor and pulled the man down on top of her. Then she rolled over on top of him and began tearing off her clothes. Shaafia was frozen in horror. Finally she found her voice.

"*Pardon*", she said as loudly as she dared.

The girl stopped, pulled her shirt back into place and turned. "Get out!" she yelled.

Shaafia was stunned. "Excuse me, this is my room."

"So, go for a walk, get drunk, just get out. Now." She lunged across the room at Shaafia and grabbed her arm. She was much larger than Shaafia and had no difficulty in shoving her out the door, which she then locked.

Shaafia stood in the dark corridor, as students came and went, carrying suitcases and calling out to each other, not always in French.

Two blonde tanned Californians said "Hi!" to her as they towed huge brightly coloured suitcases on wheels.

She waited in the corridor, marooned there, unsure what to do. Her little bag with her bus tickets and her passport, and all the money her father had given her, was still on the bed. She needed it. Then she realised that she still had the room key in her pocket. She had to go back in. She prayed for strength and protection and nervously unlocked the door as quietly as she could. As she eased it open, she heard the girl calling out *"Oui, oui, oui!!"* The couple was totally naked and the sight of the tight white buttocks of the young man, frenziedly pumping, filled her with terror. She lunged for her bag and shot out of the door, slamming it behind her, and ran down the corridor and down the stairs and away from the building. She was sobbing as she ran, wrenching breaths full of despair. The image of the twin clenching male cheeks was stamped on her inner vision. Finally she stopped under a tree and caught her breath. She crouched low to the ground and pulled herself tightly into a ball with her back against the base of the tree. Now her prayer came back and she grasped it with all her devotion. She prayed with every little bit of strength she could find: *Oh be with me. Please be with me.*

How long she stayed curled up like that under the tree she didn't know, but in the end, she pulled herself upright. At least she knew she had somewhere to go. She could return to Le Nid Des Oiseaux Serènes.

On the tram and then on the bus, she sat, pulled in within herself, as if she feared that anyone could attack her at any moment. She ran along the narrow street towards the convent and up the driveway, only feeling safe enough to walk when she reached the fountain. She stopped there and looked down at all the souls of the dead soldiers. The little birds. Then she took a deep breath and walked into the house.

She went looking for Sister Geneviève. She had to talk to someone. She heard her in the office of the convent, shouting "Why are you so stupid!" and she was not sure if she should go in. The door was open and Sister Geneviève saw her. "Oh!" she said. "You have caught me in a moment of folly. One of my greatest sins is impatience with computers." Then she looked closely at Shaafia. She got up and invited her into the room and closed the door.

"You are upset", she said as she invited Shaafia to sit in one of two wide upright leather chairs that had obviously seen many years of good service. Shaafia nodded meekly as she sat, still clutching her little bag.

"Will you tell me what has happened?"

Shaafia nodded and then, to her shame, began to cry. The nun sat patiently and passed her the tissue box.

"I am so sorry", Shaafia managed after a minute. "I did not want to cry. I prayed to be strong."

"Sometimes to cry is to be strong. It is no sin to shed tears."

Shaafia sniffed and took a breath and then as simply as she could, not in too graphic detail, she described her first day at university. Sister Geneviève listened with a quiet focus that was at first a little intimidating but then became encouraging.

"And so I had to go back in for my bag." She held it up as if it was evidence. "And they were. . . she was. . . they had no clothes on and. . ." Shaafia was not even sure how to describe what it was. Especially to a nun.

"Sometimes I am totally grateful to God", said Sister Geneviève with a sigh, "that I am well protected from so much of the modern world."

<h1 style="text-align:center">XI</h1>

The afternoon before her classes were due to begin, Sister Marie-Louise, the youngest of all the nuns, drove Shaafia to her dormitory building. The convent owned a white mini van with banks of seats and Sister Geneviève insisted that Shaafia should be taken and helped to install herself. Sister Marie-Louise was quite tall and muscular. It was she who did most of the heavy work in the convent. She could fix plumbing and she could climb ladders fearlessly.

"This girl will give no trouble, you will see", she said as she swung the van around the fountain and down the drive. Sister Geneviève had told her about Shaafia's roommate, and Sister Marie-Louise was going to make sure that Shaafia would not have any difficulties. Shaafia dreaded returning to the dorm but she knew that if she was to fulfil the hopes and expectations of her father and her whole family then she must.

When they arrived and Shaafia pointed out the way, Sister Marie-Louise set off with a purposeful stride. Shaafia had to hurry to keep pace. When they reached the room, she knocked. Nicolette came to door the dressed in a T-shirt and shorts. It was a shock for her to be confronted by a tall nun and her roommate.

"Mademoiselle", said Sister Marie-Louise, advancing into the room, which sent Nicolette backing towards her bed. Shaafia timidly followed and stole a quick glance to make sure there was no man in the room. "Mademoiselle, you have treated this young lady with very bad manners."

"So, I am sorry about that." Nicolette looked frightened. "I was not expecting her to be there and it was a difficult moment, you understand?"

"There is never an excuse to treat another person like that, no matter how the dogs of lust are chewing your entrails." Sister Marie-Louise was working herself up into quite a temper and Nicolette scooted back to the wall side of her bed. "You will swear to me that you will treat this young lady with all the respect she deserves. If I hear that you have, in any way, made her unhappy, I will come here and I will deal with you."

As she watched the effect of these words on the girl, Shaafia noticed that she was wearing a crucifix. She let herself indulge in a little private smile.

"Okay, okay. I am very sorry for what happened", Nicolette said and she did seem to mean it, although much of her tone was fearful. This big nun was frightening.

"Then I hold you to that promise." Sister Marie-Louise turned to Shaafia. "Unpack your bag and find your place." she said. There was a small chest of drawers next to her bed and she put her few things in it as the nun watched. Then she nodded. "Now walk with me." she said and turned to leave the room. Shaafia went to follow but was stopped as the nun turned back in. Her strong right hand came out and pointed a steady finger at the girl on the bed. She seemed to look along her finger as if she sighting the girl as a target. Then she turned and left. Shaafia followed her and closed the door.

As they walked down the corridor, Sister Marie-Louise chuckled. "As I said, that girl will not give you one moment of trouble, not one moment." Shaafia thanked her as they walked towards the van. "No, thank you, my child." said the nun. "I have had a very amusing afternoon."

Shaafia waved to the departing white van and with reluctant steps mounted the stairs to her room. Nicolette was on her bed, where she had been painting her toenails. When the door opened she looked up.

"Look, I am sorry." she said. "Frankly, we got off to a bad start."

Shaafia eyed her warily trying to gauge what she was feeling. The other girl then went back to painting her toenails. After a moment, she looked up. "You're a *beurre* right?"

Shaafia had not heard that slang term for North Africans and she looked puzzled. The other girl said: "*Maghrébine*? You're from Algeria or somewhere?"

"Morocco."

"So you're a Muslim, right?"

"Yes."

"So why is a Catholic nun acting like your body guard?"

"The nuns have been very kind to me since I came to France. That is all."

"*Chouette,* cute. Well I am going be careful. That one had the nasty nun look about her. I went to a Catholic school and I know that look."

And that was the end of it. They stayed out of each other's way. Nicolette did not bring any more male friends to the room and Shaafia kept herself very carefully in her half of the space. She kept it scrupulously clean, as her mother would wish, while the other side of the room was always messy. Nicolette also seemed to be permanently wired to her music player, while she was studying and often even when she was asleep. The steady *thump, thump* became the natural background sound of the room. It was rare not to see the wires running up to her ears, so there was never any need to make conversation. Shaafia never found out anything about Nicolette and Nicolette seemed to have no interest in her either.

When classes began, they barely saw each other. Nicolette was studying economics and business, so they had no classes in common. Once she found herself in the classroom again, the joy of study filled Shaafia. Most of her classes were oriented towards English and she loved the challenge.

For the first two weeks, the days flew by and she buried herself in her classes and her homework. At night she would sit on her bed and repeat her Koranic verse. She would remember her sister Adila, as if she was talking to her about her day. She would remember Dada and was sure that somehow Dada was watching over her. And she remembered the sharif and his command.

She dutifully wrote to her family each week and she also wrote to Madame Clae and to Rachi. She told the family that her studies were going well, but she did not mention the convent. Madame Clae's replies were full of her enthusiasm, as if she were vicariously reliving her own university days, while hinting that life at the school back in Casablanca was not all that she could wish. Her family's replies were written by her brother Samet, the second son. The most intellectual of her brothers, he had so buried himself in books that he seemed to have no interest in finding a job or doing anything productive with his life. He spent time in the little coffee house at the corner of the lane and loved to talk about world affairs. Shaafia found him a mystery and had never felt particularly close to him. Their father, however, had instructed Samet to be the family letter writer. He wrote whatever his father said, although he could not resist inserting some of his own comments. "Our father

wishes you to know that he prays that you be successful in your studies",
Samet wrote, adding "He thinks you are the shining light of the family;
but my dear little sister, what impact will a small Moroccan girl make on
this wide world?" What she enjoyed most were his personal observations
of the day-to-day life of the family. "Habib is learning to play football,
but he has no idea which foot is his best, so he uses them both." Shaafia
had to smile at this, for with just a few words her brother had brought
the family to life.

Rachi's letters were short and terse. Her father had begun to arrange
her marriage but she had not yet met the man she was to marry. She
was restricted to staying in the house and was forbidden to go anywhere
without her mother or one of her older brothers. Her letters were written
secretly and taken by her younger sister to be posted.

At the end of the second week, Shaafia returned to the convent for
the first time and the nuns were very excited to see her. They asked about
her studies and Sister Marie-Louise wanted to know if the other girl was
doing as she promised. Shaafia assured her it was going well. Nicolette
was behaving. "She will not dare to cross me. I'm not surprised." said
Sister Marie-Louise. Shaafia had to smile.

Going back to the convent was almost as good as going home to
Casablanca. She often longed to go home to Casablanca. She missed
the warm dry wind on her skin, the sounds of her sisters in the kitchen,
the call of the Muezzin, the smell of the couscous. But at least when she
went back to the convent, her little room had been kept for her. When,
next morning, she rose and went for nettle tea and then the chanting,
she was as happy as she could remember. She sat in the chapel and
thanked Allah for all his bounteous grace and the good company of
those who served God.

At the end of October, the nuns invited her to join them for
Toussaint. The All Saints holiday was time off from her classes and she
was glad to accept their invitation. She did not tell Nicolette where she
was going. She packed her suitcase and caught the tram, longing to
enjoy five days of peace in her room up in the eaves, the silent and still
mornings in the chapel, walks by the fountain and chores in the kitchen
with Sister Hortensia.

When she arrived, there was a small van unloading pots and pots of chrysanthemums and a French woman was standing beside the van talking sternly to a man in a cap. The woman was very unhappy about the colours of some of the plants. The man, seeming to bend under the verbal affliction, hesitantly tried to remonstrate but he could not break the flow. Shaafia had to walk around them to get to the front door.

"*Bonsoir*", she said as she passed, and the woman paused and turned to look at her. She had glasses with quite thick frames and she fixed her eye on Shaafia and glared at her. The man was glad of the shift in focus and said "*Bonjour*", then scuttled round to the back of his van.

The woman turned back to continue her attack but when she saw he had disappeared, she returned to Shaafia. "You are looking for something?" She had the imperious tone of self-assured authority.

Shaafia paused as she was about to open the door. The woman's tone was daunting. She turned to face the woman. "No, thank you. I know where I am going."

"You do not just walk into a religious house, you know. It is not a boarding house." The woman was walking towards her as if perhaps she meant to throw Shaafia off the premises.

"I am invited for Toussaint."

"Oh yes? And by whom?"

"By the nuns, by Sister Geneviève and. . . and. . ." Shaafia found herself trembling under the harsh stare of this woman.

Luckily, at this moment the man who had been trying to unload the rest of the plants dropped a pot.

"*Merde!*" he muttered, as the pot shattered on the gravel.

The woman spun back at the sound and rushed at the man, yelling abuse. Shaafia fled inside.

She found Sister Geneviève in her office and breathlessly told her what had happened. Sister Geneviève leaned back in her chair, which creaked under her weight. "You have just met our dear Madame de Fortelle. She is a great benefactress in many ways. There was a time when she gave quite a bit of money to our house. She was our most generous patron. That was before her husband lost all their money and ran away, but now she gives what she can, her time and her tireless protection. You know the dog called Rottweiller?" Shaafia did not. "It is a big and ferocious German watchdog. We do not need such a dog because we have Madame de Fortelle." She laughed and her large and soft body shook in her chair. "Oh, but she is all noise. I do not think she would hurt anyone, especially not a sweet girl like you."

Over the next five days, Shaafia ran into this woman several times and made sure that she always avoided getting too close. Then there was the day when she collided with her just outside the chapel. It had been a quiet afternoon, and Shaafia had sat in there by herself saying her prayers and feeling very at home. Madame de Fortelle was approaching, carrying a vase of the chrysanthemums and she nearly dropped them as Shaafia pushed open the door.

"Be careful, you clumsy girl", she thundered.

"Please excuse me", murmured Shaafia.

The woman put down her vase on a bench by the wall of the chapel and turned to Shaafia. "What are you doing here?"

"I was just sitting in the chapel."

"But Sister Hortensia tells me you are not a Christian."

"That is so."

"Then you should not be in there. It is only for Christians. Do you want to become a Christian?"

"Not at all."

"Then you should leave. The nuns are too generous. You have taken advantage of their charity. Go back to your own people. Go away." At this she picked up the flowers and marched into the chapel.

In the kitchen, Sister Hortensia shook her head. "Oh, she should not talk to you like that. No, no. I will tell her that you are our special guest. Don't you worry."

However for the rest of the stay, Shaafia made sure she did not cross the path of Madame de Fortelle.

She returned at the Christmas break to be with the nuns, and again the presence of Madame de Fortelle made her wary. Madame de Fortelle was in and out of the convent most days, but Shaafia began to suspect that the woman had been told not to say anything. Now, instead of accosting Shaafia, she ostentatiously ignored her. Whenever she caught sight of her, Madame de Fortelle would change direction or become focused on something else.

One day Shaafia was delighted to see M'Bella, her generous guide, in the big dining room. She was with several dark-skinned teenagers who most likely were her grandchildren, Shaafia felt such a rush of affection that she ran to the woman and hugged her. "Ah my little bird!" M'Bella said with a laugh. "So here you are!"

Shaafia wanted to thank her and stammered out that she was so sorry not to see her again. "*Ooh la!* It is nothing." The woman patted her on the shoulder; "It is enough that I see you in fine form. You are finding your French wings, I am sure."

Shaafia told her that she was doing very well. M'Bella introduced her to the two girls with her. They were indeed her grandchildren, both born in France. "These are my chickens", she said proudly. "They are French and they will be good students. They are both learning to speak English. Do you speak English?"

"Yes. I am studying to become a translator."

"Ah, then you can help them. Talk to her, girls, and show her what you can say."

The two girls, who had been chattering away to each other, when Shaafia walked in, became shy and tongue-tied, staring down at their feet and shuffling timidly. Shaafia tried a few simple questions in English but the girls were too intimidated to respond.

"Oh well" said M'Bella, shaking her head. "Maybe another day."

"Of course" Shaafia said. "I would be happy to help. I would be honoured."

"You are a good girl." M'Bella said and kissed her on both cheeks.

On Christmas Eve, there was a light dusting of snow, frosting the little birds around the fountain and drawing plumes of steam from the chimneys of the kitchen. Shaafia had never seen snow.

In anticipation of winter, she'd been taken to a second-hand clothes shop, where Sister Geneviève sometimes volunteered. Sister Geneviève had put aside some warm clothes for her, a generously padded false fur coat and a cosy bonnet made of incredibly soft alpaca wool. She paid very little for them and they kept her wonderfully warm. Sister Agnès had knitted her some bright red mittens and these too, she treasured. Now she ventured outside in all her new warm clothes to gaze at the white flakes drifting through the naked branches of the plane trees in the driveway. The water in the fountain was beginning to freeze, and when she poked at it with a stick, it crackled and splintered. There was a peace that came with the snow and she sat for a moment on the stone bench, gazing up into the last wisps of early evening pale twilight. The flakes of snow fluttered and ebbed at the whim of the breeze, sometimes even rising before settling. She followed the play of the wafting curtains as each flake found its resting place and dissolved. How peaceful and soft it all was.

Finally the cold drove her inside, but not before she had recited her verse to the sun long-since set and to the grace of the universe that given her such gifts. She felt deeply at peace with herself.

Midnight mass was celebrated by the local priest, Father Lefait, and Shaafia sat at the back of the chapel, delighting in the hundreds of candles that lit up the curved wooden vaulted ceiling, from which echoed the beautiful chanting of the nuns. There were quite a few lay people there, including M'Bella and her granddaughters and Madame de Fortelle.

When mass had concluded, the priest was at the door and everyone was wishing each other *Joyeux Noël*. Shaafia nodded to him as she passed and wished him a joyous Christmas. He was not a young man but he had a youthful face and eyes that shone when he smiled. He inclined his head as she spoke and said "The sisters tell me of you. I am happy that you could join us."

Shaafia had never spoken to a Christian priest before and she wasn't sure how she should behave, but she smiled timidly and bowed her head and said "Thank you", and turned to walk away.

"Do you realise that girl is not a follower of Christ?" It was Madame de Fortelle, who must have been right behind her.

"Oh yes", said the priest, quite loudly, no doubt so that Shaafia would catch it. "It is wonderful that she can be with us on this beautiful night."

"It is a disgrace, if you were to ask my opinion." And Madame de Fortelle was also making sure that she was heard. The harshness of her voice sent a little shiver through Shaafia as she walked away.

Up in her room, as Shaafia settled on her bed to repeat her Koranic verse and to offer her blessings to those she loved, the image of Madame de Fortelle came to her. She was shadowed and indistinct but Shaafia knew instantly who she was. In the image, the poor woman was in agony, as if her body pained her in all its joints, as if there was a darkness in her, threatening to consume her and against which she had to fight to gain a breath. Compassion rose up in Shaafia in such a wave that she found her heart pounding and tears running down her cheeks. Her repetition became more and more powerful as if she herself were helping the woman to fight. There was one moment when the eyes of Madame de Fortelle, accentuated by her glasses, seemed to lock onto hers, dark and tortured, crying out to her for comfort. As the image faded and she concluded her last repetition, she prayed with a fullness that touched her to the core: *May Allah take care of this poor soul.*

XII

It was in the late spring, just after Easter and during the university spring break, that Shaafia's relationship with Madame de Fortelle changed. Shaafia had been at the convent for several days, when M'Bella brought her two granddaughters for some English practice. The weather was turning warmer, the narcissus were springing up in great golden banks around the fountain and the sparrows were burrowing under the eaves with their little beaks carrying grass and sticks for their nests. Shaafia sat with the two girls by the fountain and they began to describe what they could see around them, in whatever English they could manage. It was soon clear that they were beginners, but this was one way that Shaafia could repay her debt of gratitude to M'Bella.

As Anouck, the younger of the two, was attempting to describe what the narcissus looked like, "It is yellow colour with green legs", the elegant old grey Citröen DS of Madame de Fortelle glided up the drive, stopped in the middle of the turnaround and subsided onto its tired suspension. Madame de Fortelle appeared to lunge out of the driver's seat and propel herself in the direction of the chapel, moaning loudly *"Mon Dieu, mon Dieu!"*

The English conversation continued in fits and starts for a while longer and then M'Bella came out of the building to take her granddaughters home. "They are successful in English?" she asked.

"It is a good beginning." Shaafia said with a smile, and the two girls giggled.

"You will teach them good English, not American." Shaafia was surprised that M'Bella knew the difference. She kissed them all goodbye and waved as they went off down the drive.

Making her way back towards the kitchen, she passed the chapel. The wailing that was coming from inside pulled at her, and she turned and went in. Madame de Fortelle was at the front of the chapel prostrate before the twisted sculpted crucifix. Her voice rose into the high wooden ceiling, crying out the name of Jesus and then calling, "Why, oh Lord Jesus, why?" Without hesitation, Shaafia went to the front of the chapel and knelt beside the hysterical woman. The glasses lay abandoned on the stone floor.

Shaafia put her hands on the broad heaving back and gently moved them across her shoulders. Madame de Fortelle did not seem to notice at first but her body seemed less agitated and her voice slowly dropped in volume until she was sobbing with her face pressed to the floor.

As she continued to rub the woman's back, her prayer came back to Shaafia: *May Allah take care of this poor soul.* She stared up at the crucifix and she began to focus her prayer on the face of the Christ. The eyes were closed and although the body was in agony, she began to recognise that the face itself seemed to be calm. She stared at this unlined and untroubled face, detached from its torment and continued her prayer.

After quite some time, the prone body became still and the voice of Madame de Fortelle spoke quietly and calmly from beneath her unfastened grey hair.

"Thank you, sister."

Eventually she pulled herself up until she was on her knees, scrabbled around on the floor for her fallen glasses and then looked up at the crucifix. She did not yet look around to see who had been rubbing her back. She stared up at the cross.

"I was not the best of mothers. I did what I could. I tried to love my sons. I tried to keep them in your sight. I did not succeed. Now you have taken Hugues. And you have taken his son, Antoine, my grandson, who I have never seen. Who I will never see. I pray that I can learn to accept that this is your will. I pray that you will look after them both, even if they did not have the love of Christ in their lives." She paused and then took a breath of deep sorrow. "Oh dear Lord, if this is a punishment for my own sins, then I must atone for them. Whatever wrong I have done, whatever sin I have committed, may I be forgiven so that they may be saved. I ask this, as this dear sister here beside me is my witness."

She turned, with her ravaged face, her ruined make-up, her dishevelled coiffeur, her tortured eyes, to see who had given her their loving touch in her darkest moment. She did not react with shock but instead became very still. Shaafia looked back at her with compassion. There was no fear of this woman any more. Madame de Fortelle stared at Shaafia and finally in a tortured whisper, uttered her gratitude.

"Thank you Lord for sending me your child in my anguish." She dropped again to the floor, but this time in silence, still and in prayer.

Shaafia quietly got to her feet. She bowed to the calm face in the twisted body and backed away from that other tortured body on the floor.

It was at dinner that evening that she heard from the sisters what had happened. Madame de Fortelle's son Hugues had gone to live in Australia many years ago, after he had graduated from his studies. He had been estranged from his parents and had cut himself off from them. He had made a new life for himself, married and had two children. Now he had been killed in an accident, which had taken his son as well. Shaafia said nothing of what she had seen and as far as she could tell, no one was aware that she had been in the chapel. Sisters Agnés and Geneviève had gone back to the château to take care of Madame de Fortelle and the nuns would organise a mass for the de Fortelle family for the next day.

The next time Shaafia saw Madame de Fortelle was at the mass. The older woman was dressed in black and veiled. She came in, walking slowly with her head down, with some other women, presumably family members, and sat at the front. Father Lefait led the mass and the chapel was very solemn and indrawn. Shaafia sat behind the nuns and the many others who had gathered, and in her own way offered her prayers.

At the conclusion of the mass, as Madame de Fortelle walked slowly up the aisle with the nuns, she stopped when she reached Shaafia. Madame de Fortelle stood still and slowly lifted the dark veil. Her eyes were red-rimmed and hollow, she wore no glasses and had no make-up, but inside her somewhere there was a dark glow. Her eyes met Shaafia's and held them. Then she bowed her head, replaced her veil, and moved on to the back of the chapel.

Shaafia stayed in the chapel and, after everyone else had left, she approached the altar and knelt in front of the sculpted sacrificial form. She felt her heart beating strongly in her chest and, as she looked up at the face, she had a startling moment of recognition. She had not seen it until then but this face was something like that of the man who put his hand on her head as a child. It was as if she was again looking up as a nine-year old into the face of the sharif in Casablanca.

Show me where to find the little bird with the crooked wings, she prayed.

THÉOPHILE

Not long after his 29th birthday, an event celebrated alone and with no joy, Théophile de Fortelle had pulled together enough money to get away from France. Years earlier his brother Hugues had done the same, going to the other side of the world, to Australia. Their father had run away to Argentina not long after. Théophile was following this new family tradition, where the men ran away.

One day in the throwaway newspapers given out at Bordeaux tram stops, he saw an ad where a flight to India with an open return was on super-special. There was just enough in his bank account and he bought one.

He'd spent a couple of days in Mumbai in a backpackers hotel in Colabar, mostly full of young Europeans like himself, and mostly keen to try as much local dope as they could. A group of them had hired a taxi to hit Goa where everybody said the best dope was cheaper than chapatis.

Now in another universe, eight months later, he lay facedown in the sand, naked and filthy under a coconut palm, until a khaki-coloured dog licked his nose and mouth. He was dreaming that his mother was trying to wash him and he was angrily dodging the washcloth. His waking spasm made the dog spring back and bare its teeth. He lay there for a long timeless suspension of sensation, trying to locate himself. Slowly the row of curving palm trees along the foreshore began to make sense and he rolled onto his side to look at the hut, where the French couple had been staying with him. His body was sending him signals of distress but he couldn't yet decipher them. Painfully, one after the other they landed. He was sunburnt and his skin was screaming. That became more and more apparent: subcutaneous torture. He had shat himself and he was spattered with it. His head pounded. No mistaking that and altogether he was a mess. When he tried to sit up, it was obviously unwise and he sank back.

He lay there trying to recreate what had happened. It seemed like another age since they had bought an ounce of pure hash behind the Goa market and made a huge omelette with tomatoes, some kind of local spinach and some very chewy potatoes. That had been at night, so he must have been lying there at least half a day, or maybe it was more.

The dog sat panting in the shade and watched him, not unlike the vultures that he had seen on every pile of garbage since he'd first hit Mumbai. Waiting for him to die? A distant but distinctly identifiable sense of panic began to overtake him; he rolled onto his stomach and pulled his knees up into a crouch to get away from it. His ravaged skin screamed while the panic washed over him like the derisive laughter of young men in a dangerous back alleyway. The after-waves of his first attempt to move made him nauseous and his body shook. Finally he began to call on whatever threads of will power he could find in the ragged corners of his consciousness, pushing his hands down into the sand on either side of his knees, preparing to move, From there he slowly tried lifting his head, like nursing a newborn, a fragile living thing arising from its birth place. He gave thought to standing but decided that upright was beyond him and he slowly crawled towards the hut. His forearms threatened to leave him facedown again in the sand but he applied the last wisps of his strength to reach the door of the hut, which lay open. When he finally made it, his arms gave out and he sank on the threshold, an anthropomorphic doormat. The dog sauntered over, sniffed at him one last time and gave him up, trotting away to some other distraction.

The young man lay there, hoping the French couple would reappear or hoping he would die. Either seemed possible.

In the end, Théophile found a little more will power and dragged himself fully into the hut. Adjusting slowly to the darkness after the harsh sun, he finally recognised that all signs of the French couple had been removed. The remnants of their omelette were feeding a family of cockroaches in a corner but the two backpacks were gone.

"*Dommage*", he groaned. He could use some company and at least they spoke French. The guy was *penible*, a pain in the arse, so full of himself, but the girl was friendly. She would sit with him in the evenings on the beach and smoke bidis.

Her name was Ariette and she loved the sunsets. While her boyfriend preferred the bars in the town, she would stay with Théophile and they would have grand conversations about how they had come to India to find God. She did anyway. She told him that she and the boyfriend weren't really a couple, having only hooked up just a week before, when she arrived in Mumbai, from France. It was mostly out of convenience, she'd said. She felt safer with someone to travel with. Théophile had hopes that the guy would get impatient and decide to move on, leaving Théophile and her to travel together. She'd told him that she really wanted to visit some different ashrams and Théophile said he wanted to do that too. Just as soon as he could get his head together. He didn't tell her he'd already been in Goa for eight months and somehow couldn't quite find the volition to move on. It was so easy to live there and he'd met so many interesting characters and had tried some pretty amazing dope. Maybe if she had stayed, he would have been ready to move on. Now as he accepted that she'd gone, probably never to be seen again, he felt an ache of loneliness.

At last he dragged himself upright and onto the wooden bed with its rattan wicking, part of the scant furnishing that came with the hut. Although he could have afforded a perfectly good hotel, there was something, basic, primitive and satisfying about living in this hut. How ironic that a handful of rupees a day went such a long way in Goa, even better when you could share the hut with others and split the cost. More than anything else, it was the opposite of Château des Mésanges. Half a world away, where he took birth and grew up, and from where he had finally escaped. The château, with its various wings built in succeeding centuries, had some forty rooms to choose from. Throughout his childhood, he had roamed in its vastness, looking for secret passageways and mysterious cupboards, oblivious to the heavy legacy of his ancestral family, the De Fortelles. He had been born into a labyrinthine world and now he chose to live in this one small hut with its rattan beds and dirt floor. He had no need of anything more.

In the wooden box that served as a cupboard, he found his tin of coconut oil and began to rub it into his skin, wincing with the pain of it. There were parts of him just too difficult to reach and he let them go. He sat on the edge of the bed and stared out of the door. The human body is a heavy burden, he thought, *le corps humain est un fardeau lourd.* He began repeating it to himself like a mantra: *un fardeau lourd.* Finally he got up and found an overripe papaya. Insects had begun their incursions and he brushed them off before he bit into it. The juice ran down his face and got sticky in his stubble, but it seemed to wake him up a bit more. He went over to the terracotta water jar that his landlord filled every few days, after the rent was paid of course. Shocked by the coldness of the water, he washed his face and neck, and then began the nauseating work of scraping away the disgusting mess, the encrusted excrement sticking to his buttocks and legs. *Un fardeau lourd, un fardeau lourd.*

II

A shadow appeared at the doorway and he turned, oblivious to his nakedness, desperately hoping it was Ariette. The narrow and short silhouette of a south Indian man stood there with his hands in *namaskar.*

"*Namaste.* You are to come." the man said in sub-continentally accentuated English.

"*Mmm?*" It was the best Théophile could manage in response.

"You. Come" said the man. He took a step inside the hut and, seeing Théophile's lack of clothes and his unsanitary state, took a step backwards so that he was just outside the doorway. Théophile wasn't quite sure if the man was real or some latent vestige of the dope. Finally he muttered, "I don' wann come wid you."

The Indian man moved his head gently from side to side. "Must. You wash body. Put clothes. Shoes, then come. My guruji say I am to bringing you." Théophile stared at this man, unable to find any further response. The man stood looking at him with such certainty that Théophile slumped back against the wall of the hut and all his resistance to this intrusion drained away.

"Okay." he muttered. "Okay." He didn't care.

The man then felt empowered to help and stepped inside. "*Bahut achha.*" he said. He now ignored the nakedness of the European and pushed Théophile towards the water jar. He was in charge. He picked up the pitcher and sloshed water over his abject charge, finding a cloth to wash him, Again Théophile had the flashback to his mother and he shook himself.

"I do it", he said and roughly took the cloth. The little man watched him, ready to step in if the young man faltered. Théophile managed to deal with the worst of his filth and then found a ragged towel to dry himself. With the man hovering near him, he put on his white Indian kurta shirt and some cotton pajama pants. His sunburnt body screamed as he dressed.

"Passport?" demanded the man. "Money? Waluables? You must be bringing everything."

"Huh?" said Théophile squinting now at his intruder and beginning to wonder how wise this was. "Where we going?" he mumbled.

The little man again rocked his head from side to side. "Not come back. I am telling you, this place bad for you. Bring." He gestured in general at the contents of the hut.

Théophile stood unsteadily in the middle of the hut and looked around him. So much shit. Maybe the guy was right. What good was any of this? He pulled his few valuable possessions together, his money pouch and passport, a few clothes, and put them in a cloth tote bag advertising a South Indian rice mill. He slung it over his shoulder and yelped in pain as it hit his sunburnt skin. The man took the bag from him, making sympathetic noises, and went out. Théophile looked back at the mess in the hut. Why had he spent so much time in this shithole?

His sandals were by the door. The Indian man must have found them, because he certainly hadn't left them neatly paired like that. As he stepped outside, the air was beginning to cool and he took in his first decent breath. He didn't even bother to close the door. He'd paid for the rest of the month, but what the hell. There was nothing for him here. The khaki-coloured dog watched him from the shade of the palm tree. Théophile stood still, checking that he could actually do this. Some vague sense of physical normality was creeping back.

A small tonga with high wooden wheels, brightly decorated sides and a skinny horse snuffling in the traces, waited in the shade. The man undid the reins from the palm tree and gestured to Théophile to get on the back. The tonga dipped alarmingly backwards as Théophile pulled himself painfully up onto the rear-facing passengers' seat. The little man threw the tote bag up beside him, and clambered up into the driver's seat. "*Chalo*! We go!" he called over his shoulder and clicked his tongue at the horse.

As the wiry little horse dug in and strained against the weight, and the tonga pulled away from the hut, Théophile experienced a wrenching sensation of loss, terrible loss. Unable to hold himself back, he began to weep. Great shudders of sadness came out of him in waves, wave after wave, with the hut disappearing amongst all the other identical huts, the palm trees leaning out to the sea, the dust rising from the wooden wheels of the tonga, the vultures eyeing the garbage heaps, the naked children chasing rusty bicycle rims with sticks, the women with their saris tucked up high between their thighs pulling water from the well— so much loss. His weeping seemed bottomless and in the end he just closed his eyes and let the rocking of the tonga and the rhythm of the horse's feet carry him to wherever the little man wanted to go. Théophile didn't care. He hugged his tote bag and braced his feet against the sway and bump of the cart.

III

The driver took the tonga away from the beach and out through the last straggling villages on the outskirts of Goa. The rhythm of the wheels and the horse's hooves and the occasional word from the driver were all Théophile was aware of. Trucks and taxis dodged around them and horns blared. Drivers hurled abuse as they worked their way past the slow moving tonga.

Darkness came on and, apart from several times when he came close to falling off the back of the tonga, Théophile dropped into a state of semi-consciousness with no sense of time or space. Thoughts would drift through his mind in disconnected episodes of momentary lucidity. He'd left his cell phone somewhere, maybe in the hut. Why didn't he think to bring his suitcase? Where was it anyway? He should have left a note for Ariette. What if she came back? Was he being kidnapped? Where was he going? He badly needed to smoke something.

Some time in the night, the tonga began to climb, the horse straining against the weight. At last it stopped and the little man shook Théophile. "Now walk", he said. "You too much heavy." Théophile searched inside himself for the means to move and somehow, holding the little side rail of the tonga, he found his feet on the ground. The human body is a heavy burden.

The little man talked quietly to the horse and sometimes sang to it, as he walked beside it. With an emerging wave of fear, Théophile recognised that he had no idea where he was. He peered around in the darkness, fiercely gripping the rail with both hands, tottering along and in danger of falling under the wide wooden wheel. There was thick jungle on one side of the narrow road while the other side dropped away to a valley where lights from small villages dotted the darkness. Somewhere off in the distance a loudspeaker was horribly distorting some Bollywood lovesong.

The horse slowly worked its way up the long incline, with the little man continuing his equine conversation. Théophile grimly held the rail and kept himself upright, willing his feet to stay under him. His breath came in short, hot jabs from his lungs and the sweat ran off him with sticky insistence, while the muscles in his legs threatened to give way beneath him. His back was raw with the sunburn.

At last they reached a flatter section of the road and the driver allowed Théophile to climb back up. To his relief, his tote bag had not fallen off. He clutched it to his stomach as his one comfort while the tonga moved off. His sweat began to cool and he shivered as they gathered speed on the downward slope. As the night passed, he clung to his bag and the rail of the tonga with an abject numbness.

When the sun rose, pale apricot fingers of clouds ran fine filaments across the sky above them and birds began to call and flutter in the predawn coolness. The driver finally stopped the tonga at a little chai shop.

"Now we are breakfast." he said.

There were various Indian men sitting in the smoky shade of the wooden chai shop and they looked up with interest as Théophile staggered in after the driver, clutching his tote bag to his chest. They talked amongst themselves and he could only imagine the derogatory remarks they were making. Their chuckling unnerved him. A boy in surprisingly well ironed Levis brought chipped-rim glasses with the incredibly sweet tea. He placed them on the dirty laminex table, ran a filthy cloth around the edges and bowed to Théophile. Without thinking, he put his hands round the glass and burnt his fingers. He very nearly dropped it in his pain. Every eye in the shop was on him. A man in an equally filthy apron that may have once been white, brought them some hot chapatis wrapped in newspaper and he devoured the flat Indian pancake bread with a greed that surprised him. Then he realised he was supposed to share with the driver.

The driver laughed. "You hungry man!" he laughed and the whole chai shop joined in. More chapatis were brought and they ate in silence. Théophile felt limp and ill but the Indian man seemed to be as alert as if he'd just had a good night's sleep. He was talking animatedly to the other patrons. The boy in the Levis came over to Théophile. "You America, right?" he said again bowing. Théophile wondered where he had learned to do that.

"I am from France", he said, aware that he was under scrutiny.

"Not America?" said the boy, obviously disappointed.

"No. You know where is France?" Théophile felt he owed some kind of explanation to the boy.

The boy turned and shoved his backside in Théophile's direction. "Good jeans from America. You have good jeans? I buy from you, good price."

"Sorry", said Théophile feeling almost guilty and opening his hands in a gesture of apology. The boy stalked off, clearly disgruntled.

Théophile paid for the meal, bought some bidis and walked out into the gathering warmth of the morning to smoke one. When the driver joined him, he climbed back up onto the tonga. As the cart began to move, the boy in Levis came out to wave.

"You come back soon. Bring good jeans!" he shouted. Théophile waved lethargically as the tonga turned away for the village.

The road became nothing more than a narrow occasionally bituminous pot-holed thread through rice fields where grey bullocks toiled in the mud, fed by thin rivulets of water. Sweating brick-makers, thin as stick figures, built their temporary kilns by slimy creeks, and hordes of black crows eyed everything from the gaunt trees. Sometimes Théophile slept but always there was the danger of falling off the tonga.

In the heat of the day, they rested by a small reeking river, the horse drinking long and deep. Several Indian women were beating rolls of laundry with rocks and Théophile wondered how they would ever get their clothes clean in such disgusting water. The image of his mother and her cleanliness obsession washed over him. The women gathered up their bundles, balanced them on their heads and disappeared through the long dry grass. The driver tethered the horse to a telephone pole whose wires dangled from either side, cut off by someone who had probably sold the rest of the wire as scrap. The driver laid out a grass mat under some trees and indicated they could rest. They lay side by side until the worst of the heat had passed, Théophile using his tote bag for a pillow. He smoked a bidi and faded away.

When he awoke, he had the strange sensation that someone was calling his name. He thought it was the French girl, Ariette, and he sat up looking to see her. The heat haze shimmered across the rice fields and he felt foolish. The driver woke and sat up.He flashed his wonderfully white teeth in a smile at Théophile. "Not far", he said, and unfastened the dormant horse and clambered enthusiastically back up into his seat. Théophile sat still and smoked another bidi before he found the will to move. Watching the butt smoulder in the grass, he dragged himself upright and forced his feet to move. The driver watched him and Théophile realised that he was expected to roll up the grass mat. His back ached as he bent and his head throbbed as he remounted the tonga and on they went.

The afternoon was an endless trail of potholes and creek crossings, rice fields and hamlets where little boys ran beside the tonga, yelling "Hello Mister, you give one dollar." Now and then the tonga was forced entirely off the road by a train of buffalo carts heavy-laden with hay or a multicoloured, flower-festooned truck with its singsong klaxon blaring and "Horn OK Please" written on the tailgate. It all passed Théophile like a parade in a nightmare. The rail to which he clung was his only support, his tote bag his only comfort.

Evening came and they ate rice and stringy chicken *bhaji* at a roadside stall, festooned with loops of little coloured lamps, run by a noisy generator that coughed every so often, making the lights blink. The meal was served on mango leaves sewn together with toothpick-thin strips of bamboo. Théophile ate in a stupor. When the meal was finished, the leaves were thrown onto the street for the crows. Théophile paid the few rupees required and the journey resumed.

In the last moments of the day, in the dying orange glow of the westering sun, the tonga began to climb again. Théophile smoked the last of his bidis, cursing that he hadn't bought more. Now there were no more villages. He kept shifting from one buttock to the other trying to find some way of softening the bumpy ride. Where they were going and why seemed to be a distant question lurking somewhere in his consciousness but he couldn't muster the power of concentration to focus, much less resist.

And then finally in the late evening the horse dragged the tonga up one long last hill and stopped in a collection of shuttered shops and stalls. There was a long wall on one side with a wide square wooden doorway over which hung a single electric light, hosting a mist of circling insects.

The little Indian man yelled something and, after a long pause, a sleepy voice answered from inside. The gate was unlocked and pulled back and the horse drew the tonga and Théophile into an open courtyard. Another man approached with a lantern.

"Come." said the driver clambering down from the tonga and taking the lantern from the other man. "You sleep. Morning comes, then *darshan*." Théophile, clutching his tote bag, meekly followed the little man with what little energy he had left. They entered a long wooden building, where the dull yellow light of the lantern revealed rows of wooden beds, some occupied by inert bodies and others empty, each with a thin mattress rolled up on the end. "Water is there", whispered the man gesturing towards the far end of the hut. "Now sleep." Taking the lantern, he was gone.

In the dark, with his mind unable to function at all, Théophile crashed into the nearest of the unoccupied beds and fell on it. The hard slats dug into his body but he had no volition left to unroll the mattress or do anything. With his last faint ray of consciousness, he pulled his tote bag into his chest and passed out.

IV

Before dawn, there were bells ringing and there was movement in the hut, quiet footfalls, doors opening. Close by a steady deep drumbeat and the calls of conch shells filled the air. After some moments, these sounds gave way to voices chanting in the still cool morning air and Théophile found himself sitting up, in pain from the hard wooden slats of the bed and his sunburnt body, but wanting to go towards the sounds of the chanting.

He found the water jar at the end of the building and sluiced his face. Leaving his tote bag on the bed, he followed the sounds, out into the still dark predawn.

Across the courtyard, light streamed from a temple with a gold-domed roof and white statues of guardians with lances, standing on either side of the steps. Inside, there were rows of glowing lanterns; as he mounted the steps he squinted into the bright light of the interior. There were maybe twenty people standing with their backs to him, women on one side, men on the other, all facing the front of the temple. At the front was a brightly painted life-size statue of a woman with four arms, brandishing a sword and sitting astride a tiger. Before her stood what Théophile supposed must be a priest, holding a large metal plate that supported a ring of yellow candles. The priest was waving the tray in circles in front of the statue while everyone else was chanting. The air was thick with incense smoke.

One of the men turned to Théophile and gave him the underhand Indian gesture of beckoning and Théophile came to stand beside him. The man was chanting from a small book, which he offered to share, but when Théophile looked at it, he realised it was in a script he couldn't read so he shook his head. Instead he watched the candles circling and circling at the front of the temple and let the sounds of the chant wash over him; somehow he seemed to know what was being chanted. He felt he had heard this before, somewhere, sometime in the long-ago past, but he couldn't grasp where or when. In a deep part of himself, he relaxed, breathing a little deeper, swaying gently on his feet and feeling that it was surprisingly good to be there.

When the chant finished, the priest raised the tray of candles high in the air and the chanters in unison dropped to their knees and bent forward in a deep bow to the statue. Théophile felt like a giant towering above them and he had the instantly terrifying experience that the woman sitting on the tiger was staring at him. The black shining eyes seemed to be very alive and to pierce into his being. To escape the intensity of that look, he dropped to his knees and, bending forward, rested his head on the temple floor as the chanters were doing. And then out of him arose a great cry of grief, as if, in the bending forward, he had unlocked some old secret store of anguish, ages of pain, layers of despair.

It poured out of him onto the cold stone floor and out into the still air of the morning. His battered voice was careening from the stones and the bricks of the temple, his inner being seemed to be ridding itself of so much rancid effluence and he utterly surrendered to it. How long he was there, crouched in the position of a child, with his head on the floor, he had no idea, but finally he quieted and his breathing evened. At last he pulled himself back onto his heels and saw the tonga driver squatting patiently beside him.

"Chapati", he said quietly. "Chai. Breakfast."

Théophile painfully pulled himself back onto his heels and then staggered as he got to his feet. The tonga driver had his elbow in support. Avoiding eye contact with the statue, Théophile followed the little man obediently out of the temple. Miraculously he had managed to dislodge his sandals before entering the temple and he now found them neatly paired at the steps.

As he moved out into the white morning sunlight, his bladder screamed for relief. "Got to peepee", he said to the little man.

The man nodded and took him behind the temple to a wooden building with a row of squat toilets without walls between them. A tiny wrinkled Indian woman was sluicing the cement floor with buckets of water. The driver spoke to her and she sent one last forceful wave of water over Théophile's sandals and left. The relief of the long urination filled him with a sweetness that was almost shocking. The smell of his urine, the sound of it on the porcelain toilet bowl, the colour of its arc. It was all so beautiful. Shaking out the last drips, he shook his head in wonderment.

"*Merde*", he said to himself, "I love my peepee", and he began to laugh.

His guide had withdrawn and was waiting for him outside. Théophile managed to stifle his laughter as he adjusted his cotton pants. They walked to an open pavilion where people were lining up to receive a metal cup of steaming spiced tea and a folded chapati, the ubiquitous Indian flat bread. In the line stood a mixture of people, mostly Indian and mostly men. Théophile was relieved to see several Western-looking people and he began to realise that he should find out something of where he was. When he received his chai and his chapati, he sat with several Western-looking young men on mats on the floor. After his first sip of his tea, which scalded his lips, he saw that no one else was drinking yet and stopped.

Finally a tall Indian man stood up with military posture, put his hands together, and said some words, which the seated group repeated in unison. Then everyone began slurping their chai very noisily from their cups. The trick seemed to be to hold the cup close to but not touching the lips and then to suck it across the gap. No one spoke. Théophile looked around him and nodded at some of his neighbours, who nodded back. He dunked his chapati as others did and with his first mouthful, his hunger came rushing to him. He felt like he hadn't eaten anything for days. Now his hunger burned inside him and he wolfed down his chapati. Once the last crumb had gone, he jumped up and went back to the serving table for more, but when he got there, the two Indian men who had been serving, put up their hands in restraint and pointed back to the mats. Clearly the rule was one each and no more. Théophile felt intimidated by the silence but his hunger was intense.

"Eat", he whispered in English.

In response one of the men held up his finger and said "*Ek*". Then they gathered up the remaining chapatis and retreated into a back room.

Glowering, Théophile went back to his chai on the mat. The man next to him grinned and muttered, with an American accent, "Chapati nazis, huh?" Not quick enough to catch the meaning, Théophile smiled weakly and drained the dregs of his chai.

The sun was gathering its heat as he walked out of the pavilion with the American. A peacock pecked at the dirt and as they passed, it fanned out its tail and turned in a half circle. "Beautiful", the American said.

Théophile nodded and then asked in his best English "Can I ask you something?"

"Sure", the man said, continuing to walk.

"Where is this place? What is it called?"

The other man looked at him in surprise. "You don't know where you are?" When Théophile shook his head, he asked "How'd you get here?"

Théophile thought for a moment, trying to craft his answer. This was both an exercise in linguistics and content. Finally he simply said "With a horse and a chariot." The English word for "cart" had eluded him.

The other man frowned. "Really? But you knew where you were going, right?"

"Not at all", Théophile said. "He just say to me I must come."

"Who was it?" The American was puzzled. "You mean someone invited you?"

Théophile stopped and looked around to see if he could see his driver, but from a distance most of the Indian men looked much the same, small-framed, short and dressed in the same white clothes. "I don't see him", Théophile said. "He come to my hut in Goa and he say to come. But he not say where."

"Cool", the American said. They walked on in silence for a moment.

Théophile felt the need to say more. Dredging up his memory of what happened at the beach in Goa, he said: « 'E say to me, Guruji tell 'im. »

« No shit! » The American was looking at him with slitted eyes, as if not sure whether to believe him. "Sounds like maybe she must've sent him."

"Pardon?" asked Théophile, not sure if he had really understood.

"See, it's my guess, and who knows why, she decided you were supposed to be here?"

"Who is this 'she'?"

"Padma Amma." He looked at Théophile for recognition but saw only his blank expression. "I heard she's done that before, you know, sent for somebody, but I've never met anyone she actually called." The American was looking at Théophile with admiration. "That is so cool."

"Who is this person?"

"Wow", said the American and eyed Théophile closely as if he doubted what he was hearing. "You mean you never heard of her?"

When the Frenchman shook his head, he went on. "Okay. Okay." He shook his head in amazement. "Man, what a trip."

He started to walk again. "Okay. So this place is called Shree Durga Prasad Ashram, right?" He spread out his hands to take in their surroundings. "And the spiritual head, the guru, is a woman and her name is Swami Padmananda. She was a disciple of Anandaji Maharaj. He died years back. This was his ashram. So now it's her. « He paused to see if Théophile was still following. Théophile dutifuly nodded so he went on. « Everyone calls her Padma Amma and she's the real thing. I mean, she's a realised guru, a saint, you know?"

"A saint?"

"Yeah, in the Indian sense. You sure you never heard of her?"

"*Pas de tout*. Not at all."

"Man, that's unbelievable." The American shook his head, then he put his hand on Théophile's shoulder." Well, in about an hour, you'll get to meet her. She gives morning *darshan* in the medan."

Théophile's most pressing need, more than meeting the guru, was to eat. When he asked the American about it, he grinned and said. "You got rupees?"

Théophile suddenly remembered his tote bag. He'd left his money belt just lying on a bed in India. He felt a rush of panic "It is in my bag."

The American clapped him on the shoulder again. "Hey! If you're paying, I'm eating." he said, unaware of the pain he had inflicted on Théophile's ravaged skin. He walked him back to the sleeping hut, talking enthusiastically, not much of which Théophile could follow.

To his relief Théophile found his tote bag untouched under the bed and his money belt inside it. He strapped it on and the American led him through the grounds of the ashram, describing what each building was. In fact the ashram was not much more than a collection of small brick buildings under coconut palms and Ashoka trees. The temple was in the centre and was by far the largest and most ornate building.

Walking through a lush vegetable garden, where sprinklers lazily pocked away, creating misty rainbows in the morning sunlight, they passed through a side gate out to the dusty road where a small boy saluted them and said in carefully rehearsed English: "You want *ganja*, change money?" The American said something in whatever Indian language it was and the boy waggled his head and sang "Good morning", before returning to his post at the gate.

Across the road the lean-to shops and stalls had come to life, clustered together under a row of dusty trees. One was a tailor's shop with rolls of different colour cottons arrayed on a trestle table in the street. Another seemed to sell only plastic objects. Bottles of all sizes sat on shelves, bizarrely coloured sandals hung like garlands from the awning, and statues of Indian gods and goddesses sat in military rows on a wooden counter. Several other shops seemed to serve nothing at all, but each had an Indian man sitting on a chair in front of it. As they passed, the American greeted each one and they returned the greeting. At the far end was a collection of wooden boxes in front of a small white stucco building.

"The local diner", the American said with a grin. "Grab a box." He ducked into the shade of a torn canvas sheet, pulled tight over several of the lower branches of a tree. Here he dropped onto a wooden box and pulled up a larger one to serve as a table. Théophile followed his lead.

"You like *uttapas*?" the guy asked. Théophile shrugged, unsure of the nature of the question. "Trust me", said the American and swivelled on his box to face the darkness in the shop. "Ram!" he yelled. "*Uttapa, dos. Chai dos. Jeldi hai!*"

A young Indian boy appeared and waggled his head. "*Ji Baba. Uttapa dos*", holding up two fingers, "*chai dos*", and again two fingers. "Soon coming", and he disappeared, yelling the order somewhere into the back of the shop.

"You'll like 'em", said the American. "House specialty. Well that's basically all they do. Hey, it's not your cordon bleu cuisine but it sticks to your ribs." Then he pulled out a pack of bidis. "Smoke?"

Normally by this time of day, Théophile would have craved something to smoke. Anything. In France he had smoked since his teens and once he had arrived in India, the cheap bidis became his habit. But now as the young American extended the packet towards him, a sudden wave of nausea hit him and he recoiled. "No thank you."

The American got up and went to the cooking fire at the back of the shop and with a twist of paper, lit his cigarette. When he came back to the table, he blew the smoke up into the air to avoid Théophile and said "Name's Brad." He then looked at Théophile expecting him to introduce himself. With his native French reluctance, he hesitated until, finally, he admitted, "I am Théophile, Theo." To an American ear it sounded like T. O. They shook hands. Théophile asked, "You have been in this ashram a long time?"

"Couple weeks. I'm at Cornell, South Asian studies. I was supposed to go to the University in Nagpur, for the next semester, but I met this guy on the train in Pune. He told me he had just been here. I don't know, somehow, when he was talking about it, I knew I had to check it out. The way this guy went on about Padma Amma, you know, there was something. . . It was like I was meant to come here. So here I am."

"And the guru? You have met with her?"

"Oh sure."

"She speaks English?"

"Not much. She says 'I love you' a lot and a few other words. When she wants to say something, usually one of the boys translates."

Suddenly Théophile had so many questions. As they talked, the Indian boy brought their chais in cracked porcelain cups with the saucers brimming. Several scrawny chickens pecked hopefully around their feet and a crow eyed them from the lowest of the tree branches. Brad had the ubiquitous American enthusiasm for sharing and so he regaled Théophile with his stories of the ashram and how it worked. Théophile's English, although not fluent, was good enough to follow most of what the American was telling him and he began to feel a kind of relief, even a happiness at what had befallen him. He wished that Ariette was there with him. This was exactly what she was looking for.

Their *uttapas* arrived, they began to eat and Brad talked on, with his mouth full of the doughy pancake. The *uttapas* were filled with undercooked onions and something green and bitter, but Théophile enjoyed his with a relish that was almost ecstatic.

"This is an amazing crêpe", he said. "Not like French crêpes, but *pas mal*. Good."

Brad grinned at Théophile's enthusiasm. "Indian cuisine!"

When Théophile had finished, he sat back and drained the rest of his chai. "It is very nice here", he said. "I did not ask to come but now think I am lucky to be here."

"I'd say it's your destiny, T. O. If she rounded you up, and it sure sounds like she did, there has to be a reason for it."

Théophile looked carefully at Brad to see if he was joking or making fun of him. "You think so?"

"You bet. I tell you, I really want to be there when you go up for *darshan*. It's going to be worth watching."

"What is that?"

"*Darshan*? It means to see. It's a Sanskrit word. It's when the guru gets to see you and you get to see the guru. Although when I say 'see' it's not just with the eyes if you know what I mean." Théophile's obvious incomprehension led him to go on. "A being like her…Well they can see not just the physical. She sees the whole thing. The big picture if you like."

Théophile felt a little tremor of fear inside. "She can read the mind?"

"Oh sure. The mind. The subconscious. Your karma, past and present. The works."

"I don't think I want someone to see all what is in my mind", said Théophile with a rueful smile. "Is not so nice, you know."

"Yeah. It takes a bit of surrender, but it's worth it. You know, it's kind of a relief to let someone see all that shit. It's like it's not it's not just yours anymore. And you know something else? She doesn't give a damn about it anyway. It's just the mind, it's all an illusion. When she looks at you, man, she sees way more than all the garbage in your head, way more."

Théophile sat there feeling oddly light-headed, as if he were already experiencing someone looking at his thoughts and seeing them all as garbage. He had the ludicrous image of a garbage truck driving out of his head and leaving it nicely empty. He felt fearful but good nonetheless. "I would like more chai", he said and the American yelled to the back of the shop for the boy.

V

By the end of breakfast, Theo had heard most of Brad's life history, not all of which made much sense, but he didn't mind. Brad was twenty-four, obviously very bright, having won scholarships to a fancy college-prep boarding school, a liberal arts college and to Cornell for his Masters. He was from Boston and his family was Episcopalian. He rooted for the Red Socks.

In his turn, Théophile had said a little about himself. He had the inbuilt French reluctance for self-revelation, but he felt obliged to offer what little as he could. However as he spoke of living in France and in a château, the open mouthed enthusiasm of his companion drew more out of him than he would normally admit.

"No kidding?" became a regular refrain as Brad called for more chai and leaned forward to hear Théophile's background. "Like a real château?"

Théophile described it, perhaps embellishing it a little here and there. He passed over the fact that it was dilapidated and in desperate need of repair. He carefully skirted any reference to the poverty he had escaped, both material and psychological. He spoke of his childhood where he and his brother would roam the château'x secret hideaways, the dungeons, the towers, the narrow back stairs. He didn't mention that his brother Hugues had slipped away from a cold and hostile domestic environment as soon as he could and left Théophile to fend for himself as their parents fought endlessly. He only obliqucly referred to how the château effectively had just the one remaining occupant, his mother.

"I tell you man", said Brad grinning broadly, "one of these days I'm coming to your house."

Théophile paid for the breakfast and they walked back into the ashram. Brad offered to show him around before *darshan* began. The grounds consisted mostly of gardens with winding pathways, banana groves and mango trees, abundant flower beds and a series of fish ponds with huge golden fish looping lazily near the surface. By the time they reached the central open area called the medan, a marble-floored square that lay behind the temple and was bounded by rows of terracotta pots holding miniature palm trees, a small crowd of mostly Indian men had gathered and were sitting on mats in tight rows before an empty wicker chair. Beside the chair stood two young men in starched white kurtas, looking rather like the guardian statues in front of the temple, but without the lances. Sandals were neatly paired on a rack by the courtyard entrance.

"You okay sitting on the floor?" asked Brad.

Théophile noticed how thin the mats were and how hard the marble looked. "How long to sit?"

"Maybe an hour or so." Brad saw the foreboding on the Frenchman's face. "You can get a blanket. It helps a bit."

There was a small shed at the back of the medan, where an Indian woman was sitting in front of the door. Brad went over to her and after quite a few exchanges of hand gestures, she reluctantly opened the shed and handed him a thin grey blanket, which he brought over to Théophile. "That woman think she owns the blankets", he muttered. "If you don't give it back afterwards, she'll kill us both."

He folded the blanket into four to make it thicker and he showed Théophile where to sit. Brad himself seemed quite comfortable on the marble and deftly folded his legs into the full lotus next to Théophile and then cracked his neck left and right, with one hand on his chin and the other on the top of his head. Théophile heard the crack and was startled. Just as he was about to say something, the entire seated group suddenly bent forward like windblown grass and Théophile was left upright, conspicuous in a sea of bent backs.

From a side door, a tiny dark-skinned woman of indeterminate age had appeared. She was wearing a rust-coloured sari and her hair was piled up into a grey bun on top of her head. As she moved towards the chair, she looked directly at Théophile with still dark eyes that pierced into him and seemed to burn his brain. He was filled with absolute terror and instantly he threw himself forward as best he could in his awkward sitting position. His head hit the marble and he held himself down in a tight agony of constraint, until a cramp ripped into his rib cage and forced him back upright. To his relief he was once again surrounded by upright bodies. When he managed to get his breath back and to work out the intense cramp, he saw that the woman was now seated in the wicker chair, talking earnestly to an elderly Indian man who was kneeling at her feet.

Brad caught his eye. "That's her", he said quietly out of the corner of his mouth. "You want to meet her?"

The terror came racing back into Théophile and he shook his head emphatically. "No, no, no", he whispered. "I just watch."

"Okay." Brad nodded. "Tell me when you're ready. I can introduce you."

However, within minutes the woman in the chair had finished talking to the older man and was looking around the group. She said something sharply to the back of the courtyard and, before he knew what was happening, Théophile found his tonga driver standing next to him saying "Come."

He shook his head fearfully but the driver was insistent. "Get up."

Unbending himself painfully, Théophile staggered to his feet and the driver impelled him towards the wicker chair. His left leg seemed to have gone to sleep and with each painful step, he became more and more aware of the intensity of the gaze that was directed at him. He could not hold her look at all and tottered forward like an unstrung marionette. As much to escape as to express respect, he dropped to his knees in front of the chair and tipped forward until his head was back on the marble. The coolness of the stone soothed his brain while above him, he heard the conversation between the guru and the driver, as if he were at the bottom of the sea and ocean liners were passing over his head.

At last the driver tapped him on the shoulder and Théophile reluctantly surfaced. He gazed at the diminutive feet of the guru and then willed himself to look into her face. To his immense relief, she was smiling gently at him. He felt a great wave of tension ebb away and managed a thin smile in response. The driver again tapped his shoulder.

"Amma says to you she is pleased you ask to come."

This made no sense to Théophile, who shook his head, but couldn't get his voice to work. The guru gazed at him for what seemed like an eternity before she said something very softly. The driver translated.

"Your heart call and her heart answer." Involuntarily Théophile found his hand going up to his heart, almost as if he were checking that it was still there. In response, the guru put her hand to her heart and nodded. Then she spoke again and the driver did the translation.

"You have a work to do. Important. Your heart wants to work."

At last Théophile found his voice. "Okay", he croaked.

The guru reached to her right to a small side table and from it took a little book, which she extended towards Théophile. She looked at him and said very clearly: "Englis."

He thought she was asking his country of birth so he shook his head but replied in English, "I am French."

A dark look crossed her face and she thrust the book at him. "Englis book."

Embarrassed beyond belief, he muttered, "Pardon", and reached to take the book with his left hand. At which the Indian driver jumped forward and smacked his hand away. "Use other hand", he said sternly.

Wishing he could shrivel up and disappear, Théophile obediently accepted the little book in his right hand and whispered, "*Merci.*" To his further horror he found he had no legs to stand on. The driver, although much smaller than Théophile, picked him up and more or less carried him back to his blanket. Brad was grinning broadly as the driver dropped Théophile onto the blanket.

"Nice *darshan*", Brad whispered.

As he sat on his folded blanket, Théophile found himself in a swirling vortex of inner movement. His face was burning, his left leg was twitching uncontrollably, his stomach seemed to be leaping about inside him threatening to unburden itself onto the marble, his heart was racing and tears were running down his cheeks. And yet at the same time there was a part of him that stood aside and watched all this with absolute detachment. He was aware of his body and his mind, the weight of the little book in his right hand; he was aware of the guru before him now greeting a group of sari-clad women who were kneeling around her in an earnest semicircle; he was aware of the coconut trees above his head where the sun made slashes of light on the marble floor; he was aware of the slowly turning planet on which he existed as if he were a disinterested tourist; and most of all he was aware that he himself was none of these things. He was something else, something solid and irrefutable, something that had no name and no shape; he was something that he had always been and had forgotten all about. And he felt waves of love, not for any one in particular or for any thing, just love itself. After some time he closed his eyes and disappeared.

When he opened them again, the medan was empty and the marble was hot to touch. He felt the most peaceful he had ever felt in his entire life. He was also totally unable to move his legs, which had been crossed in front of him. He put the book carefully in his tote bag. With both hands he worked to uncross his completely numb legs; the pain of suddenly recirculating blood made him cry out in pain. As he was trying to get up, Brad came into the courtyard.

"Hey man, you missed one hell of a great lunch. *Baji* from heaven." He squatted down next to Théophile. "You okay?"

For some reason, this seemed to be hilarious to Théophile and he began to laugh. Brad grinned at him and Théophile laughed more and more. Brad began to laugh too until the two of them were hooting. After several minutes, an Indian man in a white dhoti and a little white cap carrying a bamboo *lathi* came striding into the medan and hurried over to them.

"Is quiet time", he said sternly. "Must be in silence."

This only served to push the two young men into even stronger paroxysms of hilarity. The man shushed them and when that had no effect, he began hitting them with his bamboo *lathi* and trying to force them out of the medan. Several other Indian men appeared and as a group they finally succeeded, remonstrating in harsh whispers, in pushing the two hooting miscreants out of the medan.

Finally Brad led Théophile to a wooden bench under a clump of banana trees.

When he got his breath back, Théophile looked at Brad and said "I feel wonderful."

Brad just nodded and looked up into the lush green leaves of the banana tree.

"I get that", he said. "She's lit a fire in you."

VI

They sat together under the trees in the hot afternoon sun. The small book lay in Théophile's lap. Finally he opened it and began to flick through the pages. He showed it to Brad. "Do you know this book?"

Brad took it and nodded. "*Ashtavakra Samhita*. I wonder why she gave you this?" He leafed through the pages and then closed it again, giving it back to Théophile. "We worked through it in a graduate seminar, though not in English. The original is Sanskrit. It's a bit of a weird scripture if you ask me. It's like two guys get into heaven and tell each other how great it is. The only problem is they don't say too much about how they got there and they don't seem interested in helping anyone else get there either. Except for some pretty heavy-duty stuff like total abstinence. It's not my favourite text, I gotta say."

He handed it back to Théophile. "Good luck with that!"

Théophile opened the book and read the first verse aloud. "Janaka said 'How can I attain knowledge? How can I attain liberation? How can I become detached? Tell me, of Revered Sir. '"

"That's the question right there", muttered Brad. "And Ashtavakra gives it to him, chapter and verse from there on."

"Who is this Ashtavakra?"

Brad leant back on the bench and seemed to drop into a state of meditation for a minute. Then he grinned at Théophile. "Oh, he was quite a dude, if you believe all the stories. They say he was a boy saint who was born with a crippled body, bent in eight places. That's how he got his name. Ashtavakra means, more or less that: bent in eight places."

"I have not heard of this", Théophile said. "When did he live?"

"No one's too sure about that. Or if he's real. He could just be fictional. Indian scriptures are like that. I've read commentaries that see it both ways. It's a bit like Ganesh, you know? I mean, was there really a guy with an elephant's head or is he just a representation of something? The remover of obstacles."

Théophile shrugged. Indian philosophy was not something he had put much effort into.

"Anyway", Brad said, "this kid, Ashtakavra, is most famous for being the guru of King Janaka. You heard of him?"

"No."

"He's the other half of the dialogue in this book. You want to hear the story?"

"Maybe we get something to eat first, no?"

"Oh right, you totally missed it. Lunch is finished. You okay to try the chai shop? Not too much else to choose from, out here."

They walked back out of the gates of the ashram into the baking heat of the afternoon. The saluting boy was asleep under a tree. In seconds, Théophile was covered in sweat. When they reached the shelter of the chai shop, not a soul stirred. Bodies were strewn here and there in the shade, like some terrible aftermath, but when Brad yelled, there was a lazy stirring and the young man who had served them in the morning sat up groggily from under a table.

"Hey Babu, this French guy needs *bhaji*. You got some left?" The boy waggled his head from side to side in the mysterious and ambiguous Indian response to any question. He walked to the back of the shop and yelled until an older man appeared, sleepily scratching his armpits. The boy yelled some more and the Indian man grumbled but turned on a gas bottle to fire up his huge metal pan. He poured in some kind of viscous oil, then from somewhere he produced a bowl of cooked vegetables and threw them in. Meanwhile Brad retrieved two bottles of Thums Up from a rattling fridge in the corner, chugging away on power from an electric cord that looped through the trees. "Thums Up", he said, grinning as he snapped off the bottle tops. "They used to have a proud slogan that said 'No natural ingredients!'"

The boy came back to them and, all smiles, said "*Bhaji* soon coming."

They sat on boxes in the coolest corner of the tarpaulin shelter, sipping their Indian colas. Brad lit himself a bidi and began to recount the classic story of Ashtavakra and King Janaka.

"The easiest way to read this story", Brad said, blowing smoke above his head, "is to get the comic book but I don't have that one yet. You can get comics on every Indian saint there is. Okay, so the story of Ashtavakra. Here's the way I remember it. King Janaka was the ruler of Mithila, a kingdom in the north of India. Actually I think there was a dynasty of King Janakas but this is the story of one of them. So, one day he was asleep on his fine royal bed, lying back on his silk sheets, and he had a dream. In this dream he was a poor man wandering on a dusty road. He was so hungry that he walked into a farmer's field and stole a stalk of sugar cane. The farmer saw him and began to hit him with a stick. Suddenly King Janaka woke up yelling. But then he looked around him and he saw his handmaidens fanning him and his bodyguards on the alert and all the finery of his court at his fingertips.

"He dropped off to sleep again. But as soon as he did, he was back in the sugarcane field and the farmer was still hitting him with a big stick. So he woke up. Then he had a question. Which was real, the waking state or the dream state? He summoned all his wise counsellors and asked them. They gave all kinds of scriptural references, recommended a different diet and offered to do *pujas*, but none of them could say definitively whether one state was real and the other wasn't."

Brad paused to see if Théophile was following all this. Théophile nodded, so he went on.

"Tell me if I'm going too fast, T.O. Okay, so King Janaka didn't like any of their answers and got so royally pissed off he had them thrown in the dungeon. One of them was the father of this boy Ashtavakra. When his dad didn't come home for tiffin, he asked his mom what happened to him. When she told him what the king had asked, the boy said he would go and save his father. So this kid walked into the royal court. This must have been the first time he was there, because when they saw him, all the courtiers and the king himself began to laugh. Don't forget the kid was bent in eight places so he looked pretty weird. He stood there in the court of the king while they all hooted and hollered. Then he began to laugh too, only harder than any of them.

"Finally everyone stopped laughing and the king said 'Child, I know why we were laughing. Because of the way you look. But why were you laughing?' Ashtvakra replied 'O King, you were laughing at my physical form. I was laughing at you because that is all you could see. Only a fool would think that the human body is the ultimate reality. ' The king wasn't too impressed to be called a fool and nearly threw the boy into the same dungeon as his dad, but the boy said 'O King, you asked a question that none of your wise counsellors could answer. I have the answer. '

So the king repeated his question: What is real, the waking state or the dream state?

"This was a smart kid, so he struck a bargain. 'If I tell you the answer, my dad gets out of jail, deal?' The king agreed, so Ashtavakra said 'The answer, Your Majesty, is that neither is real. Both are states of illusion. Only the *atman* is real, that which can never be born and which will never die. You are that, but you don't know that. Because you don't know that, you live in ignorance.

"This king was a smart king so he listened carefully to this and he saw that it could be true. So he asked Ashtakavra to be his guru. And then one day by following his guru's teachings diligently, he attained liberation."

The boy brought two metal *thalis* to the box that served as their table. On each *thali* was a mound of steaming rice, another mound of stewed vegetables, a bowl of dal and two chapatis.

"And his dad got out of jail", Brad said. "*Bon appetit.*"

Théophile looked round for something to eat with. Although he had been in India for eight months, he had not yet had to face the rural habit of eating with his fingers. He watched Brad moosh the rice and the vegetables together with one hand and then pour the dal onto it, much the way one would mix cement. When he had a good blend he moulded a portion of the mixture into a small ball and scooped it expertly into his mouth with his thumb. Théophile attempted the same operation but because he was left-handed, he did it with his left hand. Brad stopped him.

"Bad move", he said. "You remember when she gave you the book this morning?"

Théophile dropped his messy attempt at a ball back onto the *thali*, looking puzzled and more than a little annoyed. He shrugged. "Of course."

"You went for it with your left hand and they stopped you, remember?"

"Ah yes."

"So in India the left hand is for wiping your ass, nothing else."

"But is natural for me, the left hand."

"Better get used to it. It's a big no-no to touch anyone or anything with the dirty hand."

Théophile shrugged and, with his clumsy right hand, attempted to mould the food into a ball. It was not elegant. Finally Brad took pity on him and shouted: "Babu, you got a spoon?" After a minute the boy appeared with a large and slightly rusted serving spoon. The boy gave it one last earnest wipe on his grubby T-shirt and handed it over. Théophile carefully accepted it with his right hand then cleaned it a bit more using the bottom of his *kurta*. He looked up guiltily to see the boy glowering at him.

The two young men ate in silence for a few minutes. The heat of the day was increased by the heat of the curried *bhaji*, and Théophile found himself again suffused in sweat. He needed a second Thums Up.

After he paid for the meal, they walked back into the ashram, moving slowly from one shady spot to the next. They both took a quick lukewarm bucket bath to reduce the sweat and headed for siesta. Brad's bed was several along from his and they both lay down in the hot afternoon with a rickety fan lazily looping over their heads, ticking in an ineffectual attempt at moving much air. Brad was out in seconds but Théophile could not sleep, feeling his body vibrating as if there were currents of electricity passing through him.

His mind seemed to be racing, recreating the events of the morning: the courtyard, the guru, the statue of the woman on the tiger. Nothing seemed to be quite real and yet everything seemed to be laced with significance. What this significance was, Théophile could not work out. He closed his eyes against so much inner activity, but even then images swirled and he could not distance himself from them. Finally he sat up and reached for the book. "Janaka said 'How can I attain knowledge? How can I attain liberation? How can I become detached? Tell me, Revered Sir.'"

As Théophile read these words, a new kind of peace descended on him. That's what he wanted: knowledge. He wanted to know, he wanted to know who he was, he wanted to know what the point of being alive was, he wanted to know how to be free from this sense of being stuck. He wanted to be free. He repeated to himself in English "Tell me, O Revered Sir." For a while he closed his eyes, expecting somehow to hear the answer to his request. But all he got was an echo of the question: *tell me, tell me, tell me…* Finally he went back to the text and began to read on. It seemed like a kind of code. The two voices in the scripture, the king and the crippled sage, talking in riddles but from a sense of certainty. They seemed to know how to be free. They were describing it. Janaka asked the question but then he seemed to know the answer as well. How come it made no sense?

Théophile lay there for a long time watching the fan going round and round, endlessly round and round. *C'est comme ça*, that's how it is: round and round and round and round.

VII

Later in the afternoon, after another bucket bath to wake himself up and a shave with a razor borrowed from Brad, Théophile went back to the medan . Once the heat of the day had passed, Brad had told him, Padma Amma would sometimes come out and sit in the cool of the evening.

Folding his blanket as thickly as possible to give himself something of a seat, Théophile crossed his legs as best he could. Brad settled next to him and seemed to go off into meditation. Around them sat groups of Indian men and a sprinkling of Westerners. Théophile began to wonder if Ariette, the French girl might turn up. They had spoken so often about spiritual pursuits back on the beach, maybe she had heard of this ashram. He was longing to talk to someone in French about what he was experiencing.

While he was thinking about her, he sensed the change in the people around him and this time was alert enough to bend forward with some grace as the tiny figure of the guru appeared. She took no notice of him as various people came up to her chair, until one very thin elderly Indian man with a little white Nehru hat in his hand bowed before her. She nodded at what he said and he bowed deeply before walking backwards away from her.

Brad leaned in close to Théophile. «That guy's the past life reader.» he said.

Théophile couldn't catch what Brad had said. «Pardon?»

Brad however did not respond but was looking to the front of the crowd. The Guru was looking at them both. In the power of her lookThéophile was on fire again, heat flashing up along his spine, and perspiration pouring into his eyes from his hairline. She stared at them both for what seemed like an age and then turned to look upwards into a coconut palm where a small bird was diligently cleaning under its wings. The entire group assembled in the medan looked up with her. Then she spoke.

One of the boys in white stepped forward and said loudly: «Guruji says, watch how even the smallest bird will take care of its wings. If it does not do so it cannot fly.»

Then the Guru got to her feet and walked through the group sitting before her. As she passed Brad and Théophileshe pointed up to the tree, as if she wanted to be sure they had understood, Then she was gone.

A number of people came forward to bow to her chair before leaving the medan and then walked away Awkwardly scrambling to his feet, Théophile felt the need to bow to the guru too, then he followed Brad out of the medan

Brad said «Right from the Guru's mouth. When she says something , you better take notice.».

Théophile nodded. Then he remembered that Brad was trying to tell him something when they were sitting before the Guru.

«You tried to tell me something, but I didn't get it.»

«Oh yeah. The old guy with the Nehru hat. He can tell you about your past lives.»

«Past lives?»

«You know, like who you were before you were born.»

«Oh» Théophile was unsure why this was useful.

«It's a trip I tell you. » Brad grinned. «You ought to get him to do yours. I'd bet he could tell you why you're here.»

«You think so? You think it is true, what he can do?»

«Oh yeah» Brad nodded. «He's got it.»

It was the following morning when Brad introduced Théophile to Nagadas, the reader of past lives. He was a courtly, formal man who bowed as Brad said his name.

The elderly man led Théophile towards a low brick hut with a thatched roof. Inside there was a small table and two wicker stools. The old man took off his sandals at the door, waited for Théophile to do the same and then ushered him inside. They sat on the stools with the table between them and the old man pulled a battered cardboard folder from a drawer in the table. He placed it in front of him and then placed both his hands palm down on the table.

"Give me your hand." demanded the man and Théophile caught himself before his left hand had moved too far. Again from the drawer in the table, the old man pulled out a pair of thick black-rimmed glasses, which he pushed up onto his nose. He peered down at Théophile's palm for a long time. He opened the folder. Inside was a large dried leaf.

He took the leaf very gently, with reverence, and laid it on Théophile's open right palm, placing his own right hand on top of the leaf. The air became very still. Somewhere outside, a truck horn sounded, a peacock screeched and a metal-wheeled barrow rattled past the hut.

The old man began to speak.

"They are like the stones on which one takes steps to cross a stream. You see? One life, one stone. Step by step. Some stones are large and easy to stand upon. Others are unstable and will throw you into the stream. If you fall into the stream, you must start again. Of course. You have tried many times to cross the stream."

The old man was speaking slowly and carefully, his hand cool and steady, his eyes gently closed. Théophile willed himself to follow the words as closely as he could. The stream imagery meant nothing to him.

"In the seeing of the past, always I see a *mala*, a rosary, of lives, like beads strung one lifetime after another on the string of *samsara*. You are knowing *samsara*?" He opened his eyes. Théophile meekly shook his head and the old man closed his eyes again before he went on. " It is the cycle of birth and death. You are born, you live, you create karma, you die. So many times have you done this. But for you there is one of particular significance. This is the one, more prominent than all others for you. In this life, not so long ago, you followed the teachings of a master in an ashram, not unlike the one where you are now sitting. You know what I am saying?" The old man opened his eyes again and peered at Théophile through the thick lenses of his glasses.

"Yes, thank you." said Théophile, not as firmly as he would have wished but the old man accepted it and went on.

"Good. It is important what I have to tell you. If you follow the *sankalpa* of Shri Guru, her will, then what I shall say will bear fruit." He closed his eyes again. Théophile idly wondered why he needed the glasses. "It is for you important and I can see for others also. You must know there were others of you in that ashram, all disciples of the same guru. So young, such pure souls, so full of devotion. Ah but you see, my friend, here is the seed of downfall." He paused, opened his eyes again and looked sternly at Théophile. "You know what is 'downfall'?"

Théophile shook his head. He had a vague sense of the word but wanted to be sure.

"If you do not follow, you must say so." The old man shook the forefinger of his left hand at Théophile. "I will explain you. 'Downfall' means to fall down. Means to lose that which you are having. It means loss. When man experiences such downfall, then he must begin again. So now I will tell of your downfall. Do not be sad." He closed his eyes again and Théophile felt the pressure of the hand on the leaf more intensely.

"This is the downfall, not just for you but for others also. Each one could not attain the goal. That much is certain. Each one fell down because each one had a weakness. I can tell you. One fell under the spell of black magic. One, oh yes, too much enjoyed sense pleasures. And one betrayed his own people. You see how it is with temptation and karma?"

Théophile urgently wanted to ask which one he was but Nagadas went on without a pause.

"In this life you, I am telling you…" The thin gnarled finger of the old man's left hand wagged in Théophile's face, even though the old man's eyes remained closed. "You, all of you, you are *yogabrashta.*"

This meant nothing to Théophile, but his inclination to ask was cut short and the thin finger pointing at him seemed almost threatening. "*Yogabrashta.* You might say means fallen yogi, yes? Or you might say such a yogi who could not complete the mission of the soul in that one life. You see this?"

At last Théophile sensed he had a chance to speak. "It is difficult to understand." he ventured. The old man opened his eyes for a moment and his look pierced, accentuated by the glasses, into Théophile's eyes. Then he grunted, closed his eyes again and the left hand dropped back onto the table.

"One day, my friend, one day." And then, to Théophile's surprise, the wizened face cracked open into a delighted toothless smile and the old man chuckled. He opened his eyes and removed the glasses. "Oh yes", he said. "Oh yes." The creases at the corners of his eyes deepened and he laughed till his body shook.

After several minutes of chortling, he took out a less than clean rag and wiped his eyes. "To laugh is God's blessing. Is it not so?"

He put away the rag and became serious again. "So much time you have spent. So much time you have lost. So little time is left." Théophile nodded. That much he thought he understood.

"Ah." Nagadas nodded as well, making for a strange moment of mutual nodding before the old man went on. "But one day you will see everything as clear as these coconuts." He was pointing above their heads where Théophile noticed for the first time a small wooden rack with a precariously stacked pile of big green fruit, which, if they fell, would probably kill him instantly. He edged his stool a little out of the way.

The old man was smiling at him. "It is the wise man who respects karma", he said. "But karma is difficult to understand. Difficult to understand."

Théophile felt the burden of questions, piling one on top of the other. He ventured warily, "You are telling me of my life, the life before this one?"

"I am indeed."

"But you say there are other people? People like me?"

"Oh yes. It is clear. In this life, in this very body, you are having destiny. Those of you have come, once again, as you did before. As it is said in the scriptures, now each must face the consequences of his action. You see, the impressions of the previous lives, not just one, create the conditions of the present life. You must be knowing this. Yes?

Théophile nodded because he had no idea what could possibly be said.

"This I will explain you also." The finger of the left hand was up again and waving in his direction. "In this life, you must know, there is the chance to correct the sins of the past. You understand?"

Théophile nodded again. The old Catholic notions of sin, long ignored, floated into his mind. Memories of enforced confession, uttered rote fashion, knowing his mother would be asking the village priest afterwards if her son had done the right thing. He thought he had left sin back in France.

"But not only that", the old man said. "There is the chance also for liberation. You know what is 'liberation'?"

Théophile repeated the word with his French accent: "*Libération*". The word could mean anything. His mind conjured up the front page of the left-wing Paris newspaper of that name. He found himself grinning with the ridiculousness of it and the old man took that as a good sign.

"Yes, yes. Liberation is the highest goal. All men crave to be free from the cycle of birth and death. That is liberation. You want that."

The left hand finger was emphatically pointed at Théophile's chest. "In that lifetime of which I speak, in that ashram, you wanted liberation. Ah, but my friend, not enough. Not any of you, not one, could resist the temptations. Like a bird flies too close to the sun, gets wings burned. Falls to earth. But you came so close. And so in this lifetime, consequently, you will meet again. It is necessary. You must. It is guru's grace. You will recognise the others when the time is ripe. That much is certain. The karma is such that it cannot be avoided. I am clear?"

"Can I ask you something?" Théophile had questions swirling in his head and he felt a torrent of them wrestling to express themselves.

The old man looked at him and then shook his head. "No. No more today", he said. "I see you are too full. Not ready to ask the right question."

And the old man got to his feet. "Is one hundred rupees." Suddenly the glasses were gone, the leaf back in the folder and the folder back in the drawer. Théophile reluctantly stood up and reached under his kurta for his money belt and handed over the grubby notes, feeling as if he must have done or said something that was a mistake.

"Excuse me." he said. "I am sorry." But the old man gave him a curt bow with his hands in *namaste*, said "Good afternoon" and left.

Théophile sat back down on the stool, stunned, unable to move, trying to remember as much as he could of what had been said. Questions and images threshed in his mind to the point where he felt he could not hold onto anything. Who was Théophile? How could he accept the notion of past lives if he could not remember them? This strange idea of 'liberation'. Liberation from what? Were there really others like him? How would he find them? Was it Brad? Was it Ariette? And if the old man was right: was he, in fact, some kind of reborn yogi? He shook his head. Maybe the whole thing was just a result of smoking too much powerful shit, too many bidis, too much sun, too much…He didn't know. His brain just couldn't cope.

He walked slowly out into the blazing afternoon sun, then immediately sought the shade of an arbour of bougainvillea. There was a stone bench; he sank down onto it and closed his eyes, both against the sun and against the incomprehensibility of what he had been told. He breathed in the subtle perfume of the arbour and in that moment he heard a voice inside his head. It was a young voice, like a child's, but clear and lucid. It spoke to him in French.

"If you are seeking liberation, my friend, then avoid the objects of the senses. They are poison. You have poisoned yourself so long. Give it up. You must find contentment and come to know what is the truth. This is the cure. Consider this body in which you sit and breathe. You are not this. You are not made of solid matter. My dear friend, you are not made of flesh; you are not earth, not water, not fire, air, nor even space. You say you wish to be liberated. It can be, but only if you come to know yourself as consciousness. You must become the witness of all this."

As the voice spoke to him, he felt a great heaviness. He felt the weight of his body as if suddenly he was carrying its weight as a burden. The human body, *un fardeau lourd*. He knew that.

Eventually he opened his eyes and stared up into the vivid purple of the shelter above him. He watched a small brown bird preening itself under one wing.

Who was saying this?

Whoever it was, they'd have to be simple with him.

He knew so little.

VIII

In the days that followed, Théophile found himself naturally adopting a regular pattern, a rhythm determined mostly by the quotidian schedule of events in the ashram. Lying on the hard bed with its thin mattress, he would sleep deeply and dreamlessly. When he heard the morning chant, he would find himself propelled into the temple. He never missed a day's chanting. The statue of the woman on the tiger never ceased to fill him with a kind of fearful awe. He had noticed that throughout the day people would come and worship the statue, sitting in prayer or meditation, often lying before her facedown, stretched out on the floor of the temple in supplication with their hands extended towards her. Afterwards they would approach the rail behind which she sat on her imposing tiger. A priest was always there, except at siesta time, and the statue worshippers would put a coin in an offering box and then receive a drop of water, which the priest would pour into their cupped palm from a little silver teapot. This they would sip and then brush their hand over the top of their heads.

After watching this ritual for a few days, Théophile found the courage to do it himself. He bowed before the statue and put a rupee in the box. Immediately the priest came across with the little teapot. By now Théophile had become adept at using only his right hand. The drop was cold on his palm, and he sipped it and found that it was delightfully sweet coconut water. He touched his damp palm to the top of his head. Feeling slightly lightheaded he had sat against the wall of the temple and closed his eyes. He felt the drop of coconut water touch his scalp. Suddenly he was floating away into some kind of ethereal universe where his body had no weight or substance. He seemed to be able to float unsupported and he felt a wave of happiness ripple through his mind and lift him. When he finally came back into his body, it was almost a disappointment to find that once again he was trapped in its fleshy weight.

He became addicted to this daily routine, although he could not always access the same delicious inner state.

Every day he would join Brad for breakfast with some of the other Westerners who needed more than one chapati and one cup of chai to start the day. He asked Brad about the statue. "Ah yeah." he said. « She is Durga. The goddess, the divine mother, the power of the universe."

"She is frightening to me." said Théophile.

"Oh, you bet." laughed Brad. "You don't mess with her. She's a slayer of demons. I have a comic that tells some of the Durga myths. They're pretty wild. I'll lend it to you." Brad had a huge collection of the children's comics that told all the classic Indian scriptural stories, legends, saints' lives and Indian historical events. He was planning to refer to them in some of his post-doctoral essays. He claimed it was the best source of information on otherwise difficult reading material. "You'll love the funny drawings too." he added.

Every day Théophile was there in the medan for the morning *darshan* with the guru. He never had the courage to go right up to her as he saw others do, and she in turn seemed to completely ignore him. He would watch her closely, trying to imagine what kind of state she was in. If she was a realised being, as Brad had said, what was that like? Very often, after watching her for a while, Théophile's mind would become very quiet and he had the impression that he was able to look at himself from outside himself. Or was it that he could look at himself from inside himself? Whatever it was, it was surely the most peaceful feeling he could imagine.

He diligently began to study the book the guru had given him, reading slowly and trying to understand what she wanted him to know. There were no words that he didn't recognise, the sentences were clear enough, but the meaning seemed to be hidden. There was one chapter that he found himself reading again and again:

Ashtavakra said:
"The state of bondage is when the mind longs for something or when the mind grieves about something.

"The state of bondage comes when the mind rejects something or when the mind holds on to something,

"Bondage comes when the mind is pleased about something and equally when the mind is displeased about something.

"Liberation is when the mind does not long for anything nor grieves about anything.

"Liberation is when the mind does not reject anything or hold on to anything.

"Liberation is when the mind is neither pleased about anything nor displeased about anything.

"Bondage is when the mind is tangled in any one of the senses, and liberation is when the mind is not tangled in any of the senses.

"When there is no 'me', that is liberation, but when there is 'me', then there is bondage.

"Consider all this carefully."

Every time he would, indeed carefully, pick his way through this passage, it would hold him in its grip. It seemed to be stating the obvious. If his mind didn't do all that—thinking, holding on, getting pleased or displeased—then he would be a peaceful person. That was clear. He had glimpses of such peace when he sat with the guru in the courtyard. But he had no idea how to get his mind to do that anywhere else. How could he control his mind? "When there is no 'me', that is liberation, but when there is 'me', then there is bondage. *Comment eviter le 'moi'"*?

After several days of wrestling with this, he showed the passage to Brad. They were finishing another breakfast, the remnants of *uttapas* and chai on their box table.

Brad read it through and said "It's the classic thing isn't it. Just do what the boy saint says and you're in paradise. You know, T. O. in all the scriptures I've studied, the Vedas, the *Mahabarata*, the *Patanjali Yoga Sutras,* they all say this, more or less. The secret is that you actually can't do it by yourself. It's impossible." He was thoughtful for a moment. "You could spend your whole life trying and lots of yogis do. You must have seen those guys standing on one leg in Mumbai, some of them for fifteen years or more. Or the bed-of-nails guys. That's supposedly why they do that. Nirvana. That's what yoga is for. To still the mind. I guess, maybe now and then some lucky yogi actually gets it right, but I have to tell you, it's rare. Anyone who does is a saint."

This wasn't helping Théophile. "So what is the point of saying all this. Why even talk about liberation, if it is not possible?"

"Hey, I didn't say it wasn't possible. I just said you can't do it by yourself. At least most people can't. You and I can't. But it is possible."

"How is it possible?"

"As far as I can see, there is only one way. And a lot of the scriptures agree." Brad chuckled. "Even the Bible agrees. 'I am the way and the truth and the light. ' That was Jesus, he said that. And what he was saying is, the only way is the guru."

"You see Jesus as the guru?" asked Théophile, thinking maybe he had misunderstood Brad's English.

"Oh sure." Brad said. "Greatest guru of his era, no doubt. The only problem was his disciples turned him into a religion, which kind of killed it."

"This is very difficult for me to understand."

"Well unless you are one of those rare Christians who have a one-on-one relationship with Jesus, you might as well forget him. No value in a second-hand guru, if you ask me. Anyway, there are plenty of other gurus. Every age has the guru and specially here. This is India's great gift to the world, man." Seeing Théophile frowning, he went on, "Oh yeah. India gets the gold medal for recognising the greatness of the guru. In other places, they tend to string them up on crosses or whatever. There's probably more than one right now in some psych hospital in the good old U. S. of A. But here, in India, they say the guru is the way. The guru has the power."

"But what is this power?"

"Well, how to explain that? I guess it's like satellites in space." He grinned, as he saw Théophile wrestle with his apparent non-sequitur. "You know about satellites, right?"

Theo circled a finger in the air to show, hoping he had gotten it.

"Okay. Once they're up there, they go round and round forever." He imitated Theo's gesture. "Liberated in space you might say, free from gravity. But they need massive rockets to get them up there. The guru is NASA. The guru gives you the boost."

"That is a nice image, but how is the guru like NASA?" said Théophile. "How can I get that rocket?"

"That's the number one big question, my friend." Brad handed his book back to Théophile. "According to scriptures I read, when the disciple is ready, the guru appears. The disciple has to recognise the guru and the guru has to accept the disciple. When that happens, they say, the guru enters the disciple and the work of purification takes place. You see?"

Théophile thought about what Brad had said. After a moment, he asked, "So for you, Padma Amma, she is the guru?"

Brad looked out onto the hot dusty street. A stray yellow dog lay panting, draped across the speed bump outside the ashram entrance. Watching the dog studiously as it licked its genitals, Brad shook his head. "I don't know. Sad to say this, but I don't think so."

A noisy three-wheeler taxi bustled up to the speed bump, carrying three sari-clad teenage girls jammed together on the back seat. A thin horn tooted, and the dog slowly relinquished his speed bump and wandered into the shade and the taxi bustled off.

"Sometimes," Brad said, "I think maybe she is. She might be. Other times, I don't know. She has not shown me any sign of it. I mean, I like being here and all. It's a good energy in this ashram. I get good meditation here. But I have to tell you, I really don't know."

"Do you think she is my guru?" Théophile recognised he was reluctant to voice this suggestion.

Brad looked at him and shook his head. "Don't ask me, man. For that question, you better ask her."

For some reason this suggestion took a hold of Théophile for the rest of the day.

Ask her. What a thought!

He was going to have to ask her.

IX

The guru however was quicker. The next morning when she came into the medan, even before she had sat down, she beckoned to Théophile to come forward. With his heart on fire, he stepped around several seated Indians and dropped onto his knees in front of the guru's chair. She fixed him with a stern look.

"Question. *Ek*." she said holding up one finger. One of the young boys in white, who were always on hand, inched closer and whispered to Théophile, "Guruji asks if you have one question."

He seemed unable to breathe for a moment but in the end he willed the question out of himself in his best English, his voice shaking. "I ask, please, you are my guru?"

Her eyes pierced him and they held him fiercely in their grip. Then she shook her head and Théophile felt a wave of nausea pass through him. Still her eyes held him.

"Book?" she said, added something else in her own language. The boy leaned in again and whispered. "She ask you if you read the book she give."

Théophile managed to nod and finally to blurt out "Not understand very well".

She smiled and spoke some more, which the helpful young man passed on with the same smile. "You must study the book from the inside."

When Théophile betrayed his lack of comprehension, the smile disappeared and she leaned forward with her eyes piercing into his. Then she spoke with such great force that it pushed Théophile back on his heels. It was not volume, simply force of energy. When the boy translated, with the same force, he was hissing in his ear.

"She say 'Now is time for action. Bird must fly. Ashtavakra now born back into the world. This why she give you book. Ashtakavra was guru of Janaka. Now you also. '"

Then the small figure on the chair seemed to grow huge in Théophile's vision. She seemed to expand out of the chair, occupy the whole space of the ashram and diminish him into a tiny bug-like creature cringing beneath her. Her voice thundered around him and rattled his skeleton. The boy's voice merged with hers.

"Now you must go. Go back. Bird must fly. Not waste time. Work. Ashtavakra there. You serve her. You serve her and she save you. Only she can save you. Go there."

A tiny little voice from some tremulous part of him, rose up, not much more than a thin squeak: "Go? Where?"

The voice of the guru was pounding inside him "Back. You go back. You home. Big house full of ghosts. Ashtavakra there. She look for you. Now is time."

And then it broke. Two small birds squabbled in the trees overhead and the guru was just a small female form seated on a chair and turning to speak to a woman holding a vase of roses. The boy motioned impatiently to Théophile that he was in the way. He pulled himself to his feet and shuffled back to his blanket on the marble. He couldn't bear to make eye contact with Brad so he simply closed his eyes.

He tried to piece together what he had just been told.

It was time to fly.

Ashtavakra was reborn. She would save him. She? Ashtakavra was female? And he was to go back? Not to Goa, not to the hut, but to a big house full of ghosts. Home. The château. The house of ghosts he had run away from. Why? Why there? And who was Ashtakavra? Had somebody come to live there? Since he had arrived in India, he'd wanted no contact with that life. He had sent one clichéd two-line postcard to his mother when he first arrived in Goa and after that nothing. The last thing in the world he would have chosen to do was to go back there.

After the *darshan*, he took himself off to the gardens. He sat under the bouganvillea, trying to piece together what had just happened. His intense resistence to going home stood before him like an iron door. At the same time there was a fire in him. He wanted to do what she said, whatever it was. But then he had asked her if she was his guru and although she didn't say no, she said, or at least he thought she had said, that Ashtakavra was his guru.

That made no sense.

He was desperate to talk to someone. He went to the hut of Nagadas, the man who had read his future but the stools were unoccupied. Unable to think of anyone else, he reluctantly sat with Brad after lunch under a banyan tree.

"What do I do?" he said.

"Go with it. In Sanskrit they call it *upadesha.* The guru speaks, gives a command. Like the bird message she gave us, remember that? It is said to be *caitanya,* meaning alive. Whatever she says, it has the power to take you a long way. You'd be mad not to follow it, and just as close as you possibly can. And, I tell you, the way she gave it you, that was powerful."

"So I go back to France?"

"If that's what she said."

"She said the big house full of ghosts. I know what it is."

"So?"

Théophile shook his head. There seemed to be no doubt in Brad's mind. The *Ashtavakra Samhita* lay in Théophile's hand. He looked at it with suspicion "And this Ashtavakra? She said 'she'. I think she said that. Anyway, the boy said 'she'."

Brad shrugged. "Who knows what that means. Listen, Padma Amma gave you the book. There had to be a reason. She tells you to get your wings in good shape. So now she says what she says. You're the only one who's going make sense out of it." Brad patted Théophile on the knee. "It's between you and her. You know what? I think she just set you on a whole new path. If it was me, I wouldn't hesitate for a second. You ask me, I say go for it."

X

The following morning his daily routine was shattered. After the early morning temple chant, which Théophile had come to love, after the breakfast that was never quite enough, after his daily recourse to the chai shop, one of the boys in white had come to find him. The boy had stood almost to attention beside the box where Brad and Théophile had just emptied their chais; "Taxi is coming, just now" he announced "You packing bag, just now. Then going" After which he had given a crisp bow and left.

Now his tote bag was packed and sitting on his bed. In a daze Théophile had carefully washed and shaved, put on the new *kurta*, which he had ordered from the little tailoring shop across the street, and entered the medan for his final *darshan*.

As he sat waiting for Swami Padmananda to arrive, his heart was pounding in anticipation. He looked around at the ashram to imprint it on his memory. So much had happened here and he understood so little of it. He had so many questions for Padmananda. Was he following her command? Was he doing the right thing? He recognised that in some subtle way, he had come to totally trust her.

When she appeared, he bowed deeply in his place and found a wave of gratitude well up in him. When he looked up, she smiled at him and his heart melted. She motioned, with the slightest dip of her head, for him to come forward. He approached and bowed deeply with genuine reverence. He felt an unfettered love for her, this tiny dark-skinned ineffable person who could reduce him to an atom with a single glance. And instead of all his questions, all he could say was: "*Merci infiniment, du fond du coeur.* Thank you with all my heart."

She nodded, her eyes absorbing him, and then reached to a side table and presented him with a little statue of the goddess Durga on her tiger, made of white stone.

"She go with you. Make safe." One of the boys in white wanted to repeat what she'd, said but she gestured him aside. From behind her chair, she produced a bunch of incense sticks with glowing tips and a fine curleque of smoke rising from it, which she wafted over his upturned face. He had seen her do this from time to time and wondered what it signified. As the smoke drifted across his forehead, he inhaled a heady perfume of sandalwood and felt a wave of intoxication rise within him. Holding the statue in his right hand, his eyes met hers as the incense sticks moved across his face and blazing light flashed unmistakably between them. He could hold the intensity of it only for a second and then he bowed deeply.

He rested at her feet until he knew the moment had passed. He drew himself to his feet and edged backwards until he found his place. He stayed there, sitting, for the rest of the *darshan* with the statue in his lap.

When she stood up to leave, so did he. She gave him a little wave, as she walked away. A moment later one of the boys in white came for him. "Taxi is waiting"..

The three-wheeler taxi was throbbing unevenly and blowing blue smoke. Brad was there, with some of the other Westerners Théo had come to know. "Well, man", Brad said, putting a brotherly arm round his shoulder. "You're on your way. Keep in touch. I really want to know how this plays out."

"I will", was all Théophile managed to say. His heart was in his mouth and he was in danger of tears. "I am grateful to you. You were a good friend."

At the last minute the little Indian man who had rescued him from the beach at Goa appeared. "Now going?" he said breathlessly. Théophile nodded and they bowed in *namaste* to each other. The Indian man gave him a little package of incense. "Remember ashram", he said. "Smell sweet." It was the same incense as the Guru had waved over his face.

The taxi driver revved the three-wheeler's tinny engine, blowing an even thicker cloud of blue smoke over the onlookers, indicating he was impatient to be gone. Théophile clambered onto the back seat and clutched his tote bag to him with the precious Durga statue carefully buried in the middle of his few possessions. He waved to Brad and the others before grabbing the rail in front of him, as the taxi hit the speed bump.

Then the ashram was gone and the taxi was rattling down the hill and away into the jungle. Théophile swayed and swung in the unstable back seat and made sure his tote bag didn't jump overboard. His mind was in much the same state. He was leaving without really knowing what had happened to him there. He knew he was certainly different from the shameful mess that had been dragged up that hill, but what he was and who he was, that was as much a mystery as before. And now he was to go back, back to all that he run away from. And there, somehow, he was to discover, what? Some kind of reincarnation of a crippled saint? There was no way he could marshal his thoughts and he eventually let himself drift. The driver was singing along to raucous Hindi techno on the surprisingly sophisticated CD player that skipped when the taxi hit the biggest bumps. .

Several hours went by and Théophile found himself at the bus station in a dusty town full of wandering cows and erratic bicycles. He bought himself a ticket for Mumbai and resigned himself to the long hours of bus-born torture. And yet even as the bus endlessly rocked and bounced, he could smell the incense that Padmananda had waved across his face. He told himself he was flying as she had commanded and he felt good about it.

A day and a half later he was at the Mumbai airport in Santa Cruz, and redeeming his open-ended return. It was no longer open-ended. The adventure was over.

When the Air France hostess bid him *"Bonsoir"* as he entered the plane, still dressed in Indian-style clothes, his sense of dread mounted. Somehow her crisp Frenchness was too much of a rapid transition. He just wasn't ready to face all that he had run away from.

And all the way across the Hindu Kush Mountains and the wastes of Northern Iran, the Black Sea and cloud-shrouded Bulgaria, he found himself inside himself and praying to Padmananda. And as he did, she began to feel like a presence to him. The more he sought for her inside, the more solid she became. By the time the captain announced the beginning of their descent into Charles de Gaulle Airport, he had unearthed some measure of peace inside himself.

The numbing queue for immigration, the perpetual announcements for departures in French, repeated in tortured English, the hunt for the transfer terminal for Bordeaux, the crush of bodies from the four corners of the earth, travellers desperate not to miss their flight…All that rushed and swirled around him as he held intently to his inner sanctuary.

His last flight rose sharply into the grey air above Paris and into thick cloud. The quick arc across the southwest of France went in a flash, with no more than cashews in a sachet and a plastic cup of tomato juice to distract him. Tilting over gently, rounding on its approach, he saw beyond the wingtip, the serpentine lower reaches of the river Dordogne and beyond it the rolling green of Entre deux Mers. He was back.

Instinctively his hands went up into the gesture of *namaste*.

KATE

It was not until she was eighteen that Kate found out that her grandmother was part aboriginal.

Lying in her hospice bed in Sydney, Ella Campagnieri pulled her oldest granddaughter close and, as best she could, between desperate breaths, whispered the family secret. The ventilator sucked and blew as the old woman hoarsely detailed a hidden story of her era. Between the inhalations that required most of her strength, she described how, like so many other half-blood children, she had been taken from her mother as a child and kept in a Christian Mission home. Ella knew little about her father, other than he was a white man and worked on the first railhead project. She thought maybe he had been Italian. Her mother, whose name had been changed from her aboriginal name to Beth, had barely ever referred to him, seemed to know nothing about him and, as far as Ella could recall, never mentioned his name. He was around, she got pregnant and then he wasn't around any more. So Ella knew almost nothing about her father and not much more about her mother, who may have come from somewhere near Geraldton. But Ella wasn't sure.

« I want you to know about this, so it wont die when I die. » she had said, holding Kate's hand. Kate nodded and squeezed the hand that held hers.

What Ella did know was that when her mother was a teenager she went to work as a housemaid for the Ungarry Station in the Murchison area. Ella had no idea how she got there. She was still probably a teenager when she fell pregnant with Ella. The child was no more than four or five years old when the authorities came, and her mother had no power to prevent them taking her child and absolutely no capacity to appeal to the courts to return the girl to her. Ella remembered the day the men took her and two other girls from their mothers. The mothers screamed and ran after the police truck that was carrying their children away. Ella remembered seeing one of the Ungarry Station owners smiling. Later she thought bitterly that he was probably pleased that there would be fewer mouths to feed.

What little her mother had imparted to her in the few years they were together, Ella now whispered to Kate. She spoke of stories she remembered her mother telling, songs half-forgotten, images of a life in the bush. These were the treasured snippets of recall that she had kept alive in the years that followed. She passed over the miserable years in a mission institution near Northam, far away to the south, alluding to casual abuse but not dwelling on it. She had left the mission when she was sixteen and been employed in Perth. She never went back.

She was lucky, she whispered. "Some girls got pregnant early, some turned into drunks and some just died. I was lucky." She had been taken care of by the family she worked for, genuinely loved. Right after the war she met her future husband, a young shy Italian who had arrived with very little English. He worked as a gardener for the family. Ella said "I think I must have inherited a love of Italians." As, step by step, they fell in love, the family encouraged them and helped them to find a place of their own. They both continued to work in that home for some years. "You see how lucky I was?" She tried to laugh but it turned to painful coughing that stopped her talking for quite a while. Kate sat with her, trying to remember her grandfather who died when she was very small. She watched as the laboured breathing of her grandmother settled and she could speak again.

When Ella was able to speak again, she told her grandaughter that she had returned to Ungarry only once, when she was pregnant with Kate's mother, Pat. Ella's own mother, Beth had died by the time she went back and all but one of her aunties had passed on as well. The remaining auntie had told Ella what she could, and Ella was determined that Kate, as her oldest grandchild would be the one to keep alive the link to her last wisps of ancestry. She had waited possibly too long, putting off talking to Kate until she was old enough to understand. Finally the lung cancer had forced Ella's hand.

Kate wondered if Ella had ever found the opportunity or the openness to share her past with Kate's mother. Did Pat know anything about what Kate was now learning? And if she did, why had she never said anything? Kate did not have the courage to ask.

As Ella shared in short gasps what little she had retained, she was sadly aware of how meagre it was, of how removed her life had been from her roots. She spoke of the bush, the smell of the earth, the calls of the birds, the starry night sky, the stories the old ones told. And although it was not much, although the old woman repeatedly rambled off into incomprehensible side-stories, her account stirred in Kate a deep questioning about her own identity.

« I won't forget. » she promised.

Holding dearly to these scraps of her heritage on the day her grandmother took her final breath, what most firmly implanted itself in Kate's brain was the urgency with which the old woman gripped her hand. The last thing Ella said to her was "I knew you would understand."

Kate decided to keep Ella's revelations to herself. After the funeral, at which no reference to anything aboriginal was made, Kate told neither of her parents nor her two sisters, as none of them had ever shown the slightest interest in anything aboriginal. She suspected that if she brought up the subject, it would be brushed off or even denied. Kate could never imagine her mother, so urban, so correct, so domestic, ever being the slightest bit interested in anything that wasn't in *Woman's Day* or *Home Beautiful*. And her sisters were just kids with gadgets and clothes. Instead, Kate read some of the books about the so-called "stolen generations" and these made her feel sad and angry. The accumulative effect was to look for some way to engage with her past. Despite her parent's hopes that she would do a university degree, she decided on a nursing career. She couldn't explain it to them but she knew she wanted to do something for the aboriginal people.

When her training was complete, holding fast to her promise not to forget, she looked for nursing positions in the areas her grandmother had talked about. She had discovered that Ungarry Station no longer existed, other than abandoned ruins, but in one of the nearest towns, Meekatharra, there were nursing vacancies. At least she could begin there.

The response from Meekatharra was fast and enthusiastic. They had chronic shortages and were so keen to have her that they paid her travel expenses and would welcome her with open arms.

II

As the small regional passenger jet banked steeply over Meekatharra on its final approach, she saw the town as an oasis. It was almost shocking to see green lawns and swimming pools after the brown and yellow country that had unfolded under the wing for so long. From the air it seemed like the town was a lush picnic someone had laid out in the middle of a dry and barren landscape. The picnic stopped abruptly at the edge of the town. And yet as Kate studied the dry country spread out endlessly to the hazy distances where the horizon seemed to fuse with the sky, she longed to be in that country. This was the country of her people.

Although the country beyond beckoned to her, at first, however, she simply dived into the predictable rhythms of hospital life. The town was small but the hospital had all the basics. Many of her patients were aboriginals, half blood and full blood. As she tended to them it was always with the inner question about whether she was somehow related. She particularly loved taking care of the children, but she found it disheartening to see how many of them came in with bad teeth, terrible skin and infected eyes. Her friend Jenny, who had already been at the hospital for two years, told her to get used to it. "These are all edge-of-town kids", she had said, not bothering to disguise her disgust. "They live in the camps and they live in shit. You wouldn't want to see it. Their parents are drunk, the older kids sniff petrol and most of them end up locked up. It's a lost cause."

Kate hadn't mentioned her own aboriginal connection and once she gauged the general attitude amongst the nurses, she had no desire to. It wasn't that they were racist exactly. It was more a hardened attitude to the fringe dwellers. Some of the younger doctors, fresh from their medical studies in Perth, were more open to seeing the potential in their young and damaged patients, but anyone who had been around for a while sneered at their optimism as hopelessly naive. Jenny had begun a casual relationship with one of these altruistic doctors, an earnest young man originally from Adelaide. His name was Allan and he had come with a mission. The relationship lost its lustre fairly quickly for Jenny when she discovered that he had born-again Christian tendencies and a steadfast disinclination to have sex before nuptials.

On her days off, a few times Kate went into town with Jenny and some of the other nurses to hang out at the pub. There wasn't much else to do. The local unattached men, mainly sex-starved mine workers, seemed to think that nurses were an easy target and this made for some unpleasant scenes. This wasn't at all what Kate wanted.

Sometimes she would go for walks by herself, venturing to the edge of the town where the suburban roads abruptly turned to red dirt tracks and the manicured gardens gave way to scrub. She would gaze off into the distance and wonder about what was beyond the low hills. However she had also seen the shanties and leanto's where the fringe dwellers lived and she'd been warned that it wasn't safe to wander near them. Again, not exactly racist but close, the other nurses would warn her of young aboriginal males, drunk or high on glue sniffing, who could be violent.

After a while Kate stayed mostly in her room when she wasn't working and read all she could about the aboriginal people and their heritage. The Meekatharra library had a reasonable range of books that didn't seem to get much use. The librarian, an anorexic redheaded girl from Perth, was delighted to see another redhead in town and helped her to find the best texts on aboriginal history and culture. They struck up a casual friendship, and Terry was the closest Kate came to telling anyone about her reasons for coming to the town. She admitted to a deep interest in aboriginal culture and over several cups of indifferent coffee in the one apology for a coffee shop in the town, they talked about what they knew. But somehow Kate never found the right moment to reveal her own connection.

She tried to find out whether it was possible to get to whatever was left of Ungarry Station. The station had long been abandoned and no one went there any more. She could rent a Ute from the BP garage in town but she was hesitant to go out into the bush by herself. It would take a full day to drive there, she would have to camp and then take another full day to drive back. It was too daunting a prospect and the more she got to know the staff at the hospital, she couldn't see anyone in whom she felt confident enough to share what she wanted to do and why. When she tentatively mentioned it to Terry, the librarian admitted to being horrified of the bush and she shook at the thought. All those creatures that crawled and bit.

And, as Kate thought about it, even if she did make this trip, what would be there once she got there? Probably just ghosts. There would be no one to ask. She let it go.

Two months after she began at the hospital in Meekatharra, she had a dream. In it her grandmother sat with her by a fire under a brilliant starlit sky. She seemed animated and pointed out certain stars. She said they were Kate's guides. She said all Kate had to do was call to them and they would come to her.

When she woke, Kate lay in the dark in her hospital staff room and felt such a desire to find the guides. In her mind, she called to them "I am ready. Show me." And then she drifted back to sleep.

III

They came for her just a week later. It was a hot still dusty Sunday afternoon. She had done her rounds and was sitting in a cane rocking chair, taking a break on the shaded verandah. Her clipboard lay in her lap and she had begun to let her eyes close against the haze, when a silent shadow moved in front of her. Silhouetted against the brightness, it was hard to see who it was. Then she heard the voice.

"You call us. Now we come for you." It was an old man's voice, thin and crackly but certain.

Kate squinted up at him uncomprehending, her heart pounding. She put down her clipboard and stood up. She was taller than the old man, who was almost opaque in his thinness but whose eyes, now that she could see them, had a dark intensity to them. It was challenging to hold his gaze.

"What do you want?" she asked gently.

"You call us."

"I'm sorry", she said. "I haven't called anybody."

"Spirit voice call", he said and he poked her in the chest with a surprisingly strong finger that seemed to almost pierce her skin and sent a shock wave through her whole body. "Now you learn your people." Then he turned and pointed to a stand of straggly gum trees across the lawn. At first Kate could see nothing but then, deep in the shade, she made out three old aboriginal women in ragged print dresses, holding little dilly bags. "Women teach", he said. "You learn good." Then the man turned and walked off the verandah, heading back to the trees.

She watched his bow-legged but sturdy walk, his bare feet on the diligently watered hospital lawn, with a rising feeling of elation, laced with fear. There was an imperative in this old man, a draw so strong that she knew she was going to follow him without being able to summon any kind of rational response. Without an articulated thought, without any sense of resistance, she left her clipboard on the rocking chair, crossed the verandah, descended the two wooden steps and followed this man across the lawn to the trees in her solid nursing shoes and her well-tailored made-in-China uniform. Somewhere deep in her consciousness, she heard the censorious and carping voice of her mother, the annoyance and concern of the Nursing Services head, Matron Harding, Jenny's voluble warnings about danger in the bush, Terry's fears, but none of that had any power to sway her now. Instead, somewhere inside herself, she listened to the breathy voice of Ella, desperate to pass on what she knew. And Kate had no doubt she must go.

When she reached the trees, the three women made sweet greeting noises, like small birds in the early morning and one of them stroked her dark red hair in admiration. It was pinned up and in a spontaneous gesture of acceptance. Kate pulled at the pins and allowed the fullness of her hair to fall over her shoulders. It was as if she had invited them to embrace her and all three began to fondle her hair and cluck together in excited chatter. This lasted only a moment before the old man impatiently clicked his tongue and they picked up their three little dilly bags, took Kate by the arm and led her beyond the trees and away from the hospital.

As they passed over a low sandy hill, she looked back just the once, not with regret, or uncertainty, or even fear, but with an acceptance so total that as surely as the hospital's corrugated iron roof disappeared from sight, so did the life she had lived up to that moment.

A thin loping dog had joined them. This dingo-cross with a long dangling tongue and a bent tail had been waiting obediently for the old man. Now it fell in behind his heels and kept pace. The women walked several steps behind.

Travelling away from the sun, they crossed several low hills and walked through low scrub and brush, not following any kind of path that Kate could see. Her shoes filled with the dry sandy earth and eventually she took them off, along with her little white socks. The warm ground felt good under her feet, though small sharp rocks began to cut into her soft flesh and soon she realised her feet were beginning to bleed. Still, she could see that her shoes were of no use. After carrying them for a while, she put them down under a tree. The man and the dog continued to walk in an unbroken rhythm but the women waited for her without a sound. She put the socks in her pocket and left the shoes behind. Looking back at them from a distance, she smiled. How silly they looked there: two sensible nurse's shoes, side by side. Maybe a lizard would come and live in one of them.

Her guides had walked mostly in silence and she had simply followed, little bubbles of excitement welling up in her again and again. She would smile at herself and brush away the bush flies with a lack of irritation that came from a deep tranquillity. There was a rhythm to it all. Even though her feet were painful, she felt it was all right.

As sunset approached, the man stopped by a rocky outcrop that formed a half circle round a sandy clearing. Once the women caught up with him, he gestured, muttered something and left them there. The women talked quietly to her but in a language of their own, indicating that they should gather firewood. Now that they had stopped, Kate recognised that she had in fact quite badly cut her feet. She sat on a rock and used her socks to attempt to clean away some of the encrusted blood. One of the women came to her. She squatted down and held the bloody feet in her hands, making a gentle singing sound. Then, still squatting, she pulled up her dress and urinated into her cupped hand. Then very gently she applied the urine to Kate's feet. The warm liquid stung but somehow the Western medical training that had been so well inculcated for the last four years did not resist. Kate stared at this old woman lovingly managing her feet and felt wonderfully taken care of. The woman stood and found a broad flat stone and placed Kate's feet on it. It was warm from the sun and seemed to draw the sting out of her wounds.

Kate watched as the three women brought back armloads of sticks and laid them for a fire. Kate knew that once the sun had set, the air would be cold and the fire would be essential. Expecting to see the women make fire by some traditional method, she had to smile when one of the women pulled out a plastic Bic lighter from her dilly bag and lit a pile of dead leaves. By the time the fire was blazing, the old man returned with the dog at his heels, carrying a filled water-skin and a dead goanna. They drank with their cupped hands and watched as the goanna cooked in the red coals of the fire. In the last rays of daylight, they pulled the roasted lizard from the fire and tore it apart. The taste was deeply pleasing to Kate, a flavour of her unexpected new life. When they had eaten, one of the women who had saved some of the tough oily skin, rubbed it against the flesh of Kate's feet, speaking gently to her all the time. The old man walked away from the fire to sleep by himself with the dog up against him. The women lay close together and they pulled Kate into their warmth.

She lay there between them as the fire died out, feeling their breathing, smelling the saltiness of their bodies, the comfort of them, and she felt as if she was a child again, protected and belonging. The hospital, Sydney, that other world, all seemed like some remote illusion, as unattainable now as the daylight that had gone with the sun. Before sleep overcame her, she wondered at how effortlessly she had turned her back on it all. She had told no one, left no note; she had just walked off the verandah without her clipboard and without regrets. Harding would come looking for her, Jenny would know nothing, Terry would wonder. The police would be called, they would check her room and find all her things, nothing taken or disturbed, there would be a hunt, her mother would receive a call…then what? And then she fell asleep.

IV

When the sun rose, the air was cold and the ground was hard. Even before she opened her eyes, Kate, was shocked to reconnect with her surroundings. Far off she heard the caustic commentary of a crow, while close there was the gentle breathing of her human comforters. She had never slept outdoors before. She had gone on a few camping trips with her high school, but none of those had involved sleeping in the open air. When she opened her eyes, the pale blue of the morning sky stretched infinitely away above her. The women on either side of her began to move. They sat up and chattered quietly to her. She looked down at the crumpled mess that was now her uniform. The white blouse was streaked and one sleeve was torn. The tailored dress, dusty and twisted. If only Matron Harding could see her. She had to smile at that. Matron Harding lived in another universe.

One of the women blew on the embers of the fire and brought it back to life. The man and the dog had gone. Kate took a little of the water from the skin and rinsed her eyes and face. She knew the water was precious but felt the need to perform at least the basic steps of her usual morning ritual. She found some of the hairpins still in her pocket and pulled back her hair as best she could. It was already matted and full of dust and sticks.

One of the women had climbed to the top of the rock pile and was facing the rising sun. She began to sing and waved her arms in rolling motions towards the sun. The simple beauty of it struck Kate and she stood still, letting the sounds bathe her, just as the first warmth of the sun was beginning to do.

Her feet were now a nasty mess of encrusted blood and the woman who had treated them the night before gestured at her that she should take care of them with her own urine. The three women stood over her expecting her to do as she was told. Peeing in front of other people was not easy, but there was no sense of embarrassment in the women. They were simply making sure she did what was necessary. At last she managed to overcome her resistance. She cupped her hand beneath her to catch the golden flow; she sat in the dirt and massaged her feet. It felt good and strangely natural and the women acknowledged that she had done the right thing. She had kept her bloodied socks and she put them on her treated feet.

The women threw dust on the fire till it died and then gathered up their dilly bags. Obviously it was time to walk again. She began to take careful steps and was surprised to find that her feet did not hurt as much as she feared. They walked with her, not in any hurry, letting her set the pace.

Mid-morning they came to a small water hole where the old man with the dog was waiting for them. The water hole, not much more than a soak, had enough water for drinking and refilling their water-skin.

After everyone had drunk, the man came close to Kate. "You sleeping. Now waking", he said with a bony finger pointed at her chest. Kate was not sure how to respond, so she smiled and nodded. He did not seem to like her response. "Sleep all life. Now wake up." Then he seemed to lose patience with her and said a few words to the women and strode away with the dog at his heels.

Throughout the day they moved slowly, resting under a rocky outcrop in the hottest part of the afternoon. Later, once the heat had eased, they went on. As they were scrambling up a rocky incline, Kate slipped and fell, smashing her wrist against a rock. Fearing the worst, she looked down and saw the wrist was bleeding and she had broken the face of her watch. On closer inspection she saw that the bleeding was not serious, not much more than a skin tear. Without even thinking, she peed into her hand and dressed it. As the watch was useless, she took it off and put it under a rock. Walking on, she remembered some tourist promotion she had seen somewhere: "the timeless outback".

Once evening approached, they settled in a narrow rocky ravine, sheltered from a cold wind that had sprung up. They made a fire, roasted a small furry animal, a rat-like marsupial that the old man brought and for the second night, Kate slept deeply and without dreams, coccooned by the three women.

In the morning, they made no sign of leaving and Kate wondered if this was their destination. The old man had slept with his dingo a few yards from the women and he too stayed. The women tended the fire, building it with more sticks until it blazed quite high. The wind howled across the top of the ravine and whisked the smoke away as it rose against the rock wall. One of the women began to treat the small skin of the animal they had eaten the night before. She scraped the skin clean and stretched it carefully with green twigs to spread it out. Then she began to heat the skin, holding it to the fire but beyond the reach of the flames.

Kate watched her for a while and then, seeing that there was no sign of moving on, she began to walk a little up the ravine. Her feet were healing and her socks had worn through. She decided to get rid of them and to let go of her underwear as well. The only point in having underwear is when it's clean, she thought. She made a little ball of the discarded clothes and scooped out a hole in the sandy bottom of the ravine. She buried the clothes.

"It's like I'm burying the old ways." she thought. She smiled, imagining someone looking at her now might think she was at a funeral. She sat by the little mound she had made and put a ring of stones round it. Now it really looked like a grave.

As Kate sat there, her eye travelled along the yellowish brown rock wall of the ravine. It was a surprise to realise that just above head-height were drawings, faint but discernible, in reddish brown. She had seen aboriginal paintings often, especially since Ella had talked to her. She had been to the Gallery in Sydney regularly and loved the intricate designs of the traditional painting. Some of the artists had been there and she had spoken to several of them. She knew rock painting existed and now here it was, in the middle of nowhere. There were human figures, birds and animals, mostly small rodents with their skeletons showing. The birds had large wings and flew in a formation above the other figures. On the periphery, there were several male human figures with exaggerated genitals, holding raised spears, but most of the figures were female, also genitally defined, grouped in a circle. She got as close as she could to the drawings, trying to work out its narrative. She traced her fingers along the fine ochre lines, trying to imagine the artist who had put them there. She became lost in it, as easily as if she was in a darkened cinema or watching television.

This was suddenly broken by the sound of the women by the fire calling in birdlike cadences, each one differently pitched, but hauntingly harmonious to Kate's ear. She thought it was for her and she came down from the rock face and turned towards them. They were standing, all three, facing up the ravine in the other direction, where a slow-moving figure made its way through the rocks. It was an old women, entirely naked except for a green peaked cap that advertised John Deere tractors and a long brown emu feather that swung from a leather thong round her neck. She walked with the help of a stick and was followed by a female dog, which seemed to be about the same vintage.

As she approached, one of the women looked around for Kate and called her, beckoning her with enthusiastic gestures. Kate hurried towards the fire. She and the old woman arrived together. The other women chattered excitedly and clasped the older woman's hands then pushed Kate towards her. The woman had a milky film over one eye, but the other had a bird-like intensity. Her face had an infinity of lacework wrinkles that made her dark skin look like crinkled paper. Kate couldn't imagine what age this woman could be.

The man, with the dingo at his heels, came from behind a turn in the ravine. When he approached the fire, he and the old woman exchanged words and then he came very close to Kate. Once again his long bony forefinger was digging into her chest.

"This is sacred woman's place." Hhe gestured back along the ravine, where Kate had seen the rock drawings. "This place, learn woman spirit." Then pointing to the old woman, he said: "She come for you. She make good medicine, so you learn. You do what she says." Then he turned and walked away. His dog was sniffing at the female that had come with the old woman. The man called it, and when the dog ignored him, he simply walked away, out of sight up the ravine.

Kate looked back to the old woman. She had bent to the fire and had taken out a burning stick and was already walking slowly along the ravine. The smoke from the stick was carried up into the air by the swirling wind in the ravine. The other women pushed Kate to follow her. The woman stopped and lit a small fire in some spear grass and then further on, did so again. Soon there was a trail of smouldering grass. When she came to the little mound that Kate had made for her underclothes, she looked down at the ring of stones and poked at it with her stick. She uncovered a bra cup and looked up at Kate. She said something to the other women and they all cackled with laughter. She buried it again. Kate wanted to apologise, she didn't know this was a sacred place, but it was clear none of these women could speak to her or understand her.

Not far from the mound, the old woman pushed the burning end of the stick into the ground. When she pulled it back out, no smoke rose from it. She used its blackened end to draw a circle in the sandy bottom of the ravine, leaving one small section unclosed. Then she pointed to Kate and chattered rapidly with her one intense eye fixed on Kate's face. Kate had no idea what was expected of her, until the woman pointed at the opening in the circle. She was being asked to enter it. As soon as she stepped in, the woman used the stick to close the circle entirely. The woman motioned for her to sit, looking toward the rock face and drawings. The four aboriginal women now sat round the circle each holding a pair of stones. They began to click the stones together in a steady rhythm. Kate found herself gently rocking to the sound. The old woman began to chant, her voice beginning high and getting lower and lower until it faded away. Then she would start again while the clicking of the stones continued. This went on for perhaps an hour or more. When it stopped, there was silence. It was as if the women were waiting for something. The wind howled and faded along the top of the ravine. They all sat very still until, high on the rock face, there was a movement and they all looked up. A crow had landed there and was adjusting its wings.

The old woman pointed and the others became very excited. Then they began to chant together, a different cadence whose echos bounced back off the ravine wall, adding body to the form of the chanting. The crow stayed where it was for quite a while and as soon as it flew off, the chant ended.

The women stood up, chattering animatedly and the old woman scuffed away the circle. Kate stood still, unsure what she should do until the old woman took her hand. Her skin was leathery and hard. She stroked the soft pink palm that she held and talked quietly, her one good eye steadily peering into Kate's face. She led Kate to exactly the same place at the wall of the ravine where she had stood earlier. There the woman pointed at the female figures in the circle, gesturing back to the place where the circle had been. Kate understood that what they had just done was being depicted on the wall. Sure enough in the middle, faint but unmistakable, there was a circle. She nodded, saying "Like us".

The women took her stick with its blackened end and pointed to the painting where birds were flying above the other figures. She touched them, one after the other, constantly talking. Kate ached to know what she was being told. One of the birds was different from the rest; its wings were not outstretched but pulled in, jutting at an angle, as if it had been injured. It was this figure that the woman now concentrated on. Pointing to Kate and then back to the bird figure, she made it clear that there was some relationship between them. She pointed up the cliff face to where the crow had perched. Now the three were linked in her gesturing, the drawn bird, the crow and Kate. "I think I get it", said Kate, hoping that at least her tone would indicate what she meant.

Next, the woman took the end of the stick and rubbed the charcoal from it onto her face. Then she took her hand and led Kate farther along the ravine floor. Some fifty metres along, the wall had a cleft that dropped from an open top into a Vee-shape at the bottom. Where the rock joined, there was a small roughly verticle crack. The woman put her hand deep into the opening and came out with water cupped in her palm. With her right forefinger she took drops of the water and touched Kate's eyes, ears and lips. She gestured for Kate to open her blouse. When she did, the woman also put a drop of water on each of her breasts and dried her hands on Kate's hair. Kate was about to button up her blouse again, when the woman put her hand on her chest between her breasts and shook her head. She turned to the other women and spoke to them, and the three other women encircled Kate. They began to chant again and, after a few moments, the old woman took the emu feather from around her neck and stabbed Kate with the sharp end between her breasts, where her hand had been. The pain was intense but something in Kate held her back from crying out, or stepping back. It was important what they were doing. It was necessary. It was what she had come for. And then her head began to swim and she fell onto the sandy floor of the ravine.

How long she lay there she couldn't be sure. When she opened her eyes, her shirt had been buttoned and tree branches had been propped above her body to make a shade. She could hear the women talking quietly close by. She looked up through the lattice of leaves, at the face of the ravine, at the drawings, and especially at the drawing of the bird with angular wings. She closed her eyes again and spoke inwardly to her grandmother. "This is for you, Ella. This is for you."

Her chest hurt. She slowly pulled herself until she was sitting. Seeing her move, one of the women came over. The others joined her and talked in quiet voices, their hands gently rubbing her arms, soothing her. She loved the sound of their voices. One of them offered Kate the water-skin and she drank. The animal skin the woman had been treating earlier in the day had been cut into thin strips and knotted together to make one long strand. One of the women now knelt next to Kate and wound this string around her hair, pulling the hair back into a thick bunch behind her head.

Kate looked at the women, each in turn. It was the original three; the old woman had gone. "Thank you", Kate said. They replied and nodded and gestured up the ravine, to the fire. Kate asked "Where is she?" making the gesture of the feather round her neck and fanning her hand out. They pointed up the ravine. It was clear however that they were not to go in that direction, they were going back to the fire.

Kate took one last long look up at the drawings on the wall, trying to commit them to memory. Then she turned and, moving with care, left the sacred women's place.

V

The old man was waiting for them. He had put the fire out. It was time to move on. They walked out of the ravine and continued following the dry watercourse that led into it. Kate walked in a state of wonder, replaying again and again what had happened. How she longed to find someone who could explain what it meant. She had tentatively asked the old man, but he instantly rebuffed her and said "Women's business." with such finality that she knew he would say nothing at all about it.

In the late afternoon, they walked into a camp by the creek bed, where children ran and played and women tended fires. There seemed to be no males older than puberty.

As they arrived, the group was greeted with shrieks of delight and everyone came to see the strange girl with the red hair. Looking around, while children tugged at her clothes and fingered her hair, Kate realised she could no longer see the old man or his dog.

Several of the women in the encampment spoke some English and one, who seemed not much older than Kate, told her that she would stay with them. Her name was Millin, she said, and that Kate and she were sisters. At first Kate wondered if this could be some kind of relative. But when Millin introduced her to other women and said they were her sisters too, Kate understood that this was a general greeting, a way to tell her that she was being accepted. It became clear that the three older women were the elders of this group and were sisters to each other but not to Kate. Millin said that they were wise women who would teach her many things.

"They say they know you come from this country long time", Millin said. "You, me, we part of this land. This land happy you come back."

"Can I ask you about something?" said Kate, so happy to find someone she could talk to and a woman, perhaps not much older than herself.

Millin grinned at her "First you like to wash, eh?"

The idea of cleaning up was delicious and Kate nodded. Millin lead her away from the camp to a place where the creek bed opened out into a water hole. "This water safe, no crocs here", she said laughing, which was reassuring. Crocodiles were not something Kate wanted to encounter.

Millin gestured to Kate to go ahead, as she shucked off her own simple dress and waded into the water. Kate looked at Millin's dark skin, the sinews of her muscles, the natural rhythm of her body. Unclothed, she moved with a grace and certainty that filled Kate with a sense of wonder. .

Kate carefully untied the long strand of knotted skin that held her hair and, after a moment's hesitation, and so aware of her own white body, she shed her uniform, now totally filthy. The relief at getting rid of its restrictions allowed her to breathe. She felt the gentlest warm movement of a breeze against her skin and as she waded self-consciously into the cold clear still water. She glanced down at the wound in the centre of her chest. A small scab had formed and there was an aureole of bruising around it. Millin had watched her until she entered the pool then let herself sink from sight. When she came to the surface, she began to scrub herself with the orange mud from the bottom. Then she rinsed herself off, dropping beneath the surface several times, before wading out of the water. Once again Kate was aware of the unself-conscious beauty of this woman, the water draining from her as she walked up the bank. Then Kate sank down until the water covered her head and she briskly ruffled her hair to get the dust out. It was matted and tangled beyond belief and she had to work at it until she could get her fingers to run through it. When she finally got the mess under control, she saw that Millin had gone and she was alone. She scrubbed at her body as she had seen Millin do, finding the mud to be wonderfully cleansing.

Finally feeling fresh and clean, she let herself float on the surface, looking up into the cloudless sky, marvelling at what had happened. She thought of Ella and she sent her a thought or a prayer: "Thank you, Granny. Thank you."

After a while she became aware of someone standing on the bank. Millin had come back and she was laughing.

"You sleep in the water!" She was holding a simple print dress in her hands and gestured to Kate. "You put on this", she said. "Better for you."

As Kate left the water hole, she was acutely aware of Millin regarding her body. She could not tell whether she was critical or had any judgement at all. She merely observed. Kate looked down at her own chest and pointed to the wound.

"What does it mean?" she asked.

Millin smiled at her and put her finger lightly on the wound. "Sisters", she said. She pointed to her own chest. She had a scar in the same place. "I will tell", she said." Not now."

Kate nodded. She could wait. She brushed as much water from her body as she could before she put on the dress. It was cool and big enough to flow around her in a way that was so much more comfortable. She would throw that nurse's uniform, the last vestige of her European-ness, into the fire.

They walked together back to the encampment and saw the children running with a pack of others. One of them had seen an echidna and they were chasing it through the saltbush.

The fire was still burning and Kate went to throw the uniform into it but Millin stopped her. "No", she said. "Keep. Good for children." Kate passed it to her and wondered how the children could really use it.

Now they were in a larger group, the three older women had their sleeping place and their own fire a little apart from the larger family groups. Millin showed Kate her own sleeping area with her two little children tagging along. She said Kate was now their auntie. They had no inhibitions and crawled all over her and hid little objects in her hair.

After the sun had set, they all ate together. Kate not really sure what the animal was she was eating but happy to go along with whatever she was given. They prepared the sleeping area and she lay with Millin and the children all snuggled up together. The minute she closed her eyes she was gone.

Sometime in the night, she woke into a half-waking, half-dream state in which she could see the crow with its angular wings. It was preening, using its beak to poke deep beneath its shining black wings. Its eye was intense. Or was that the one eye of the old woman? When Kate became fully awake, the wound in her chest throbbed sharply. One of Millin's children snuffled and cuddled in closer to Kate for warmth and Kate put her arm around her, as she dropped back into sleep.

In the stark cold morning, feeling stiff and sore, as she had after each night on the hard ground, Kate felt that she had passed some very important kind of test. They had taken her in. She was a part of them now. This was her world. She took herself off to the water hole and splashed her face. As the ripples flattened out she looked at her reflection in the early morning sunlight. "Who are you?" she asked her own reflection. Then she shook her head and went back to the camp.

Millin told her that the younger women were going hunting and that she could come. "Children stay here", she said. "Not good for hunting, too much noise." The children continued to play and didn't seem to notice the party of five young women head off together. By now her feet were beginning to harden and Kate had less trouble walking. However as they walked in single file through some low hills she was acutely aware of how the other women moved without disturbing the ground. They seemed to glide, almost above the ground, while she felt herself to be ploughing through it. They were light and she felt like a bulldozer.

Finally they stopped on a rise above a stand of saplings. Millin told her quietly that this was a good place to hunt for lizards. "Lizard, he is quick and he hear good, so we quiet."

Kate nodded and waited to see how the hunting would take place. The women formed a circle round the sapling and began to move in slowly, precisely placing their feet in the soft earth. Kate tried to imitate this as best she could but inevitably stood on a twig or a dry leaf and was horrified at how much noise it made. Close to the trees, the women became very still. Kate watched them and was thinking about how they must have been trained to do this. Millin pointed her finger at her and shook her head. Kate did not understand, so she simply stood still. She was thinking about how the women seemed to be able to communicate without speech when suddenly she saw Millin look annoyed. She came over to Kate and pointed back up the hill. Kate felt chastised but had no idea why. She obediently backed up the hill and sat on a rock to watch the hunt from a distance.

Stealthily the women closed in on the saplings and suddenly one of them flung herself on the ground amid a cloud of dust. Seconds later she stood up with a brown reptile limp in her hands, which she thrust into her dilly bag. The women spoke animatedly as they climbed back up the hill.

Millin squatted down beside Kate. "Him good", she said pointing at the dilly bag. Then she looked at Kate with a penetrating gaze. "In hunt, no think. Lizard he hear you think." This made no sense and

Kate shrugged her incomprehension. Millin pointed to her head. "You thinking, lizard he hear." And then Kate understood perhaps what had happened. Maybe animals could pick up the vibrations of thought. She could believe that, but the idea of not thinking, or rather being able to choose when to think and when not to think, that was beyond anything she had ever considered. "Not think?" she said. "How?"

Millin shrugged and tipped her head on one side. "You talk, you not talk. Same." Although that made logical sense, the methodology was not apparent.

"I don't know how to do that", Kate said. "I'm sorry."

Millin looked at her for a long moment as if trying to sense why Kate could not do something so easy. Then she got up and they joined the rest of the women who had already moved off along the rise. As they made their way along the edge of the rise, Kate tried not to think. She soon realised that she was thinking about not thinking. At the same time she was acutely aware that everything she did was noisy: her feet, her thoughts. She was just horribly noisy. She began to feel more and more annoyed with herself. At the peak of the rise, they saw another clump of trees. Off to one side a larger thicker eucalyptus with a white twisted trunk stood on its own. "Ah", said Millin. "Good. Tree take thinking."

Although this made no sense to Kate, she obediently followed Millin to the tree. "Put thinking in tree", said Millin. "Like this." She leaned her head against the white trunk and made a hand gesture as if waves were flowing from her head into the tree. "You stay."

Kate sat with her back to the tree and rested her head against a gnarly lump of striated bark. She watched as the women once again made a circle around the other group of trees. She was still angry with herself as she leaned her head back and she distinctly felt the moment when there was a tangible transference from her into the tree. As if there was a magnetic current that was pulling her into itself. Her first impulse was to resist it, not wanting to lose herself but, remembering the look in Millin's eye, she let herself go and felt a rush, a cathartic outpouring of some inner tension that she had been holding until she felt deliciously still and peaceful. She could still see the women and marvelled at their statue-like stillness. Now their stillness seemed to match her own. The complete suspension of outer movement held them all for a timeless period in which she came to feel as if she had just woken up from a long dream. This was broken by the sudden lunge and dust cloud as they caught another lizard, snapped its neck, and dropped it into the dilly bag.

The hunting went on for much of the day and Kate became more at ease with sitting still against trees. There was a gathering feeling of euphoria that seemed to get deeper every time she did it. She began to think she would be happy just to sit against a tree forever.

Although Kate was not aware of it, the hunting had moved in a circle and so it was a surprise when suddenly they walked into the camp to a riotous reception from the children. Fires were lit and the lizards were tossed into the ashes once the fires had developed. Millin took her two children back to the water hole and Kate followed. Once they had all washed, the two children ran and splashed in the water, while Millin and Kate sat on the warm rocks at the edge.

Kate felt almost shy about asking Millin, but she knew she must. "Can you tell me about this?" she said, pointing to the centre of her chest.

Millin nodded. "Heart." Then she leaned over and ran her fingers from the wound radiating out, up her to throat, out to her shoulders and down across her belly.

"Like sun."

"And the crow. You know about that? There was a crow there. They pointed at it and then they pointed at me."

"That your spirit. She come so you know her. You bird spirit person."

"Are you a bird spirit person?"

Millin smiled broadly at her and Kate was aware of her beautiful teeth. "Sisters, you me."

"I am very happy to be your sister."

The children ran out of the water and off up to the camp as the sun had dropped behind the rock beyond the waterhole.

"We eat them lizards", Millin said enthusiastically as she jumped to her feet.

Once they had shared out the lizard meat, which they ate along with some green bitter leaves that Kate had not seen anyone pick, some of the women began to sing and others accompanied them with the rhythmic clicking of sticks. The older woman who had sung to the rising sun when they had brought Kate into the bush was the main singer. Her voice was thin and high but had a resonance that seemed to reach up into the star-studded night. The other women sang a lower accompaniment and then some of the other women began to dance, slowly shuffling their feet in the dusty earth in time to the rhythms.

Kate felt such a rush of love for these women as she watched them in the flickering light of the campfires. Millin came and sat with her. "This women's song", she said. "Story of ancestors dreaming."

"What does it mean?" asked Kate.

Millin watched the movements swaying with the rhythm until she took Kate's hand and stroked it. "One time we all lizards. You, me, live in the earth. Other times we red parrots in the tree. Sometimes just wind making dust dancing." She twirled her fingers to illustrate the *willy willy*, the miniature vortexes of wind that carried the dust into the air. "Sometimes we born as people. Walk. Hunt. Sometimes we man, sometimes we woman." Millin said no more for a while, until the dance became very quiet and slow and the song was no more than a murmur. "All time, this song says, we go back. Come back. Go back. All time."

As she slept that night the echoes of the song played at the edges of her consciousness and in the morning she found herself trying to repeat one phrase under her breath. She shyly approached the singer and asked her. The old woman at first did not recognise what Kate was trying to do but finally she recognised her very approximate version of the song. She patiently repeated several phrases until Kate had been able to sing them. They sang them together. Later Kate asked Millin what it meant.

"The spirit is like a snake; it can make a new skin. The spirit is like a snake; it moves fast in the grass. The spirit is like a snake; when it bites, you die."

For the rest of the day the song played endlessly in Kate's mind. She found herself trying to understand what it was saying to her. She wanted to know the spirit. Everything about this kind of life seemed to touch the spirit. She wanted to know how to touch it, how to be a part of it. She wished that she and Ella could have been there together.

VI

As each day passed naturally into the next, Kate began to let go of any sense of time. Without her old ways of measuring time—without the clockwork life of hospitals and shifts, medications and rounds—her life had no temporal distinctions. The sun rose, arced and set. She rose, she did whatever everyone else decided to do and she slept.

The women and children stayed together as a group and only on occasions did they see men. When Kate mentioned this to Millin, she was told that the men had gone to a men's gathering, "Men's secret stuff", she said, and they would not be back for quite a while.

Kate began picking up some words so she could talk to the children and understand what they said to her. She began to teach them English words and they created a midpoint of communication that was part their language, part hers and lots of miming and laughing. The children innocently and openly accepted her and were loving, tactile, warm little creatures that she was totally in love with. The other women seemed to have fully embraced her as one of their own as well. Her feet hardened, her hair became bleached and matted and her skin peeled and then began to darken. At the same time, she noticed how her mind was beginning to become quiet. There would be times during the day when she had no thoughts at all and was deeply peaceful. She would sit by herself with her back against a tree and become so still that she began to feel as if she no longer existed. At other times the snake spirit song would play itself and she would begin to hum its simple melody. Whenever she saw or heard a crow, she would stop and think, "Maybe that's my spirit."

It was the beginning of the oncoming rainy season when the men returned. Dark thunderheads had begun to appear in the west but so far had brought nothing more than distant rumblings. The old man who had first approached her at the hospital came walking into the camp with his dingo. She was sitting by the cooking fire with Millin's children turning fat greasy grubs over in the ashes and then eating them on the end of sticks like marshmallows. He squatted by the fire and Millin deferentially offered him a grub. He blew on it for a moment then popped it into his mouth. When he finished chewing, he looked at Kate.

"Your child is born", he said.

Kate was amazed and assumed she had misheard. "I don't understand you", she said

"A child", he said. "You have child. She is born. You must go now and take care of her."

"I sorry", Kate said softly. "I don't have a child. I mean, I haven't given birth to one."

He shook his head impatiently. "No. In the dreaming I see your child. It has come into the world for you. Spirit child. You take care of her. She has a body but it is not strong. You take care of her. She teach you." Then he held up his hand, open palm towards her. "Now you must go. Be with her."

"Where?"

"In the place you born, she born."

"In Sydney?"

"Now you go." He said this with absolute conviction. "Tomorrow, the Ute come for you."

Kate stared at him as he chewed on a second grub, watching the fat dribble into his beard.

"But I would like to learn more about our life, our people." Kate felt a rising sense of panic. "I want to stay here."

He shook his head. "What you learn, you learn already. You learn nothing more. Now rains come, you go."

Then he got up from the fire and walked into the darkness.

Kate asked Millin if she could explain what he meant, but Millin shook her head. "He knows things. He says what he sees, you know, in the dreaming."

"So I really should go back to Sydney."

"It is the dreaming."

That night as she lay with Millin and the children, she looked up at the sky, the vast speckled universe and she wondered what it could mean. She knew that coming into the bush had been what she had to do. There was no doubt. It was true: she had learned so much, not by anyone teaching her but by a kind of absorption, a knowing that developed inside. These were her people and yet of course, they were also not her people. She thought about Ella and felt a deep contentment, sure that her grandmother was pleased with her.

As she fell asleep, the presence of her grandmother was palpable, as if Kate was a child again, lying in her lap, with her grandmother singing softly to her. It was not the spirit song but it seemed to be a song of her own, one that was at once deeply familiar and also touching, drawing on her heart and bathing her with its cadence.

VII

In the morning, not long after sunrise, a battered Toyota Land Cruiser bumped and rattled its way into the campsite. There was no road that Kate had seen. The driver, a skinny young man with a lopsided grin, seemed to have found his way by instinct or some other guidance system that didn't rely on technology.

Millin greeted him with much affection and told Kate that he was called Digger and he was one of her brothers. He worked in the mines in the Pilbara and came back always just before the rainy season. Digger grinned at Kate and said he had heard about her and that she needed to go back to Meekatharra. He could take her there. He had to return the Ute anyway, he said, because it belonged to his uncle.

Before she knew it, she was saying goodbye to Millin and to the other women and hugging the children. The old man was not to be seen. The three older women who had escorted Kate at the beginning were very sweet with her, caressing her and telling her, with Millin's help, that she was a good girl and that she would take care of the new child, just like they would. They sang the spirit song for her softly as she walked away from the camp. She found herself in tears and hugged them all before finally hauling herself into the cab of the Ute.

The truck felt strangely claustrophobic after having been outside for so many months. She wound down the window and shouted her goodbyes as Digger engaged the clutch and the Ute lurched off across the rocky surface. As long as she could see them she waved, the children running along behind in the dust. Finally she let herself sink back onto the seat, which cushioned her as the Ute careened and bounced its way across the dry creek bed. Every now and then Digger would grin at her but he seemed tongue-tied now they were in such close proximity and they drove for hours in silence.

It was dark by the time they reached Meekatharra. As the Ute passed from sandy track to bitumen, the sudden silent running of the tires after so much bouncing brought a sharpened awareness, and Kate knew that she was not at all prepared. The hours jolting along in the Land Cruiser had lulled her into a thoughtless numb state. Now she knew she had to wake up to a new reality. What would she say about where she had been? What kind of trouble would she face? There would be the matron to deal with, maybe even the police. And her family. She marvelled at how easily she had left everything behind her. Where would her stuff be? Would her room still be there? And then she realised that she didn't really care. The stuff was from another world and now the people she would have to confront were equally from another world. The sudden silence of the bitumen surface was as obvious a landing as if she been to another planet and was touching down again on earth.

Digger pulled up outside the hospital grounds, not wanting to go up the drive. The engine rattled as the Ute idled and Kate found herself afraid to get out. "I better get going", said Digger. "See you later." In effect, he was politely asking her to get out.

"Thanks for the lift", she said and reluctantly pulled on the door handle. Even the air in Meekathara smelled different: smoky, plastic, industrial and someone had a barbeque going and it wasn't lizard. She felt a nervous churning in her stomach. She slammed the door, Digger gave her a shy little wave and drove off, with the accumulated dust of the bush wafting in spirals from the tray.

She stood there in the road, terrified. Stuck between her two worlds, in her dirty plain cotton dress and no underwear, possession-less; she knew she was at the edge of a cliff and she had to jump off.

Each step up the driveway to the hospital was like lifting a heavy weight. Her bare feet on the warm cement felt unreal. Pushing open the fly screen door to the nurses' quarters seemed to sap the last of her strength and she stood in the doorway, too drained even to close it behind her. A voice yelled at her, from inside the building, to close the door to keep the mozzies out and with a jolt she was back in the world of nurses.

And then the voice that had yelled at her came out of the darkness and Jenny was staring at her. "Kate?" Kate realised in a rush that she was probably barely recognisable. Her hair was much lighter and a matted mess pulled back by the skin thong, her skin was dark and she was dressed like a native in bare feet.

"Jesus. What happened to you?" Jenny was staring at her. "We thought you'd run off with some mining bloke. You didn't leave a word."

Kate shook her head trying to find the right words. "It's a bit hard to explain. I'm sorry."

"Oh shit, don't be sorry. I'm just glad to see you're in one piece. The cops've been looking for you. Your family think you came unstuck. Officially, you're a missing person. Not a word for three months." Jenny shook her head. "Where were you?"

And there it was. This was going to be the question Kate would have to answer, again and again. She shrugged. "I went walkabout."

"You what?"

"I went, you know, off into the bush."

"What the hell for?"

"Because, well, because I wanted to know about…" And finally she had to say it. "I know I don't look aboriginal to you, but my grandma was. She told me and, well…I just had to go and find out."

"Holy shit." Jenny was looking at Kate as if she wasn't sure she was in her right mind. "Did you find her?"

"Oh no, she's dead." Kate realised she was smiling as she said this. She took a breath. "She only told me just before she died, about where she came from. It was from near here. That's why I came here."

"Jesus." Jenny shook her head in disbelief but at the same time she was getting angry. "Why didn't you say something? I mean, I don't care if you're aboriginal or what you are. You could've said something. I mean, you just disappeared. We found your clipboard on the verandah. You didn't even finish the shift. Matron threw a pink fit. And we thought maybe, well, anything could have happened to you. Kidnapped, raped or I don't know, anything."

Kate sighed. "I know. I'm sorry."

"And look at you. You look like shit. You went native didn't you, the whole abo thing. And they're just like that, they suddenly take off."

"I don't expect you to understand Jenny. I don't expect anyone to understand. It's just something I needed to do."

Then Jenny took a breath. "Well, you're back. What are we going to do?" Then she took Kate's arm. "You do stink a bit. At least have a shower and wash your hair. I haven't a clue where your stuff was put, but you can have some of mine for now."

"Thanks." Kate suddenly felt utterly weak and exhausted. The idea of a hot shower seemed unbelievably inviting.

Jenny led her into her own room and watched as Kate stripped off the cotton dress. She laughed. "Well you look like a real abo now. You got the all-over tan."

The hot water was the most exquisite sensation on her skin and she stood and let it run through her matted hair and down her sun-baked back. She had loved the water hole and the mud wash with Millin but there was nothing like hot water and then the luxury of shampoo and conditioner. Finally Jenny poked her head round the shower curtain. "You're going to go down the plug hole soon."

She handed Kate a towel and gave her some shorts and a T-shirt. Then she said, "No undies?"

Kate managed a grin. "You don't need them in the bush."

"And no shoes either", added Jenny looking at Kate's hardened calluses.

Once she was dry and dressed, they sat together in Jenny's room. So far no one else had seen her. It turned out to be a Saturday night and most of the nurses had hit the town. "You can sleep in my room tonight. But what are you going to do tomorrow?" asked Jenny. Then she laughed; « Hey it's sunday, you could go to church! »

Kate grinned. How ludicrous the idea of going to church seemed after where she had been.

Nonetheless the future had to be considered. "I think I'd better go straight back to Sydney. I've got some explaining to do, to my family, my mum, and anyway I won't be welcome here any more, will I?"

"It's going to be interesting to watch Harding's face when she sees you."

Kate frowned "Did she get a replacement?"

"Oh yeah, but it took a while and even then only a temp. She was pissed as hell. But she'd probably take you back."

"You think so?"

"Oh for sure. You were good. But she'll give you a lot of shit first."

"I don't blame her."

Jenny went off to an empty room and dragged back a spare mattress and a pillow. She found sheets and a pillowslip and made up a bed. When Kate lay down on the mattress, she couldn't believe how soft it was. She laughed. "I can't sleep on this. It's so soft. I slept on the ground out there."

Jenny was getting undressed as Kate was talking. Obviously she slept naked and as Kate looked at her white skin, she remembered the beauty of Millin, naked in the water hole. She missed her already.

As they lay in the dark, Jenny asked Kate. "What was it like? I mean living out in the bush?"

Kate tried to frame some kind of answer that would be understood. At last she said, "It was pretty hard at first. My feet were too soft and the sun was hot and I missed all the comforts, you know, the things you take for granted. I would have killed for a cappuccino, but after a while I kind of worked it out and then it was Okay. It was really good."

"Did you eat bush tucker?"

"I ate what they ate. Lizards and grubs and snake, you know, whatever they hunt."

"Geez, I couldn't do that", said Jenny, and Kate felt her shudder in the darkness.

Then Kate said very quietly "It's what my people do."

VIII

Despite her doubts, Kate slept deeply on the soft mattress and without dreams. When she woke, it took her a moment to reorient herself. It was a shock to see the white painted ceiling above her head and then to hear the radio coming from someone else's room. She couldn't hear any natural sounds. No birds.

Jenny got up and put on her nurse's uniform.

"Stay here." she said to Kate. "I'll sneak you some breakfast." Then she grinned. "Couple of slices of croc do you? On toast?"

While she waited for Jenny to come back, Kate began to think about what she would have to deal with. She would have to face the matron. She would probably have to explain to the police and then she would have to call her mother. She wasn't looking forward to any of it.

Jenny came back carrying a tray with orange juice, cornflakes, toast and coffee. While she delighted in the forgotten taste sensations of European food, Kate's stomach threatened to rebel with her nervous anticipation. This was heightened even before they finished breakfast when one of the other nurses had wandered into Jenny's room and the circus began. Soon there was a whole crowd of nurses and then some of the younger doctors. Everyone wanted to hear the story. Before it got completely out of hand, Jenny took charge by standing on her bed to get everyone's attention.

"Alright shut up everyone!" she shouted. Kate was cringing at her feet. Jenny now had the room's undivided attention. "So this is the deal. I am Kate's press agent and we are selling the story to whatever channel pays the most." Everyone laughed and some shouted suggested bids. It had the desired effect and cut the tension.

Into the moment's silence that followed, Kate said "I will tell you what happened but I need to do some urgent things first. I'm Okay. Nothing bad happened and I will tell you, I promise."

Jenny pushed them all out of the room and turned to Kate. "You've got ten seconds before Matron breaks the door down. Get ready."

It wasn't much more than that before the stentorian knock announced her arrival. Jenny opened it and there she stood. Matron Harding had built herself a professional persona that tolerated no bullshit. She was short and stocky with a thick thatch of brown hair that was always pinned. Her glasses had heavy burgundy frames, which added to her severe look.

She stood with her arms crossed and her lips tight. Her eyes were steely pinpoints as she scrutinised the spectacle of what used to be one of her most reliable nurses.

"So you have decided to show up again have you?"

"Matron, I am truly sorry. I don't have any excuse. It happened kind of sudden and I had to go."

"You sound incontinent." And there was something of a humourous glint behind the forbidding glasses "You have your reasons, I'm sure, but you have to know you left me in a hell of a spot."

"I know."

"So the question is, are you back with us or is this a social call?"

Kate licked her lips trying to find the right way to explain. "I can't. I am so sorry, Matron. I have to go back to Sydney."

"Well then I won't ask what you have been up to. That's your own business. Your things are in the shed out the back. You can get the key from Kevin. I had a feeling you would eventually put in an appearance. You have pay owing to you that you can pick up at the office and then you will have to talk to the police. They wasted some of their supposedly valuable time looking for you. Not today. It's Sunday. And don't ask for a reference because you won't get one. You can continue to stay here but I will charge you rent. Is that acceptable?" She locked eyes with Kate for one long second, waiting for Kate's nodded response. Then she turned on her sensible heels and was gone.

Jenny had to begin her rounds and left Kate to herself. Others came and went for a while, hearing that Kate had reappeared and she got very sick of saying the same thing again and again. However as the working day got going, she was finally left alone. She sat on Jenny's bed looking for the starting point to the rest of her life.

Almost reluctantly she decided to retrieve her belongings. She went looking for Kevin, the groundsman and keeper of the keys for the shed. Kevin was part aboriginal and had worked for the hospital for years. He himself had had a few episodes of going walkabout. When she found him, he was in the maintenance workshop oxy-welding a hinge to an iron gate. She stood near the door watching the blue sparks flying around the hooded figure. Finally he pulled back the face guard and looked up.

"Hey look what the cat dragged in." He grinned at her with his face guard sitting on top of his head. "We heard you went bush. That true?"

She nodded.

"Where'd you go?" He turned off the blue flame.

"I don't really know. Out there", she said, pointing off into the sandhills. "I wanted to find out more about my people, our people."

"And did you?"

Again she nodded, recognising that she wasn't sure how to talk to Kevin. With the nurses and doctors it was actually easier. They were Europeans. She was not, at least not any more. Now she was talking to a man who was like her, part of this world and part of that other world.

She came into the workshop and sat down on a toolbox. "I never knew I had aboriginal blood. I grew up white. My family never said anything and hid my grandma's past. I only found out when she told me herself, just before she died."

He put down the oxy torch, pulled off the face guard and sat on a box facing her. His face was caked with sweat and his hands were grimy, but there was something about the way he sat carefully and turned to face her that made her want to cry. He spoke gently. "It must be tough to find out you belong somewhere else after all those years."

"I haven't a clue where I belong now." She blew her nose and grinned sheepishly. "I wasn't much good at living the way they do out there."

"Nah", he said with a nod. "You gotta be born to it. The black fella's world is hard for whites to understand. I grew up out there, but I had a hankering for the white man's things." He was looking around the workshop at the tools and the equipment. "Yeah. This is my world now."

"How did you decide? I mean, you're a bit of each aren't you?"

"Yeah I'm fifty-fifty. You know what made me decide what world I wanted to live in?" He grinned sheepishly. "It was footy."

"You used to play football?"

"Me and my brother. We played and we were both good. He's down in Fremantle now. Trained with the Dockers for a while. I busted my ankle when I was nineteen and that killed it."

"That's a pity." Then she frowned, looking at him in his dirty jeans and sweaty T-shirt. "Are you happy in this world? I mean living here, Meekatharra, and working in the hospital. Don't you miss the bush?"

In answer to her question he got up and went over to the workbench. He came back with a framed photo of himself with his arm round the shoulders of an Asian- looking woman and two little boys.

"I was a bit of a lost soul for a while", he said, passing her the photo. "But when I met Rosey and we got married, that got me straightened out. My boys are my world now."

"She's not aboriginal is she?" Kate was looking at the woman in the photo.

"Rosey?" he laughed. "She's a mongrel. Her dad was Filipino, a pearl diver up in Broome. Her mum was a bit Irish, a bit Chinese and God knows whatever else. But you know what, Rosey doesn't care about all that. She just loves the boys like I do."

At that moment a small flatbed truck drove up to the workshop and a grey- haired man, whose shorts rested low in the shade of a massive belly, climbed out. They sat in silence as the man came into the workshop, pulling on the belt that secured the shorts.

"G'day." said the man adjusting his eyes to the shade. "New assistant?" he said, jerking his thumb at Kate.

"No such luck. » Kevin said, getting up from his box. He went off to the back of the workshop. The man came over to Kate and saw that she was holding Kevin's family photo.

"Proud of his nippers is our Kev", he said. "You work here in the hospital?"

"I'm a nurse", she said automatically. Realising what she'd said, she added "Or I was. I'm heading back to Sydney."

"Jesus", muttered the man. "Why would anyone want to go to that hell hole?"

"It's where I'm from. I mean it's where I was born.

"Well that explains it. Once a city slicker always a city slicker."

Kevin came back pushing a small orange lawn mower. "There you go mate." he said. "Works like a charm now."

"Good on yer." the man said, digging out his wallet from his back pocket. "What do I owe yer?"

"Twenty'll do it. Didn't take long."

"Old Kev's a bloody genius." the man said with a grin. The money changed hands, and the man pushed the mower towards his truck. "See ya." he yelled over his shoulder and hoisted the mower onto the flatbed. "Have fun in Sin City."

As they watched the truck reverse and head out, waving the way people do when it's an automatic action, Kevin asked. "You want to get your stuff?"

"My stuff." Kate laughed. "Isn't it funny that we have to have 'stuff'. Out in the bush I had nothing and I was so happy about it."

"Yeah, it's a different world alright." He took her to the shed behind the workshop sorting through a bunch of keys, as they walked. "Like this eh? We lock everything up and worry about losing things. Nobody nicks my stuff, alright?" He found the right key and unlocked the shed door. Inside she found her belongings all carefully labelled. She looked at the little collection of boxes and her suitcase and for a moment she couldn't remember what was in them.

"Welcome back to the world of 'stuff.'" Kevin said. « Look familiar?»

IX

The small plane kicked up off the runway so abruptly that she wasn't quite ready for it. Meekatharra slid away at an angle and was gone in seconds. Then there was just the great rolling red-grey, yellow and brown landscape of the hinterland, unfolding in an array of shades and shapes that offered no detail. That's where she had been. Now, so high and removed from it, there were no people, just scant traces of human habitation, vague lines on the vast continent scrolling away below the wing. There were roads and bush tracks and the rail line, hinting that people moved through the landscape, but there was nothing to show that anyone lived there. Then the plane lifted up through a thin veil of cloud and it all disappeared.

Kate sat back with her eyes closed, trying to find a perspective. Had she found what she'd come for? If her grandma could see her now, would she be pleased? The hostess brought her a plastic cup of tea and plain biscuits in a plastic wrapper. Kate had a flash of eating fatty grubs round the fire with Millin and her kids, and she had to smile. The hostess took it as a compliment and said "You're welcome."

The plane droned on above the undulating white under-clouds and Kate leaned her head against the window. The vibrations dulled her mind and she dropped into a vacant place inside herself. Fleeting images of Meekatharra played at the edges of her consciousness. Returning a couple of books three months late, explaining to Terry as best she could, and seeing nothing but puzzlement on her face. Kevin saying goodbye to her and giving her a shy hug with real warmth. The matron handing her a typed reference in an unsealed envelope and telling her they would miss her; anytime she decided to come back, she'd be welcome. Jenny going with her to the only hairdresser in Meekatharra and watching the great tangled mess of red hair come off. She pulled back from the window to look at her new short-haired profile. Somehow the letting go of her hair had been a strong symbol of whatever it was that she was becoming. But even with her newly cropped head, she had kept the skin thong that had tied her hair. It was her only souvenir.

Kate went through the motions of changing planes in Perth, walking through the airport, over-lit and garish with its fake-looking didgeridoos and stuffed koalas, the take-away cappuccinos, the racks of magazines promising celebrity scandal, and then becoming part of the great anonymity of a transcontinental flight to Sydney. She knew when she arrived in the early morning, her mother would be there, nervous and twitchy, to pick her up. Kate was not looking forward to it.

Flying east through the short night, she dozed. She awoke, finding herself aware of a presence, aware of someone hovering close to her, trying to touch her. She opened her eyes and looked around the darkened cabin of the Airbus as it droned on across the Nullabor. No one was near her. Everyone was in their own seats with their eyes closed.

She lifted the shade and stared out into the darkness. There were no lights below, just the dark void. Then she saw it from out in the darkness: the vaguest outline of a face with an eye, the only visible eye, fixed on her. The face surrounding the eye became clearer and a voice spoke inside her: "I am waiting for you. Waiting." Her heart was flooded with a feeling of love and involuntarily she said softly back to the image "Thank you, thank you. I will find you." And then she dropped into a deep dreamless sleep that lasted until the plane banked over the harbour.

When Kate felt the plane tilt for the landing, she looked out at the busy commuter ferries crisscrossing below; the endless bays of the north shore lined with the trophy homes of millionaires, precarious on the cliffs; the high-rises of the inner city; the white crouching shell of the Opera House; and then descending over the chaos of rooftops of factories and truck depots beyond the city. As the plane's wheels hit the ground, Kate took in a deep breath.

Her mother was waiting. Pat's initial shock at how Kate looked, short hair, darkened skin, lost weight, made her waver and they embraced with a tentative contact that revealed how much of a gap there was between them. It was as if each thought the other might break if they held on too long. When Kate was growing up, there had been the inevitable mother-daughter clashes but they had also been friends, confidantes almost, though with carefully defined boundaries. The huge gap between them now was the sharp divide that came from all their previously unspoken history.

They made the obligatory post-flight small talk as they waited for Kate's bags and walked to Pat's Nissan, hidden deep in the oppressive concrete layers of the Mascot Airport car park. With the cases in the boot, they got in and each put on her seat belt. Then her mother, stolidly looking forward, unable to hold back any more, began to cry. Kate sat very still and waited.

Pat reached across her, after a minute, to get a tissue from the glove box. Kate tentatively put her hand on her mother's.

"I'm sorry.", Kate said. "I should have told you when Grandma first spoke to me about it."

Her mother nodded and blew her nose. "I was so worried." she said with a sniff. "I thought…Well, I thought maybe something aweful had happened to you."

"I know."

"I'm sorry I'm being emotional. I didn't want you to see me like this. I wanted to be calm and to talk sensibly."

"We will." Kate patted her mother's hand and Pat started the car and they made the journey home, running against the morning's peak traffic. Her mother gripped the wheel as she concentrated on driving and Kate watched the metallic waves of commuters coming at her with a relentlessness that was depressive. Looking away from the road, she found endless billboards silently screaming their promises, shops and houses and factories all jammed together, a tumultuous concentration of man-made things filling her vision. It all seemed so oppressive and encroaching. After the desert, she knew it no longer had anything to do with her. To blot it out, she tried to imagine that once all this was bush, virgin and natural. The visual cacophony that had taken its place seemed ridiculous. In the end she simply closed her eyes.

When they pulled into the drive of the neat brick house in which Kate had grown up, she felt a sense of relief to be somewhere that was at least familiar. But as she looked at the old giant quandong tree and the rambling bougainvillea and the house itself, Kate felt as well a flash of dread. There was a heaviness in returning to the very place in which the secret of her ancestry had never been mentioned. Fallen Jacaranda blossoms swirled, brown and brittle, around the concrete statue of the stork by the entryway, as they carried her bags up the front steps. Pat unlocked the door and stepped back. She was inviting her firstborn back into the family home.

Kate's father had gone to work, that being the way he habitually defined himself. He had been an engineer, he was an engineer, he would always think of himself as an engineer. His lack of sons had perhaps accentuated his focus. Although he had been in every way a dutiful husband and responsible father, Kate could not remember ever having had a conversation with her father that was important to her. He had been a fixture of her childhood and adolescence, like the living room furniture: always there but never much mattering. She was relieved that she would not have to speak to him just yet.

Pat put on the kettle for the expected cup of tea. Kate's suitcases had gone to her old room and sat there on the floor, looking like they were ready to go somewhere else very soon.

Kate perched on a barstool in the kitchen as the kettle boiled and her mother arranged "Ladi's' Fingers" on a plate. Kate had to smile. "Are you trying to make me feel at home with those?"

Her mother glanced up to see if Kate was upset but when she saw the smile she softened. "I don't suppose you can get them in the west."

"I never saw them in Meekatharra. And certainly not in the bush." She took one and the soft crumbly pastry fell apart as she bit it, the crumbs falling onto her shirt.

"You still like your tea…" Her mother wanted to say ". . . the way you used to", but now that question felt awkward, pointing as it did to what had changed her daughter.

Kate felt the pain of it and said, lightly, "Same as always." When the tea was ready, they sat side by side at the breakfast bar. There was a moment as each sipped her tea and then as so often happens when two people are nervous with each other, they both spoke at once. Kate had decided it was the moment to explain, while her mother was making small talk about some neighbor whose dog had been run over. They both stopped. Then her mother said "I'm sorry. Go on."

Kate looked at her mother, searching her face for signs of understanding. She did not want to hurt her mother but she had to be clear. She had to be extremely clear. "I don't really expect you to understand what I did. I didn't mean to scare you, or Daddy, or to be a trouble for anyone. I just had to go. Like I told you on the phone, I went out into the bush because…because of Granny. No one made me go. I wasn't kidnapped or anything."

"You hear these terrible stories about the outback", her mother said.

"I know. Nothing terrible happened. It was actually incredible and… and important." How was she going to convey this to a woman who had never said anything about her origins? "You knew Granny was aboriginal didn't you?"

"She was mixed race, I knew that."

"But you never said anything."

"No. I…we…we never did. It was better. I suppose it was to protect you."

"From what?"

Her mother sipped her tea, obviously trying to find the right response. "When you were growing up there was prejudice, you know, about aborigines and I thought it would be better if you just felt like normal kids, growing up without any ambiguousness. Your Gran and me, we both thought that."

"You talked about it with her?"

"I think I mentioned it to her, once or twice."

"Were you ashamed?"

"Me? No, of course not." Her mother let out a forced laugh. "We were Italian too, don't forget, and there was a lot of prejudice about that, especially when I was young. Being called a wog is not so different from being called an abo."

As Kate gazed at her mother, she saw the shadows of the pain that was hidden there. Her mother had never mentioned prejudice before. "It must have been horrible."

"Oh well, these days it doesn't seem to matter any more. Now we discriminate against Muslims, don't we! Always the latest arrivals." Her mother was making an enormous effort to be light. They drank more tea.

Kate felt the need to go to the heart of what she had come home to say. "Just before Gran died, when she was in the hospital, she told me about her early life. It was important to her to tell me. She told me everything she could remember. She didn't want it to get lost, you know? And then after she went, I kept thinking about it and I knew I had to go there. I just had to find it for myself. I know for you it must be different. But for me, it was something I had to do. There was something missing. That's why I never went to Uni, that's why I did nursing, that's why I went out to Meekatharra."

"And did you find what you were looking for?"

Kate thought about this. "I don't know. I can't say yet. But at least I felt it was a real part of me, of who I am. Does that make sense?"

Her mother shook her head. "Maybe it was a mistake not to tell you."

"Mum, you did what you thought was best. I don't blame you."

Her mother nodded. "I tried."

And somehow that seemed to restore a certain peace between them. Kate felt free enough to talk about what she did out in the bush. Her mother listened with wide eyes, the rest of her tea growing cold. The reason for coming out of the bush, Kate did not reveal. There was no way her mother was going to understand that. Neither did Kate for that matter. By the time she had described most of what she had done out in the desert, her mother was gazing at her with maternal admiration.

"Well, I would never have imagined you had it in you. You're a wonder. It was so brave of you to just take off and trust those people, and live like that. I think it's incredible."

"Really?" Kate was surprised.

"I couldn't have done it." said her mother. "I'm city born and bred. But bare feet in the desert and eating lizards. Maybe some of Gran's genes jumped a generation or something. You were always her favourite. Maybe she saw it in you." Pat began to clear away the tea things as she went on talking. "So now what are your plans?"

Kate hadn't thought too much about concrete plans and she had to think. "Get a job I suppose. Matron gave me a terrific reference, even though she threatened she wouldn't. So I shouldn't have any trouble."

"Good for you." said her mother and her tone suggested that she had arrived at a state of, if not contentment, then at least acceptance. Her daughter had come home, after a bit of a wild adventure, and was now going to settle down. She'd tell Don all about it when he came home and she'd reassure him that his daughter had not gone off the rails. Everything was going to be all right.

X

It was strange going to sleep back in the bedroom where she had grown up, as if she had left this room as one person and returned as someone else, someone she barely recognised. Treasured knickknacks, objects that once meant so much stood dusty on the dressing table. Novels she had loved and texts she had studied occupied the bookshelf, testament of what she had been. The wardrobe was packed with clothes for all the various occasions that were her old life. A trip to the Brotherhood of Saint Lawrence bin would be one of her first actions. It was just so much stuff.

It was even stranger living in the same house with her parents and their uneasy caution with her. They too looked on her as a stranger in their midst. All their dinner table conversations stayed strictly in neutral non-threatening territory. Her father acknowledged her return politely, asked her no difficult questions and continued with his carefully ordered life.

Kate reconnected with a few of her old high school friends, but that too seemed peculiar to her. They were the same as before but she was not. Sitting in a coffee shop by the harbour, they were full of who had what kind of new boyfriend and who was planning a holiday to Phuket. It was almost impossible to plug into the stream of their culture and she had nothing to say. She told them about nursing in Meekatharra and they made appreciative noises and went back the excitement of the latest cell phone apps.

With her two sisters, Kate tentatively aired the possibility of telling them about their own hidden past, but found there was no interest. Whatever questions they had about her adventures seemed to be more accusative than interested. She had been the cause of family disruption and they didn't like that. She got the feeling they had been happier when she wasn't there.

She began to feel caged in and she knew she had to do something to break away. She scanned the nursing sections of the employment supplement of *The Sydney Morning Herald*. There was no shortage of positions on offer.

The larger city hospitals all had a general shortage of nurses and they all seemed keen to have her, but she knew she could no longer work in a big institution, with all the big machines, the stale air, the noise and the reliance on pharmaceutical routines. Whatever it was that had happened to her in Meekatharra had made her want to work with people in a more personal way. Although this was where she had trained, now the big hospital environment felt utterly inhuman, coldly regimented, a zone of drug dispensers and body shops.

As an alternative, she looked up some of the inner city organisations that work with urban aboriginals, hoping that maybe here she would find not only a connection with the people of her ancestry but also perhaps the child that the old man in the bush had described. How she would be able to recognise this child was a mystery to her, but she held a secret certainty that somehow it would have to happen.

She visited an aboriginal women's social centre in Newtown, Kookaburra House. It was a huge old mansion of a place with a massive Norfolk pine dominating the front yard. There were kids everywhere, kids of all shades. Some were obviously only part aboriginal, maybe as small a part as she was. Kate had phoned in advance and spoken to the director, and now she asked a girl, who was attempting to push another girl up into the tree, where to find Sheila Curran, the director.

"Ah, dunno Miss. Probably in the office." And she returned to the task of trying to wedge her friend into a cleft in the lowest branch.

Kate considered knocking or ringing a bell but from the noise in and around the house, she realised it would not do much good. She went inside, looking for the office. This turned out to be the first door on the left, which said, in brassy stick-on letters, "Off". The last three letters, the "ice" had been torn away and something less than polite had been written in magic marker in front of the "Off". She was about to knock on the door, when it flew open and an overflowing laundry basket barrelled out with a pair of bandy legs underneath it. Kate jumped back and the laundry basket took off down the corridor. From behind, she saw the broad backside of a dark-skinned woman in a housecoat.

"Excuse me." called Kate to the rapidly disappearing back. It paused in mid-step. "Sorry to disturb you. I'm looking for Mrs. Curran."

"Aren't we all." said the back and rounded the end of the corridor.

Two small boys ran up the corridor towards Kate, dragging between them a cardboard box with a small squealing passenger. They flew out the open front door and Kate wondered about the state of the passenger as she heard sudden shrieks. She hurried back to the front door expecting to deal with broken limbs and bloodied noses, but the box had miraculously made it down the steps and onto the grass without losing its load. She turned back to the "Off".

From the floor above there were continual thumpings and the sounds of kids yelling excitedly. The office was a chaotic jumble of boxes and jars. There appeared to be no one in the room until she heard a noise in a corner and found a small girl with a mop of frizzy hair sitting in an empty box eating what appeared to be blackberry jam with a pencil. She was dipping the pencil into the open jar and then sucking the end.

"Hello." Kate said.

The girl paused, looked up at her, then down at the jar. "Jam's good for you." she said with definitive assurance and then went on with her ritual.

"Do you know where Mrs Curran is?"

The girl looked up again and squinted at Kate. She thought about her answer, then she shook her head. "Nup." she said and went back to the jam.

A woman in a print kaftan appeared at the door, carrying yet another cardboard box. "Ah." she said putting down her cargo, "You must be Kate. I'm sorry for the anarchy. It's school holidays right now and we are, to say the least, understaffed."

Before Kate could reply, the woman, clearly Mrs. Curran, spotted the girl in the box. "Oh Kylie, what are you up to?"

"Snack." said the girl.

"Oh yes. But you know those jams are for us to sell at the bazaar. Still you must have found one with a loose lid, so it's probably just as well. However I don't recommend that you eat the whole jar." Mrs Curran looked at Kate. "Can you get salmonella from blackberry jam?"

Kate considered that for a moment. "I don't know. Probably not."

"Give it to me", the director said and the girl meekly handed over the jar and emerged from the box. She sucked the remaining jam off the pencil, stuck it into her frizzy hair and marched out of the office.

Mrs. Curran peered under her desk and, finding a waste basket, threw in the jam jar . "Please find something to sit on." she said to Kate. Kate removed several heavy boxes from a chair and sat on it. Mrs. Curran had done the same behind the desk and they faced each other.

"So how can we help?"

Kate gave her a short version of where she had been and Mrs. Curran listened with rapt attention. "Well, well", she said. "You will meet other women here in something of the same boat as you. Children of the children of the lost generation, you might say. Of course not all of them have ventured out into the bush as you have."

Kate nodded. It was not clear to her if Mrs. Curran was aboriginal herself. She had tanned European skin, Mediterranean perhaps, and brown hair cut sensibly short. She was perhaps in her fifties and solid. She decided not to ask.

"I don't really know what you do here," Kate said, "but I am looking to do some kind of work in the aboriginal community."

"That's laudable", the director said, "but it might not be lucrative. We work on a piddly little budget here, a miserable dribble from the government, handouts from whoever we can lean on and flogging jam." She was waving at the various boxes dominating the room. "Honestly, we don't have a position for a nurse, although I certainly could do with one. To tell you the truth, I don't have any vacant positions at all. With a salary, that is. You are welcome to volunteer of course. We'd love to have you, if you can stand working with some of the most rambunctious individuals you will ever meet, not to mention their kids."

Kate liked this woman's no-nonsense way of looking at her situation.

"I will have to find some kind of paid work," she said, "just to keep going, but I would love to help out when I can."

Mrs. Curran got up. "Let me show you around and you can meet some of the others. Most of them are volunteers and the rest exist on the smell of an oily rag, if you know what I mean."

They walked down the corridor as Mrs. Curran opened doors and showed her rooms with workspaces, some clunky old computers, art rooms and a makeshift carpentry shop.

"Although we are ostensibly a women's centre, it's really the kids we spend most of our time on."

And that's how it seemed to be. There were children all over the building, most unsupervised and running and shouting. Kate met the other staff, only three of them in fact. The woman who had been carrying the laundry basket, Dorry, turned out to be the housekeeper and general caretaker of the building. She greeted Kate absently and seemed to be deeply angry. As they left her, Mrs. Curran told Kate that Dorry was dealing with all sorts of domestic challenges and not to mind her too much. "Her old man's back in Long Bay Gaol on assault charges, one of her sons got badly beaten up in a street riot and her daughter's pregnant, again."

Upstairs where the noise seemed to be strongest, they came across a room of children excitedly juggling balls and dumbbells. It was a decidedly dangerous arena to step into with loose balls rolling around and lost dumbbells crashing to the wooden floor. In the middle, stood a young man in jeans and a long sleeve "Bran Niu Dae" sweatshirt, watching his circus with a huge grin on his face.

When he saw Mrs. Curran come in, he yelled in a surprisingly loud voice, "All balls down!" There was a resultant crash and clatter and all the children turned to look at him. "We have an audience." he announced.

"This is Marco," Mrs. Curran said, "without whom, we would be running a madhouse."

"Oh," he said, with mock severity, "I thought the whole idea *was* to run a madhouse."

"This is Kate." Mrs. Curran told him. "She might be helping us out. She's a nurse."

"Could be very handy." Marco said, shaking hands with Kate.

"We will leave you to it." Mrs. Curran said, as she ushered Kate to the door. "We are all looking forward to the big day." She turned and faced the children who were waiting with their balls in hand. "You will be the best little circus in Sydney."

After she had closed the door, she said, "Marco is brilliant with them. He used to be in that famous Canadian circus. Have you heard of it?"

Kate shook her head.

"Anyway, he doesn't do that any more. But he lends his skills to the kids and they adore him. We are going to have a kids' circus day soon so they can show what they are learning. It'll be on the same day as the bazaar. Jam and juggling."

The other staff person was a young woman, Ashley, perilously thin and nervous who was the officially assigned social worker. In a tiny back office, full of papers, she greeted Kate with effusive good cheer and seemed awestruck when Mrs Curran gave her a short version of Kate's background.

"Oh! That is so beautiful." she gushed.

Mrs. Curran explained that Ashley's work focused on the women, especially the younger mothers, helping them to establish themselves and learn practical parenting skills. "It's an uphill battle, but Ashley is a battler, aren't you, dear?" she said as they headed out the door.

Ashley was smiling shyly under the glare of the compliments.

"I do what I can." she said "Nice to meet you", she called after Kate. "I hope you can come back."

As Mrs Curran took Kate back downstairs, she lowered her voice to say "Poor Ashley is way out of her depth here and constantly in danger of drowning but we try to keep her afloat."

They returned to the office. "So what do you think?" asked Mrs. Curran. "I know it all looks a bit chaotic but some very important things are happening."

Kate felt a warmth for this woman and felt genuinely drawn to the place. "I will have to look for some kind of paid position." she said. "But for now I want…Well, I would like to help here, if I can."

"I am very glad you said that. I felt instinctively you were our kind of person."

They shook hands and Kate promised to return the next day. As she left the building, the girl who had been attempting to hoist her friend into the tree had finally succeeded, and she and her friend were sitting in a fork some three meters off the ground, singing together.

"Bye, bye." they called, as Kate walked underneath.

She looked up at them, two little birds in a tree. "See you soon." she called up and she meant it.

XI

Kate signed up with a nursing agency and there was plenty of work for her. She would be called to different places, mostly the smaller private hospitals and often with elderly patients. She did what was required and earned enough to keep herself together. With the back pay from Meekatharra, she had enough to rent a little flat on the top floor of an old Georgian house just minutes from Kookaburra House in Newtown, where she began to spend as much time as she could. The house quietened somewhat after the school holidays had finished, but there were always things to do. She found herself packing boxes of jam as often as bandaging scratches.

At Mrs. Curran's suggestion, Kate went out on home visits with Ashley, to help the women with health issues. It was a shock for her to see how most of the families lived, even after Ashley had warned her. Many of the houses were barely furnished, with broken windows patched with torn plastic, garbage bags overflowing in unkempt yards full of bike parts and abandoned cars. Often whatever furniture there was, was broken, hand-me-down, Brotherhood of St. Lawrence. Empty beer bottles were the dominant decoration. Kate soon saw that the root of many of the health problems she saw in these families was their junk food diet, their erratic eating, and the way no one had much of an idea about cleanliness. It was a challenge not to show her disapproval, even though Mrs. Curran had cautioned her about showing her feelings.

"You have to understand where these families come from." the director had said. "This is just my perspective. I think of how the aboriginal people were before we came. Maybe what you got to see out in the desert is one of the last remnants of that. They were part of the landscape. They were integrated with it so completely that when we came, we utterly changed it, destroyed it and them with it.

I know what I'm saying is a bit of a cliché but still, that's the way it was. They lost their world and many of them haven't found how to be a part of the new world. Not all of them, of course. You will see some of our women who are just heroic in what they achieve. But there's been one hell of a lot of collateral damage along the way. The men are the most lost. Look at their expected life span, less than half of a white Australian man."

Kate listened to Mrs. Curran with a growing anger. How could this be? How could she have grown up comparatively happily in her family, having everything they had, while these families in the same city, not so many kilometers away, were living in desolation?

Mrs. Curran could see her churning. "It doesn't do us much good to get angry about it."

"But it's just not fair." Kate said.

"No, it's not fair. But I have to say, there's only one way to make it more fair."

"Like what?"

"This is another cliché: help them to help themselves."

"How? I mean when they're living in those places and the kids have no decent food or clothes and the men are all in gaol? How?"

"Women", Mrs. Curran said with a smile. "I believe it will be the women who will find the way for modern aboriginal families to do well. And that's why I do what I do."

Kate looked at Mrs. Curran, sitting in her office, and marvelled at her serenity. This was a woman who knew what she wanted and was going for it. "So you really believe that the women could change the situation?"

"If we can help the women to work out how best to live in this modern age, if they can become familiar with the tools of modern living, if they can keep their children in line, then the aboriginal people will have a future. In the meantime, we try to help the kids have a decent life, have some fun. And you know what? Even though they live in difficult circumstances, and some of them are going to get into trouble sooner or later, still they are mostly happy kids."

"But they don't stay happy, do they." Kate was remembering some of the teenage girls she'd seen, pregnant already, some alcoholics, some on other drugs, many of them showing clear signs of domestic violence. Not happy. And then there were so many depressing stories of where the young men were heading.

"I know." Mrs. Curran nodded. "But we try. Look at what Marco is doing. Who knows, one of these kids might be the next great circus performer."

Kate had begun to spend quite a lot of time with Marco. While the holidays were on, she loved to watch him work all day with the children. They obviously adored him and were quick to pick up what he taught them. Later they would come for after-school practice and then again at weekends. He pushed them but with such good humour that they loved to banter with him. Even on the hottest days, he was always in his long-sleeved sweatshirt.

A week after she had started offering her time at Kookaburra House, he invited her to go to a pub where performers would do try-outs. She hesitated, not having been out since her return from Meekatharra, but he chipped away at her until she gave in.

The pub was on the inner harbour. Originally it was a workingmen's waterhole, but the suburb had gentrified and now the clientele was anything but working men. Marco seemed to know everyone and introduced Kate to dozens of people of all shapes and sizes and hair colour. The performances were also dazzlingly varied, from the banal telling of old jokes by a terribly overweight young woman in a waistcoat and a painted-on moustache, to some sophisticated political songs lampooning the current state premier, sung to a banjo. Marco told her that he often performed here and was preparing a new act. By the end of the night, Kate was laughing and feeling freer than she had for a long time. She had a few beers and not having drunk much alcohol recently, it loosened her up, perhaps more than she realised.

As they left the pub, she draped her arm round Marco's shoulders and told him it was the best night she had spent in ages. He walked her home and she very nearly invited him up.

They spent more and more time together, and after a while she did invite him up and he stayed. In her life, men had not played much of a role. She had had various semi-serious boyfriends during her nursing training years but nothing that meant very much to her. Marco was fun to be with and his humour was infectious. He helped her to draw herself out. She told him something of her background and gingerly aired her desires to find out more. One night as they lay together in her bare little flat, she took the plunge and told him the story of the child. He listened with his hands behind his head looking up at the ceiling as she spoke.

"Oh man", he said "That is the coolest thing I ever heard. I want to be around when you find him or her."

It was relief to have shared that with someone.

After several weeks, Mrs. Curran observed to Kate that she and Marco seemed to have hit it off and Kate had blushed. It was then that Mrs. Curran asked if Kate had noticed anything, unusual about him. Kate was puzzled until Mrs. Curran gently asked if Kate had ever seen Marco with his shirt off. They had become intimate together, affectionate but not to the point of taking off their clothes. Neither had seemed keen to go to that next step. Now as she thought about it, Kate felt a tremour of unease.

"I have hesitated to say anything", said Mrs. Curran, "I thought maybe you would work it out for yourself."

Instantly Kate knew what she was alluding to. "Tracks?"

Kate realised that there were aspects to Marco that had been on the periphery of her awareness and that she should have recognised. His pupils had that look, his pale skin, his edginess. She had seen heroin users often enough, working, as she had, in inner Sydney hospitals during her training. Somehow she had allowed herself to be blinded. What was admirable about Marco had shaded what was otherwise there to be seen.

She thanked Mrs. Curran and thought about it for quite a while before deciding to confront him. One night up in her flat, as they lay together on her bed, she turned to him and gently began to remove his sweatshirt. He watched her with hooded eyes and let her do it. There they were.

She ran her fingers lightly along the ragged lines. "Were you going to tell me about this?"

"What good would that do?" he said and there was a hard undertone to his voice. "I can do without your moralising."

"That's what you expected I would do? Moralising?"

"That's what happens."

"Why do you do this Marco?" she asked looking into his eyes. This was important. His answer would determine whether she could still be in his company.

"Just because. That's the short answer. I went through some tough times and I got in, it kept me going and now I can't get out." He put his sweatshirt back on and got up. "I'll see you around maybe. This isn't for you is it?"

She stared at him. Now he was cold and distant. The funny, quirky Marco was not there. She shook her head. Then he sealed it. He went over to her bag, took out her purse and helped himself to the notes. She didn't try to stop him.

"For services rendered", he said and let himself out.

She sat and stared at the closed door and her pillaged purse. And then she told herself it was better that way.

The hard part would be telling Mrs. Curran that she wouldn't be coming to Kookabura House anymore. What Marco was doing for the kids was more important than what she was doing. She knew that, despite what he was wrestling with. At least he had that. But she knew she could not be in the same place.

She told Mrs. Curran a few days later on a cold blustery morning as they sat together in the cluttered office. Mrs Curran nodded as Kate described her decision.

"I am not surprised", she said with a sigh. "I thought it might go like that."

Then she leaned forward in her chair and smiled at Kate. "You know, I have been thinking about you for something different. It's not working with aboriginal people but it is a very special kind of a task."

"You mean work?"

"Oh yes and well paid too." Mrs. Curran got up and went to the mantle piece above the old coal fire that was no longer used. She picked up a photo from the collection on the mantelpiece. Kate had seen these photos many times and was vaguely aware that they were family photos. Mrs. Curran brought it back and handed it to Kate.

The photo showed a child in a wheelchair. She was thin and pale, sitting at an angle that made her look uncomfortable, almost as if she was suspended slightly above the chair. One eye seemed to be turned upward while the other was focussed on the camera. The face was expressionless, the mouth slightly parted.

Kate stared down at the photo, riveted by the one eye.

"This is my granddaughter", Mrs. Curran said. "I would like you to meet her."

BOOK TWO
CONVERGENCE

P IA

They named me Pia.

It will do.

My resistance to being born has become my struggle to accept that I must continue to live in this difficult body.

The terrible descent that the soul makes from the celestial plane to the earthly plane, inevitable, predestined, impelled by that force against which there is no defence.

The heaviness of it, the strain, the desire to pull back, hold back, go back. No, please no, not again.

To be enshrouded in the womb, where growing and forming is no consolation. No longer free to fly and no space to move. The unnatural knots hobbling the flesh and bones that I was becoming.

And then that frenzied compulsion of the host, my mother's body, to evict me. Inexorable, impossible to fight.

Born.

I was born.

Crouched inside this small misshapen shell, fully aware, I hear them discuss what is "wrong" with me. They assume that I take nothing in and so they speak freely. It has a long and ugly name but no matter what they choose to call it, it means I cannot control most of the outer systems of this body. I cannot walk, speak, feed myself, or perform any of those unpleasant daily functions that whole people, normal people, manage on their own. It means that I wobble and tip, I dribble and make unintelligible sounds.

And until I decide to reveal otherwise, it looks to them as if my brain is not working very well either.

I have been propped against pillows, mute and apparently unconnected, as endless doctors and therapists have discussed "my case". But unlike them, I know why it has to be like this. They call it a "congenital" birth defect, a malformation of my body while I was in utero. I did not develop properly, they say. They believe a vital part of me is missing.

Although that is obviously the case, in terms of the body, I have a different way of understanding it. I know this is how I was supposed to be born. This is how it has to be done in this life. It is not a "defect" but a vehicle. I cannot say why it has to be exactly like this, why this particular form, why this type of human existence, why this dis-ease. I do not have access to the vast record of what has led to this birth, all that has taken place before. It is recorded in the great library of all knowledge to which I have not been granted access.

What I am is the consequence of whatever I was before. And it does not really matter what that was. All I know, all I need to know is that my assignment for this life is that I have to learn to live in it, while making sure I do not forget where I came from and why.

I am here for love.

It is the one and only reason. If it were not for love, then I could not bear to keep going. If it were not for love, I would return to the adoring beings that I have left behind in that other place, that other sky, where no one needs to have a body at all, where no one has to struggle with a mind that fabricates endless and pointless thoughts.

There, our only conversations are beams of divine presence. There, I was perfect. I was undifferentiated. I was whole. There, I bathed in continuous love. It is that, and only that, I have brought with me. It is both a memory and a gift. I have so much to give. There is a fire in me and its flames light my life. I am here to give that to whoever has the ability to see what I have to give.

The time will soon come when I shall begin. And it must be done in this angular, undisciplined skeleton, these alien muscles, this unworkable machine through which substances pass and over which I have no control.

This is the vehicle.

I am Pia and I have come to give love.

CLAIRE

The double funeral began at home. It had to be that way. Tonino's beloved triple-finned Thruster surfboard had to be there. How could it not, when he lived his beautiful short life for the water? How could it not, lying parallel with his father's board, when Hugues, "Le Roi de son Château" was always beside his son? And how could it not, even as the two lives had ended in the turbulent water that they had both battled and loved. The coffins sat side by side, each resting on the surfboard of its occupant, each pointing out to the ocean as if ready to launch at any moment from the middle of the great open family room—this room which they had imagined, designed and built together, in which they had lived. Lived and now not lived.

Claire floated through it all as if she was some kind of supernumerary in a great and splendid opera. There were flowers everywhere, great bouquets and wreathes, some with messages, others simply redolent in their own right. The funeral functionaries did what they do. In their dark suits, with their carefully composed faces and their hushed professionalism, they moved, practiced and choreographed. The event coordinator bent to her task, omnipresent and brusque, occasionally asking soto voce for an opinion on something but mostly demonstrating that she had control.

Like the waves audible beyond the pool, the guests flowed into the house and eddied into corners and out onto the terrace. Hugues's partners, Allen Moore, heavy and lachrymose, Vito Zagni, nervous and tight, made themselves the hosts. Without Hugues, they were a tripod with a leg missing, but they worked the room and represented the firm with a diligence that was touching. Claire was grateful for them but could afford them no attention. She had to keep herself carefully intact. Her mother was everywhere, knowing most of Claire's friends and greeting whoever else was there with the social prowess that allowed her to be comfortable in whatever company she found herself. She paid special attention to the nervous little clutch of ten-year-old boys, Tonino's friends, and their parents. The adults were themselves dealing with the vicarious shock of a parent losing a child. It could have been any one of their children.

The messages had been sent to France, written in English. No invitations were extended, simply the news. There had been no immediate response.

The girl who looked after Pia was a mess, but seemed to manage, just. Claire was grateful for that too, because today she could not let herself be too close to Pia. If she did, she would fall apart. This was not how she had planned to spend Pia's eighth birthday. At least Pia was dressed and her hair had been brushed. The girl had parked Pia, in her wheelchair, close to the coffins. Claire determined that as soon as possible the girl would be replaced. The girl was crouching down beside the wheelchair, trying not to cry. Pia had a clean cloth on her lap to catch her dribble. She held Roo to her in left hand. Her right arm, bent deeply at the elbow, angled out to Tonino's coffin and she ran her forefinger along the wood, gently back and forth, tapping with her fingernail. She was crooning. Did she really know what it was?

At the appointed time, the event director nodded to the celebrant who moved to the microphone set up in front, where the flat screen television could be raised from its concealed recess in the huon pine cabinet. Claire watched him and the ironic thought crossed her mind that he was being operated by a remote control exactly like the one that made the screen rise up. He had a fine head of white hair, which he carefully realigned with his long elegant fingers before he spoke.

In mellifluous tones, he invited the guests to arrange themselves around the room and, as they did, the event director gently ushered Claire to her place and nodded to the girl to bring Pia beside her mother. The two coffins pointed out to the ocean. How often had the two of them headed down past the pool with their boards, dropping along the zigzag path to the beach below.

Beautiful words were spoken. Allen spoke of Hugues, and then Vito of his friend Tonino. Claire's sister Asha and her partner, Imogen, sang "You Are the Wind beneath My Wings" as Pia gently crooned. Claire did not speak, but held herself afloat, brittle as a cuttlefish shell at the water's edge.

At the appointed moment, the coffins were lifted up and carried away from the beachscape, away from the family room, away, side by side, in a hearse. How like wave imagery it all was. The room emptied and the surfboards remained.

The motorcade diligently wound its way to the crematorium. The coffins were carried in, laid onto the automated conveyer and journeyed through the automatic doors, swallowed up. Unseen, the bodies in their boxes turned to ash, the smoke whipped away in the afternoon breeze.

The mourners returned to the house and the formalities of the obligatory gathering took place as they must. The unoccupied boards became repositories for cinzano glasses and cubes of goat's cheese.

The caterers had everything impeccably prepared and the event director was pleased. Claire performed her duties. Her husband and her son were remembered, honoured, missed. So many of those well-meant but essentially hollow words were spoken while discrete waiters eased by with avocado dip and shrimp. Such a tragedy. Taken in the prime of their lives. Terrible accident. As the strong late afternoon sun bathed the terrace and glittered on the rippling water of the pool, people stood in small knots with their drinks and their canapés, inevitably drawn to look down at the beach and the rolling breakers beyond. Seeing again the father desperately trying to save his son in the unpatrolled waters. They had been so at home in that water, so accustomed to its vagaries. Yet on that one day there was an unexpected, treacherous current and the boy misread it and the father could not overcome it. Their bodies and their boards had come ashore like sea birds returning to their nests. They had been carried up to the house, undamaged in anyway except for their loss of life and breath.

At the end of the day, the guests reluctantly paid their last respects and Claire allowed the hugs and kisses to be bestowed as was required. Some mourners dropped down to the beach and threw flowers into the breakers. Curious passersby stopped to watch, an Indian family from the western suburbs asking if it was a festival. When they were told it was for a funeral, they paused to offer their prayers for the departed.

When at last the final stragglers had withdrawn, the cleaners appeared and the caterers packed their van. The remaining flowers were placed decorously on the surfboards and all over the house, the event director was thanked and cheques were dutifully signed for all those whose skills had contributed to a well-run event. The girl had kept herself together enough to put Pia to bed and had left, a miserable hunched-over orphan on her motor scooter.

There was no more to be done.

Claire sat on the terrace as the waves rolled in to the beach below, now shrouded in the shadow thrown by the setting sun. Far off, up to Barrenjoey Head, the sun still bathed the lighthouse, as if it was functioning as its traditional beacon of warning, in the daylight. A single surfer sat gently bobbing in the dusk, well out, just beyond the line of the light, waiting for the opportune wave, as her boys had done so often.

Her mother brought her a cup of tea and they sat together in silence until Claire shivered. "Mum," she said, "I can't live here any more."

HUGUES

He had escaped, run away, gone as far as he could, to start again. Sydney was literally the other side of the globe, and there he would begin a new existence that carried none of the scars of the old world. The freshness of the air, the brightness of the sun, the raw horsey laughter of the women in the bars and the willingness of strangers to be friendly opened Hugues up like one of the tulips rising from the cold ground at the end of winter in his family's château. He was twenty-three, imperfect in his English, recently graduated with high distinction from a prestigious *ecole* in Paris and desperate to disappear.

While his classmates jostled for the best positions in the fiercely competitive arenas of the civil service, Hugues turned away. The freedom that came as he crossed into the southern hemisphere was a release as palpable to him as if chains had dropped away. Between the constant friction in his family—his father's catastrophic business follies and his mother's desperate and smothering attempts at control—and his ambiguous relationship with a girlfriend who wanted to be married and pregnant, Hugues felt a pressure too heavy to be borne. He had bought his open-return ticket with a tearing sense of urgency, telling no one where he was going. He hesitated as he thought of his younger brother left behind to deal with the family dramas on his own, but the desire to be free was too strong. Théophile would have to fend for himself. Hugues had no intention of ever using the second half of the ticket.

On his first morning, bleary from the claustrophobia of the long plane journey, he breathed in the exhilarating ozone at the bucking prow of the ferry heading for Manly Beach at the mouth of the harbour. He'd met a couple of German girls in his backpackers' hotel and they hooked up and went out to the surf. Near-naked girls lay on the beach. Children ran and played and yelled and the coffee was good. His spirits rose and rose.

He travelled with the German girls for a while, going up the coast into the lush wonders of the Australian eastern seaboard. Byron Bay, the Gold Coast, and on up towards the tropics, everything he saw seemed to be full of promise and new energy.

By the time he returned to Sydney, he knew this was his place and he was determined to stay. He found work in a Wooloomooloo pub and learned how to pull an Aussie beer with a decent head on it. His French accent was considered an exotic asset and although he took some ribbing from people who had never forgiven the French nuclear tests in the Pacific or the blowing up of the Rainbow Warrior, and the constant mockery of the Australian Rugby fans, still he revelled in the relaxed and friendly atmosphere.

One evening he was more or less ambushed by a wild girl who lusted after his Frenchness. A few random Gallic syllables seemed to turn her into a rampantly hungry sexual animal. This went on for several conjugally athletic days until he was exhausted. Kerry had a tiny flat in Rose Bay overlooking the naval dockyard. Once the fervour had died down a little, she loved to lie naked with him on the floor of her flat and stare out at the water. She asked him about France and his life. She wanted to go there. When he had told her about his studies in Paris, she got very excited. She worked for a temp agency and was sure she could get him a good job. And she was as good as her word.

Within days, she had him interviewing with a Swiss bank, whose Australian branch was just opening. They took him on in a temporary capacity but seeing what he could do, offered him a permanent position in less than a month. Although he had come in on a tourist visa, they paid an immigration lawyer and had him fast tracked.

The work was absorbing, the life in Sydney was vibrant and the beaches so accessible. Very quickly he began to feel at home. His relationship with Kerry went on for several months, but as his exoticism wore off, her fervour died down. He came back to her flat one evening from work to find her exploring new territory in the form of a muscular naval attaché from Iowa. Hugues packed his bag and, without regrets, moved on.

Within a year he was speaking with a distinctly flat Australian twang in his vowels, renting a top-floor flat above the beach at Bronte and learning to surf. He had made several good friends at the bank, and as they talked about their hopes and plans, they began to plot and speculate. Each had his specialty. Alan Moore had come from a mining engineering background. He was quiet, paunchy and domestic. He could see potential but lacked the personal confidence to act on it. Vito Zagni was an accountant, mercurial and prone to singing aloud. Although they were very different, they were somehow complementary. When they met Hugues, who was both European and an economist, they instantly formed a triumvirate. There was an opening for financial services to link European investors with the vast mineral wealth that was Australia's inexhaustible under structure. Although the Swiss bank did a little of this kind of financing—established mining was seen as dull—it was mostly interested in investment brokering in high tech start-ups.

The three talked through long nights, imagining how to create their own enterprise. Alan was the most conservative, frightened to leave the guarantees of a salaried existence at the bank, worried about his mortgage and swayed by his wife's insecurities and the arrival of their first child. Vito was defiantly single and an inveterate risk-taker. Hugues revelled in their arguments and plans with a newfound enthusiasm that consumed him. Finally Alan was convinced, and they made their move just as some of the bigger mining firms were consolidating and several new and aggressive young entrepreneurs were establishing new ventures. The bank was not as upset with them as they feared and they were able to negotiate an ongoing professional relationship. The bank saw them as strategic partners and backed them.

The three newly minted businessmen found themselves on a swift upward curve that was breathtaking. They were in demand and at the very centre of what was happening. They called themselves Formorzani and Associates, Financial Services, a somewhat messy agglomeration of their three names that they settled on after a long night of alcohol fuelled debate. They leased their first offices overlooking the harbour in North Sydney. Although deeply in debt to begin with, they enjoyed the trust of their backers and began to establish a vibrant crew of young and hungry financial whizz kids, taking risks and reaping the benefits. They rode the mineral boom at just the right time.

Two years later when they were signing for their new office suites, Hugues met Claire Curran. She was an interior designer whose work Vito already knew. She was quick and creative and she seemed to sense the energy of the three and she crafted her sense of it into a stylish threshold that opened into fluid workspaces, revealing discretely secluded areas without confinement. They loved what she accomplished for them. By the time she had finished and they had moved in, she and Hugues had begun to enjoy each other's company.

She was quintessentially Australian and so, to Hugues, wonderfully not European. She was open and friendly, uninhibited physically and quick to laugh. She loved netball, which he had never seen, and Sunday *yum cha* in Chinatown. At the same time she was sophisticated enough to appreciate some of the same artistic expressions that Hugues enjoyed. She had been to Europe several times and loved it. He half-heartedly promised to show her France one day, but she sensed his reluctance. He was not ashamed to be French but he was so keen to be something new. She set about showing him her own continent, taking him for long walks up in the Blue Mountains, where he marvelled at the colours of the birds, the powerful smell of eucalyptus and the untamedness of it all. It was so unlike France.

Coming off an ugly grasping relationship with an older litigation lawyer, she was wary of commitment. While Hugues was just the perfect rebound vehicle, urbane, polite, gentlemanly almost, she kept him carefully at a distance. He was fun to play with and so wonderfully not Australian. For their first year, while the company occupied his every waking minute and her own career was accumulating new accolades, they would meet for drinks, weekend rambles, restaurant outings and simple uncomplicated sex that made no promises. She had her own flat on the north shore and her own life.

They had birthdays just a week apart and she loved to remind him that she was a week older than he was, two Sagittarians. When they turned 28, he took her to Noumea in New Caledonia for a week of pseudo French society. It was there, that he felt confident enough to began to share something of his own life and why he had wanted to turn his back on it. While they breakfasted on baguettes and *grands cafés crémes*, he described his boyhood in the château.

To have grown up within the double-moated walls of Château Des Mésanges seemed like a fairytale to her, but as Hughes described the travails of his family, she understood why he had wanted to escape. They were an aristocratic family and could trace their line back to the sixteenth century with all the baggage that went with that. The château was bought by the family in 1890, it having been in the illustrious De Montrichard family since it was first built as a fortified outpost of the English during the Hundred Years War. Several De Fortelles had fought in Napoleon's army with distinction and later two of them had served for short and inglorious periods in disasterous short-lived governments between the two world wars, but in its current form the family had sunk into obscurity and endured a run of misfortune that seemed to speak of an inauspicious destiny.

The château had three wings, he told her, each built in a different century. The inner defences had been partially demolished to let in more light in the early nineteenth century but in most respects it was much as it had been since it was built. The walls were more than a metre thick in places and the towers had slit openings for archers to defend the interior. The moats had long been drained and were now grassy ditches while the barbican defended nothing any more and served as a handy storage place for firewood. Several floors in two of the wings had been abandoned because the flooring was riddled with holes and runnels of Capricorn beetles and no longer safe to walk on. The château sat on the highest knoll of rolling extensive grounds, famous in better times as a hunting ground for deer and wild boar. There were still many hectares of red and white wine grapes, although the *chai,* the cellars and the acreage were now leased to local *vignerons*.

The family fortune had plummeted in the unfortunate hands of Hugues's father. Alphonse De Fortelle had invested in a number of ventures, including several start-ups in Senegal, which, one after the other, turned out to be fraudulent or quixotic. Whether a cause or outcome of his business failures, he had a serious drinking problem. He seemed to have placed certain moneys in locations where they could not be traced and, then, he himself disappeared. As far as the local gossips were concerned, Alphonse had been spiriting money away in Lichtenstein or had taken a mistress to Argentina.

The family sank to its nadir as Hugues entered his teen years. He heard his parents fighting furiously behind closed doors. He witnessed his father moving into the far end of the chateau's south wing, denying entry to anyone. He watched his mother grow angrier and angrier, lashing out at whoever crossed her path. Hugues and his younger brother, Théo, learned to read their mother's moods as a survival tactic. Even before his father finally absconded, Hugues's main strategy was to throw himself into school. He was a brilliant, quick and confident student and he sailed through college and the *lycée* with top grades. It was inevitable that he would score high enough to go to the Science-Po and he could decamp to Paris.

His family history came out in episodes as he and Claire swam in the tepid lagoon, lay on chaise longues under coconut palms and dined alfresco under the moon. To Claire, he admitted that at times he felt guilty leaving his younger brother to suffer at the hands of his bereft mother, but not enough to do anything about it. He knew too that his mother had very little money and was trying to live and run the château solely from the money that the leasing of the vineyard brought in. Perhaps he would get to the point where his own business was doing so well he could afford to help. But not yet.

As Hugues talked, Claire sensed his conflict, the mixture of shame and regret. She said little as he poured out how he felt. Perhaps he could have been kinder to his brother, perhaps it would have been nobler to have supported his mother, but he was in too much pain himself. At least here, on the other side of the world, he could make a new life for himself.

"I would love to see the world that you grew up in." she had said gently, holding his hands under the table.

Hugues had stared out to the placid aquamarine lagoon beyond the patio where they sat. He shook his head. "I ask myself if I will ever go back to France."

They crossed a threshold together in the francophonic tropics, and by the time they returned to their working lives in Sydney, they had made a deep commitment.

They married the following year on the bluff at South Head, witnessed by Vito, Allan and his wife and Claire's mother and sister Asha. Claire's mother had been delighted when she met Hugues. She admitted to him that Claire's previous relationship had "given her the willies" and that she was sure Hugues would treat her daughter with all the respect she deserved. Sheila was so unlike his own mother that they became good friends right away. Where his mother was stiff and traditional, Sheila was warm and generous. Where his mother had bitten down on her hardship and turned to acid, Sheila radiated a personal confidence and light-hearted fellowship. Where his mother had clung to her rigidly orthodox catholicism, Sheila bathed in a warmly universal acceptance of life. Hughes had thought about inviting his mother and his brother to the wedding. He wasn't even sure if Théophile was still living at home. However when it came time to think about whether his own family should be present to witness his new life, he was certain they should not. He sent his mother a letter and a set of photos after the event, and asked for her blessings. It was the best he could manage.

Another year passed and Antoine was born. Vito appointed himself chief mentor and re-christened the boy Tonino and that was who he became. Claire worked on the design of their new home overlooking the ocean not far from Barrenjoey Road. As the rambling old weatherboard that had occupied the site was demolished, its stubborn reluctance to open to the seas sealing its doom, she kept as much of its tangled garden as she could. She kept some of the best timber as her conception turned into wood and glass. The running water and the existent trees held their position with the house flowing around them. She scaled back her other design projects and took to fulltime motherhood and home creation with a passion. As they moved in and began to delight in the expansiveness and the sunlight of her design, she fell pregnant again and her whole life took a new turn.

Pia's condition was diagnosed early in the pregnancy and they agonised over the question of termination. Several specialists were strong advocates of immediate action. They painted pictures of what life would be like. Hugues felt ambivalent about it, perhaps more than a trace of his strict Catholic upbringing still afflicting him. For Claire, it was constant emotional turmoil. She questioned her ability to take care of a child with such disabilities, she felt threatened by the unknown. Researching what Athetoid Dyskinetic Cerebral Palsy looked like gave her the horrors. She met people who had children with that disability and marvelled at their courage. She didn't think she had that in her. Her mother, however, was a tower of strength and support and, bouyed by the protection of her mother's indefatigable confidence, Claire battled on. In the first trimester, she was physically sick the whole time, not at all the way she had been withTonino, who sailed through his gestation like a gently rising soufflé and floated into existence with an ease that would be the style of everything else he did.

As they approached the critical cut-off point, the decision becoming more and more alarming to contemplate, Claire had a dream. It was not that she could see or hear her child but more that she felt the force of its being. For one thing, it was a female child, and whoever this was, she was coming and would not be stopped. The decision was made. She was coming. She had to come. In the morning, Claire lay next to Hugues, sweating and in agony. When she told him about the power of the dream and the presence of the person who was waiting to be born, he held her in his arms and he promised to be the perfect father to his little girl, no matter what challenges she would face.

And then Pia was born.

KATE

The photo of the child had fixed itself in her mind and Kate kept coming back to it. As Mrs. Curran's Subaru crossed the Harbour Bridge and headed north, she began to explain her daughter's situation. It was just days since the death of her Claire's husband and her ten-year-old son. In fact this would be the day she was to receive their ashes. Claire's daughter had Athetoid Dyskinetic Cerebral Palsy and Sheila gave a quick summation of what Kate should expect from the child. Mrs. Curran was clinical and precise but underneath, Kate sensed a very different feeling. It was almost an afterthought when Mrs. Curran added "But there's more to her than meets the eye." Kate decided not to pick up on it. She would see for herself.

The girl who had been looking after Pia had quit. The deaths were too much for her and, in fact, Mrs. Curran confided, she rather thought the girl had more than a crush on Hugues, Claire's husband. He was French after all. It was a relief that she had gone.

As the Subaru crossed from the sedate suburbia of Pittwater to the more flamboyant Barrenjoey Road side of the peninsula, Kate could see they were entering serious money real estate. Every home was spectacular, with ocean views and pools, swooping angular rooflines and arching ceilings. Mrs. Curran pulled into the open parking area at the front of her daughter's home. It was as beautiful a house as any, but more secluded and discrete, giving away little to the street but everything to the sea. A curving ramp led down past a series of pools on the left, rippling down, one into the next, until close to the wide dark wood front door, the water ran off under a little wooden bridge and away to the right.

Sheila Curran pushed the door open without knocking and called "Yoohoo, here we are!" Kate followed her into a wide marbled foyer brightly lit from a skylight. An acacia with a twisting serpentine trunk looped up from a small inner glassed-in courtyard and a fountain ran droplets of water over quartz projections on a wall of white stone.

Claire appeared and Kate could recognise her mother in her. She had the same colouring but was slimmer and her hair was tied back in braids. She was barefoot and wearing a tracksuit; she had dark rings under her eyes. She kissed her mother and held her for a moment. With her arms still around her mother's neck, she looked up at Kate.

"Hello." Claire said, pulling back a bit from her mother. "Mum says you are exactly what I need." She let her mother go so she could shake hands with Kate.

"What a fabulous house." Kate said and meant it.

"Ah, this house", Claire said with a sigh. "This house was a dream come true. We dreamed it, we designed it, we built it and now it's…well, it's a nightmare house." She turned and led them into the lounge. The wide vista of the sea opened before them, all the glass doors drawn back into their alcoves. "I am sure Mum has filled you in, so I don't have to go over everything. The house is on the market. Somebody will fall in love with it, no doubt and we will move on. I won't be sorry."

As she was speaking, she walked out onto the terrace and Kate followed her. The wheelchair was facing the sea.

"Pia", said Claire, "someone's here to see you." She turned the chair and Pia swung round to face them. The minute she saw her grandmother, she let out a strong "*Haaa!*" and thrust out her arms, her stuffed kangaroo tumbling to the terrace.

"Hello my darling", Sheila cooed and knelt down to hug the frail figure. From behind, Kate watched the matchstick thin arms bat themselves against Sheila's back as the child tipped forward from her chair into the arms of her grandmother. The movement took Sheila off balance and she fell slightly to one side with the child in her arms. Instinctively Kate dropped down to stop her from falling and as she did, the child pulled back to look at her. Kate knelt on the floor so that their faces were quite close together and their eyes locked. The child's right eye held her in its gaze while the left eye rolled autonomously in its socket, unfocused. The intensity of the right eye was, however, unequivocal.

Sheila recovered her balance and she saw that they were looking at each other. "This is Kate", she said to her granddaughter.

Without losing her one-eyed contact, the child leaned in closer to Kate and said "*Haay*."

"That's right", Sheila said. "Kate."

A long slow thread of saliva ran down from the child's open mouth and Sheila instinctively wiped it away with her own sleeve.

"*Haay*." Kate was pleased. It was a distinct attempt to say her name. She

smiled, keeping her eyes locked on the child's face. "Hello Pia", she said softly. "I am very happy to meet you."

Suddenly the child made a strong jerking movement to dislodge her arms from around Sheila's back and dropped into Kate's chest. She was as fine-boned as a sparrow. Kate put her arms around the frail filigree of bones that was this person's body, afraid that she might crush her. The child's head was against her chest and Kate felt her own rapid pulse where the head touched her own body. Over the top of Pia's head, Kate saw Sheila Curran smiling and nodding.

"I knew you were the one", she said.

THÉOPHILE

His mother was not at the airport. Why he had even imagined that she would be was a mystery. Théophile had not told anyone he was coming, so why, as he walked out from the sliding doors with his tote bag over his shoulder, did he look around as if expecting to be met?

Suited businessmen with wheeled carry-ons and computer bags hustled past him to the taxi stand, while he stood in his Indian cotton *kurta*, a white sheep amongst the dark wolves. As he made his way outside into his first breath of French air, past the fugitive smokers huddled close to the doors, he shivered. He used to be one of them. Now he was not what he used to be. The shiver was not because of the cold, although the air was not like Indian air. Was it fear? He couldn't marshal his feelings beyond the obvious turmoil in his belly.

His credit card still worked at the ATM and gave him, not very much, but the means to go…where? Should he get the bus into the centre of Bordeaux and go straight out to the family château? Could he do that? Even before he had flown off to India, he had been living away from home. Unlike his brother Hugues, Théophile had not gone to some prestigious *ecole* and obediently climbed on the career ladder as young men in France are expected to do. He had dropped off the competitive conveyer at the end of high school, leaving the *lycee* with indifferent results and no motivation. He had been a disgrace.

He'd left home to escape the oppressive and desperate maternal clutches of his remaining parent and the sadness as palpable as the mould on the walls in the cellars. He had drifted, moving from one group house to another on the wrong side of the river, where no one monitored his hygiene or his appearance. He had worked in a paper shop and then in a factory that made cardboard boxes and, in between, he had survived perfectly well on the generosity of the French State to take care of its own.

There had been a period when he'd gone up into the Dordogne, not far from Josephine Baker's château, and had lived with two girls who grew hydroponic marijuana. In the 1920s the African American exotic dancer most famous for wearing not much more than a bunch of bananas had sashayed herself into a fortune, which she'd spent on a vast estate and some forty orphans. To avoid the entrance fee, Théophile used to slip over the estate's stone wall and wander in the grounds, so well manicured and posh, so different from his own family's decaying domain. When the two girls got busted, Théophile was lucky enough not to be there and he moved on.

He had gone to Paris and met his brother just once. He and Hugues had sat in a bistro in the *quinzième arrondissement,* at a time when smokers were still legal indoors, and had talked about their parents. His brother had said he felt guilt about leaving Théophile behind, but what else could he have done? Théophile looked into his brother's eyes, searching for some sign of real remorse. There was none. They shook hands and promised to stay in touch, but Hugues took off to Australia not long after and Théophile wandered from one place to another, working on the black, taking the benefits and finding nothing to anchor himself. He rarely gave his brother a moment's thought.

So where was he to go now? Padmananda had been very clear: the house of ghosts. But did she mean for him to live there, visit there, or what? Somehow the forward movement that had brought him this far now fell away. Near the token vineyard planted to impress the toursits, in the forecourt of the airport, Théophile sat on a bench and opened his tote bag. He stared at his pathetic collection of possessions, most of them totally useless for living in France. He unwrapped the small statue of the goddess and ran his fingers over the white stone. He imagined himself back in the ashram, in the temple, lying facedown in full submission to the imperious presence of the rider of the tiger. He was lost in that other world, when someone approached him.

"Excuse me." the person said in Indian-accented English. He looked up. A young man with a large red suitcase was standing in front of him. "You are speaking English?"

Théophile nodded.

"Yes?" said the young man. "I am thinking you are coming from India."

Again Théophile nodded, squinting up against the light to better see his questioner.

"You are French?"

"Yes, I am French", Théophile said, almost as if it was a burden to have to admit it.

"Then maybe you can tell me where I can find the university. I am here to learn to speak good French and to work in IT."

"Yes, I can show you." And somehow that seemed to be the motivation he needed. Théophile put the statue back in its cloth and, closing his tote bag, he stood up.

"We can take the bus."

As they walked together, the young man chattered away happily. He was from Gujarat. Had Théophile been there? His hometown was Surat, a great city. This was his first time in Europe. He had heard many wonderful things about French cooking and he was hoping to eat lots of croissants. Théophile let all this flow over him and made occasional noises of affirmation, but inside himself he was deeply grateful for this distraction. It was as if he had been sent a little help. He could even imagine that it was a small gesture of divine intervention from the lady on the tiger.

They bought their tickets and took the local bus. When the young man introduced himself, his name was Shivji, Théophile felt he should add a little more to the conversation. He told him that he had been in the south and had spent time in an ashram. The young man had never heard of it or Padmananda either.

"In India, so many ashrams. You should be careful. Too many gurus. Most of them are charlatans: give you mantra, take your money."

Théophile shrugged and let it pass.

They caught another bus, which passed through the neat and tidy suburbs, the *banlieux* of Bordeaux and terminated at the university. The young man had various papers indicating where he should go and

Théophile walked him to the office. He waited to see if Shivji would manage and was relieved to hear the woman in the office speaking strongly accented but workable English. He shook hands with Shivji and wished him luck. The young man was effusive in his thanks and asked if they could meet again. Théophile hesitated and then reluctantly gave the young man his mother's phone number. It amused him that after all this time he still knew it without having to look it up.

As he walked away, he smiled. He had given his mother's number as if it were his own. He knew he had to go home. The guru had said that's where he should go, so why was he resisting? It was time to let go of the old and allow whatever was going to come now to come. And there was the mysterious question about Ashtavakra. Théophile had read and reread the verses on his journey. There were times when he had a sense of something about to lift, some veil about to be removed…There would be a moment in which he could almost see. . . But he could never hold it. It was like a vague impression at the periphery of his vision and if he turned to look at it directly, it would disappear.

There was a phone booth outside the student canteen and he called his mother's number.

The female voice that answered was a surprise. He asked if his mother was there and said who he was. The person on the other end was a nun, Sister Geneviève. She asked if he was in Bordeaux and when he told her he was and that he was planning to come to the château, she gently asked if he had heard the news. When he said that he had heard nothing and that he had been away for a long time, she said that he should know that his brother and his brother's son had been killed in Australia and that his mother was very upset. The nun said she was sorry to have to bring him such terrible news, and when he said nothing in response, she went on to say that it would be very good if he came to the château, that his mother would be relieved to see him.

Théophile tried to feel some kind of response to her news and felt simply disconnected. He told her he would catch the bus to the nearest small town and then perhaps someone could pick him up from there. Sister Geneviève said she would do that herself. He put down the phone and stood for a moment, motionless. The pale afternoon sun threw long shadows and he studied his own. He felt numb as if he was his own shadow, ephemeral, thrown at the whim of some far off light source.

Then he picked up his tote bag and went into the student canteen and ordered an espresso, his first proper French coffee. He took the cup to a seat by a window where the outside world was masked by posters promoting rap concerts and Irish pubs He breathed in the aroma of the coffee and let the news of Hugues's death pass over him. He didn't even remember that Hugues had a son. Had he ever known that? And now Hugues and the son were both dead. He had been an unconscious uncle. How he felt about his brother was an unknown to him. It was an unknown while he was alive. Now he had a dead brother. The news had been just too big, too sudden, too ungraspable. He could feel no immediate sadness or sense of loss or even regret. It was as if he had read it in *"Le Sud-Ouest"* as an item of local news about someone else's brother and someone else's brother's son.

After a while he dug out the *Ashtavakra Samhita* and randomly opened at a verse. "My brother is dead", he thought to himself. "What has the crooked saint got to say about it?" The verse on which his finger fell read: How can there be birth, how can there be karma, or even death, when you are that one unchanging, peaceful, untarnished, and limitless consciousness?

Students came and went around him. A girl sat opposite Théophile for a while with wires coming out of her ears, while she bopped along to whatever was playing on the little device hanging round her neck. She was oblivious to him. And he was trying to be that limitless consciousness for which death did not exist. Finally he gave it up and walked out.

He caught the tram into the centre of Bordeaux and the bus out to Créon. The motion of the bus lulled him into somnolence. With his head against the window and his tote bag on his lap, he drifted across landscapes of Goa, bumping along on the back of the tonga, sipping chai, chanting in the early morning, bowing before the chair of Padmananda. When the bus finally pulled into the bus station at Créon and Théophile opened his eyes, it took an act of conscious recognition to remember where he was.

It was dusk and much cooler as he walked from the bus. He dug out a thin Indian shawl he'd haggled over at one of the little shops outside the ashram. It featured an almost gothic representation of the goddess Durga that he'd thought would be perfect for early morning meditation, but now it was the only protection he had against the rapidly cooling air. After making his call, he went to a dingy café where three old men sat at the bar watching the Simpsons dubbed in slangy French. He drank a horrible bitter coffee while the woman behind the bar eyed his kurta and shawl with undisguised suspicion. After ten minutes, despite the cold, he went outside to wait for the car.

His mother's old Citröen appeared with the nun at the wheel. Théophile walked across and threw his tote bag on the back seat. As he let himself in, the smell of his mother's perfume hit him. He very nearly gagged on it. Sister Geneviève looked at him.

"Are you not feeling well?"

"Exhausted", he said.

As they drove, he allowed the sister the indulgence of asking where he had been and he painted a vague picture of travelling in India. She said she was so sorry to be welcoming him home at such a tragic time. He thanked her. As he talked with the nun, he was aware of holding himself carefully and quietly intact. The narrow country roads threading their way out towards the château, through patches of forest and the endless ranks of ordered vineyards were as familiar to him as his own hands and yet now seemed more alien than the jungles of Goa.

The Citröen turned into the long gravel drive, gently climbing past the line of august platane trees and the crumbling stone wall. The ruts seemed to have deepened and held more water. Groups of spring narcissus waved amongst the weeds along the way. At the final turn, the château came onto view with the last light of the day outlining its two towers, and the spiked roof of the barbican

As the nun brought the car to a stop, Théophile took stock of his inner state and the unbidden thought rose up inside him: *Welcome to the house of ghosts.*

He threw his tote bag over his shoulder and willed himself to go in. Crossing the outer moat, he looked up at the barbican, cracks in the stonework, ivy all over it. The door to what was now the firewood store stood ajar. There was very little wood there. As he crossed the inner moat, past the low stone wall, the dread of what he was about to enter rose up in his throat.

The nun pushed open the massive oak door and ushered him in as if she were his host. He thanked her and he meant it. At least he would not have to face his mother alone.

His mother was sitting in the main parlour, by the fire. Above her towered the two old portraits of Fernand De Fortelle and his wife Odile, who represented the apex of the De Fortelle fortunes and whose likenesses Théophile had hated since he was a very small boy. The room was painfully cold and his mother seemed intent on drawing comfort from the warmth of the fire in the grate. She had a dark shawl around her shoulders, which were bowed down by more than just the weight of the shawl. She appeared to be perhaps half the size that he remembered her being. He puzzled over this. Was it the dark shawl or had she in some way diminished? How had she looked when last he saw her? He could not even remember exactly when that was. When he'd decided to go to India, he had just called from Paris and left her a message.

Now as he entered the room with Sister Geneviève, his mother turned from the fire and rose, almost in pain, to greet him. He crossed the parlour with the sense that he was measuring and assessing each step. He watched as if from outside himself. *Here is Théophile walking to greet his mother who he has not seen for years and who is grieving. He puts his hands on her shoulders and kisses each cheek. She kisses him and holds him. She seems fragile.*

"It is a miracle that you have come." she said with her face against his shoulder.

"I was commanded to come." he replied and was a little shocked at what had popped out of his mouth.

She pulled back to look at him. "By whom?"

He looked down at her ravaged face, her red-rimmed eyes searching his and he knew he had to be scrupulously honest. "Three days ago, maybe it was four, I was in an ashram, a spiritual retreat, in the south of India. The spiritual master of that place, it was she who said I must go home immediately."

"Then she must be a saint." his mother said, "and I bless her with all my heart".

This came as such a shock to Théophile that he stared at his mother wordlessly and found, to his horror, there were tears running down his cheeks. They stood there holding each other and grieving, and in their grieving many of the defensive layers of whatever had been constructed between them crumbled away.

Eventually she pulled back. "Ah my Théo. My Théo. You must be so tired. I will make up your bed in your old room and you can rest. Have you eaten anything?"

He was relieved to see a little of her old self re-emerge. He had to think, when did he last eat something? It must have been on the short flight to Bordeaux, a packet of pretzels and tomato juice with celery salt. He shook his head.

"So we must take care of our son. Our only son." And that was a mistake. What little energy she had gathered to welcome him, fell away. He put his arms around her again and was heartily glad when Sister Geneviève spoke.

"Agnès is in the kitchen and she is preparing for you. I will see what she has made."

It broke the fall, and his mother gathered herself. "Yes, yes. Thank you, Sister." She turned back to Théophile. "Where are your things?"

He had unconsciously kept the tote bag over his shoulder while he held his mother. Now he swung it off.

"This is all I have in the world."

She shook her head in disbelief. "So little?" She took his arm and led him up the winding broad stair that seemed to be noisier than he remembered. Certain stairs he remembered having creaks and groans but now nearly all of them had joined the chorus. At the top she took him along the worn carpet to his old room.

As she opened the solid oak door, adding her weight where it now caught the undulating floor boards and switched on the bare single globe that hung inside the tattered lampshade, his old life seemed to flood out of it and envelop him. It took more than a little self-will to cross the threshold. Once inside he felt almost too large for the room, as if he had somehow expanded since he had lived there, or it had begun to shrink away without him. His old desk was there in front of the wooden casement window with its swirly glass panes. His narrow bed was covered with a worn coverlet that he did not remember at all. There were schoolbooks on the shelves and in the oak closet, with its sagging hinges, there were shirts and pants he had not worn for perhaps fifteen years. And all of it smelled mouldy.

"No one has slept in this room since you left it." His mother stood tentatively in the doorway. "I have not had the money to fix anything so I am sorry that you see the house in such a condition."

"*Maman*, it is not important."

"I must find you some clean sheets and a better pillow." She seemed to gather herself and to become more businesslike." And you will want a shower of course. Sadly we do not have hot water upstairs as the plumbing has some problems. Downstairs there is hot water and I will find a fresh towel for you." And she turned and was gone.

Théophile stood in the middle of the room and sensed the ghosts of lost years floating about the ceiling. Then he grinned to himself and went to one corner of the room and lifted the loose floorboard, behind the closet. It was all still there, his little hoard of treasure, the jars he had kept his hash in, his bong, his porn magazines, all the toys of his late adolescence and early adulthood. He stared down at them and he knew that none of them were of any value to him any more. He would go out into the woods tomorrow and burn the lot.

As he heard his mother returning, he slid the floorboard back and went to open the window. This took some strength as the window frame had jammed, the wood expanding with years of moisture, but he finally managed to get it to swing inwards. He looked out into the forecourt in the last light of the day and beyond the inner and outer walls of the château to the darkened oak woods. He turned back from the window as his mother came in with sheets, a blanket and a towel.

"There is something that I would like to do and I hope you will help me." She was stripping off the old coverlet as she was speaking.

"Certainly. How can I help?"

"You are good in English, I think."

"I am Okay. I can speak it well enough."

"I need to write a letter and it must be in English."

"I can do that."

She straightened up from the bed and looked at him bleakly. "Théo, I have not been a good mother to either of you boys and I have not been a good mother-in-law to the wife of my son and I have not been a good grandmother to my two grandchildren." Having no idea where this was going, Théophile simply nodded. She watched him do this, trying to gauge how he felt. When he said nothing, she plunged on. "I must write a letter to the wife of Hugues. I must tell her that I am full of remorse. I must ask her to forgive me if she can do that."

"Hugues has two children?" Théophile realised how little he actually knew about his brother's life on the other side of the world.

"A son and a daughter. Now there is just the daughter."

Although the water was no more than tepid in the only shower that now ran in the château, he felt refreshed—until he had to put on his old and mildewed clothes. It was like trying to wear a different skin, and he determined that he would go shopping as soon as possible, to find clothes for whatever sort of life he was going to have back in France. When he appeared in the old kitchen, so familiar and so full of remembered aromas, he found the other nun had heated some excellent soup and there was decent bread and some good cheese. He and his mother sat to eat with the nuns in the kitchen, perhaps the only warm room in the whole château, while he recounted a carefully edited version of his experiences in India. The nuns were more interested in the ashram than in any of his other discoveries in India, and he ventured tentatively into the sort of spirituality that he had begun to discover for himself.

"It is a blessing to find God's grace in whatever form it may come", Sister Geneviève said and he detected no irony or reserve in the way she said it. He smiled at her and nodded, both amused and ashamed that he had presumed the nuns to be anything other than strictly and myopically Catholic. It was beginning to look like nothing about his previous existence was going to be the same as it had been.

PIA

I do not count the years. To celebrate passing from one year to the next doesn't make any sense to me. I just count the time to be served. They thought I didn't understand what happened to my brother, but I knew. How could I not know? Their souls, both of them were there, but not where their bodies were. Not any more. Antoine, who knew me better than anyone, his soul spoke to me. "I am sorry." he said. I am sorry too. I am so sorry to lose him. He was the one person I could communicate with. He knew what I wanted, what I liked and what I didn't want. He was the part of me that worked. He was my arms, my legs, my fingers. He was there whenever I needed to make contact with the world around me. To lose him is to lose my agent of action.

And my Daddy. He was a wonderful cuddle. He was warm. He was soft. When he held me, I could let go. I could forget that I have a rigid, nerve-jangled body and I would become soft. His love was warmth. His love was without judgement. His love gave me strength. When he held me, his body took the place of my body. I will miss that.

Now they are both gone. His soul and Antoine's floated above us and I could see them and they knew I could see them. And they knew I was the only one who could. We said our goodbyes like that.

Now that they are gone, I cannot hide behind them any more. They were the two who let me be as I am. Without them I must now do it on my own. I must learn to fly on my own. I will find others, of course I will, but none will ever be like Antoine and Daddy.

It's not that my mother doesn't love me. She does, with all her being. But it comes with all those layers of other feelings. She cannot truly know who I am. She can't see me. She is not free. She tells herself it is

195

her fault that I am the way I am, and it puzzles me. Why is she guilty? Why is she so ashamed? Why is my mother angry with herself? Why is her heart always twisted with worry? Does she really think it is to punish her that I was born the way I am? Even now as she drowns in the loss of half our family, she feels so bad about neglecting me. She feels sad that she did not give me a birthday. My eighth birthday means very little to me. What does it matter that eight years have brought me to this point? The pain for her, of losing Antoine and my Daddy is only worse because I am still here. There is nothing I can do to help her with that pain. Not yet. Of course she has no way of knowing that I can see it. The layers of her pain are too thick for her to hear me.

And so the souls that were sent to help me to begin, they have finished their work and they have gone.

I am grateful to them both.

Now I must rise up and show myself.

Now I must fly.

Letters

Château des Mésanges
Entre Deux Mers
France

My dear Claire, my daughter-in-law,

Although my heart is in pain, I can imagine that your pain is more unbearable. We have both lost a son but you also have lost your husband. That loss I have known already. To lose both in one moment is a tragedy impossible for the mind to comprehend. Although we have never met each other and our worlds are so far apart, I offer you my love and my deepest regrets in this terrible event in both our lives.

I write no English and so this letter is written by the younger brother of Hugues, Théophile. He is here with me and for this I am grateful. I write to you now, not only to offer my deepest condolences but as well I wish to say that I regret profoundly that I do not know you. That I never met Antoine, my little grandson, I regret more than you can imagine. That I have not met Pia, my little granddaughter, also. I ask you sincerely for your forgiveness, as I have asked God for his mercy. That I have been not the best parent or grandparent I regret.

As I hold the pain in my heart, now I ask, in the names of those who we loved and we have lost, can we make a rapprochement between us? How can we do this? Do I dare to ask you if you are willing, perhaps, to come to France? I ask if you are willing to bring my granddaughter to see me? That I have not thought to make this invitation long ago is now painful for me to recognise. But God has willed that Hugues and Antoine should leave this world and He reminds me that I have so much behaved not well. You must know that I do not have the means or the ability to come to you. You will understand this, I am confident. Perhaps it will help to lighten your heart to see the château where Hugues was a boy, though it is a humble place.

I pray to God that my past sins of omission and commission be forgiven and I pray that I may make amends.

I await your response.

May God in His infinite love and wisdom spread His benevolence over us all.

I respectfully kiss you and my granddaughter.

Thérèse Beauville de Fortelle

Barrenjoey Road
New South Wales
Australia

Dear Therese,

Your beautiful letter has warmed my heart. I am sorry that I cannot write in French and my computer does not do the accents that I see should be in your name.

My dear Mother-in-law, I too am sorry that we do not know each other. I am so sad that you never saw my beautiful, strong, good-hearted son, your grandson Antoine. Here is a photo of him with his father and his surfboard. He lived for the sea. And it was the sea that took him from us.

Your letter came just as I began to think deeply about what to do with my life and how best to take care of the future for Pia, your granddaughter. Without Hugues, it is so hard to even imagine how to begin a new life. Your letter helped me to see that there are important steps that I must take. So, thank you for your generous invitation and yes, Pia and I will come to see you in your chateau. It must be very beautiful. Hugues told me many stories about his childhood there. We would like to come soon.

I am selling our house; I have already put it up for sale. This house, where we lived as a happy family, holds only memories for me now and we cannot live on memories. The house will be sold, I am sure very soon. After that we could come at any time that would be suitable for you.

You may not know about Pia. I should tell you that she has some handicaps and so, if you are willing, I would bring someone with me to help with her. I should also tell you that Hugues, my wonderful husband, your son, has provided for his family so well, that we have no financial worries at all and we are well able to provide for ourselves in every way.

I am looking forward to getting to know you and to meeting Theophile too.

We send you all our love.

Claire and Pia de Fortelle

BOOK THREE
REVELATION

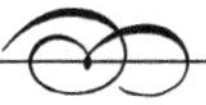

I

As the semester drew to a close and she studied intensely for final exams, Shaafia began to give thought to her summer. She dearly wanted to go back to Casablanca to see her family, but she knew she would have to make enough money for her own needs and even more if she wanted to buy an airfare. In the letters she had written to her father, she had said she could only come if she had the money to pay for it herself. By her brother's hand, her father had told her that he was proud of her and that he knew she would bring honour to the family and to God. He was sorry that they did not have the money to bring her home but whatever happened, he was certain it was God's will and God would take care of her.

She studied offers of summer work posted on the boards at the student centre but felt frightened to make any effort. So many of the vacation jobs available did not seem wise. Working in a bar was not what good Muslim girls did. Waiting tables, serving pork or non-halal meat and alcohol, she could never imagine her father approving of that.

There were several options for being a nanny for the summer but when she finally plucked up the courage to phone, the jobs were already taken. She felt annoyed with herself that she had waited so long. In the end she turned to her friends at the convent who by then had become as close to her as if she were part of their family. Without hesitation Sister Genevieve invited her to spend the summer with them if she wished. They would love to have her. She shyly brought up the subject of finding some kind of work.

"Well you never know what the universe has in store for us." the sister said. "Who knows, maybe something will appear." Then she laughed. "Let's leave it up to God, shall we?"

The nuns had become a central part of her French experience. Tthey were an anchor in the turbulent sea of her first year at university, her first time on her own. They were a powerful antidote to her loneliness and her longing to be with her family.

"Thank you sister, *merci infiniment.*" Shaafia said with her heart full.

"You come just as soon as you are finished with your exams. Marie-Louise will pick you up. We have missed your sweet presence."

As the year unfolded, Shaafia's relationship with her roommate had found an uneasy rhythm and both managed to live with it. They never exchanged more than a few words and kept to their own space, although Nicolette's dominated Shaafia's. Nicolette was always still asleep when Shaafia left for her first class, spent her waking hours with her ears wired to her iPod and stayed up long after Shaafia went to bed. Shaafia had learnt to sleep with the pillow over her head, although her sleep was always shallow and troubled. The room, and in fact the whole building, seemed to vibrate with constant tension, as if an electric current crackled endlessly in the air. Shaafia spent as little time in there as possible and instead lived her waking hours between classes and language labs in the library, surrounded by the heavenly comfort of more books than she could ever read.

On the final day, when her last exam was done, Shaafia pulled together her belongings and cleaned her smaller half of the room. Nicolette appeared toward the conclusion and was stunned.

"Why do you clean this stupid room now?" she demanded. "We are leaving and never coming back."

"It is respectful to leave it well for the next person."

Nicolette shook her head in disgust. "They have cleaners who do that. They get paid for it. And don't touch anything of mine."

It was their last conversation. Nicolette turned on her heel and left. Shaafia finished the cleaning in her area of the room and carried her belongings to the door. She stood there in the corridor looking into the room. Then she carefully removed her name from the door and went downstairs to wait for Sister Marie-Louise. The nun had called Shaafia several times to make sure she knew when to be picked up in the van.

Shaafia sat on her suitcase under a large pine tree that whispered in the brisk late spring wind. Looking up into its branches, she watched a crow cleaning its beak and preening its feathers. She had begun to notice birds more and more, wondering when the bird with crooked wings would appear. She was lost in that thought when the horn of the van startled her.

Sister Marie-Louise sat in the van laughing at her.

"Your head is in the clouds, or is it in the tree?" she laughed as she opened the door for Shaafia to put her suitcasein the back.

The van crossed the river and threaded its way through the vineyards on the other side, and Shaafia felt the weight of her last year begin to soften. It was as if she were going home. If she could not go back to Casablanca, then the convent was surely the right place to be.

Sister Marie-Louise happily chattered on as they drove. She asked Shaafia how her exams had gone and Shaafia said that she thought maybe she had done well enough.

"Well enough?" The sister snorted. "*Alors*! I have an idea you have done better than that. You are a smart girl."

When the van turned into the familiar driveway, Shaafia sighed with contentment. Whatever residual tension was left in her body ebbed away. As soon as the van stopped, she went to visit the fountain with the little bird statues. Fresh flowers had been planted, and there were tulips and crocuses all around the base. The air was gently scented with spring, and she knelt by the fountain breathing it in. She stroked the little stone birds and looked up into the platanes where their living counterparts were twittering.

Then Shaafia went into the chapel and sat in the front row. The sun poured through the windows and dappled the stone floor in the blue light from the stained glass. The statue of the Jesus seemed asleep, although not very comfortable in that position.

She closed her eyes and began repeating her Koranic verse. As she continued, it began subtly to quieten to the point where she could barely hear the words. It was more that she sensed the words were going on within her on their own. It was as if the verse were receding to make room for something to arrive, like the host at the door of an inn who steps aside in order to usher in a traveller. Shaafia found herself wondering *who was coming, what was coming?*

The door of the chapel opened, but it was only Sister Agnès who came in. Shaafia got up, inclined her head to the statue of Jesus and went upstairs to unpack her bag.

II

After the first days of re-entry into his old haunt, Théophile began to doubt whether anything had really changed and it gnawed at him. Had his time in the ashram been some kind of extended hallucination? Had the seemingly prophetic words of the guru been a hollow promise, maybe just to get rid of him? If not, then where was this supposed reincarnation of the crippled saint? Was it real or something metaphoric? Had it all been some kind of illusion that he had bought into? And even if it wasn't, what was he supposed to do now? What was the point?

With nothing better to do, Théophile reorganised his room, getting rid of much of his now irrelevant paraphernalia, his adolescent toys, the diversions of another lifetime. He ended up burning most of it, deep in the oak woods. He pulled together a mound of dry leaves and sticks and, when he lit them, he watched the small flame jump up. He'd had to find matches in the kitchen as his old treasured cigarette lighter with the nude girl who stripped when the lighter was tipped up, had run out. The girl still stripped but she had no gas. The other nudes offered no joy either. The old magazines curled and writhed in the flames, the naked bodies of glossy pornography browning and blackening into twisted and tortured caricatures of themselves. He watched the destruction, detached, amused. His other old toys and pleasures followed. Throwing his bong into the fire was the hardest. It was tempting to think about going back to the comfort of those old supports. As the glass bong shattered in the coals, he longed to have some confirmation, some sign that the path he had embarked on was real, that it went somewhere.

He read and reread the *Ashtavakra Samhita*, trying to break the apparent code, trying to penetrate the words or find a crack in the wall of his own seemingly impenetrable ignorance. The statue of the Durga sat by his bed and in a flimsy attempt to recreate the feeling of the temple, every day he lit a tea-light candle and waved it before the statue on a little metal tray, while murmuring what he could remember of the morning chant.

Several visits to Bordeaux had enabled Théophile to get a few new warmer and not-mouldy clothes and to reapply for unemployment benefits. It felt depressingly regressive to re-enter the French safety net but he needed the money. He looked up a few of his old friends, but most seemed to have moved, changed addresses, bought new cell phones or just disappeared. Those who were still around seemed as indifferent to Théophile's return as he felt towards them. Sitting in his once favourite bistro along the *quai*, he had told some old acquaintances about being in India, but he left out the part about the ashram. A few thought it was cool being in Goa and getting all that cheap dope, but Théophile found no joy in their company and he caught the bus back to the château feeling depressed.

From their long history together, he and his mother were wary of each other, but certainly their relationship was very different from before. It did seem as if she was trying her very best to be civil and to treat him as an adult at last. Nonetheless it was not yet a comfortable relationship. Once the nuns had returned to the convent, they found themselves in each other's company more than he would have wished. Writing the letter to Claire had been a most intimate experience for them both and after that Théophile felt he needed to draw back.

His mother had prevailed upon him to go to mass with her and he had reluctantly done so. To his surprise he found himself calm and indrawn in the convent chapel. His old antipathy to all things Catholic had faded away and instead he felt, almost shockingly, that he was in the same kind of atmosphere as the ashram temple. Without thinking, at the end of the mass, he accompanied his mother to receive communion and with an even greater shock, saw an image of the Durga statue when he closed his eyes as he took the wafer. He sat with his mother in the chapel after the mass and attempted to make sense of it. At least his mother would be pleased to see him behaving like a good Catholic. He was aware of her next him but felt a vast gulf between them as he tried to align his inner world with his outer circumstances. To transcend the forms was the best way he could think of it. Jesus on a cross or Durga on a tiger, what difference did it make?

They went to the convent often and he become quite content to be there. It was the closest he felt to being back in the ashram. His mother often brought flowers from the overgrown and rambling gardens of Château des Mésanges. Sometimes he and his mother would join the nuns in the kitchen for lunch and again he was amused at his own newfound tolerance for these previously anachronistic impositions on his childhood. They had always seemed to be nasty-tempered disciplinarians, sent by God to give him hell. But now here they were, an eccentric group of interestingly opinionated women and he began to enjoy their characters. How had he not seen them like that when he was a child? How could he have hated them with a vitriolic resentment when they were so funny?

With the exchange of letters, Madame de Fortelle grew more and more nervous about the impending visit of Claire and Pia. Where would she put them? How could she take care of them? She agonised over the crumbling state of their home. What would her daughter-in law think? It was all in such terrible condition. Such an embarrassment to have a guest see how impoverished it all was. For the first time in his life, she admitted to him that she had no money at all. It was painful for him to see the excruciating embarrassment that contorted her face as she said it. He told her they would manage somehow. He felt a twinge of guilt that he had no means to help. He had just seen his credit card balance and he himself was living beyond his slender means.

The photo of Hugues and Antoine with their surfboards now sat in a solid elegant wooden frame on the mantle piece above the fire. The two tanned athletic lovers of the surf looked free and buoyant while above them lurked the intimidating de Fortelle forebears. The contrast struck Théophile every time he entered the room.

His mother had also shown him the wedding photos that Hugues had sent. How happy his brother looked, his hair blown back in the wind and his arm round a very attractive woman who must surely be his new wife. He looked at the single photo of Claire in her simple bridal outfit for a long time. As always, thought Théophile, my brother did well. Now she was coming and he would see for himself.

Claire had written regularly to describe their preparation for the journey. She seemed full of enthusiasm and her letters glowed with her anticipation, which Théophile found himself echoing as he translated the letters for his mother. She had booked their tickets, she wrote, and there would be, as she had mentioned, three of them, the third person being a nurse to help with Pia. She hoped that would not be an imposition for her mother-in-law. She described some of Pia's needs, especially the wheelchair. Always she seemed to accentuate that they would be no financial burden, as if she knew of the difficulties already. Perhaps Hugues had told her.

Preparing the château seemed to represent a huge undertaking and Madame de Fortelle was in a constant state of agitation over it. She wanted her son to help make her decisions about the visit: where the guests should be housed, how to cope with the child, where they would be fed, what they would eat, how she would be able to communicate with *les anglophones*? Théophile shook his head as he remembered the headstrong woman of his childhood, so certain of herself, so assured of her own rightness at all times.

Together, they looked at the different ground floor rooms to see which one would be easiest for the wheelchair and closest to the one bathroom that still ran hot water. Every room was crying out for renovation. Floorboards were loose and some were rotting; the wood-chewing beetles, the capricorns and the termites had taken up residence long ago and were eating the château room by room. The walls had seen no paint for years and the aging wallpaper had a universal greyness that was deeply saddening. Many of the windows did not close well and there were drafts everywhere. The furniture was not much better, but they chose the best there was. Thérèse came to the conclusion that her own room was the only one good enough for Claire and Pia and she determined to move herself upstairs. They spent days lugging dressers and beds up and down the stairs.

In all this, Théophile said little, feeling himself caught in constant ambivalence. On the one hand he was not looking forward to the invasive disruption that the Australian guests would create and in which he would have to be present to function, if nothing else, as the translator. He began to wonder how his mother was going to cope. Most likely she would not and he would have to be there for her as well. On the other hand, he was interested to meet his brother's widow. And in a secret part of himself, he couldn't help but wonder if the visit was part of the reason he had been sent back. There was no other sign of anything resembling what had been predicted. Was this it? Was this all part of the plan? When he tried to reason with it, the whole idea became ludicrous in his head. And yet the impending arrival was the one event that seemed to have portent. He had no real faith that the arrival of their guests would be anything significant, but at least it was something.

III

The luxuriousness of first class flying was a revelation to Kate. The multi-lingual cabin crew, in their neat beige outfits with the small token headscarf, a nod in the direction of the airline's Arabic traditions, were constantly attentive. The food was superb and the seats smoothly converted into beds with elegant sheets and pillows.

Pia, dwarfed by her generously plush seat, seemed to have sunk deep into herself and was oblivious to her outer surroundings. From time to time Kate would check to see how Pia was but found her remote and indrawn. Roo was enfolded in her arms as if she were protecting her stuffed toy from the world while she herself was somewhere else entirely. She ate almost none of the never-ending temptations they were offered, occasionally letting Kate feed her some small delicacy. Tiny fragile vol-au-vents with artichoke hearts and sips of fresh guava juice did little to draw her out from her inner focus. Kate was not worried about her, however, as she seemed calm and still. She certainly had no interest in any of the 500 channels on offer on her personal screen.

Claire, too, was indrawn. As soon as it was possible, she had her seat converted into the flatbed and she lay inert with an eye mask on. With Kate in charge of Pia, she could now let herself drop down and down, carried by the weight of the last month's endeavours. The immensity of all she had endured seemed to crush her into oblivion. As the plane spanned the red desert wasteland below, so at last Claire let herself descend into the wasteland of her own submerged turmoil, held at bay for so long. She did not weep. Rather she turned to the deep reservoir of her grief and let herself merge with it.

Watching the vast continent pass below her in the fading light, far to the north of Meekatharra, Kate offered her grateful blessings to the gentle souls who had sent her on this beautiful journey. She smiled to herself as she remembered her own grandmother and her first guides, the women with whom she had become family and the naked aboriginal woman who had initiated her into the sisterhood of the desert crows. Her hand gently rested on the spot where the emu feather had penetrated her chest. She imagined Millin with her children by the waterhole and she hummed the melody the old lady had taught her as she left. Her lay back in the soft upholstery and bathed in the deepest of contentment as the plane left the coast and soared away across the Timor Sea.

On the day when Kate first met Pia, she knew this was "her child". There was no doubt. What passed between them had been a tangible palpable recognition, instant and unequivocal. Kate's heart had pounded as she held the flimsy limbs of the child and she knew with such certainty not only that she had found what she was looking for but also that her experiences in the bush had been real and true. This deep confirmation, this certainty, thrilled her and seemed to break open such a depth of love in her that she could barely contain it.

As she had held Pia in her arms, Sheila and Claire had discussed how it might work for Kate to come and live as Pia's nurse and carer. The details sailed over Kate's head, as irrelevant as the gulls in the breeze above the terrace. She would readily have done the work for nothing because she knew she had found her way. They had worked out a salary and arrangements, days off and having her own room, all created without her commenting, as she held Pia in her arms. From time to time the child would murmur "*Haay*" and pull back to look at her, then drop back into her arms. The battered stuffed kangaroo, badly in need of a good wash, had been retrieved and sat alone on the wheelchair.

Kate moved in the next day. Pia sat upright and expectant with a glow about her that made Kate's heart ache to see her. She dropped to her knee and they enfolded each other in their arms for so long that finally Sheila had to break them up, so she could have her own hug, unload Kate's few belongings from the car and go back to work. As Claire took Kate through what Pia needed, Pia followed Kate with her one good eye, constantly murmuring her "*Haay*". Whenever she could, Kate would stroke her arm or gently say to Pia, "I see you." Claire made them a cup of tea, Pia sipped orange juice through a straw, and they sat together on the terrace.

"It is so good that Mum found you. Truly you can't imagine how relieved I am. After, well, after all we've been through. Thank God. Thank you so much for doing this."

"I feel the same", said Kate, not sure how to respond to the emotion flickering behind Claire's eyes. "It's perfect for me. I was really looking for something to dedicate myself to and the minute I saw Pia, I knew she was just what I wanted. Thank you for inviting me."

They sat in mutual contentment.

It was easy for Pia and Kate to find a comfortable way to be together. Although Pia was totally dependent physically, her personality was strong. Her few words had a subtle range of inflections that were astonishingly clear. She certainly knew what she liked and didn't like. But more than words was the power of her touch. When she hugged, although her limbs were clumsy and angular, there was a wave of energy that went with it. Kate became addicted to holding this child just to be flooded with the feelings that she invoked.

The physical requirements were simple and the child was light and submissive as Kate bathed her, exercised her reluctant limbs and combed her hair. She soon sensed Pia's needs by the subtle signals she gave out. On the other hand Pia had little interest in much of the outer world around her. Loud noises shocked her and she would jump and shake. She loved music, especially soft classical music, and she would make humming sounds when she heard it. Otherwise she seemed largely unaware of her surroundings. Saliva would dribble from the corner of her mouth and she seemed not to sense it.

Very often in the afternoon, Kate would sit with Pia on the deep leather couch looking out to the sea, and they would simply enjoy the comfort of each other's physical presence. Kate would sometimes talk to Pia as if they were having a conversation. Pia was apparently inattentive, even her good eye unfocused, but every once in a while she would murmur and Kate took this to be confirmation that Pia was taking in what she was saying.

The first time Kate softly sang the melody she had learned in the desert, the effect on Pia was startling. She sat very upright as if holding herself as attentively as she could. The song seemed to rivet her. She rocked herself gently making a sound not unlike the song itself and they continued together. From then on it was a precious shared moment every day. For whatever reason, Kate only sang it when Claire was not around. It was just their own private song. At other times, they would sit there quietly and Kate found herself as still as she had learned to be in the desert, her mind at rest and her heart open. It was a mutual stillness, as the child had a capacity to be completely at rest.

Meanwhile Claire busied herself with the sale of the house and the direction of

her new life without her boys. Resolutely, she gathered their belongings and had them picked up by a crew from the Brotherhood of Saint Lawrence. When the van turned up, the two scruffy young men could not believe the quality of what was being offered. Claire secretly wondered how much of it would actually make it back to the warehouse, but she said nothing. The triple-finned Thruster would thrill some new young owner and she privately wished that whoever it was, he would not…She dared not even frame the words for herself.

She had an emotional reunion and business meeting with Vito and Allen, where they promised her she would be the silent third party in the firm. They were deeply committed to taking care of her and fulfilling their responsibilities. It touched her deeply that they wanted her to know just how well they were doing and that they would ensure she had everything she would ever need. She would receive the full one-third share of everything the firm made just as if Hugues himself were still there. At the end of the meeting with no more to be said, the three sat in silence, close to tears. When she left, Claire hugged them and called them her guardian angels. Saint Vito and Saint Allen.

The arrival of the letter from her mother-in-law was perfectly timed and gave her a welcome new burst of purposeful energy. Yes, of course, they would go to France. They would all go. Kate was surprisingly unaffected by the proposal. For her, wherever Pia was going, she would go too. There was not a moment of hesitation. She applied for her passport as Claire arranged one for her daughter, while at the same time the sale of the house went through. It would all work out perfectly. By the time the new owners took occupancy, they would fly away across the world.

When the time came, Kate had almost reluctantly gone back to say goodbye to her parents and her sisters. There was a strained last meal in the family dining room, where, over the years, so little had been communicated during endless rounds of her mother's colourless cooking. Her father was taciturn, her mother prattled on, her sisters surreptitiously texted and checked their mobile phones under the table, probably to each other. Kate did her best to be bright and enthusiastic about going to France, but underlying the brittle conversation was a thread of relief on all sides.

When she finally left, they all pecked at each other's cheeks and exchanged dutiful emotionless hugs. They promised they would stay in touch as people do when they don't really want to, and she drove away in Hugues's soon-to-be-sold BMW. Inching her way across the Harbour Bridge in the packed evening traffic, Kate felt a finality about her farewells to her family. If she could have burned that bridge she would have.

The farewell with Sheila at the airport was entirely different. She enfolded her daughter and her granddaughter in her arms and cried gentle tears. Kate watched the three of them all entwined and bathed her heart in the sweetness of it. Sheila gave Kate as full a hug as she had her own family and thanked her again and again. Kate looked deeply into Sheila's eyes. "You are an incredible person", she said, almost in tears herself. "You can't imagine how grateful I am to you." Then Sheila laughed her full confident bellow and said "Well then, let's be grateful to each other."

They had wheeled Pia through the sliding doors to immigration, waved back to Sheila one last time and spent an hour indulging in the deferential welcome in the first class lounge. Claire and Kate accepted flutes of champagne and there was fresh squeezed orange juice for Pia. The two women raised their glasses and Claire said "So here's to the new adventure. Here's to our new life!" And Pia pulled back from her orange juice and said loudly: "*Ha!*"

IV

The day the Australians were due to arrive, Théophile awoke soaked in sweat. He stared up at the greyish paint peeling from the high ceiling in his childhood bedroom with its now cobweb-encrusted plaster centrepiece and felt utterly dislocated. He had dreamed he was back in the ashram in India but it was not exactly as he had lived it. The temple had become a fire pit and the statue of the Durga was enormous, alive and terrifying. Devotees were dancing before it and burning up in the flames, oblivious to the heat. He however was outside and wanted, desperately wanted, to be part of the fire, part of the dance, but he couldn't find the entrance. His shoes were glued to his feet and there were people around him, French people, laughing. Some of them seemed to be contacts from his life before India and they held his arms and pulled at his clothes. He had begun to weep in anger and frustration and it was this that woke him.

He lay on the narrow bed with the morning light slanting across the far wall, patterned by the fresh growth of the oaks reaching up from the woods below. The small white statue stood inert by his bed. His copy of the *Ashtavakra Samhita* lay beside it. Somewhere outside a merle announced her sweetly voiced presence.

His body ached, as if he had been twisted and torn in his sleep. He rolled painfully out from under his old patchwork coverlet and lit a small candle and a stick of incense from the little packet given by the tonga driver. He waved them in a little circle before the Durga statue while he willed himself to imagine the temple as he knew it, not as he had just seen it in his dreams. Despite the sweet smell of the sandalwood, there was no peace in the ritual and he finally groaned and went in search of cold water to sluice his face.

Staring at himself in the gilded but flaking mirror of what was once an elegant bathroom, he shook his head. Who is this person? What is he meant to do with his pathetic apology for a life? The temptation to fall into a state of abject hopelessness, stared back at him. He stared into the eyes of the other, the image of Théophile who was no more Théophile than…than who? What? Had he learned anything from the hours of trying to understand Ashtavakra and Janaka? Had he gained anything from Padmananda? Was he worthy of receiving anything more than ridicule?

His mother's voice was almost a relief, like an alarm pulling him back from an irresistible descent into self-recrimination. She was calling up from downstairs. He pulled back from the mirror and dried his face. He gave a last look in the mirror and a wry self-deprecating smile as he turned away, and went to the top of the stairs.

"The sisters are here to help." called his mother.

He dropped down the creaking stairs and was grateful to see Sisters Geneviève and Marie-Louise. The sisters as a group had become regular enough in his life that he bent to kiss them both on their cheeks without thinking about it. He even caught himself rather wishing he had showered before he greeted them, feeling foolishly unclean.

There was a hasty breakfast in the kitchen, while Sister Geneviève apologised that they could not bring more of the convent vegetables to stock the kitchen for the new arrivals. "It is too early in the season for our best", she said. "But carrots and radishes are a start are they not!"

His mother had propped the photo of Claire and Pia in the middle of the table and kept staring at it as if she was making sure she would know who they were. Claire had sent the photo so that her mother-in-law would recognise them at the airport. Thérèse had found an old, chipped but gold frame to put it in. Around the photo, coffee was poured and chunks of baguette broken up to be dunked. And then before he knew it, after excusing himself for a quick shave and shower, Théophile was behind the wheel of his mother's Citröen, with the white convent van following along behind for the luggage. Sister Geneviève would stay at the château to prepare the welcome. He wondered at the generosity of the sisters towards his mother. Didn't they have anything else more important to do? Perhaps not. And he was aware that his mother had been equally generous with her time, and long ago her money, at the convent over the years. Maybe it was merely quid pro quo. He grinned to himself, as he used the Latin. His mother caught his smile.

"You are happy this morning?"

He turned to look at her. "What does it mean to be happy?" he asked, as he worked the Citröen over the bouncy back roads towards Bordeaux.

The soft suspension gave the old car a floating movement that sometimes threatened to waft it sideways off the narrow country roads.

His mother looked steadily forward, still clutching the photo frame and he was unsure how she was responding to his question. He asked her "Would you say that you are happy?"

"As you say, as you say." she agreed. "On the one hand here is our daughter-in-law and her little daughter coming to see us. On the other hand they are grieving the loss of Antoine and of Hugues. The Lord gives and the Lord takes back, as it says in the Bible."

"So how would you say you are feeling this morning?" Could he remember having this kind of conversation with his mother, ever? As he waited for his mother to reply, he made sure the white van was following. Sister Marie-Louise was a typical French driver so she was right on his tail.

"I feel, I feel…" His mother was struggling. Finally she sighed and said " I am nervous to meet this Claire. I am anxious to see the child of Hugues." She looked down at the photo. "I am terrified that I will not be able to understand what is being spoken. I am ashamed that I have not been a better person, a better parent. There is all that. And then, I wish to say, I want to say, that I am grateful that you are here, my son. Voilà, so many different feelings."

He nodded and they drove on in silence.

Bordeaux has a ring-road called the Rocarde, which carries not only the morning peak hour traffic but great caravans of *pantechnicons*, sixteen-wheeled monsters from Spain and Portugal going north and from Holland and Belgium going south. At both peak periods on most days the Rocarde freezes up in both directions. As soon as Théophile edged the Citröen down the ramp onto the Rocarde, they saw the bottleneck in front of them. The French call it a *bouchon*, a cork. It had been so long since Théophile had driven in Bordeaux, that he had completely forgotten that this would be the case and would greatly inhibit their passage to the airport, halfway round the Rocarde. They should have predicted this. He sensed his mother begin to panic that they were going to be terribly late.

The traffic inched its way forward down the long hill towards the François Mitterand Bridge crossing the Garonne. The van was right there behind and as he looked at the nun in the mirror, he saw her gesticulating at him, to get off the Rocarde. He only knew this way of getting to the airport. They were locked in until the other side of the river, travelling at little more than walking pace with his mother becoming more and more agitated. Finally they were still well short of an exit, when the van suddenly took off into the emergency lane and he swung out violently to follow her, narrowly missing the bumper of the huge Polish semi-trailer in front of him. His mother was horrified.

"What are you doing? Where are we going?"

"Following the church." he said tersely, as the van sped along the emergency lane and shot up the exit ramp. From there it turned right into a narrow busy road lined with apartment blocks and small shops that Théophile did not recognise at all. She took rights and lefts through a maze of little back streets, past tiny workers' cottages wedged between more salubrious *maisons bourgeois*, until finally breaking out into open fields on a rise.

The morning sun bathed wide expanses of verdant green manicured vineyards, and Théophile recognised the famous and expensive chateaux of Haut Brion, where the ground yielded such wondrous grapes that no one had ever dared to develop the land into housing. Around these august vineyards on lower ground was the sprawl of Bordeaux suburbs, with the university on one side. The traffic was much lighter through the vineyards and they gathered speed. Sister Marie-Louise ran several orange lights, leaving Théophile to risk the red, but he kept up, despite his mother's developing hysteria. Now they were running against the inward flow of morning traffic and the pressure eased. They crossed over the Rocarde on its western circumference and a few minutes later rounded into the airport approach not all that much behind schedule.

Just before the airport precinct, Sister Marie-Louise pulled the van over into a parking bay and Théophile pulled up behind her. His mother was breathing heavily, clutching the photo frame, but she had a wan smile as the sister jumped from the van and approached the Citröen.

"We are in good time, are we not?" she grinned, evidently proud of her
navigation skills. "Did you like our little detour?"

Madame de Fortelle politely responded in a less than steady voice, "Yes thank you, Sister."

"Good. So now I will wait for you here and when the Australians have their valises, you call me and I will come." She brandished the convent's newly acquired cell phone, their belated attempt to keep up with the technological revolution. Théophile had replaced the one he had left in the hut in Goa. They had already agreed on this strategy. No point in paying for two lots of parking.

"At least we are here." he said with careful neutrality as he started the Citröen. "Shall I leave you at the terminal while I park the car?" he asked, knowing exactly what his mother would say.

"No, no! You must come with me." He shrugged and drove into the midterm parking, not convinced that the "Arrette Minute" would give enough time. You get ten minutes free but then you pay a lot if you stay a second longer. His mother carefully stowed the photo in her big black handbag, and he helped her from the car and took her arm as they walked through the ranks of attendant Renaults and Peugeots, most of which are always that ubiquitous and anonymous dull grey.

Inside the Air France terminal, he checked the arrivals screen and saw that their flight had landed. Their Gulf carrier did not do the short hop from Paris to Bordeaux, so they were reduced to the commuter flight. He and his mother stood attentively behind the ceiling-high glass partition that separated them from the baggage carousels. She took out the photo again and kept glancing down as if she was worried that she would instantly forget what they looked like. Théophile craved another coffee, as hints of the brew wafted across from the small kiosk just behind them.

And then the lift opened and a disciplined Air France attendant in a tight skirt and perfect posture, wheeled out a very slight little figure in a wheelchair followed by two women with wheeled carry-ons. Théophile murmured to his mother, who had been staring fixedly at the escalators on the other side: "I think they are here." She jumped as he pointed to the group. She stared down at the photo and then at the group.

"Yes! Yes! Bonjour! Bonjour!" she shouted through the glass. He shrank back from his mother's sudden outburst and also realised that the glass was fairly sound proof. He tapped on it with the car keys and Claire turned. She saw them both and she smiled and waved. Then she bent to the wheelchair, turned it and pointed to the glass. The tiny figure in the wheelchair seemed inert. Meanwhile Claire had spoken to the other girl who also waved.

"Oh I am feeling so nervous." said his mother. They watched as the group turned back to the carousel.

Théophile tried to see what kind of child was in the wheelchair. He had not dared to articulate the thought for himself that perhaps this was the child that Padmananda had spoken of. She had said, at least he thought she had said, that Ashtavakra was now reborn in his château. The problem was that this child was already eight years old, not newly reborn. At the same time the child was in a wheelchair and seemed to be bent, or at least not like a normal child. Could this really be Ashtavakra? And even if it was, how would he know?

A different wheelchair was brought and the child was moved and then the first bags that emerged were theirs with bright orange priority stickers all over them. Several Air France staff were on hand and seemed to be taking extra care of the group. Trolleys were loaded and the group headed for the exit.

As they emerged, it seemed to Théophile that there was a strangely still moment, as if everyone had frozen for a split second. Claire broke it by embracing her mother-in-law and then Théophile. She smelled exotic to him and as her hair brushed his face,an instant intoxication flooded through him and he found himself thinking of Padmananda. The sensation seemed to paralyse him and he could not function. But then he realised that he was vital to what was happening. He was the only means of communication. His mother and Claire were already talking to each other but this was more like a ritualised dance of greeting than meaningful words. They both had tears in their eyes and he saw that maybe there was no need for translation just yet. Claire had indicated Pia and Madame de Fortelle bent automatically to kiss the child on both cheeks. Pia jumped at the unexpected intrusion and the kisses went wide of their intended target. Claire hastily wiped a gathering thread of saliva with her handkerchief and smiled apologetically at her mother-in-law.

Théophile shook hands with the other girl and welcomed her in English. "Did you have a good flight?"

Kate smiled up at him and nodded. "It was fantastic! I have never flown first class in my life. They treated us like bloody royalty."

"You came on first class?" Théophile was not sure he had properly understood her quite strong Australian accent.

"You have to do it once in your life, don't you." She grinned and turned towards her charge, crouching next to the wheel chair. "Pia." she said putting her hand gently on the head of the child and turning it so it faced Théophile. "This is your uncle. His name is Théophile." Théophile winced as he heard her literal rendering of his name. *Thee-oh-file*. Of course, she had probably only ever seen it written. As Kate turned Pia's head, the unfocussed eye floated away into the air above his head and he was unnerved by it, thinking she was blind. But then the other eye came into contact with his and rested on his face.

The look was powerful and seemed to strike into him. He instinctively dropped down to be at her level and the eye followed. *Who are you?* he thought even as he was saying, "Hello Pia. I am Théophile and I am happy to meet you."

V

The whirlwind of arriving in Bordeaux took Kate by surprise. Everything had been so elegant, so easeful, so dignified. The two hours on the ground at Charles de Gaulle airport in Paris had been simply a haven of peace and sophistication in yet another first class lounge. They had been escorted and greeted like celebrities, taken showers, changed clothes, nibbled canapés amid endless deference and soft leather upholstery. Pia had floated into and out of focus, both her own and Kate's. It was almost as if she were taking a different journey from the adults. Her body was carefully wheeled from place to place and her bodily needs were seen to, but her presence was no more than a fine thread of existence, as if her real self was a kite flying high above her somewhere linked only by the finest of kite-strings.

When the time came to catch the Navette to Bordeaux, their boarding passes had already been taken care of and, before anyone else boarded the much smaller Airbus, they were escorted to their front row seats with Pia. No luxurious seating here for such a short flight but they were handed copies of *The International Herald Tribune* and good coffee, unlike anyone in the seats behind them.

The deference continued when they landed, the tight-skirted Air France attendant crisply taking charge of the airline's wheelchair along the jetway and into the lift. By the carousel, Pia's own special wheelchair was retrieved and Kate transferred her. Not that Pia seemed to notice. Kate knelt beside her and held her hand, squeezing it and talking to her softly as they waited for the bags to come. Pia's only outward movement was to clasp her stuffed kangaroo, making no sound, slumped back in her chair.

When the automatic doors from the customs area opened, they were ejected into a different world. All the calm, sophistication, peaceful deference vanished. Now they encountered Madame de Fortelle and Théophile in a sea of other greeters and arrivers. Claire impulsively threw herself at her mother-in-law, Kate introduced Théophile to Pia and the journey of the travellers entered a new phase.

Moving away from the press of the inevitable crowd that blocks all arrival gates, the tearful reunions, the hugging of children, Théophile explained that there was a van ready to take their luggage. He got on his cell phone and led their party towards the exit. Standing outside, not far from the little airport vineyard, Kate watched fascinated as Théophile began to translate the platitudes of first encounters. Are you tired? No, no it was all very comfortable. It is such a long journey. Yes but we had beds so we could sleep. Oh you had beds? Théophile added his own commentary, telling his mother that they had travelled first class and Madame de Fortelle looked at him with astonishment.

The white van appeared and Théophile introduced Sister Marie-Louise. Claire politely shook hands as did Kate, both mystified as to why their baggage attendant was a nun. Neither dared to ask. Sister Marie-Louise looked at Pia and seemed unsure about her. Then she bent abruptly and kissed the child on both cheeks. It was done as a matter of social requirement, barely making physical contact. Pia did not seem to notice. Then the nun stood up and wished them *"Bienvenu à Bordeaux"*, which Théophile dutifully translated, before occupying himself with the bags with the help of Kate and Sister Marie Louise. The sister noted the style of the bags and said to Théophile *"Haut de gamme!"* Top of the range. He smiled enigmatically at her. All the luggage was stowed away except for the wheelchair, which would be folded and placed in the boot of the Citröen. Pia would have to be wedged between the two adults in the back seat, as no one had thought about a child-sized seat for her.

"Allez!" Sister Marie Louise called, climbing into the van and taking off.

Théophile pointed the way across the parking lot towards the Citröen. As they walked, Kate pushing the wheelchair, Claire was speaking to her mother-in-law via Théophile. She wanted to tell Thérèse how grateful she was to be in France, how moving she found it to meet Hugues's family. She wished that Hugues could have been with them. This brought the two women to an abrupt halt in the middle of the parked Renaults, where they impulsively hugged each other and wept. Théophile stood awkwardly to one side and glanced back at Kate. She smiled at him and looked down at Pia.

Pia had turned her face up to the sun and had closed her eyes against it. Kate dropped down beside her.

"Are you asleep?" she asked quietly.

Pia opened her eyes and looked at Kate. "Nah."

"Oh that's good," Kate said, "because we are in France and there will be lots of new things to see."

Pia's left hand came out looking for Kate's and, when she found it, gripping it, squeezing with some urgency. "What is it?" Kate was searching Pia's face trying to catch her intention. "Do you need to go to the toilet?"

"Nah." Pia was most clear indicating what she did not want.

"You can't be hungry."

"*Ha. Haay.*" she said looking past Kate. It then became clear. She wanted to do something with Théophile. Kate stood up.

"Pia would like to see you." she said.

Théophile looked at his mother and his sister-in-law hugging each other, then stepped closer to the wheelchair. He squatted down so he was at Pia's level. Her left hand came out and reached for his face. Her fingers were long and delicate, unbelievably soft and they gently ran along his jaw. He was grateful he had taken the time to shave. She was humming, in short quick murmurs, almost as if she was following some kind of tune. Her good eye fixed on him.

Kate watched and let the moment be. She knew this needed no intervention from her. Pia suddenly thrust the ragged stuffed kangaroo into his hand, moving so unexpectedly that he nearly dropped it in surprise.

"You want me to look after it for you?"

"*Ha!*" said Pia and seemed to be laughing.

He stared at her, trying to reach into her, trying to see who this was. He felt almost as if he was looking at someone with a mask. If only he could remove the mask, he would know who she was.

Then the moment broke, as his mother announced that they should go. Thérèse still held Claire's hand but they were both looking down at Théophile. He took the child's hand and kissed it. Then he tried to stand up and found himself dizzy. He took an awkward step sideways and crashed into Kate, who grabbed him.

"Are you alright?"

"Sorry. Excuse me. I stood up too fast."

"Hey." she said with a grin, "We're the ones who are supposed to have jetlag, not you."

It took him a second to decipher what she meant, but then he got it and smiled weakly. "Oh yes, sorry."

They arrived at the Citröen and organised who would sit where. Theophile ended up with the stuffed marsupial in his lap. They pulled out of the parking area, and from then on there was very little conversation because the front seat couldn't really hear the back seat. The Citröen was in need of a new muffler. Pia receded into a semi-dormant state, as she usually did in cars, and Kate watched the tree-lined Rocarde fly past. There was not much to see as the ring road mostly ran below ground level, burrowing unobtrusively around the Bordeaux suburbs to reduce traffic noise. Looking forward over Théophile's shoulder, it unnerved her at first to have the driver on the left side of the car and to be driving on the right, this being her first exposure to the way most of the world drives.

When the Rocarde began to open out, Théophile called over his shoulder, "Now we are about to cross the river Garonne. You will see the city of Bordeaux to the left." They looked out the window as the wide muddy-brown tidal flow appeared below the bridge. The city of Bordeaux lay off downstream, but there were no high-rise buildings at all, just a few church spires.

After a few more minutes Théophile took them off the Rocarde and they headed east, beyond the last suburbs and out into the vineyards of Entre Deux Mers. Claire looked across at Kate. "Beautiful isn't it!"

Kate nodded. Then they saw their first château and both exclaimed together "Oh look!"

Madame de Fortelle turned to see what they were looking at and she said "Beaucoup de châteaux". Théophile added, loudly over the engine, "She says there are many châteaux. As you will see, the countryside has very many, some big, some small, many very old."

"I can't wait to see yours." Claire shouted over the noise.

"Oh." Théophile said over his shoulder, equally struggling over the revving of the Citröen, "You will see our château is not so important as many others in this region."

Claire leaned forward to make sure she was heard. "You can't imagine how excited all my friends were when we said we would be living in a real French château."

"I hope you are not too disappointed." He did not translate this for his mother.

As the Citröen wound its way through the undulating vineyards and patches of oak forest, the neatly manicured hedges and stately stone dwellings, Kate caught herself remembering the desert landscape of her grandmother's people. Compared to the parched red-brown earth, the scant blue-green plants beyond Meekatharra and the wide-open sky, this was another world, as opposite to anything she could ever have imagined. She gently put her finger up to the spot in the centre of her chest, where the emu feather had penetrated.

She thought : *I have come a long way.*

VI

Turning into the rutted driveway by the crumbling stone wall, Théophile stopped the car.

To one side, partly obscured by ivy and badly tarnished to the point of being unreadable, was the small plaque imbedded into what was once a fine stone arched entrance. The iron gates had long ago fallen off on both sides and were now buried under brambles of blackberries and nettles. "This is Château des Mésanges." He said it without pride, as if he was no more than a tourist guide.

Madame de Fortelle turned awkwardly in her seat, having said little throughout the journey. "*Bienvenue chez nous et maintenant chez vous.*" Her voice wavered with emotion.

Théophile was about to translate her welcome speech, when Claire replied "Thank you so much. It is wonderful to be here." This he dutifully translated back and his mother was pleased.

He drove carefully up the incline along the tree-lined approach. He had to concentrate, the soft suspension threatening to scrape the old girl's bottom on the high centre of the track between the deeper waterlogged ruts. Behind him the exclamations of delight, as the château revealed itself through the platane trees, made him smile. Happy tourists.

Sister Marie-Louise had already unloaded all the bags and had arranged them in a neat row. She now stood with Sister Geneviève as the welcoming committee. The Citröen came to a stop next to the bags and the suspension subsided like an old grey bullock lowering itself with a sigh of relief to the ground for a rest. Théophile got out and the stuffed kangaroo fell to the ground. He had forgotten about it. He jammed it into the pocket of his jeans and opened the rear doors for his guests while Sister Geneviève did the same for his mother, who struggled up out of the front seat. Sister Marie-Louise went to the boot to retrieve the wheelchair.

Théophile watched Claire's face as she came out of the low back seat of the old grey Citröen and looked up. He was imagining what it would be like to see the château for the first time, if you had never seen one close up before. He had always taken it for granted. What you grow up in is your norm. Her eyes widened as she looked up along the massive slightly inward-leaning outer battlements, the huge stones towering over the grassy ditch that had once been the outer moat. And then beyond those stone walls rose the two turrets of the château proper, with their black slate conical tops.

"It's incredible." she said in awe. « You live in this?"

He smiled sheepishly. "I was born here."

She turned to help with Pia, as Kate lifted her from the car. "Look", she said, gently directing her daughter's face towards the château. "This is where Daddy was born. This was his house when he was a little boy."

The child looked at the walls then back at her mother. Then with her left hand she stroked her mother's face.

Claire hugged her. "I wish he was here, too." she whispered.

Sister Marie-Louise had mastered the challenges of unfolding the wheelchair and brought it round. Claire smiled at her. "Thank you."

Madame de Fortelle then introduced Sister Geneviève to them all. She shook hands with Claire and then Kate and then carefully and slowly bent down towards Pia who had been strapped into the wheelchair.

"*Bonjour ma cherie. Bienvenue*" she said very softly. Pia turned her head to the sound of her voice and her good eye focussed on the nun's face. "*Coo-coo.*" she said quite clearly. The nun was delighted "*Coucou! Tu parle français!*" She kissed the child lightly on both cheeks and Pia gently crooned her new *coo-coo* as she did.

Claire bent down to be close to her daughter. "This is Sister Geneviève." to which Pia continued with her *coo-coo*-ing. Claire straightened up, looking surprised. "That's a new one." she said to Kate. "I wonder where she got that from?"

She stroked her daughter's face. "My darling, we are going to have fun here."

As the sisters began to organise the bags, Kate took a moment to gaze up at the château in much the same way as Claire had done. Théophile found himself grinning. "You have not seen a château such as this before?"

She shook her head. "No, never. It looks like something out of King Arthur or Robin Hood. You know what I mean?"

"To us, it is not so important. It has a long history, of course. Every château will have such a history. To me it means that there are many ghosts."

"You're kidding? You mean it's haunted?"

"I hope I have not made you frightened." He realised that there might be some culture clash with his newfound family. "I was meaning that this château has many memories. I did not mean bad spirits. Spectres. You know what I mean?"

"Oh. I wouldn't have been surprised if you had said there were real ghosts. It kind of goes with old castles doesn't it?"

He smiled. "I suppose so." He thought of his marching orders from India, going back to the house of ghosts. What did that really mean?

Sisters Marie-Louise and Geneviève had begun to wheel the various bags under the portcullis of the outer wall. Théophile turned to help and Kate joined him. Claire wheeled Pia and followed her mother-in-law under the high arched entrance with its narrow defensive vertical bow-slits above it. Madame de Fortelle was speaking nervously to Claire and looking back for her son to translate. He hastened forward towing one of the bags.

"I wish to tell her that I am embarrassed that she will find our home not in the best condition. You must explain to her that we, how shall I say, we must make do, as best we can."

Instead of translating for Claire, he said gently to his mother: "There is no need to be embarrassed. They think they have landed in a fantasy world. They will be full of wonder at everything they see."

"Oh but everything is in such bad condition, so poor."

"They will not notice, *Maman*. They are from a land without chateaux." Then he told Claire that his mother hoped they would feel comfortable and that she was very happy to welcome them into her home. His mother eyed him suspiciously, sensing his subterfuge.

Claire however was effusive. "Oh, thank you again. I am sure we will love it here. I mean, just look at these walls and these towers and the stonework. It's incredible. I can't wait to explore. You must have so many rooms."

"I think there are forty, something like that."

"Oh my God. Forty rooms!"

His mother glowered at him. "What are you telling her?"

"I said that there were about forty rooms and she is amazed, like I told you."

"Did you tell her that we cannot live in most of them because they are in ruins, Did you say that?"

"She will find out for herself, soon enough. Right now she is in love with our château. Let her enjoy it."

"It is dishonest."

"*Maman*, no. You must see that she is delighted, let her enjoy it. I promise you she will learn about us and this family all in good time."

His mother sighed. "Maybe you are right."

Madame de Fortelle led the entourage across the inner moat, also now just a grassy ditch below stone embankments, past the little stone barbican, which now guarded nothing but firewood, and into the inner courtyard. The sun had risen enough to flood the stone flags of the courtyard with welcoming warmth. Geraniums flourished from a series of cut-down wine barrels, an ancient wisteria webbed across one facade up to the third floor and ivy insinuated itself over most of the other walls, above wooden benches crying out for paint.

Théophile pointed to the low stone wall facing the inner moat. "In the nineteenth century, they took away the high wall from here. It was important for defence in the earlier times, but it did not let in the light. Now you see it is only the sun that attacks us."

The two adult Australians gazed up at the high walls, the panelled windows in criss-cross glass, the sculpted figurines, rendered vague by several centuries of weather, above the arched doorways. Here and there martin's nests were glued to the walls in the shelter of the eves. It was all so exotic.

Madame de Fortelle pushed open the huge oak door and stepped down into the flagstone foyer beyond. Claire skilfully manoeuvred the wheelchair down the single step and the luggage porters followed her in.

The entrance hall was dark, both from lack of natural light and from the dusky oak panels, and there was a moment to adjust eyes before the visitors could see where they were. Again, once they did, the oldness of it, the regal nature of the lofty ceilings with the single chandelier and the cold hard worn stone floor awed them.

As Madame de Fortelle opened the door to the parlour and ushered them inside, she said: "This is the room where I spend most of my time. It is the warmest room in the winter because we have the fireplace." Théophile translated, as the newcomers gazed around the room. The portraits of Fernand and Odile de Fortelle glowered down from the far end, and Madame de Fortelle gave a little introduction to them as the most prosperous of the de Fortelle ancestors. As Théophile translated, he softened his mother's continuing tendency to self-pity. Somehow he did not want Claire to be exposed so early to his mother's self-denigration. He described his ancestors as significant forebears but in no way alluding to the diminution of the de Fortelle destiny that unfolded after them. Claire gazed up at the portraits and then her eye dropped to the photo below: her own son and her husband with their surfboards. The contrast was stark.

"You know," she said, drawing away from the luminous bronzed bodies of her men, back to the medieval interior, "Hugues did not say very much about all this. I mean he told me where he grew up, but not so much about all this incredible history."

Before he translated for his mother, Théophile said, "Maybe it is because he did not think of it as incredible history. I am like him. I do not. We had to live with them staring at us, but we would ignore them." Then he told his mother that Claire had said that Hugues had described this room to her and that she was glad to see it at last. This was deeply pleasing to Madame de Fortelle and Théophile congratulated himself on his tact.

"Do you take tea or do you prefer coffee?" Sister Geneviève asked the Australians, surprising Théophile with her attempt at English, thickly accented though it was. He imagined that she had practised it quite a lot beforehand.

"Oh, I'd love a cuppa." Claire said. Then she saw the puzzlement on all the French faces. "Tea would be nice." she corrected herself.

Kate said: "Yes, tea for me too please."

"And for *la petite*?" Sister Geneviève asked, gently laying a hand on Pia's head.

"Do you have juice? She likes apple juice, if you have it." This was translated for the sister who could not follow the Australian accent. "*Jus de pomme*." She nodded and disappeared into the kitchen.

"Please come and sit." Thérèse indicated the faded stuffed fauteuils in a semi circle before the empty fireplace. They wheeled Pia between two of them and everyone sat. The luggage stayed by the door and Sister Marie-Louise turned and followed the other nun to the kitchen.

Once they had all settled, Thérèse looked, perhaps for the first time, closely at Pia. The child was back inside herself, unfocussed and still. Thérèse leaned across and now looked intently at her.

"She does not speak." she said, which Théophile translated.

Claire laid a gentle hand on her daughter's arm. "She can say a few words."

"But she is not, how do you say, handicapped in her mind?" Théophile struggled to find the kindest way to translate this and failed.

Claire turned to her mother-in-law and shook her head. "No. Not at all. You will see, as you get to know her, that she is very alert and present, when she wants to be."

Madame de Fortelle nodded, still regarding Pia with a frown. Then she looked across at Kate. "And she is the helper?"

"Kate is a nurse. She is fully trained and she understands Pia incredibly well. I am very grateful to have her."

"She is a nurse?" Madame de Fortelle frowned. "Your daughter is sick?"

"No. It just so happens that Kate is a trained nurse. Pia is quite healthy."

"She does not look healthy to me" Up to this point Théophile had simply conveyed the messages back and forth; now he intervened.

"*Maman*, that is not a polite thing to say. You don't know."

"Translate what I said. And do not tell me what is polite. She is my grand-daughter, and it is obvious to anyone that she is not well."

Théophile took a breath and then said "My mother insists that I translate exactly what she says."

"Yes, you must." Claire was troubled by what was happening. "I want to know exactly what she said. It is very important to me."

"What does she say?" demanded his mother. He told her and she was pleased, looking at her son with satisfaction. "It is good we are sincere with each other." she said, looking directly at Claire. "I will insist that Théophile translate exactly what we have to say to each other."

So Théophile dutifully conveyed his mother's concern. Claire looked thoughtful but Kate leaned forward. "You know." she said looking at Madame de Fortelle, "It is good that I am a nurse because I can tell you, in my professional opinion, that in most ways, Pia is quite healthy. I can tell you that for her age she is a little underweight and she is lacking in iron and calcium in her bones but, otherwise, she is good."

Théophile conveyed that opinion and there was silence.

The awkwardness of the moment was broken and everyone was grateful for Sister Geneviève pushing a rickety wooden cart with teapot and cups rattling on the top and a plate of what looked like thin brown upside-down cupcakes.

"It is English tea." she said proudly in English.

"Sister, you are very good to be doing this. I feel embarrassed that the blessed sisters of the convent are working like servants in my house." Madame de Fortelle had risen to serve the tea as she made this short speech. Théophile was unsure if it was to be translated. He looked at his mother and when she caught his look, she shook her head ever so slightly, and he let it go.

"And Sister Agnès has sent her most beautiful *canelés*" added Sister Geneviève pointing to the cakes. Then she asked Théophile in French, "You will explain about *canelés*"

"These little cakes are a tradition of Bordeaux. There is a story that many years ago there was a *patissier* who made a mistake and his cakes looked like this. I am not really sure about the tradition."

"*Oof!*" Sister Geneviève said in disgust. "*Quel muuvaise histoire!*" Her comprehension of English was obviously good enough to catch what he had said. Then she went on to describe what she felt was the true history. Théophile dutifully translated. "It was we", she said proudly, "Who first made *canelés*. It was nuns before the revolution who made them. You see the shape? It is like the columns in a church. And there was a secret recipe that was lost in the revolution, but in our order it was kept. And if you really want to know, Sister Agnès puts in real Armagnac! Voilà!" Then with a flourish she handed around the plate of the bronzed fluted delicacies. They were a little sticky to the touch but they had a crusty outer shell. Claire broke a little from hers to give to Pia. When it touched her lips, she spat and it landed on the floor.

"Oh, I am so sorry." Claire bent down to retrieve the piece, but Thérèse stopped her, putting a hand on her shoulder. "It is nothing", she said. "The child will not like the alcohol."

Kate took a tissue from the back of the wheelchair and dealt with it.

The tea was poured and everyone had a cup and a *canelé*. Pia drank juice with a straw, also pulled from the stock behind the wheelchair. Claire and Kate expressed their delight at the custardy insides of the pastries, with their powerful brandy flavour, and a sense of peace descended on the room.

Théophile, sitting on the edge of one of his family's fading armchairs, realised he still had a stuffed Kangaroo in his back pocket. He pulled it out and Kate laughed when she saw it. "You're in her good books if you get to look after Roo", she said.

Pia looked up when she heard the word "Roo" and looked at Théophile. "*Ha*", she said with a dismissive wave of her hand. "Looks like you're meant to keep him." added Kate.

"I am honoured." Théophile made a little bow in the direction of the child, with his cup perched on his knee. Then as he sat back in his chair, he began to recognise how incredibly fatigued he was. The translating, the caution in dealing with whatever his mother wanted to be said, the impact of the three Australians, it was all gathering into a stormy headache that threatened to overwhelm him. He put down his teacup, let the Kangaroo drop into his lap and closed his eyes.

"*Ca va mon fils?*" his mother asked.

He opened his eyes and managed a weak smile for his mother. "I am not so practiced at being a translator. It takes an effort." Then he noticed that the others were also looking at him so he had to convey to them what was being said.

Claire smiled at him warmly. "You are doing a wonderful job. I totally understand how challenging it must be. I am sorry that I can't speak much French. I did a tiny bit in high school, but not much. I would love to take a class and learn."

Wearily Théophile conveyed this to his mother. She replied: "My sons both learned to speak such good English, but I did not and for this I am sorry. And I will try to learn. You will teach me perhaps?"

They laughed gently at the idea of teaching each other.

Then Sister Geneviève spoke. "There is a young girl who is staying at the convent. She is studying to be a translator in English and she is also in need of employment for the summer." She turned to smile very sweetly at Madame de Fortelle. "I think you have met her already. Her name is Shaafia."

VII

Shaafia's summer vacation offered the balm of tranquil days, following the convent's quotidian schedule. In the serenity of pre-dawn, she found herself naturally waking at the right hour, bathing, now with a comfortable acceptance of hot water, and descending to the chapel with enthusiasm, taking tea with the nuns almost as if she were becoming one of them. Her own prayers were deep and fulfilling. Her repetitions of her Koranic verse filled her with such contentment that at times she found herself in tears of pleasure, as if those she loved and to whom she dedicated these repetitions were with her, repeating the verse by her side. Shaafia found the chanting in the chapel no different in essence from the chanting in the mosque back in Casablanca.

From the first day, she had joined in with kitchen and garden duties and was happy to do whatever she was asked. The nuns delighted in her company and they had many lively discussions about religion and their relationship with God. Though there were the exceptions, in most of the nuns she never sensed any desire to convert her in any way from her own path. Rather, they seemed to want to appreciate how it worked for her. She was as happy as she could ever remember.

On one memorable day, Sister Geneviève had asked her if she had spoken to her family since she had come to France. When she admitted that, other than her weekly letters, she had not, the nun invited her into the office and handed her the telephone. Shaafia felt astounded and flustered. She had to admit that in fact her family did not have a telephone. There was a neighbour who did, but she did not know the number. "Then, when next you write to your family", Sister Geneviève said, "you must set a time so that you can call them at the neighbour's house. It is important, I think, for you, is it not?"

Shaafia's heart was full of longing as she nodded. "Yes it is."

When the day came, she felt nervous to speak to them. She had not actually told them about the convent. In her letter, she had said she was staying with some generous friends while she looked for work for the summer. There was no way her parents would ever understand her staying in a Catholic convent.

At the appointed time, once Sister Geneviève was sure the connection had been made, she gently slipped out of the office. Shaafia sat dwarfed by the big office chair capable of bearing the bulk of the nun, with the large black telephone to her ear. The neighbour answered and told her that her father had been waiting by the phone for an hour. Shaafia took a deep breath. Then her father was on the line, distant and formal in his speech, not used to speaking on the phone. He told that she brought great honour to the family and that he trusted that she was steady in her devotions to God and conscientious in her efforts at study. He said that he asked the blessings of God for her safety and prosperity every day in the mosque.

His words made Shaafia cry, and it was even worse when her mother got on the phone and wept as well, saying that she missed her daughter. Several of her other sisters said a quick: "Salaam", but none of her brothers had bothered to come to the neighbour's house. Nayla was not there. Her father took the phone back after a moment and told her to be good and to remember God.

"*Wacha Ba*" Shaafia said and the phone went dead. She sat there for a long moment with conflicting feelings and thoughts.

She missed them all terribly, along with the sounds, the smells, the atmosphere of home. And yet she also recognised that there was now a distance that she had travelled. She was not the same person as the girl who left Casablanca just six months before. She looked up at the crucifix across the room feeling blessed, and it was this feeling that stayed with her as she struggled up from the copious depths of the chair and left the office.

She took her father's parting instruction with her into the chapel. She sat in the front row, looking up at the crucifix with the face that seemed so familiar. She felt a peace descend and her Koranic verse arose inside. She sat there, letting it course through her, as if filling her veins and arteries with sustaining warmth. "Very soon", she thought to herself, "Very soon I will find the bird with crooked wings."

The vineyard that had served the convent for centuries had become too much for the diminishing number of nuns to take care of and had finally been subcontracted. It was now managed by another vineyard close by. The convent enjoyed the benefits of the sales and also, of course, the wine itself, but the nuns no longer did the labour, except at the *vendange*, the grape harvest, when everyone joined in. Several days after her phone call to Morocco, Yves, the man who now supervised the vineyard, asked if Shaafia would help with translation. From time to time tourists would visit the *chai*, the building where the wine was blended, matured and stored. The *chai* had a little boutique attached to it andhere they could taste the wines, "*la degustation*", and they could also buy bottles at wholesale prices. On occasions these visitors came from abroad and usually whoever worked at the sales and degustation was expected to be at least bilingual. A week earlier the girl who had been doing this work had left to have her first child, and no replacement had yet been found. Although Shaafia had never tasted alcohol, she had visited the *chai* and the boutique with Sister Hortensia and had seen how the wine was made. The smell had been quite strong and she had felt it was almost a sin to breathe in.

Yves had met her then and knew about her studies. He had asked Sister Geneviève who had thought for a moment and nodded. Why not? Shaafia would indeed be good for that. She needed to earn some money. Her hesitation was in knowing that Shaafia knew nothing about wine and would never taste it herself. Then she shrugged and said, "A translator must learn to be a good transmitter of whatever is said. She does not have to be an expert on the subject."

When Yves asked her, Shaafia had the same reservations. "I know nothing about wine." Yves assured her that this would not be a problem; she would simply translate whatever was being said. Could she do that in English?

"I will do my best."

She spent the following day with Yves and the girl who was about to have the baby, and they talked about the wine and how it was made. Shaafia soon realised that there was a whole vocabulary specific to wine that was completely new to her. There were words about growing wine, making it, the taste of it, the back taste and the fore taste. It was a new world to her and she began to doubt if she could do manage. Yves gave her a dictionary of wine terms so she could learn and he, basically, begged her to take the job. He had a party of New Zealanders coming the next day. The heavily pregnant girl said maybe she could come and help, but the baby was due any minute. The amount of money that was being offered made Shaafia's eyes widen with amazement and so she accepted.

The rest of the day she spent tremulously trying to learn all about oenology. She was good at studying, she told herself, and it was just like a class exercise. The good Muslim girl in her railed against the connection with alcohol and the dutiful daughter could not imagine her father's reaction, but at the same time the money offered would keep her very well. She buried her head in the book and studied all afternoon.

At dinner that evening she shared with Sister Agnès about her dilemma. The sister laughed generously. "Ooh la", she chortled. "How the Lord will play with us!" Then she held Shaafia's hand. "You will do perfectly well, I am sure, because you have a good heart." And when Shaafia admitted she had been studying the English/French dictionary of oenological terms all afternoon, the sister said to her "Would you like me to be your practice subject?" Shaafia felt embarrassed to involve the sister in her own troubles but the nun insisted. "It will give me such a good excuse to pull out some of our own wine after dinner. And I will invite Sister Albertine to join us. You know how she just loves a little wine!" She winked cheekily and went off to whisper to her fellow guinea pig.

When the other nuns had gone off to their evening activities, Shaafia ran up to her room for her dictionary and returned to the kitchen.

There the rosy-cheeked Sister Albertine had arrayed three bottles of red wine on the table. She was a round little woman who walked with a distinct roll. Of all the nuns she was the only one from the local community. She had proudly told Shaafia that in her family, always the oldest girl would be given to God and become a nun. "Since *La revolution* this has been the case." she said "This has been my family's convent for generations. My two aunts both died here."

Now she stood behind her bottles like a sommelier. All of them had been partially used and then recorked. Sister Agnès set out some wine glasses.

Sister Albertine peered at Shaafia over her half-moon glasses. "This is wine we would only use for cooking now because it has been opened. The characteristics will not be the same, but it is good wine. It is ours."

As it turned out Sister Albertine was a fine explainer of wines, her family were after all from the next village. As she talked, Shaafia repeated what she said in English. Neither of the nuns spoke any English but just the chance to practice was incredibly comforting for Shaafia. And of course both nuns sampled the wine as they talked. They discussed the different flavours. "*Parfums*" in French was not "perfumes" in English; it was "bouquet" or "fragrance". "*Bien en bouche*" was not "good in the mouth"; it meant the wine had a "full taste". As she wrestled with the new terms, the two nuns happily went on with their degustation. As they did, they talked faster and faster and drank more and more. Shaafia did her best to keep up and to find the right expressions for what they were describing. The pages of the dictionary were flipping back and forth, and the wine level was going down in all three bottles. At the point when Shaafia was just about exhausted, and both nuns were getting the giggles, the door opened and Sister Geneviève appeared. There was a hasty explanation as to why the two nuns were demolishing three bottles of wine, but she smiled sweetly at Shaafia, recorked the remnants of the wine and told them all to go to bed.

As they trooped out Sister Geneviève smiled at Shaafia. "So you will begin tomorrow?" The girl nodded nervously. "Do not be too worried, you will do fine. And don't worry about these two sisters, they have had a very enjoyable evening's entertainment. But", she said with a glint in her eye, "Don't let them make a habit of it!"

Shaafia prayed in the chapel, in the early morning, that God would support her efforts, but she also wondered if Allah approved of wine tasting. As she walked across to the *chai* the next morning, she kept opening the dictionary to check words and nearly fell over a fence as she walked with her head in the book. Yves was happy to see her and was sure she would be ready for whatever happened. "I have faith in you", he said.

Before the visitors arrived, there was no sign of the pregnant girl and Shaafia reluctantly accepted that she would be on her own. Yves did not really seem to be expecting the girl. He told her that having a baby was the hardest thing a woman can do. He knew all about it. His wife had twins and she nearly split into two, he said. She won't be coming. "It will just be you and me."

The visitors were Kiwis, he said. This meant nothing to her. "You know the Kiwis!" he said, "The All-Blacks!" Then he suddenly dropped into a crouch with his hands on his knees, poking his tongue far out and making a reasonable imitation of the famous Maori Haka that frightens the French rugby team before any international match against New Zealand.

Her look of slight horror made him stand up and quickly explain, just as the New Zealanders pulled up in a big black Audi. There were three very tall broad-shouldered men and a tiny yellow-skinned lady in dark glasses. Yves came forward to greet them with Shaafia beside him. She was absolutely terrified. She tried to smile, but she felt weak at the knees. She wondered if maybe they would do what Yves had just done.

"*Bonjour*", Yves said. "Welcome to ze Domaine du Nid des Oiseaux Serènes." He had some little English. "Zis eese Shaafia oo will translate for us."

"G'day. Ha-ya", said one of the men shaking hands with Yves and then Shaafia. His hand was huge and crushed hers. "Gary sma nime, this's Les'n Brett and this ere's me Mum, Tossie."

Shaafia had no idea what he said, but she warily shook hands with everyone except the lady who kept her hands behind her back. The driver of the Audi had reversed the car and parked it under a tree. He then sat on the bonnet and smoked a cigarette.

Yves invited the group into the *chai* boutique and began speaking about the wines. While he spoke about the basic processes, Shaafia managed to keep up with the English but there were moments when she stumbled and Yves would patiently repeat what he said. She knew her voice was trembling but there was nothing she could do to steady it. He told them a little of the history of the vineyard, how the nuns had looked after the vines even before the revolution, and how they managed to repossess the property later on and keep up the tradition until just ten years ago. The Kiwis listened carefully and luckily asked no questions. Yves then produced various bottles and opened them. They were three and four years old, he said, and were very good examples of the soil and the climate of the Entre Deux Mers style of wine. He would give them both red and white to sample.

The men were obviously connoisseurs because as soon as the wine was poured, each lifted his glass carefully, between thumb and forefinger, up to the light, sniffed it, rolled it around the tilted glass to watch the wine rise and then let it drain slowly down from the rim to look at the "legs". Finally each took a sip, swished it around in the mouth, opened their lips slightly to breathe over the top and then they spat it out into the *crachoir*. The lady simply drained her glass in one go and looked for a refill.

"Gettin' a hint of liquorice", one of the men said. "Watcha reckon?" Shaafia was dumbstruck, thinking she should translate this for Yves. He simply smiled at her and nodded benignly.

One of the other men responded. "Nah 'smore like a tarry kind of thing, I'd say."

Then the third man said. "I'm gettin' blackberry." Obviously they weren't looking to be translated, so Shaafia let it go. She badly wanted to go to the toilet, she was so nervous.

The man, who had introduced himself as Gary, turned to the woman. "What you gettin' Tossie?" She held up the empty glass and said out of the corner of her mouth: "Thirsty." The three men laughed, and Yves politely joined them. He poured some more of the red for the woman and she threw it back like vodka. One of the other men said: "We're gonna hafta carry ya home if ya don watchit!"

Yves was a little disturbed by this, so he decided it was time for a short tour of the *chai* and asked Shaafia to convey that. She managed and the group put down their glasses, the woman more than a little reluctantly.

Inside the barrel-store of the *chai*, as Yves described the processes of mixing the different grapes, the percentages, the blending, the testing, the different kinds of barrels and the importance of acids and alcohols and the men began to ask more questions, Shaafia began to perspire. The conversation now involved both languages at once, and sometimes more than one person at a time. Her brain seemed to tighten under the strain, and she became more and more confused. She tried to find the words for what was being said, but the more she did, the worse it got. And finally she knew she was lost. What she said no longer made any sense and the visitors were clearly unable to follow anything she tried.

She froze. They stared at her in confusion and Yves saw that something was not working. Then to her horror she began to cry. It just burst from her. She dropped her dictionary, and she blindly out into the morning sun and away from the *chai*.

She ran along the fence between the *chai* and the convent, her breath coming in short sharp stabs of distress. She ran into the chapel and threw herself on the floor at the front. There her crying intensified and it poured out of her body, as she lay there, shaking on the cold stone floor.

It was only after she had been lying there for a few minutes that she realised the organ had been playing when she came in. Now it had stopped. She raised her head and saw that Sister Agnès was sitting in the first pew behind her.

"So", she said gently, "the Lord's play was not so much fun."

Shaafia pulled herself up to a sitting position and turned to face the nun. She shook her head, not yet willing to speak.

"He will test us", the nun said, "but he will never give us anything that is not, in the end, beneficial. Something good will come from it, you can be sure."

Finally Shaafia had the courage to speak. "I knew in my heart that this was not a good thing for me to do. I should have listened to my heart."

"What you say is very wise." The nun gingerly lowered herself onto the floor to be at the same level as the girl. "If you have learned nothing else from this adventure, at least you know that." Then she gently hugged her and Shaafia melted into the welcoming embrace, the scent of some kind of incense, the gentle brush of her habit and the feeling of being protected.

Finally she pulled back and looked at the nun. "Thank you", she said.

In the evening she found the courage to tell Sister Geneviève what had happened. The sister nodded and said she had heard from Yves. She had something to give to Shaafia. She followed the sister to her office and there the nun passed her an envelope. Inside was fifty euros and a little note from Yves. He apologised for forcing her into the job before she was ready and said he hoped that she would be willing to try again once she'd had more time to prepare.

"I cannot accept this money", Shaafia said. "It was a disaster."

The nun said "You must accept it, my child. It is given in good faith. We did not recognise the difficulty it caused you." She smiled. "I am sure something more convenient will come."

VIII

When Kate woke, it was light outside.

She had been given a small room on the first floor just above Claire and Pia's room. Her bed was a three-quarter size with a massive solid dark headboard with a footboard almost as high. Whenever she moved in the bed, the two boards rocked dangerously. It was clearly a bed for deep sleepers only. The mattress was lumpy and she wondered what it was made of and also how old it was. It bore the distinct odour of lack of use. The coverlet was quilted and had once been quite fancy. It was threadbare now in the corners and with frayed sections that threatened to disgorge its contents. Her cylindrical pillow was full of feathers, and a lot of sneeze-inducing dust. The room was roughly square, almost cubed, given the incredibly high ceiling. There was a high wardrobe with bas-relief carvings of oak leaves in the doors, standing in one corner and a small porcelain sink in the other. The sink had a high copper faucet with a sculpted handle and in the sink a deep green stain ran down the centre. The wooden floor had an Eastern style rug that had borne many footprints. The camels and the desert fortress on its sand dune were barely visible.

The previous night, even before the sun had set, the travellers had all wilted. They had managed to stay awake through the afternoon, taking a short walk to circumambulate the château, pushing Pia in the wheelchair. She had seemed uninterested in anything outside herself and bobbed and rolled like a ragdoll over the uneven ground. Claire and Kate, gazed up, marvelling at the vast walls and the huge stones, although Claire's practiced eye had seen the wide cracks and the water damage. Around the château, the grounds were exotic and beautiful to antipodean eyes, the unkempt gardens had huge rhododendrons and camellias, lilies and roses, abundant in their early summer enthusiasm. The woods beyond the château revealed endless stands of oaks and elms, plane trees and cypresses. They took a short walk to the vineyards, now leased out to a local *vigneron* who was supposed to share the proceeds with the de Fortelle family.

Madame de Fortelle gloomily supposed that he was cheating them, as the money she got from him was barely enough to keep her alive and left nothing for any repairs to the château. There was a time, she had said, when the label "Château des Mésanges" was a sought-after *marque* of both red and white wine but not any more. You could buy it at the supermarket now. "It is regarded as no better than a wine from Spain", she had said with disgust.

For dinner they had a hearty soup and convent-made bread prepared by the nuns, who had gone home. It was then, at the table, that they all began to nod off. Théophile showed Kate up to her little room, toting the suitcase. He had apologised for the lack of hot water but she didn't care. She sluiced her face in the little sink and was asleep on the lumpy mattress in seconds.

In the early morning light, she lay there, now very aware of the shortcomings of the mattress. She smiled to herself remembering how, not so long ago, she could sleep on bare ground. She listened to the birds, so unlike what she would have heard on the other side of the world. There was the hard *clack-clack* of the magpie, the twitter of sparrows and the melodious song of the merle. She got out of the bed and went to the panelled window with its criss-cross glass. She looked out into the woods, brilliant green and shining in the morning light. She felt deeply drawn to the forest and, putting on some clothes, she went downstairs. To her alarm and amusement, she found that the stairs were incredibly noisy, every step making a different crack or squeak, and she hoped she was not disturbing anyone. The heavy front door had all kinds of locks and bolts on it and she didn't even try to work it out. She recalled that the previous afternoon they had gone out by the kitchen door, which led to the end of the inner courtyard. In the kitchen she saw that someone had already organised breakfast but there was no one there.

She let herself out and breathed in the sweet cool morning air, redolent with the early summer fragrances of trees and flowers for which she had no names. She walked out under the portcullis and across the outer moat. Then, just following her instinct, she wandered off into the woods. Not far in, she found a huge oak with a massive trunk with strands of ascendant ivy. The oak had twisted roots, like knees and elbows, above ground that made for little niches close to the trunk, cosy to sit in. She dropped into one, first checking for spiders. Then she wondered if they had spiders in France. She settled back with her head against the trunk as she had done so many times in the desert. Would it feel the same? Would it have the same calming effect on her thoughts? As soon as the back of her head rested against the ancient wood, she felt it. That same drawing inward, that same wave of calm as if the great tree could inhale her thoughts. She closed her eyes.

How long she stayed there, she wasn't sure but at some point she became aware of being watched. She opened her eyes and saw a crow on the branch of a small mimosa bush, the yellow flowers instantly reminding her of Australan wattle. The crow was indeed eyeing her and she smiled to herself. "My sisters are on this side of the world too." The crow called and Kate was surprised to hear that it made an entirely different sound from Australian crows. "It probably speaks crow-French." she thought. The crow took off, and Kate heard a rustle of footsteps in the leaves near the tree. She looked around and saw it was Théophile.

"Good morning", he said in English. "I hope I am not disturbing you. I saw you from my window. You like our forest?"

"I do", she said scrambling up from her nest. "It's very different from Australian bush, but I like it. Everything is so green."

"Not if you come back in the winter", he said. "It is depressing. Everything is grey and brown. You are seeing the best of it."

"The trees are beautiful. Look how big this is. How old do you think it is?

" There are trees in this forest that are older than the times of Napoleon. This is probably as old as that."

"I love the feel of it. I was just sitting there with my back to it. It felt very good."

"You looked very happy. Were you meditating?"

She smiled. "I suppose you could call it that." She brushed dry leaves from her jeans as they began to walk back towards the château. "I learned to do that when I was in the desert."

He looked at her quizzically, as if he was not sure he had heard her properly. "You were in a desert?"

"I used to be a nurse there, in the Australian desert. It's a bit of a long story, but the aboriginals who live in the desert taught me how to sit like that. They told me it I would give me a quiet mind and it works."

He was impressed. "To have a quiet mind is not easy." They walked together under the oaks and then he turned to her. "I also have learned a little of how to do that. It is why I asked if you were meditating. I have just come back from India and it was there that I began to learn."

"It would be great to visit India. I would love to do it one day. Where did you go?"

"In the south." He had paused before he spoke, considering what he would tell this girl. She reminded him a little of Ariette, the girl he had met in Goa. "I was in an ashram. You know what is an ashram?"

She shrugged "Not really."

"It is like a place for monks, but anyone can go there. There is a guru and you learn how to meditate."

"Is it Hindu?"

"I don't know. Maybe. There was a temple with a big statue of the goddess Durga. She is a goddess who rides on a tiger, so I suppose that is Hindu."

They were entering the courtyard of the château as they spoke. Kate stopped and looked up at the massive building. "It's hard to believe I am in a real castle in France."

Théophile smiled gently, enjoying this girl's enthusiasm for the house of ghosts. Maybe he could learn to regard the place of his birth and his childhood as being something other than a horror house, maybe even something wonderful.

"I am happy that you like it." Then he stopped and turned to look at her directly. "I am happy that you have come, all three of you. I think you will make my mother very happy too."

Kate smiled warmly at him. "It's good to make other people happy isn't it."

IX

Several days after the disaster in the *chai,* Sister Geneviève sat with Shaafia at breakfast. There had been no further invitations to translate for degustations and she had furiously thrown herself into whatever chores she could find in the convent. She had also spent more time than usual in the chapel, where she repeated her Koranic verse and prayed to be a better student.

Sipping her tea, the sister leant in close to Shaafia and said "I think we have found something more suitable. You are aware of Madame de Fortelle of course." When Shaafia nodded, the nun went on. "Today we will have a mass for her and her family. She is offering the mass in gratitude for the arrival of the rest of her family. I would like you to be there."

Sister Geneviève watched as the girl thought about this and, speaking so quietly that none of the other sisters could hear, she added "Oh, I know she has not been so polite to you, but you must not worry about that. I want to introduce you to the other members of her family. They are not as frightening as she is. You will like them I think. I also think that they will like you. And they need a translator."

The mass was at ten o'clock in the morning. The sisters were in attendance, except those who had other duties. The same priest who had conducted the funeral mass was there and he had nodded to Shaafia when he noticed her, several rows back. When the de Fortelle family arrived, he came forward to greet them and Shaafia kept herself low in her pew so she would not be visible. Between the heads of the nuns in front of her, she saw the familiar and formidable form of Madame de Fortelle take a front row seat, followed by a tall young man that she took to be the son. There were also two other women, one of them pushing a wheelchair, although from where she sat, Shaafia could not see who was in it.

Father Lefait took up his position in front of the altar below the crucifix, and the mass began. As she had always loved to do in the chapel, Shaafia closed her eyes. Instantly there was flash of light behind her eyes and she heard a voice very clearly: *I am here. I am here. Now. It is time for us to begin our work.* She opened her eyes with a shock and looked around. The priest was reading something that she could not follow and no one seemed to be focused on her. The son of Madam de Fortelle was translating for the two women. She looked up at the twisted figure on the cross above the priest but it too seemed remote. A ray of bluish light slanted across the chapel from the stained glass window on the eastern side. Shaafia watched the tiny motes of dust swirling in this light and, after some time, she closed her eyes again.

Instantly the voice was back: *I have looked for you.* Was it speaking French? Was it Arabic? It didn't seem to be any particular language so much as a very clear communication, one that she totally understood. In response and partly out of fear, she turned to her Koranic verse. As she repeated it, the voice picked it up as an accompaniment to it. In harmony, the voice did not say the words but created a descant for Shaafia's beloved verse. Its message was *I am here.*

Within herself Shaafia felt drawn down and down inside. *I am here. I am here,* called the voice. She felt a deepening excitement, a tremor of expectation that made her heart pound. As if diving into some ocean looking for a pearl, she went inside and down, looking and looking. *Are you the bird with crooked wings?* she called out within herself.

Suddenly she was thrust up and out of her deep state into the silent chapel. Everyone was staring at her, Father Lefait, Madam de Fortelle, the family and all the nuns. Sister Hortensia came from her seat across the aisle and sat with Shaafia. "Are you alright my child?"

Shaafia was stunned. "What happened?" she whispered.

"You screamed very loudly", the nun said.

"Truly?" Shaafia's heart was still pounding and she lowered her head away from the staring eyes. "I am so sorry", she whispered. Then she said "I am fine, really. I don't know why I screamed. I am very sorry."

Sister Hortensia looked up and said to the priest. "It is nothing. She is fine. Please go on."

Father Lefait nodded and invited everyone to pray and the chapel became silent. The nun sat with her and Shaafia kept her eyes on the priest. She dared not close them again. The mass went on, through prayers, hymns and then communion. Shaafia steadfastly kept herself still and open-eyed. But even while outwardly she remained calm, inwardly the volcano that had erupted with the inner voice was still churning. How she longed to know what it was. How she yearned to find out who was calling, who was here, what work she was being called for. Where was it coming from?

As the communion concluded, Sister Hortensia checked that Shafia was all right before she went forward, and the de Fortelle family began to make its way up the aisle. Only Madame de Fortelle and her son had gone forward for the communion, the others were waiting in the front row for them. Madame de Fortelle then led the family up the aisle nodding to the sisters and the others who were present. Shaafia kept her eyes lowered but as Madame de Fortelle was about to walk past her, the woman paused. She seemed to make an effort to prepare herself before she looked straight at Shaafia and said in a clear voice, "Thank you for coming." Shaafia lifted her eyes, nodded and then lowered her eyes again. She did not see the rest of the family as they passed her.

When the chapel was empty, she went towards the altar and knelt down in front of the crucifix, the statue with the face of the sharif. As she gazed up at it, she asked that the source of the voice, so strong inside her, be revealed. "Please show it to me. If this is the bird with the crooked wings, please, please let me see it."

Outside the chapel the sun was shining, a beautifully warm summer day. The family had gathered on the grass and were talking to the sisters when Shaafia finally came out into the bright light. She paused by the door to watch the group. Father Lefait had joined them and was speaking in tortured English to the two women, looking down at the occupant of the wheelchair as he spoke, while the son of Madame de Fortelle looked on.

Sister Geneviève noticed Shaafia and called her. "Shaafia, come and meet the family."

Both the woman and her son turned and watched Shaafia as she self-consciously crossed the grass. Sister Geneviève took her hand and drew her into the group.

"You know Madame de Fortelle, I think", she said gently.

Madame de Fortelle had a pained look on her face as if she was struggling to find the right look. She had made a supreme effort in the chapel but still she was uncomfortable in facing this girl. To cover herself she turned to her son. "This is my son Théophile", she said.

Théophile smiled at Shaafia and held out his hand to shake hers. She shyly took it, looking at him rather than at his mother. She said "I am sorry about the loss of your brother and his son. It is very sad."

He nodded his head awkwardly and said "Thank you." Then into the difficult pause that followed, he added "I understand that you speak English and that you are studying to be a translator".

Shaafia nodded and Sister Geneviève said "I have told them about you and I think perhaps this is perfect for everyone. You see, the family will need an English translator, because it is too much for one person, for Théophile. They would like to employ you for the rest of the summer. What do you think?"

Glancing shyly sideways at Madame de Fortelle, Shaafia was unsure what to say. It was noticing this glance that prompted Madame de Fortelle to say "My child, I have been most unkind and unjust to you. And you have shown nothing but kindness to me. I stand before you ashamed of myself and I ask you to forgive me."

Madame de Fortelle had used the formal French "*vous*", indicating deep respect, and this speech touched Shaafia deeply but she could find no words to reply. Sister Geneviève filled the gap. "Thérèse, Shaafia will find it in her heart to forgive you, you can be sure. It is my belief that you will become friends. It is my hope."

"And mine also", Madame de Fortelle said. "Are you willing to be our translator?"

Shaafia nodded and dared to look briefly into the eyes of the older woman. There were tears there and this moved Shaafia. She put her hand up to her heart, nodded again and managed to say "Of course, *bien sur.*"

Sister Geneviève was very pleased. "Now", she said, "you must meet the other members of the family. Perhaps Théophile, you will introduce them in English?" She led them across the lawn where the others were still talking, as best they could, with the priest.

"Excuse me, Father", she said in French. In her best attempt at English she said to Claire, "Zere is someone to meet you." Then she looked to Théophile.

He turned to Shaafia with embarrassment and said in French: "I am so sorry but I have forgotten your name."

The minute she said her name, quietly, shyly, "Shaafia", the figure in the wheel chair seemed to leap up, yelling "*Ha-ee-aa*!!"

Everyone turned with a shock, it was so loud and her movement was so sudden. She was up, out of her chair somehow and she threw herself forward into Shaafia, who took her weight but staggered back to catch herself from falling. The child was feather light, but still the energy that took her up and out of the chair had force and drove Shaafia backwards. The child's arms wrapped themselves around her and she wrapped her arms instinctively around the child, so they stood locked together.

The child was crooning now, softly, "*Ha-ee-aa, ha-ee-aa*", and inside Shaafia could hear her: *Here I am. Here I am.*

And in a great rush of ecstatic recognition, Shaafia knew she had found her bird with crooked wings.

X

The shock of seeing Pia launch herself from her wheelchair transfixed everyone and there was a moment of utter stillness. A warm summer morning on the lawn outside the chapel of the convent of Le Nid Des Oiseaux Serènes, where a frail child lay enfolded in the arms of a shy Moroccan girl, watched by a clutch of nuns and a priest, the de Fortelle family and an Australian nurse.

As the child continued to croon, her arms alternated, back and forth, between batting against the girl's back and enfolding her in a hug. The first of the others to move was Kate. She came round behind Shaafia, so that Pia could see her. Then Kate gently stroked Pia's hair.

"You found a new friend", she said.

Pia pulled back at the sound of her voice and lifted her head to face her. "*Ha-ee-aa.*" She had a brilliant smile on her face and her eyes sparkled. "*Ha-ee-aa.*" The girl looked round at Kate and her face too was glowing. She had tears in her eyes.

Kate smiled at her. Knowing that Shaafia spoke English, she said "This is Pia." The girl nodded and then faced the child whose face was so close to hers. Their eyes locked, and the child's errant eye seemed to flicker as if trying to focus. They gazed at each other.

Claire moved gently forward. Her face was pale with fright, having wondered if Pia was having some kind of fit. Now she saw her daughter beaming and smiling, her was relieved. She rested a hand on Pia's shoulder and heard her daughter murmur "*Ha-ee-aa.*" Claire as well quietly introduced herself to Shaafia: "I am Claire, Pia's mother."

Shaafia pulled her gaze away from the child and finally managed to speak. She spoke in English, her accent strong but clear enough to understand. "I am so happy to meet you. I am so happy to meet Pia. I am so…I am so happy."

Sister Geneviève also moved closer and in her own quiet voice invited them all to come inside for coffee. Madame de Fortelle took up her cue and said in a very strong business-like voice "Ah yes, Sister, thank you very much. Yes, let's all go into the refectory for some coffee. Come Théophile."

He had stood to one side, as if he was witness to some powerful piece of theatre that riveted his attention. Now his heart thumped in his chest. The kind of love he had felt in the temple in India flooded through him. He was consumed with the fire of it. He too had come to a sudden recognition. Now he knew who this crippled flimsy-bodied soul was. This was Ashtavakra. There was no doubt. This was the reason he had come back to the house of ghosts. Suddenly all the anxiety, the questioning, the lack of trust he had been harbouring dropped away. He was amazed. He felt waves of gratitude for being there, for the guidance of Padmananda, for his sheer good fortune. He wanted to laugh, he wanted to bow down in the temple, he wanted to embrace this child.

When his mother spoke to him, it was like a call from far away, barely discernible. In some part of his consciousness he recognised her voice and tried to find a way to respond. "Are you alright, my son?" She was looking up at him with concern.

"Oh yes", he said and to his amazement he felt tears in his eyes. He wiped them away. "Oh yes, I am fine."

"We will go with the sisters", his mother said, obviously very flustered by all the unconventional behaviour around her. "We will have coffee now. You must tell them."

Théophile took a breath and approached the tableau of Pia enfolded in the arms of Shaafia with Claire and Kate very close. "Excuse me", he intervened as gently as he could, trying to keep any emotion from his voice. "We are invited for coffee." His words had the effect of breaking into the tableau and bringing it to life.

Claire drew the crooning Pia from the arms of Shaafia and lowered her into the wheelchair. Kate turned to Shaafia. "Hello", she said. "I am Kate."

The group followed the sisters, but Théophile could not. He watched as the Moroccan girl walked beside the wheelchair holding Pia's hand, the child gripping the hand with both of hers and looking up as best she could and crooning still. Kate and Claire, pushing the chair, were talking to each other with their heads close together. His mother scuttled ahead with Sister Geneviève and the priest, as if she couldn't wait to run away. He stood there, unwilling to move, trying to capture for himself what it was that had just happened.

If this was the reincarnation of the crooked saint, crippled in eight places, how did he know that? What was it that had suddenly slid away to reveal what she was? And was this real or just some hallucination? He replayed what had just taken place in his mind. It was no hallucination. In the moment when Pia launched herself at Shaafia, he had seen that there was a power there, an independent free energy, previously veiled to him by the angular body. He was sure of it. The inner sensation of opening, the powerful thrust of revelation, it was too potent not to be real. Then why had he not seen it before? Had she been trying to show him what he couldn't see? He remembered how she greeted him at the airport. He had felt something then. Was she trying it then? Was he just not able to see it? He was both in awe and utterly puzzled.

Finally, he sighed and let it just be as it was. He felt wonderfully light inside himself, opened up and full of joy. The journey had been worth it. The coming back, facing the doubts, it was all fine now. He smiled to himself and went in to have coffee with the others.

XI

Watching Pia launch herself into Shaafia's arms, Kate had felt a strange surge of emotion. It was a curious mix of elation and a kind of jealousy. On the one hand she was amazed to see the frail body eject itself from the wheelchair with such force. It was thrilling to see that Pia could do such a thing. And yet it was not to her that Pia had thrown herself but to this small shy dark-skinned girl who she had never met.

As she walked beside Claire into the convent, Kate could see that Pia's mother had also been deeply struck by what had happened. "What was all that about?" Kate asked her.

Claire shook her head. "I don't know. I was scared at first. I thought she was having one of her 'turns', you know?" She had warned Kate about the several fit-like attacks that Pia had experienced, mostly when she was quite small. Medication had helped to avoid repeats. "But you know how she is. She is independent and she likes what she likes. This girl must be someone special."

"Has she ever jumped out of her chair like that?"

"Never." Claire shook her head. "She just doesn't have that strength. Not normally anyway."

"If she's done it once, than maybe she can do it again. This might be the beginning of a new phase."

"Maybe."

They had been speaking quietly, walking together behind the wheelchair, with Shaafia holding Pia's hand. There was a squeeze to get in through the front door but Pia was determined to keep hold of the hand. Now they wheeled the chair in through the high double doors of the convent's elegant front parlour, where the sisters had prepared morning coffee and plates of petit fours. Most of the nuns were not going to be present so they said their farewells at the door and went off to their duties. The priest also apologised. He had a funeral to go to in Castionne la Bataille.

Once the nuns and the priest had left, Claire backed Pia's chair in beside a huge leather couch and Shaafia settled down on the floor next to it. She seemed as intent as Pia on maintaining physical contact. Claire looked down at her and smiled.

"Your name is Shaafia? Am I saying it right?" The girl nodded and Pia added her own version: "*Ha-ee aa*." "And you speak English?" Again the girl nodded. The girl seemed to be embarrassed about speaking, or was it something else?

Kate watched her carefully, as she looked up in answer to Claire's questions. Kate wanted to see what was happening between Shaafia and Pia. She sensed a close, almost electric connection between the two, not just their linked hands but something else she couldn't quite identify.

Claire went on "Sister Geneviève told us that you are training to be a translator in English."

Finally Shaafia found her voice, which sounded small and remote, as if she was trying to break through some kind of barrier. "Yes", she said. "At the University of Bordeaux."

"The sister told us you were looking for some work during your holidays. I was hoping you would be able to be our translator."

"Yes."

Pia added "*Ha!*" very loudly, and her mother laughed.

"Pia is very happy about that", Claire said, patting her daughter's knee. "I'll get some juice for Pia. Can I get you a coffee?"

"Thank you."

While Claire turned to the coffee table, where Sister Geneviève was pouring, Kate crouched down in front of Pia's chair. Pia had kept her gaze firmly on Shaafia. Kate rubbed the child's bony little knees to attract her attention. "You just did something amazing you know. You just jumped out of your chair."

Pia shifted her gaze back to Kate. Her good eye engaged strongly and then she let go of Shaafia's hand and came forward into a hug with Kate, burying her head on Kate's shoulder.

Shaafia suddenly said "She loves you."

Kate looked across at her, over Pia's head. "I know. She is full of love, this girl. And it looks to me like she really loves you too."

"Yes." Shaafia gazed at Kate for a moment in silence and then said "Pia says that you must trust her love."

Kate was startled. "What?" Thinking she must have misunderstood, or lost something with the accent.

"She says…" Shaafia was looking into Kate's eyes with an intensity that was unsettling. "Pia says 'You must trust my love.'"

"I don't understand. How do you mean 'Pia says'? I mean, can you…? Do you understand what she says?"

"Yes." It was said in an awed whisper.

"How?"

Pia pulled back from her hug enough to look closely at Kate. Then she let out a loud "*Ha!*" and dropped back into her hug.

Kate went on, "You understand that?"

"No." Shaafia leant in very close so she could whisper to Kate. "She speaks to me, inside."

Kate felt her heart begin to beat, thudding as if from a flash of fear, an adrenalin rush was working through her body. At the same time, Pia began to bat her hands against Kate's back, flapping them in and out and murmuring, "*Haay, haay.*"

In the same kind of whisper, Kate said to Shaafia: "You mean, you can hear her, like, in your mind?"

Shaafia nodded. "She speaks to me."

"How do you know it's her?"

Shaafia shrugged.

"It could just be your own, I don't know, just your own thoughts."

"I don't know what to say. I hear her."

Easing back from the child's hug, Kate looked into Pia's face. "Can you talk to us?"

A long string of saliva ran from the corner of her mouth and her head rocked from side to side. Instinctively, Kate reached up and wiped away the dribble. "*Coo-coo*", Pia said in a light lilting voice.

Shaafia whispered. "Pia says that she will show you. She says you must trust her."

Kate gazed into her face. Suddenly she reconnected with how her own thoughts had ruined the hunt in the desert. She accepted that thoughts travelled in ways she had not known about before. But could Pia do this?

Claire joined them with a juice for Pia and a cup of coffee for Shaafia. "I forgot to ask if you take sugar or milk", she said.

"No, thank you. It is fine. Thank you." Shaafia took the coffee and held it. Kate held the juice, in a glass, up for Pia, and, as there was no straw, there were some dribbles. This necessitated going to the back of the wheelchair for wipes, so Shaafia moved back, out of the way. Claire sat with her coffee on a chair next to Shaafia, still on the floor. They both watched as Kate took care of Pia.

Suddenly Pia jerked upright and made a very loud "*Ha!*" pointing roughly in the direction of the door. Everybody looked up, poised with coffee cups in their hands. Sister Marie-Louise had just entered with a plate of *pets-de-nonne*. She stopped in the doorway, struck by the attention she received.

"*Qu'est-ce qui arrive ?*" she demanded

Pia made an even louder "*Ha!*" and everyone looked back at her.

Shaafia put down her coffee cup and stood up, visibly nervous, looking at the sister in the doorway. She spoke in French. "She says that you must forgive yourself."

The nun froze in horror.

Shaafia's voice shook as she spoke again. "She says that the child you killed forgives you."

There was an electric silence in the room in which Claire quietly asked Theophile what Shaafia had said. When he bent close and repeated it, she was alarmed.

Sister Geneviève's voice came strong and clear from beyond the coffee table.

"Who says this?"

"*Ha!*" issued from the wheelchair and Shaafia added "It is Pia who says this. She says, you were just a child yourself and you released him. It was an act of compassion. You have suffered much pain. He forgives you."

Sister Marie-Louise dropped to the floor and the small sugar coated fritters scattered across the carpet. The nun was sobbing uncontrollably. Sister Geneviève was beside her in a second, cradling her and murmuring to her. The rest of the room was utterly still.

Pia began coughing and Kate reached for a wipe.

Shaafia now shrank back into herself, as if whatever force had driven her to speak had subsided. She sank back onto the floor by the couch, partially hidden by the wheelchair.

The two other sisters in the room, Hortensia and Agnès went over to Marie-Louise. They gathered up the fritters and put them back on the plate, then Sister Geneviève motioned to them to take the stricken nun from the room. They stationed themselves on either side of her and pulled her to her feet and guided her, limp and ragged, as she staggered from the room. Sister Geneviève rose awkwardly to her feet and surveyed those assembled in the room. Madame de Fortelle sat like a statue, her coffee cup poised delicately in front of her, her eyes wide open, her face ashen. Théophile, too, was apparently shocked into stillness. Claire had bent to help Kate with Pia. Shaafia sat immobile beside the wheelchair.

Sister Geneviève moved to the middle of the room, her motions spare and her face expressing no emotion. She looked down at the half-hidden form of Shaafia. "My child", she said, "I must ask you to explain what you have just said."

Shaafia knew that she must answer, and she willed herself to come out from her shelter. She made herself stand and face the sister, before she dared to speak. "You asked me to be the translator."

"Yes."

" I am the translator, but not in the way that I expected"

"What do you mean?"

Kate and Claire were blank-faced in this exchange as it was in French. Théophile came out of himself and, recognising his role, told them what was said.

Shaafia had hesitated to speak again. How could she put words to what had come to her? She looked at Kate, and it was Kate who spoke. "Shaafia can hear what Pia wants to say."

Although he didn't understand it, Theophile translated this into French.

The electricity in the room intensified.

Claire stared at Kate.

"Child?" Sister Geneviève took a step closer to Shaafia, who dared not look into her face.

"It is as she says. » Shaafia finally willed herself to look up into the face of the nun she trusted. « Pia speaks to me. Yes. I can hear her inside. She has many things to tell us."

Then Sister Geneviève looked around the room. The tension was palpable. "Please sit everyone."

Once they had done this, she settled herself into a copious leather armchair and retrieved her own cup of coffee. She sipped it thoughtfully, her eye travelling around the group to make sure she had their attention. "I am not such a nun that believes easily in miracles. That may come as a surprise to you, as I am a good Catholic nun and miracles are the work of God." She looked to Théophile to translate then continued. "What we have just witnessed is of that order. Only one person in this convent has been aware of Marie-Louise's history. I am that person. We have kept it to ourselves, she and I. I will tell you now, because of what has been said. I ask you for your confidence in this matter."

She paused and drank her coffee. Everyone else took that as their cue and all carefully drank theirs. Théophile took up the plate and passed around the *pets-de-nonne.* He wanted to give one to Pia but she seemed oblivious, slumped back in her wheelchair, looking off across the room to the wide bay window that opened out onto the lawn and to the fountain beyond. As he gazed down at her, it was as if she wasn't there at all.

"This is what I must tell you", Sister Geneviève went on. "When she was just a teenage girl, Marie-Louise had a brother. His name was Guyaume. He was severely handicapped. He was epileptic." Théophile hesitated, looking to find the right word but Kate said it and he realised it was the same in English. Geneviève continued "It became more and more difficult for her to bear his suffering and one day, when he had a grand mal, the parents were not there. She covered his face with a pillow and she held it there, until he no longer breathed."

The nun waited for the translation, letting the room absorb what she had said.

"She was sent to an institute for criminal girls and when she became an adult, she took the vows. Her history is never spoken of."

Sister Geneviève put down her cup, gathered her considerable weight from deep in the armchair, and moved across the room to the wheelchair. There she lowered herself as if kneeling for prayer in the chapel.

"And so", she said, studying the apparently inert Pia. "Who is this child that knows this history? Who is this child who will speak through the voice of another? We must think about this most carefully."

XII

The coffee was finished in fraught silence. Everyone seemed to be occupied with their own thoughts. Théophile let his eyes roam the room, wondering how each person was trying to grasp what had taken place. For himself, he was wrestling with his destiny. If this was indeed the reincarnation of a sage, the reason he was sent home, then surely what just happened was a confirmation. He felt a throb of delighted anticipation. What else would she do? If she knew about the nun, did she know about him? What would she tell him? Could she give him a resolution to the mystery that had been alluded to, when his past life was recounted to him in the ashram? Could she make the impenetrable verses of the *Ashtavakra Samhita* come to life for him at last? Could she show him what liberation was? His mind was on fire.

He gazed at the child, looking for her to open to him. Could she feel his longing to know? But she was sitting absently staring, perhaps out of the window, perhaps at something entirely different that only she could see. He longed to be able to explore this new potential that was surging up in him. If Shaafia could hear what Pia wanted to say, then he could ask her. He had so many questions. He urgently wanted to be gone, back to the château, so they could talk.

He looked to see if his mother was ready to move. She sipped at her coffee as if it were arsenic. The pain of incomprehension etched her face, deepening the lines and darkening her complexion. He recognised that she had no way to understand what had just happened. Her trust in Sister Geneviève was probably all she had to cling to. He felt sorry for his mother, the weight that she carried, the litany of unending disappointments she had endured. She had relied on the coming of her far-away family to renew her and uplift her, but suddenly it had become mysterious and alarmingly alien. She was lost, troubled, anchorless. He realised that he felt love for her. An unexpected, gentle flood of love for his mother was welling up inside him. He leant over and laid his hand on her arm.

"*Ca va, Maman?*" he murmured.

She dared to glance up at him and subtly shook her head.

"Perhaps," he said in a louder voice and in English, "it is time for us to go home."

It seemed to wake everyone up and they all began to prepare. Even Pia seemed to return from her introverted place and look around. Shaafia was near her and they touched each other's hands, and immediately Pia began to croon. Everyone looked at her as if she was saying something important. Now they were expectant. Shaafia however made no eye contact with anyone else and said nothing.

It was Madame de Fortelle who asked the obvious: "Does she say something?"

Shaafia shook her head.

There was a distinct release in the room, as if everyone had somehow held their breath in anticipation. Now they were free to gather up their belongings. Kate manoeuvred the chair and they all headed for the door.

Once out in the morning sun again, Sister Geneviève motioned to Théophile. "She should go with you now."she said nodding in the direction of Shaafia.

"But *Maman's* car?" said Théophile. The Citröen barely held five.

"Of course." the nun said, now all business » I will drive someone."

"*Maman*, I am sure, would be happy to go with you." He saw the advantage of not having his mother in the car. He hoped she would be able to feel some small sense of relief in the down-to-earth company of the nun. She could also take good counsel from the nun as they drove.

"I will ask her." And the nun turned to take his mother to one side.

To the others, Théophile mentioned what had been decided and they all walked towards the Citröen. His mother gave him a distracted little wave and followed Geneviève. He walked beside the wheelchair with its non-communicative occupant. Her body rocked along with the motion of the chair, her head rolling a little from side to side. In her silence, it was as if there was nobody there. Nonetheless, Théophile kept willing her to say something, something for him. If she could only give some sign that she knew who he was. Shaafia held Pia's hand while Kate pushed the chair and Claire carried Pia's bag of supplies.

When they reached the car, Théophile came round to help Kate and Shaafia but he found himself in the way. Pia was so tiny that there was no need for him. Kate propped her in the middle and sat next to her with Shaafia on the other side. Claire stood for a moment, looking at her daughter between the two young women. Perhaps she too was looking for something new from her daughter. Then she opened the front door and got in.

Théophile was left to stow the wheelchair. He struggled with its folding mechanism and felt the resentment of being left out. Finally he managed it, closed the boot and came round to the driver's side. Then it occurred to him that while Shaafia was effectively coming to stay with them, she'd had no time to collect her luggage, her things.

In French, he asked her "Do you need to get anything?"

She looked up at him, not understanding.

"Your valise and your clothes and everything."

Then her face cleared and she smiled. "Oh," she said, "it will be fine. I will get them at some point. Do not worry."

He shrugged and got in. Claire turned to him. "What did you just say?"

"Oh, yes I am sorry." he said, the role of translator still not natural to him. "I just realised that if Shaafia is coming to stay with us in the château, then she will need to get her, how do you say, the things she will need. Clothes and everything."

Claire nodded and asked "She is coming to stay? It has been decided?"

He looked at her to gauge her reaction. He couldn't tell if she was all right with it. "What do you think?" he asked.

"I don't know what to think." She turned to face him in the front seat. "I have just had my world rocked by something so strange that I'm having trouble making sense of anything."

He started the car and took it round the circle past the fountain with the bird sculptures. Nothing was being said in the back seat.

Claire watched the tall trees of the driveway and, as they swung out into the road beyond the convent, she looked round at the three passengers in the rear seat. Shaafia and Pia still held hands, but Pia had closed her eyes. Kate looked up as Claire turned. She smiled at her, looking at the two beside her. Claire turned back and watched the road ahead.

Finally she said to Théophile "It's good that she is coming to stay. I will be happy to pay her for her work as a translator. I think something is about to happen in my daughter's life that I could never have imagined, or hoped for. It's just…It's taking a while for me to accept it, that's all."

"You have never seen anything like this before?" he ventured.

"No, never." She shook her head. "It is not something I ever believed would have been possible. It's not…It's not normal."

"But you are convinced that it is real? She can do this?"

"I suppose so. I mean how else could it be? How could she, Shaafia I mean", dropping her voice to make sure those in the back seat could not hear, "How could she say what she did?" It was a relief to be able to talk about it. She turned to Théophile "What about you? Do you believe it?"

Théophile swung the car into the château driveway. Looking in the rear vision mirror he saw that all three passengers seemed to be indrawn and far away. "I think so." he said, speaking equally softly so as not to be heard. " It is very strange, of course, but I think it is as she says. I can…" He glanced at Claire, selecting his words carefully. "I can feel that there is something very powerful. I am sure of it."

"Powerful." Claire thought about the implications. "I am frightened of it."

He pulled the old Citröen up to the front of the château and turned the engine off. In the silence, the car's suspension subsided with a sigh and they all sat where they were.

Pia suddenly came to life and made a long sharp "*Heee!*" which made everyone jump. Kate immediately responded. "Okay." she said. "I don't need a translator for that one. Off to the toilet right away."

They all engaged themselves in extricating Pia from the car, setting up the wheelchair and heading inside. Théophile went ahead and opened the door, Kate pushed the chair and Claire and Shaafia came behind.

Claire took Shaafia's elbow to hold her back while Kate took Pia inside. Standing just outside the front door, she said: "What happened with you and and my daughter, I have to say I have never seen anything like that before." As he heard this, Théophile turned back to listen, perhaps feeling needed for translation.

Claire continued "Have you ever done anything like this before? I mean have you ever, I don't know what you would call it, read someone else's thoughts?"

Shaafia looked up at Pia's mother, whose face was troubled, whose eyes were searching hers and she felt deep compassion. Shaafia shook her head. "This has never happened to me."

Claire went on, glancing round to be sure that Pia was not close. She noticed Théophile but ignored him. "Can I ask you, how it happens. How do you hear her?"

Shaafia thought for a moment and said "I can hear a voice. It is not exactly like her voice but it is clear, and the message that I hear I know it is for me to say. I don't know how to explain it. The voice is there and I translate it."

"I don't want you to think I am upset with you or anything like that. I'm not. It's just…It's just very new for me. Pia is eight years old and I always thought she could only communicate very simple things. I never dared to hope that she could…I wasn't sure how intelligent she was." There were tears in Claire's eyes.

Shaafia gently touched her arm and stroked it. "She is very special. She has many things to tell us. We must listen to her."

Then Shaafia looked searchingly at Claire and turned to look at Théophile too. She said "I have looked for her all my life."

XIII

Shaafia felt her heart beating fast as she spoke these words. There was no way she could explain her quest for the bird with crooked wings. And yet she knew as the other two stared at her without comprehension that she must say something.

"When I was a very small girl", she began timidly. "I was maybe the age of Pia. There was a man. He was a holy man of my tradition. I am Muslim and in Morocco there are holy men who are very close to God. They are called sharif. Such a man touched my head and gave me a blessing and told me to look for, I don't know how to say it in English." She shook her head. The words seemed too private to be able to share them, at least for now. She said instead: "When I met Pia, I knew it. And she told me inside, that she had been looking for me."

Claire gazed at this serious, timorous, girl, so young, so innocent. And she knew she was being told the truth. She let her tears flow and she took the much smaller Shaafia in her arms. "I don't know what to say to you. But at least I can say thank you. Thank you for being able to translate. Thank you for coming." Then she simply hugged her. Théophile stood awkwardly near them, feeling like an intruder.

It was at this moment that the convent's big Peugeot minibus, with its three rows of seats, pulled up to the château. They turned to greet it. Sister Geneviève was at the wheel with Madame de Fortelle beside her. Shaafia pulled carefully back from the embrace of Pia's mother, but as she did, she whispered "Thank you."

Théophile moved to the van to open the door for his mother while Sister Geneviève went to the back of the van and retrieved Shaafia's valise. When she saw this, Shaafia was overwhelmed by a wave of gratitude for this endlessly thoughtful nun. She ran towards her saying *Merci infiniment.* In much the same way that Claire had hugged her, Shaafia hugged the very wide waist of her benefactor.

The sister stroked her hair and murmured quietly so no one else would hear her: "My child, you have brought us nothing but blessings from the day M'bella gave you to us. I thank God in my prayers that I have had the great good fortune to know you."

Then they broke apart and Shaafia picked up her suitcase.

Madame de Fortelle had alighted from the car and was making an effort to be practical. She turned to Shaafia and said, in French, "We will make a nice room for you upstairs."

"*Merci Madame.*" Shaafia replied and followed her with her suitcase.

As they stepped down into the entrance of the château, Kate reappeared with Pia. As soon as she saw Shaafia, the child hooted with a strong "*Haa-ee-ah*" and put her arms out for a hug. Shaafia left her suitcase and dropped down in front of the wheelchair and they hugged each other as if they had been parted for years.

Slightly behind them Claire and Sister Geneviève had to stop. The nun smiled at Claire: "*C'est geniale n'est-ce pas?*" Théophile caught it and translated: "It is wonderful isn't it." Claire simply smiled and nodded.

Madame de Fortelle had surged purposely onward but finding herself alone, she had to stop and come back. The ritual of greeting disturbed her sense of mission and she looked slightly annoyed.

Buried deep in her hug, Shaafia heard Pia's voice, imperative and clear, and she gently withdrew to face the rest of the group. "She asks that I can sleep with her", Shaafia said in English, facing Claire.

Madame de Fortelle looked annoyed. "*Qu'est elle dit?*" To which Shaafia repeated what she had said in French. Claire and her mother-in-law spoke simultaneously: "No."

"There's not enough room", Madame de Fortelle said and Claire said much the same in English.

Shaafia stood up and turned to face Claire. "She says you must begin to let her go now. You have given her everything. She says now you must let others take care of her. She asks that Kate and I sleep with her and that you sleep by yourself." She saw Claire's reaction, a rapid play of conflicting emotions rippling across her face. "This is what Pia asks."

"Théophile?" His mother wanted to hear what was said. He apologised and gave her a summary. She looked at Claire, as everyone else was, except for Pia.

Pia sat back in her chair and said "*Coo-coo!*"

They turned to look at Pia, as if expecting her to speak, but she was looking off over their heads as if she were totally disinterested in what was being said.

"How can we be sure this is right?" demanded Madame de Fortelle. She turned on Shaafia with something of the old fire. "You are sure this is what she wants, not what you want?"

Sister Geneviève took her elbow. "Shaafia has already shown us that it is possible to read the child's thoughts."

"But that was something different." Madame de Fortelle's voice was beginning to sound shrill.

Claire took a breath and then spoke loudly enough for everyone to hear her. "I think it is good idea. It took me by surprise, that's all. I have always slept with Pia because I thought she needed me to be there. But Kate is here and I trust her." She looked to Théophile who told his mother and the nun what had been said.

Kate had said nothing yet, fascinated by the play that was unfolding. For herself she felt a growing elation, that Pia was coming to life and would be able to communicate and that she, Kate, would be there. "I'm sure it would be fine. It's fine with me and I don't mind sharing with Shaafia."

"It will be good for you too." said the nun, looking at Claire and making sure Théophile followed what she said. "To have been her mother for the first part of her life was a big task. Now she would like you to rest. She has compassion for you."

Claire waited for Théophile's translation, and then she nodded. "I think I have a lot to learn about my own daughter." she said.

The decision was made and so they organised beds and rearranged situations, so that Claire would be by herself in Kate's room. A small bed was dragged into the limited space in Pia's room, leaving just enough room for three to sleep and room for the wheelchair.

Sister Geneviève waited until it was all done before she said her goodbyes. Just before she left, she bent to kiss Pia on both cheeks.

Pia gave a joyful "*Coo-coo*" and grabbed at the nun's habit. The big nun picked her up and hugged her. Then the nun pulled back a little and said "*Coo-coo ma belle!*" Pia's left hand came up to the nun's eyes and brushed them.

Shaafia was beside her. "She tells you that if you keep your eyes closed, you will see Jesus again. When you were young, Pia says, you could see him but you do not see him now. Pia says you must close your eyes and you will see him again."

The nun kept her eyes closed and held the child close. "*Mon Dieu, mon Dieu*", she said with reverence in her voice. "*C'est la verité*" and tears rolled from her closed eyes.

Théophile had not remembered to translate into English so Claire and Kate could not follow but they sensed the importance of the moment. There was a hush as they watched the nun's tears, holding the small frail body in her arms. It was too much for Madame de Fortelle and she took refuge in one of the benches along the wall of the courtyard, making an audible "*Oof*" as she landed. She slumped there staring at the nun.

Finally Sister Geneviève opened her eyes. She looked at Pia, who was slowly waving her arms in the air as if they were being blown in the wind. There was no expression on her face and her more focussed eye looked off into the distance beyond the nun's shoulder.

Sister Geneviève took a step towards Claire with Pia in her arms. "Truly," she said, "this child speaks from God." Shaafia repeated this in English, without even thinking. "I entered the order of nuns," Geneviève said, her voice quavering, "because our Lord Jesus Christ came to me in visions. I was just a girl. I knew I must be a nun and be married to him. I did not grow up in a religious family. My father was a socialist and did not believe, but when our Lord asked me to come, I had to come.

Somehow, I am sad to tell you, once I had taken the vows and entered the convent, something came in the way. I cannot say what it was and I no longer had His vision. I have grieved and I have prayed to discover what was my sin. I have done penance without end. There was no response. I have lived in diminishing hope but strong faith. And now this child, this child…Ah, *ma belle, ma belle!*" and she hugged Pia again and again.

Now Pia came to life and offered a singsong version of "*coo-coo*" to which the nun joined in and together they chanted it. The nun, holding the child, began to dance in a circle in the courtyard, and Pia began to laugh and laugh. The others caught it from her and they too began to laugh. The high stone walls of the château courtyard rang with the sound of their joy. Even Madame de Fortelle found herself gently chuckling and then letting go into full-bodied hilarity.

XIV

Finally, happily bathed in sweat, Sister Geneviève made her *adieux*. She hugged Pia again and again before she finally handed her back to her mother. The group waved as the white Peugeot disappeared down the château driveway. The wild joy of Pia's laughter hung in the air long after it had echoed back from the château walls. And yet as they made their way back inside, there was a sudden sense of let-down as if there had been the imminence of some new opening that had not quite happened.

Nonetheless, they smiled at each other in the afterglow of the morning and Madame de Fortelle announced that they should have lunch. This gave everyone something to concentrate on and they all went into the kitchen. Théophile cut slices from a huge loaf of *pain de campagne*, Kate was given a thick wooden spoon to stir a pot of chicken soup and Madame de Fortelle produced an array of cheeses from her *garde manger*. While the silverware was laid out, serviettes found and plates arrayed Claire organised a cushion for Pia to sit in a high-backed armchair at the venerably solid kitchen table and Shaafia sat beside her,

When at last they all sat with the vast soup pot before them and on a board, the pile of cut bread and the cheeses, Madame de Fortelle presided at the head of the table.

"It would be appropriate for us to say a grace." she said. She looked to Théophile to translate. "Although I know you are all not such religious people." She glanced at Shaafia with an enigmatic look, before going on, "Nonetheless, I would like to thank God for all that has been bestowed on us today."

The room looked expectantly at her to proceed, but she had a firm idea of what she wanted. "Théophile, as you are the only man present, I would ask you to say the grace."

He squirmed under her gaze. "*Maman*, as you say, I am not so, you know…You should say it."

Without thinking, Kate turned to Shaafia. "In your tradition, do they say grace?"

Shaafia looked first at Madame de Fortelle then she looked at Kate. "In my tradition, in my house, in my family, we ask God for his grace and we thank God for what God has given. It is not the same exactly as in the Christian tradition but the purpose is the same."

"Would you be willing to say it in your language?'

"In Arabic?"

"I would love to hear that." Kate looked around at the rest of the table. "Is that alright?" Théophile had to fill his mother in and she was obviously not happy. He chose to ignore her and he said in English "I think it would be very nice to hear grace in Arabic."

Shaafia dared to look at Madame de Fortelle and something like a look of resolve crossed her face. She was going to say grace in Arabic whether Madame de Fortelle liked it or not.

"This is the prayer that my father offers before every meal." Then she began. Her voice was light and high, the throaty consonants rose above the table and the room became still.

Into the silence that followed Claire said "That sounds so beautiful." And Pia added her own "*Ha-ee-ah*!"

Kate asked what it meant.

Shaafia said: "It is a little hard for me to translate into English but it means 'Oh God please bless what you have given us in your abundance. You are the great provider of all things. ' Then she turned to face Madame de Fortelle and repeated the grace in French. Madame de Fortelle listened carefully and then said with a formal voice: "Amen".

"May I say something?" It was Claire. "I have no religion at all. Not really. I believe in God, I suppose, but not much else." Shaafia repeated what she had said, in French, for which Théophile was very grateful. Madame de Fortelle allowed a small frown of annoyance to pass across her brow, but she nodded. Claire went on hesitantly. "What I would like to say is: At last I am in the wonderful château where my husband was born. I have met his family. I am sad that Hugues is not here and I am sad that my son, Antoine, was never able to see this and to know his family. But I am so grateful. And now my daughter has begun to reveal…I don't know what to say about this. She has…She has begun to reveal herself." Claire paused to smile at Pia who was watching her with interest. "It fills me with so much gratitude. To God, whatever form or name you might believe in, we are grateful." As Shaafia completed the translation, there was a deep and peaceful silence.

Once again Madame de Fortelle added her "Amen" and then she added *"Bon appetit."*

As they shared out the soup and the bread, Madame de Fortelle leaned over to Théophile and nodded at him. He frowned, but when she turned to speak to Claire he realised he was required. "It troubles me that you have had no religion, » his mother said « But I am bound to say that the grace you have spoken was with good heart. I wish to thank you for it."

Claire smiled, unsure what sort of response was required and the lunch proceeded.

Although Madame de Fortelle had not thanked her for her grace, Shaafia felt the glow of achievement at having dared to share her Arabic grace and she took her first spoonfuls with reverence.

Pia had a large towel draped around her entire upper body while Kate took charge of her spoon. Every now and then Pia would let out a little chortle of laughter, so much of the soup ended up on the towel. She seemed to be very happy and her good eye roamed the table, as she smiled and *cooed.* She was intent on making eye contact with everyone. She even managed to draw a hesitant little *"coo-coo"* from her grandmother.

"Ah!" said Madame de Fortelle suddenly, tapping the side of her head in the French gesture of annoyance. "We must have wine of course!" She pushed back her chair and disappeared, to return a few seconds later with a dusty bottle. She handed it to Théophile. "It is from our own vines, from the time when we were the *vignerons*. I have kept just a few bottles from that time. It is today that we should open one, in honour of this occasion." Théophile dutifully uncorked it and carefully sniffed, perhaps dreading the possibility that it would not be good. He brought glasses to the table and then poured for his mother just a small amount.

She lifted the glass to her nose and closed her eyes. She sipped a bit and sighed "It is good. Please…", gesturing to the table. He poured for each, hesitating when he reached Shaafia. Her subtle shake of the head was enough and he moved on. His mother noticed. "You will not taste our wine?"

Théophile was quick. "*Maman.* You know that it is not permitted in Islam. You know that."

She huffed. "I thought maybe when you are a guest…"

Shaafia smiled at her with her new confidence. "Thank you for offering it to me." Then turning to Théophile "And thank you for understanding that I am not able to accept it. I do not wish to cause offense." It was not an apology but simply a statement. With equal calm she turned to Kate and Claire and explained in English what had just been said, adding her own explanation about alcohol and Islam.

Claire nodded. "So you have never had any alcohol in your life?"

"My experience with alcohol has been difficult", she said and bravely decided to share her experience of her attempt to be a translator in the convent *chai.* They sipped their wine and it pleased her make them laugh, even Madame de Fortelle. The wine was very mellow and full-bodied, and the others finished the bottle with great pleasure.

Once the lunch had been cleaned away, there was general consensus that what was needed was *la sieste.* The morning had been fraught with energy and everyone was coming down after it. The jetlag for the Australians was lurking in the background as well.

Claire kissed Pia and went upstairs to her new room, while Shaafia and Kate took Pia for her nap. She lay down without complaint and, closing her eyes, she was asleep in seconds. Kate was feeling drowsy too but it was the first time she had Shaafia totally to herself.

"Can I ask you something?" she said, quietly not to disturb the sleeping child next to her.

Shaafia had been down on her knees pulling a few things from her suitcase. She looked up.

"Pia speaks to you inside your mind, right?" Shaafia nodded, trying to gauge what was behind the question. Kate went on "So, when she does, do you just repeat it? I mean do you say everything she says or do you give a general idea of it? You get what I mean?"

Shaafia nodded. She thought for a moment how best to describe the way it worked. She remembered what she had told Claire earlier. "There is a voice. I know what it says. And so I say what it says. It is exactly as I would do when I translate from French into English. What I hear, that is what I say."

"But you always say 'Pia says'."

"Yes, I must do that. Otherwise you might think it is me who says these things."

"Ah yes, of course." Kate nodded. Shaafia watched her face knowing there was more she wanted to say. Kate asked. "So she hasn't said anything, I mean, like, no messages or anything for me?" Kate felt more than a little guilty putting forward the question.

Shaafia knew what was coming and she was ready. "Yes, she did."

"What was it?" Kate was electric with anticipation.

"I told you already. You must trust her love."

"Oh." Kate felt embarrassed that she had forgotten.

Shaafia saw it. "It is a beautiful message."

"Yes, yes, of course it is."

"But you were hoping for something more?"

Kate thought about it for moment. "Maybe I was. And you're right. She is just a bundle of love, and I should trust that. I mean, when I first saw her, I knew she was someone special. Not just in herself but someone special for me."

"You have been looking for her." This was said as a statement of fact.

"Yes!" Kate sat upright and stared at Shaafia. "How do you know that?"

"It is the same for me. I have said this already to Claire and to Théophile. I have looked for a long time." Then she told Kate about the sharif. And Kate in turn told her about her grandmother, and about what led her out into the desert and what the old man in the desert had told her.

They hugged. They were like sisters, Shaafia said. Kate felt closer to Shaafia than she had ever felt to either of her own sisters. This was like the feeling she'd had with Millin and her other aboriginal sisters. It filled her with the warm glow of belonging.

"Yes.", Kate said with emotion, "We are sisters."

At last, the jetlag caught up with Kate and she lay down next to Pia. In minutes she was asleep, deeply and dreamless.

Shaafia quietly sat on the floor and opened her Koran. She read for a while and then closed her eyes in prayer.

She felt the presence of her sister Adila, she felt the loving presence of Dada and she felt the power of the sharif.

"Here I am." she prayed. "By the grace of Allah. *Bismillah*. Here I am."

XV

In the quiet of the afternoon, Théophile sat up in his own room, drawing together the events of the day. In one short morning, so much had changed. He sat there trying to accept as a certainty that downstairs in his own château, in the house of ghosts, the reincarnation of the child sage Ashtavakra was taking a nap. The evidence was there. Not that she had said anything to him personally to indicate who she was. But she had used another person to communicate knowledge that was otherwise unknowable, and that was enough. She was no ordinary child.

On the side table by his bed was the battered and rumpled stuffed kangaroo that she had given him. It sat next to the statue of the Durga with his copy of the *Ashtavakra Samhita*. He gazed at the three objects. They were like the threefold God of Christianity or Brahma, Vishnu and Shiva, the three main deities for the Hindus, or the three wise men looking for the baby Jesus, or the three…He laughed to himself at the wayward workings of his own mind.

And he thought about Shaafia and Kate. Were they like him, drawn to follow a path that led to this decrepit château, so in need of renovation, just as each of them were in their own lives? Here we all are, looking in wonder at this child. We are each wanting to hear our own message, what we are supposed to do, how we should live, what is the point of our lives. And, as Ashtavara says so often, we want to achieve liberation. Trying to make sense of it all made his mind swirl and his body restless. He was impatient. He wanted to get on with the next step, whatever that would be.

As he had done so many times, he took up the book and let it fall open to a random page. He read a few lines, but they meant nothing to him. What had he expected? Sudden enlightenment? The scales dropping from his eyes? He closed the book and put it back on the table beside the statue and the rumpled Roo.

Towards the middle of the afternoon, he could stay still no longer. He stood up, stretched and left his room. He met Claire on the stairs.

"Did you sleep?" he asked

She shook her head. "Too much to think about." she said ruefully, and he agreed. They descended the stairs together. She noticed the noises they made.

"Are the stairs alright?" she asked.

He shrugged. "I don't know. They are very old. I believe they are made of *peuplier*. It is a wood that lasts very well."

"It would be good to make sure they are safe." This was not meant as a criticism, but a professional opinion tendered by an interior designer.

"I am sure you are right, but as you can see, there is no money to look after the château." He stopped and put his weight on the solid oak banister and it shifted visibly against the uprights. "Perhaps my brother told you something of the sad story of the family fortunes."

"Not so much. I think he wanted to have a different life in Australia and he didn't want us to know that he was unhappy here. I hope you don't mind me saying

that?"

Théophile looked at her steadily and shook his head. "It was the same for me. Hugues was more courageous than me and smarter. He went as far away as he could."

"It seems such a shame that such a wonderful building as this, all this history, is falling apart."

He shrugged as they reached the bottom of the stairs. "Maybe it is natural. Manmade things finally fall, don't they?"

"They do for sure, but I can't help feeling this château is crying out for a chance to be something again, you know?"

He wasn't convinced. "Perhaps."

She gazed admiringly at the high ceilings and the solid walls. "Would you take me on a tour? I would love to see it all."

"Okay. All of it?" He grinned at her. "Even the *donjon*?"

"There's a dungeon? How fantastic! Yes, please!"

"Follow me."

She was so excited about the prospect of exploring the château's hidden treasures that she had forgotten her daughter. It suddenly struck her. "Oh. I better check on Pia first."

He waited while she went to the downstairs bedroom and quietly opened the door. Then she closed it and came back. "They're all asleep."

Behind the kitchen was a narrow wooden door, and when Théophile opened its reluctant ill-oiled hinges, the smell of cold and mould wafted out. "I hope the lights are still working down there." he said as he went in. "I haven't been down here since I was a boy." He felt his way down the stairs that turned at right angles twice. Then he felt for a switch and a pale yellow light flickered on farther down.

Claire followed him down, placing her feet carefully on the worn stone steps and imagining the various romantic and horrifying stories about dungeons she had read over the years. A real dungeon in a real castle.

The stairs ended in a long dank corridor with two naked bulbs shedding their jaundiced light into shadowed alcoves. Théophile felt himself inadvertently shiver as he moved along the corridor. When he was young, it had always been Hugues who led their adventures and who had no qualms about delving into the darkest corners. Théophile had always kept his tremulous imaginings to himself, not wishing to show any weakness to an older brother. Of course they had never found anything like a skeleton, or instruments of torture, caches of treasure or even decent antiques.

After several steps, there was the sound of running water. In one alcove a glistening wall revealed greenish water running down the stones. "What is this?" asked Claire.

He shook his head. "I could not say. Most probably it is a broken pipe somewhere. Our plumbing is, as you have seen, not very modern."

She dared to put her finger on the wall and then smelled it. "I think you are right. It needs to be fixed."

He felt no need to comment on that and turned to move farther down the corridor. His face was suddenly meshed in a vast spider web that he hadn't noticed.

"*Merde, merde, merde!*" He leapt back clawing at his face.

As she approached him, she saw the body of the web-maker heavy and black scurrying away from her ravaged tapestry.

"Are you alright?"

"*Quelle horreur, déguellasse!*"

Still tearing at his face, he turned and stumbled back along the corridor, leaving her there. He threw himself up the stairs and stood in the kitchen heaving for breath. It took him a moment to realise that his mother was in the kitchen staring at him. She had been at the kitchen table with her head down but had sat upright in alarm when she heard him charging up the stairs.

"*Qu'est-ce que tu fait?*"

"Spider webs, in my face."

She looked at him with her troubled eyes. "Why were you down there?"

"Claire asked me to show her the château. I mentioned the *donjon* and she wanted to see it."

"She is down there?"

His heart rate was coming down and he now felt embarrassed that he had left his sister-in-law alone with the spiders. He nodded.

"I do not like her to see how this château is falling to pieces." His mother looked up at him and he saw the deep lines around her eyes. " It is a terrible humiliation", she added. "It brings shame on our family. Please ask her to come up."

He steeled himself. "*Oui, Maman*", he said and turned back to the stairs.

He hoped Claire was on her way up by herself, but when he turned the first corner there was no sign of her. Nor at the bottom. He called her name and got no response. He then had to will himself to move along the corridor. There was a length of pine board propped in a corner and he took it with him to make sure he did not get into any other spider webs. He moved on down the corridor, waving it in front of himself. Off to either side from the central corridor, there were more alcoves and dark rooms, cellars perhaps in the old days, now shadowed and unrevealing. He peered into several of them and called her name. Farther down, the corridor made a T-junction and he had to decide which way to go. Once again he called "Claire", and this time he heard her.

"I'm down here." She didn't sound afraid. He couldn't trace the direction of her voice, but the left turn showed another dim light bulb while to the right was in darkness. He chose the light. At the end of that corridor she appeared.

"It's so incredible!" she said. "Is this a well?" pointing off to one side.

He walked towards her still vaguely waving his pine board.

"I am sorry I left you." he said. "I have a, what you call it? A phobia? I hate spiders."

"Oh, don't worry about it. I realised that's what had happened. Are you alright now?"

"Yes, thank you. My mother asks that you come back upstairs."

"Okay." Claire seemed totally relaxed in this hellish place and he marvelled at her, while writhing in his own inadequacy. "Do you think this is a well?" She was pointing off to one side, where a low stone wall surrounded a hole that went off down into the darkness. He leaned over it cautiously and heard the water.

"Yes." he said pulling back from its dank emptiness. "In the middle ages, all fortified châteaux had to have their own water. If the English or some other enemy attacked and made a *siège*." He paused, realising he was using a French word. "I don't know the English word for that, when an army will block the fortress."

"Oh it's the same word, more or less: 'siege'. So this is a really old well?"

"Probably thirteenth century, from the first fortified château."

"How fabulous." Then she turned and began to walk back with him along the corridor. "Can you imagine over all those centuries who has been down here, who pulled the water from that well? It's just amazing to me."

He shrugged but he liked her enthusiasm. "If I let my imagination go free, about this *donjon*, I see ghosts. Who knows what terrible things happened here, during the revolution, the hundred years war…I do not like to think about it so much."

They mounted the stairs and found his mother, still at the table anxiously waiting for them to appear.

Speaking in French, his mother said "It is so dark there, and so dirty. I do not think it is healthy." She looked to her son to translate her concerns.

Claire sat down at the table and smiled at her mother-in-law. "I can see that you are embarrassed by the state of your wonderful château, but to me, I don't see it that way. I see the history, I see the stones, I see the potential to bring it all back to life. In Australia I was an interior designer. I would love to work on the restoration of this château!"

Madame de Fortelle studied her daughter-in-law's face as her son translated. It moved her to see this young woman, her elder son's chosen partner, so full of joyful enthusiasm. It warmed her.

"Ah, but you see," she said, "there is no money to do that. To live in this château, for us, is to live in a crumbling prison."

Claire took a moment to take this in: the meaning and the pain behind the words, the weight of the shame they carried. She said. "I have money. We have money. Your son, your brilliant son, was very, very successful in Australia." She waited and watched while the translation arrived and was digested. There was a rapid play of emotions on her mother-in-law's face: disbelief, hope, embarrassment.

"We could not take your money" the woman said. "It would take so much."

"How much?"

"One could not imagine."

"Thérèse," said Claire. "May I call you Thérèse?" She waited to see the outcome of this before she would go on.

Her mother-in-law had to think for a moment. "Why not?" It was said hesitantly as if the older woman were in unfamiliar territory. The French tradition of using "*tu*" and "*vous*" is imbedded in protocols that somehow did not quite fit modern Australian daughters-in-law.

"Thérèse," Claire began, looking searchingly at her mother-in law. "Hugues was the most wonderful thing that happened in my life. To have lost him and Antoine has been my greatest tragedy. But still Hugues has left me with so much. He would want me, I am certain, to use what he has given me. I want to do this. I want to bring his home back to its glory." She paused for the translation. "Does that make sense to you?"

Thérèse de Fortelle put her hand up to her face, perhaps anticipating tears or perhaps from a long-held weariness. Her glasses came off and she looked down at them as if they were no longer a part of her. "I do not know what to say to you, my daughter. You are very generous to make such an offer but I fear you do not know what it will take."

"Then we will find out."

XVI

When she woke, Kate felt groggy and slow. Pia remained inert and Shaafia had curled up on the floor. Kate dragged herself up from the double bed where she and Pia had napped side by side. Shaafia heard her and sat up. Together they looked down at Pia and she opened her eyes.

"*Coo-coo.*" she said softly.

Kate dropped down onto the bed to give her a cuddle. Shaafia watched from the side.

"Ready to wake up?"

"*Coo-coo.*" Pia's voice was soft and remote. She was sweaty so they changed her clothes and Kate carried her out to see if Claire had resurfaced. Coming into the kitchen, they found her with Madame de Fortelle at the table, Théophile hovering in the background. Pia let out a strong "*Ha!*" and her mother came to greet her.

"Hello, my darling. Did you have a good snooze?" She took her from Kate's arms.

"*Ha!*" said Pia and reached for Shaafia's hand.

Shaafia looked at Madame de Fortelle, then spoke to her in French. "Pia would like you to know that there is too much sadness in this château, but the sadness can be removed. She asks you to take off your clothes of mourning."

Madame de Fortelle stared at Shaafia and then looked at Pia. Pia was plucking at her own shirt in a fair gesture of removal. Madame de Fortelle turned again to Shaafia. "How can I know this comes from this child? How can I know that?"

Théophile quietly filled Claire and Kate in on what had been said. As had happened that morning in the convent, the air seemed to be electric.

Shaafia was not put off by the question. "Pia says that her father will pay for the removal of sadness. He wants that you should live in the château of good will."

This worked. Madame de Fortelle rocked back in her chair as if she had been struck on the head. "She knows this!" Now it was not a question, but an affirmation. She hunted for her glasses and put them back on. When Théophile translated for the Australians, Claire was stunned.

"My God, Kate!" Claire stared down at her daughter. "I have just been talking to Madame de Fortelle about exactly that. I told her I wanted to pay for the renovation of this château. I even said Hugues had left us the money for it and I knew that's what he would have wanted."

Kate's hand gently caressed the child's hair as she said "I think we'd better get used to being amazed by her."

"It's frightening." Claire's voice shook.

Théophile had heard her comment. "I think it is wonderful", he said.

Shaafia looked around the kitchen table. "That is all she would like to say." she said and repeated it in French. Claire passed her daughter back to Kate and came to sit opposite Madame de Fortelle.

"Thérèse," she said reaching across and taking her mother-in-law's hands in her own. "Please let us do this. Let us do it for you. Let us do it for Hugues, and for Antoine. Please." Théophile stood behind his mother to translate. She looked up at him.

"What do you think, my son?"

"*Maman*, there is no doubt in my mind. It should be done."

"But…" It was so hard for her to grasp.

"Stop." The word worked for both languages. He continued in French: "*Maman*, listen to me. You must let go of your old life and your old hardships and your old prejudices. You are being offered a chance to renovate yourself. Can you not see that?"

She stared up at her son, as if he were a stranger.

Quietly in the background Shaafia was translating into English for Kate and Claire.

Madame de Fortelle sat rigid and troubled. And then, suddenly Pia, who had become still and quiet, began to laugh. It was like a clap of thunder. It was strong and full and rocked her frail little body in Kate's arms. Her thin arms waved in front of her and the laughter rippled through the kitchen. In seconds Kate and Shaafia, and then Théophile found themselves laughing too. It was contagious and unstoppable. It took Claire just a few seconds, after her first alarm when the sound erupted, to start laughing too. Finally Madame de Fortelle, although valiantly trying to hold onto her dignity, allowed a tentative smile to cross her face and then she too let go. Her laughter shook her tired worried body and gave it a good shake. The kitchen rang with it until they all had tears in their eyes.

Finally they settled, and the feeling in the room was warm and convivial. Kate hugged Pia. "You are brilliant!" she said.

Pia grabbed her hand and let out a triumphant "*Haay*!"

Madame de Fortelle pointed at Théophile. "I wish to say something." He dutifully stood beside her. "It shall be as Claire asks." she said. "Who am I to stand in the way of the wishes of my beloved son, when he chooses to speak through his daughter? Let it be so."

He translated and looked to Claire to respond.

"Thérèse." she said. "Thank you, thank you." Then she stood up and took her daughter in her arms. "My darling, I have so much to learn from you. So much." and she enfolded Pia against her chest.

They made tea and spoke of other things. What had just happened to them all was so immense, it could not yet be spoken of lightly. When tea was over, Théophile led a casual late afternoon walk through the forest along rutted tracks that challenged the wheels of Pia's chair. Pia was chirpy and made little happy sounds as they bumped along. The others often turned to check with Shaafia to see if she had anything to add, but she always shook her head. High in the oaks, the merles called to each other and deeper into the oak wood, a small deer lifted its graceful head, watching them warily and then flitting from view across a stony rivulet.

When they returned to the courtyard of the château, Claire reminded Théophile that he had promised to lead a guided tour of the building. Kate took Pia in her arms as they went up the creaking stairs and into room after room. Pia hugged Kate and *cooed* now and then to Shaafia who kept eye contact with her as much as she could. As they went along, Madame de Fortelle was endlessly apologising for holes in the floorboards that were so bad in some rooms that they could not go in past the doorway. Théophile became impatient with his mother's endless embarrassment.

Finally he stopped. "*Maman*, it is enough. *J'en ai marre!* They know what is the condition of our home. You do not need to tell them every time we enter a new room."

His mother coloured under his assault. She was still not used to this new aspect of her son. She heaved a breath. "It is so. You are right. They can see for themselves."

High up under the gables of the slate roof, beyond the last very steep narrow staircase, it was clear that major work was desperately needed. The tiny rooms had been servants' quarters back when the château could afford them. Now they were repositories of dusty broken furniture, copious evidence of rodents, thick wefts of cobwebs that Théophile constantly edged around and holes in the roof that had obviously let in water for years.

When they reached the farthest end of the attic area, all of them coughing from the dust, Théophile said: "So now you have seen what we have. You can see how much it would take to fix it."

Claire looked around her. Her eyes shone, despite the dust. "It's a big job, no question. But can you imagine what this will look like when we have fixed it up! Just imagine what we could do up here. Look at these huge beams. They are so solid. Look at the stones. They will last another thousand years."

When Théophile translated that to his mother, she came up to Claire and said "*Tu est formidable.*" When this was translated too literally, Claire had to laugh. "I never think of myself as formidable. Am I that scary?"

"Oh no, no", Théophile realised he had just discovered one of those endless *faux amis*, words that sound the same but have different meaning in another language. "She means that you are, *comment dit*, wonderful."

"Oh okay", Claire said with a smile. "Then you are formidable too."

In the late evening, when Pia had been put to bed, the adults sat again in the kitchen and Claire again brought up the subject of restoration. "This is what I would like to do. I would like to open a bank account here in Bordeaux, so I can transfer whatever money we will need. I will do that tomorrow. Can we go into Bordeaux?"

Théophile nodded. "Of course."

"I want to find people who know how to renovate châteaux: artisans, stone masons, plumbers, carpenters. Do you know such people?"

Théophile shook his head and when his mother heard the translation, she did the same. "Sister Geneviève will know", Thérèse said.

"So we will ask her. Do you have any documents about this château? I would love to see anything you have that might give us some clues about how to bring it back to life."

"The parents of my husband were very good archivists." Thérèse said. "I will find many documents for you, but you will not be able to read them."

"I will help of course. » Théophile was experiencing a surge of energy inside him that was hard to contain. He almost wanted to shout aloud: Yes! Yes! Yes! Now he had something to work on and someone to work with and he was on fire with it.

They spent the rest of the evening discussing how the château might look when it was restored to its old glory. It took Madame de Fortelle a while but even she began to imagine, at least draft-free rooms, a watertight roof over their heads and plumbing that could be relied upon.

Kate and Shaafia played no real role in this, just listening and nodding. Every now and then they would smile at each other like conspirators, as the enthusiastic château planners talked and talked.

When they all at last went to bed, Kate and Shaafia spoke quietly by the sleeping Pia.

Kate said: "I am hesitating to ask you, but I can't help it. Has Pia told you special things for yourself?"

"What do you mean?"

"Has she given you a message, like she has for the two nuns, for Claire and for Théophile's mother? And of course for me too."

Shaafia thought about that. Then she nodded. "When I first heard her voice, she told me she had been looking for me. She said we have work we must do."

She smiled as she remembered how she felt when she had heard those words. "It was the most important message of my life."

Kate came over to her and hugged her yet again. "I am very happy to have met you. You are, what was the word? 'Formidable', a wonderful person, and I am so grateful that you are Pia's translator. I think this has been the most formidable day of my life."

Shaafia nodded. "It is true. Today, it was the day of the promise. Do you say that? What I mean is, from long-time ago I made one promise.

Today it has come. I am sorry I cannot say it in better English, but I hope you can understand."

"I understand totally." They hugged each other all over again.

XVII

The sweet cadences of the merle woke Théophile early, spurred into alertness by a sense of anticipation. He turned to face the statue of the Durga. In the pale dawn light, she seemed to be glowing, the tip of her upraised sword a delicate pink. He pulled himself up into a cross-legged sitting posture, wrapped himself in his Indian shawl and closed his eyes.

"It is good." he said to himself. "Although I do not see why I have been given such good fortune, I must be grateful. Although I understand almost nothing that has happened to me, I must accept it. Padmananda, you sent me here. You knew my destiny. May I learn to surrender to this unfolding mystery. May I be worthy of what I have been given." He dropped deeply into a silent, utterly still world, devoid of images or qualities. When he finally came back to the room, it was almost a shock to find that he had a body and a mind. It was as if he had been away on an effortless, bodiless, mindless journey and now had to reintegrate with his old world. He had to find himself once again, layer by layer. It was delicious.

It took him quite some time to recognise the gentle tap on his door. He found his voice. "*Entrez.*"

The door edged open with a creak. It was Claire. "I know it's still early," she said, "but I couldn't sleep. I would love to go to Bordeaux soon. Will you take me?"

"Yes of course."

She looked at him, sitting cross-legged on his bed. "Do you sleep sitting up like that?"

He smiled, still very much under the sweet euphoric influence of his meditation. "No. When I was in India I learned to meditate."

"Ah. That's nice." She looked around his simple room. "So this was your room when you were a boy?" They had looked in briefly the night before on their tour, but she had not really studied the room closely.

"Yes. I never had any other room but this one."

She came and sat on the edge of his bed and looked around. "I keep trying to imagine Hugues growing up here. His room didn't seem like him at all. I can't visualise him here, you know?" She glanced up at him sitting almost behind her, "I hope you don't mind me talking about Hugues."

He shrugged, surprised by her question. "*Pas de tout*…er, not at all."

"I only knew him in Australia. He seemed so exotic to me when I first met him. He had good manners and was so, I don't know, sophisticated, I suppose. But he was always French in Australia. If we had come back here maybe I would have seen a different side of him."

"I think he did not wish to ever come back.

"He said that." She sat there thinking about him. Théophile looked at her profile. This was the woman his brother had chosen. Good choice. He felt a stirring of the never quite hidden envy he had always held for his older, cleverer, quicker, more confident sibling—who was now dead." That seemed like a cruel irony.

"I miss him so much." Claire said, jumping to her feet. "It's not good to talk about him. It brings him too close." She walked over to the window and he caught himself admiring her silhouette. She turned and he flushed, but she didn't seem to notice.

"So let's go to Bordeaux and find ourselves a bank." she said, heading for the door.

He hauled himself off the bed feeling a little ashamed. "I will shave and we can have some breakfast and then we go. Okay?"

He eyed himself in the mirror as he shaved. Was he attracted to her? Or was it just something that he could dream about because he was free to, or she was free. She wasn't his brother's wife any more. He shook his head at his own meanderings. Then another thought struck him. Was she his guru's mother? The razor poised under his chin was frozen in midair by the thought. Was Pia, was Ashtavakra, his guru?

The question pounded in his head, as he faced it. Could this tiny misshapen ragdoll person be his guru? The closest person to a guru he had ever come across, Padmananda, had indicated she was. Was that so strange? After all what did he really know about gurus? So far Pia had certainly shown every sign of not being the usual eight-year-old, so why not? And if she was, if she really was, then he would ask the questions he yearned to ask. And if she was, then he could find out what the little book was trying to teach him. And if she was, he would live a happy life. And if she was, then Claire was like…She was like the Virgin Mary, mother of Jesus. And then he laughed. He laughed long and fully. He laughed at the fool in the mirror with the half-shaved face. He laughed at the upraised razor. He laughed at the small chipped mirror hanging on its rusty chain, on the grey wall in the dingy upstairs bathroom. And he laughed at his own good fortune. Life was good.

When he went downstairs, he had to compose his face before entering the kitchen. His mother was there with Claire. He kissed his mother on both cheeks and she held him for a moment at arm's length looking at him.

"You look healthy today. You must have slept well."

"*Oui, Maman.*" When he turned to face Claire, she smiled at him warmly and he caught the first up-swell of embarrassment tingeing his own cheeks. The thoughts that he had been having, he realised, could well become conversation. Even though she probably did not read thoughts, her daughter most certainly did. As he sat at the table and broke off a hunk of the *pain de campagne*, he remembered the lines from the *Samhita* about controlling the mind. Now he had a really good reason to work on it.

There was no sign of the other three. He was glad of that. He wasn't at all ready to have his thoughts discussed. Finishing her coffee, Claire slipped away to check on Pia. His mother took the opportunity to speak her son privately.

"Do you think she really knows how much money it will take to fix up this château?"

He thought about it. "She has worked as an interior designer, she said, so maybe she has some idea."

"Théophile," she said, dropping her voice to a whisper, "It will take millions of euros, millions. Do you think she has that much money?"

"I don't know. Maybe she does. She said Hugues had been very successful at what he did. In Australia it is maybe easier to become rich than in France."

She looked at her surviving son with a look of pain. "Hugues was always the brilliant one. If only…" She sighed. "What is past is past."

He chose to let her sit with that and poured himself more coffee. Always Hugues was the brilliant one.

His mother took a deep breath, finished her own coffee and passed her bowl to her son for a refill. As he poured, she asked "Where will you take her? Which bank?"

He shrugged. "A bank is a bank. I don't know. One of the big national ones I would suppose."

His mother shook her head. "No, no. She will be cheated by a French bank. She will not understand how it works. And you have no experience with that. If Hugues were here, then of course he could do that."

Théophile chose to let that pass without rising to the bait. "If not a French bank, then where?"

"I have heard of an English bank. It is the bank for the wealthy English people who come and buy old French houses in the Dordogne and renovate them. That would be much better."

"That's a good idea, *Maman*." What did he care which bank she went to? If it was a British bank so much the better. He wouldn't have to translate.

"I will find it in the *annuaire*." His mother was already at the sideboard hunting for the phonebook. "It is called Banque Clae or something like that." She spread the phonebook out on the table and he came round behind her to look over her shoulder. He inhaled the old familiar perfume and he felt like a little boy again, under the control of his vigilant parent, the onlooker a little behind the action. He shook off the image as he watched her finger trace down the list of banks, there were so many. There was no Banque Clae. He leaned in and reread the list. Then he noticed a tiny listing for Barclays Bank.

"Perhaps it is this?" he ventured although the two-line listing did not look like something that would attract rich Englishmen.

"You must call them and ask." she said firmly. "Speak in English and they will respect you."

At that moment Claire came back. "They are asleep in there." she smiled. "They are like three little girls all in the same bed. It is so cute." Théophile translated and his mother nodded. "Such a long journey for the child." She turned to Théophile. "Tell her what we have decided."

Claire was happy with the idea and keen to go. Théophile noted that the bank would probably not open until nine, so they would have to wait until then to call. Claire was restless. "How long does it take to get into Bordeaux?"

"Forty-five minutes, depending on the traffic."

"So let's just go and explore and find the bank. Can we do that?"

Théophile smiled at her. She was so enthusiastic. Thank God for that. He nodded. "Of course."

"Would your mother like to come with us?"

When he asked her, the response was emphatic. "No! You must only speak in English with them. I would be a burden to you."

He chose to soften the image in his translation, and Claire came round the table to kiss her mother-in-law on the cheek. Then she turned to Théophile. "I'm ready when you are."

The way she smiled at him, the lilt in her voice, he felt his rising attraction for her. He would have her all to himself all morning. This would be very pleasant.

With her travel documents and her tiny laptop in a small briefcase on her lap, Claire sat beside him in the grey Citröen as it humped and bumped down the driveway. "We must fix the driveway too", she said, "and rebuild the entrance. Just imagine the arch, with the big gates and the plaque with the name engraved. What is it again?"

"Château des Mésanges."

"What does it mean?"

"*Mésanges* are small birds. I do not know their name in English." He kept his eyes on the track. "I hope you are aware of just how big this project may become."

"We'll see", she said. "Right now I feel very strongly that I owe it to Hugues. And after what Pia said, I have no doubt."

He drove onto the winding tree-lined road beyond the château, through vague swathes of morning mist. Here and there, vineyard workers were already out with their high-wheeled narrow tractors threading along the rows of green burgeoning vines. Several were towing tanks spraying liquids in high arcs.

"What are they spraying?" she asked.

"Poison. The vineyards have many, how would you say, adversaries. Is that the right word?"

"You mean like pests?"

"I don't know the words for them all in English: diseases and insects and fungus. The grapevines are very sensitive. You see the roses planted at the end of the rows? They are the guardians of the vines. If the roses get sick, then the vine will also get sick. So the *vigneron* watches the roses to see what poisons to use."

"I always imagined that the grapes just grew and you picked them, squashed them and put the juice in a bottle. After a while that turned into wine."

"In principle. The science of oenology is a little more complicated."

"You must know all about wine. Did you work on your father's vineyard?"

"Never." He drove for a moment while he thought about his father. What should he say about the father-in-law she had never met? "He was never at all interested in the vineyard, so he made a contract with our neighbors. It is that family who run it now. My father, he thought of himself as a businessman, an entrepreneur. When I was quite small he had the Domaine de L'Aigle D'Or become the managers, so he would be free to, I don't know, make a fortune I suppose. As my mother told you, we are supposed to share in the *recolte*, the harvest. That is all we do about the vineyard now."

"And she believes she is being ripped off?"

"Pardon?"

"Being cheated."

"Who knows?" He arrived at a T intersection and as he turned, he pointed across to the left. "That is the Domaine de L'aigle D'Or."

She looked at the sweeping hill of green vines, neatly manicured with a fine Maison Bourgeois rising beyond it. A little farther along, he creamy stone *chai* stood closer to the road. The entrance to the vineyard had gracious inward curving stone walls and an antique looking sign offering "degustation".

"It looks well kept."

"Oh yes. Jacques knows what he is doing. I went to school with his brother. Their father was one of the most prestigious *vignerons* in this appellation."

"One day our château will look like that."

He smiled at the "our". « Maybe. »

«Maybe you will take over the vineyard again, bring it back to the family.»

The idea of him running the vineyard, Théophile the *vigneron,* that was a notion too far.

«It is not likely.» was all he could manage.

After a few moments of silence, she spoke again. "You said your father was an entrepreneur. What did he do?"

"Actually," he said, "I said he thought of himself as an entrepreneur." Then he made a decision to tell her just how it was. What was the point in trying to pretend? "My father was a man who had many different ideas about how to make money. Unfortunately, he did not have the patience or the discipline to study or to research. He would hear of new ventures and embark on different things, but each time, as far as I know, he only lost his money. There were some cocoa plantations in Senegal, and something about eucalyptus trees in Brazil, and another project for gas in the Ukraine. I don't know so much about any of these. I just heard my parents fighting about how the *patrimoine* of the family was being thrown away."

"What is *patrimoine?*" She gave it a fair imitation.

"It is, how would you say, what you have to give to your family when you die."

"Inheritance."

"Oh yes."

"So that's why there is no money to take care of the château?"

"And perhaps there is one other thing. My mother will never speak to you of this, but as you are now part of this family you should know it. My father is still alive and he lives in *Argentine.*" Théophile used the French pronunciation for the country.

"Hugues never spoke of that."

"He would not. It is not something of which he would be proud."

"Your father did something bad?"

"He took what was left. I do not know how much that was. He went with a woman from the village, a young woman. He tried to contact me one or two times some years ago, but I did not reply to him."

Claire stared out of the window as the vineyards gave way to the beginnings of the Bordeaux suburbs. Théophile glanced sideways at her to see how she had taken the new information. She seemed to be still.

"I hope it does not upset you that I tell you about this."

"No. It is important that I know." She put her hand on his knee. "Thank you for telling me." The hand on his knee was warm and the warmth of it infused a chemistry that he feared would show. After a moment she took it back unaware and gazed out of the window. He crossed the Rocarde and began the descent towards the wide curve of the river Garonne.

He indulged in a little running commentary on what they were seeing as they passed through the Bastide suburbs of the city, the right bank, the less prestigious side. They joined the traffic waiting to cross the Pont de Pierre into the old city.

Claire was impressed by the elegant uniformity of the Bourse, the stone warehouses and customs offices from the days when Bordeaux exported wine to the world. All had been scrupulously restored and her decorator's eye loved the lines and the textures. The city curved away from the Pont de Pierre, demonstrating why it is called the half moon city, and the organised solidity of the creamy four-storey buildings lined the curve, giving way farther down to the quayside warehouses, now restored as modern restaurants and boutiques. It was a cityscape of European sophistication, elegance and understated self-confidence. No high-rise modernity ruined the skyline, leaving its punctuation to the church steeples. The sleek blue-grey seven-car trams slid along the quay and away into the labyrinthine city itself. Everywhere there seemed to be an air of prideful purpose. She loved it as soon as she saw it.

Near the shallow reflective pool in which already a few children were running barefoot, Théophile found a tiny parking spot, taking several attempts to wedge the Citröen into it. As the car sank thankfully back on its haunches, Claire smiled at Théophile. "I like Bordeaux. It feels like a city I want to explore and get to know."

He smiled back, happy in her close company. "I will enjoy being your guide."

Barclays Bank stood resolutely behind its stone exterior, in the company of other august financial institutions. The solid glass revolving security door allowed entrance to just one at a time, so Claire came in on her own. She smiled at the woman behind the curved counter and said "Good morning" brightly, not thinking to try anything French.

The response was immediately in English although French accented. As Théophile came in, Claire had already begun to explain why they were there.

A few moments later, a pink-faced man in expensive jeans and an open neck shirt appeared and, in strongly Geordie-accented English, introduced himself as Jeremy Wheeler. They all shook hands and gave their names. He indicated a side door and led them through a series of connected corridors past open-doored offices, where Théophile imagined obsessively ambitious financiers played all day with other people's fortunes. As they walked, Jeremy was asking the questions he needed, to get a sense of who he was dealing with.

By the time they had reached his office overlooking the inner courtyard of the renovated eighteenth century building, he was very enthusiastic. In her descriptions of what she wanted to do, Claire had used the word "we", while Théophile had said not one word. She seemed very comfortable in this kind of surrounding, where he was an alien. They settled into chairs facing a fine oak desk and Jeremy settled himself behind it, turning his computer screen round so they could see it.

"So," Jeremy began, "you have a very exciting project. I am sure we have just what you need. You will want liquidity, flexibility, am I right?"

"My intention is to transfer funds from Australia, as we need them. I suppose we would pay workers by cheques?" She looked at Théophile for confirmation.

He was surprised to be asked anything and felt more and more like a spectator. At this he shrugged. "That would be the way."

"Will you need it to be a joint account?" asked Jeremy.

Claire looked puzzled. "What do you mean?"

"You and your husband."

"Oh!" And she laughed a rich free kind of laugh that Théophile adored. "Théophile is my brother-in-law. That's why we have the same surname."

Jeremy was suitably apologetic. Théophile on the other hand, allowed the sweetly wistful thought that being her husband would be rather good. And then, as Claire and Jeremy talked on, he caught himself and he remembered his resolve to control his mind.

After an hour, in which Théophile mostly sat quietly, Claire stood, carefully inserted a thick wad of brochures and contract papers into her briefcase and shook hands with Jeremy. Jeremy escorted them back to the bank forecourt, heartily shook hands again and hoped to see them very soon. He wished them great success with the venture and said he would love to see some of what they were planning as it evolved. Théophile imagined Jeremy was very pleased with the morning's proceedings, and he acknowledged that his mother had made an astute assessment of the financial institution, even if she didn't know its name.

As they walked away along the nobly named Rue Esprit des Lois, Street of the Rights of Man, honouring the philosophical writing of the local hero Montesque, Claire looked around her. "This all feels so good." She looked up at him, smiling warmly and his heart melted. "Thank you Théophile. I am so glad that I have met you and that we can do this together." Then she gave him an impulsive hug, while two high-heeled tight-skirted French women, both glued to cell phones, had to dodge around them. He tentatively put his arms around her, breathed in her subtle perfume and drowned in it. After a second she pulled back and said: "Let's celebrate with some really good French coffee."

He took her to an elegant coffee shop under the columned extravagance of Le Grand Théatre with the statues of the muses dominating its facade. This was an establishment he would never have thought to patronise on his own, and he wondered if this was a sign that his lifestyle was about to make a radical shift. They were served two *grand crèmes,* which came with a little platter of petit fours. The bill was deftly slid under his cup and he dreaded to think how much it was.

She gazed up at the immense ceiling and out across the stone edifices of Place de Tourny. She admired the sharp triangle of the building opposite, which he told her was the school for wine. Beyond towered the great column of Quinconces with its flamboyant fountains sparkling in the sun. She looked at home here, and Théophile, considered that, while Claire wasn't French, she would find her place in France. He let himself imagine that he would be part of that place.

XVIII

Shaafia became aware of Pia while still deeply asleep. The child had slept between her and Kate, and for most of the night Shaafia has sensed Pia there. Early in the morning, however there was a change. It seemed that Pia was trying to reach out to Shaafia. The call drew her from her deep sleep, and she felt her consciousness rising to meet the call. Then as a dream image, Pia was there, but not in the physical form that Shaafia slept next to. In this subtle form Pia was tall and erect, fine-boned and airy, silvery in colour and radiating light. Nonetheless Shaafia knew instantly who it was.

"Now you can see me as I truly am." the radiant form said. "If you can see me as this, then you will always know me, always."

Then Shaafia woke. Pia lay on her side, her good eye fixed on Shaafia, her breath coming in laboured, stertorous gasps. Shaafia stared into the eye for a moment, holding the silvery form in her mind as she became conscious of the sound of the breaths. She sat up and saw Kate still sleeping on the other side. She moved Pia a little so that she was more on her back, but her breathing became even more laboured. Shaafia leaned over and tapped Kate.

Kate snapped awake in her nurse's instant response mode.

"She is not breathing very well", whispered Shaafia.

Kate sat up and listened. Then she knelt on the bed and pulled Pia upright, tapped her smartly over much of her back until her breathing became normal again.

"She does that quite often", Kate said. "Her lungs are weak and her bronchioles clog up." She looked at Pia. "You gave her a fright, you did."

Pia said *"Ha!"* and dropped into Kate's lap for a cuddle.

Kate looked at Shaafia over the top of the child's head. "You'll get used to it", she said. "Our baby has a lot to deal with on the physical level."

They got up and Kate prepared Pia for the day. Shaafia watched as the flimsy arms and legs came out of the white linen nightdress with the flying angel designs and the utilitarian night-diaper. Kate ran the shower, waited for the hot water to kick in and then gently soaped and rinsed her charge. Shaafia was moved by the frailness of Pia's body, so brittle in its whiteness, so absent in musculature. She also admired Kate's ease, her skill, her smooth actions, her thoroughly trained nurse's competence. All the while, behind Shaafia's eyes, the divinely erect silvery form shimmered.

Once Pia was dried and dressed, they went out to the kitchen. Madame de Fortelle was there by herself. Pia gave her a sweet little "*coo-coo*" greeting and the woman got up to kiss her granddaughter on both cheeks.

"Did you all sleep well?" Madame de Fortelle asked. And before Shaafia could translate Pia gave a big "*Ha!*" which made them all laugh.

Madame de Fortelle poured juice for Pia and the others helped themselves to coffee. As they did, Madame de Fortelle told them that Claire and Théophile had already left for the city to find a bank. Pia kept her eye on her grandmother and Madame de Fortelle became aware of it. "She watches me all the time", she said to Shaafia. " Can she see with the other eye?"

"It doesn't focus." Kate, said when she heard the translation. "But she can see you very well."

Shaafia translated this and added "Pia tells you she sees you with the eye of knowledge."

Madame de Fortelle frowned. "What is meant by this?" She stared fixedly at Pia, but she found the eye regarding her to be intimidating and she soon looked away.

"Pia says do not be afraid."

Madame de Fortelle was speechless. The colour rising in her cheeks, she glared at Shaafia as if she was responsible for this message. Her fingers agitatedly tore apart a small piece of *pain de campagne* and scattered the crumbs on the table.

Kate quietly asked Shaafia what had been said. As the translation came Pia gave her a little "*coo-coo*." Kate put some fig jam on a small piece of the bread and fed it to Pia. As she popped the bread into the child's mouth, Kate said "You are giving your grandma a hard time, you know!"

Pia let out a wild "*ha!!*" and threw her arm up in the air, so that bread and jam went all over the table and her juice hit the floor. Madame de Fortelle took advantage of the mess to get up from her chair and clean it, obviously trying to hide her inner discomfort.

Kate started to jam up a new piece of bread and said: "Alright, no more hysterics till you have eaten some breakfast."

Pia ran a jammy finger along Kate's cheek as she fed her and said, without making any more mess, "*Haay.*"

Getting rid of the crumbs and the broken glass into a bin, Madame de Fortelle chose to avoid coming back to the table. The others drank their coffee and Shaafia poured more juice for Pia. Once Madame de Fortelle had left the kitchen, Kate looked at Shaafia.

Shaafia shrugged. "I must say what it is she wishes to be said."

"I know." Kate said. "Poor lady, it must be so strange for her."

They both looked at Pia. Kate watched the child chewing on her bread. Her chewing was irregular and messy, bits falling out here and there. But her good eye had a twinkle in it and she smiled at them both with her mouth full.

"So now you have found your voice, Miss Pia, I want to ask you all sorts of things. Can I do that?" Pia simply nodded. "You know things about people. People you have only just come across. How do you do that?"

Pia looked at her and stopped chewing. Her jammy finger reached for Kate's hand and grabbed it.

Shaafia said "Pia tells you, love."

"Love?" Then Kate shook her head. "I'm sorry, that's vague for me. What does it mean?"

"She says that when you understand love, you understand everything."

"How do you understand love? I mean what do you do?" Kate looked at Pia. "You are asking a pretty difficult thing."

Pia coughed and little crumb rolled across the table.

"She says it will come to you."

"Okay.» She grinned at her charge. «I can wait."

They drank their coffee in silence because there was nothing that could be said. Finally, Kate tried a different approach. She caught Pia's eye and asked "Why didn't you do this before?"

Kate looked at Shaafia, who shrugged. "She has nothing she wishes to say."

" Maybe I'm asking a dumb question. Maybe you just weren't ready or maybe you were waiting for Shaafia."

"*Ha-ee-ya.*" Pia said and laughed a little chuckle of a laugh and lost a few more crumbs.

Kate couldn't let it go. "Do you know about me?" Her eyes were searching the child's face. " I mean before I met you. Do you know where I was and what I did?"

In response Pia suddenly lurched forward and her forefinger hit exactly the point in her chest where the emu father had pierced. In so doing she came out of her chair and began to fall from the table. Kate grabbed her and held her to herself. The finger went back to the same spot.

"Okay. You know about that." Shaafia had been watching but saying nothing. Kate settled Pia into her lap and fed her another piece of bread. Then she began to explain to Shaafia the significance of what had just happened. Kate went back over her desert experience until she got to the emu feather woman. As Kate spoke, Pia chewed happily on her bread in Kate's lap and seemed disinterested in anything else.

After breakfast they cleaned up and decided to go outside for a walk. Kate told Shaafia about the tree she had found in the woods, the one where she could settle into a little niche and sit in like an armchair. She wanted to show them. Instead of the wheelchair, they took it in turns to carry Pia and her little bag of the things she always needed.

As they left the château courtyard, there was no sign of Madame de Fortelle.

It was a sunny, still, early summer day. A cloudless morning early summer sky speckled through the canopy of fresh green oak leaves to the forest floor where timorous new ferns were springing up. They found the tree and Kate asked Pia if she would like to sit in one of the niches. She gave her a happy "*ha*" and they made a spot for her where she immediately lay back against the tree trunk, much as Kate had done the day before. Seeing that she was comfortable, Kate and Shaafia chose niches on either side for themselves and they all settled in with their backs to the trunk.

As she became quiet within herself, Shaafia began to repeat her Koranic verse, drawing the presence of the sharif, of Dada and of Adila. With her eyes closed, she could see them and she made her salaam to each of them. She saw the face of the sharif as he looked down at her outside the mosque in the market place, she sensed the subtle jasmine smell. She remembered how Dada used to sit with her head back against the old fig tree, outside the house in Casablanca, when Shaafia used to read to her in French. She remembered the sweet smile that Adila would give her first thing in the morning when they woke on their mats. She thanked them for being with her and she told them how happy she was. Truly she told them, her prayers had all been answered.

As her inner state deepened, she could see the silvery form of Pia and they were all together. They could see what she could see. Pia knew them and they knew this beautiful form. The unity of it, the love between them all, thrilled her, rippled through her and lifted her spirit into an ecstatic state unlike anything she had ever known.

High in the oak above her a merle added her sweet voice to the morning.

XIX

It was Claire's voice that brought them back from their own inner worlds. She was calling them from the château courtyard. "*Cooeee!*" Kate called back with her own *cooee* and they gathered up Pia and her little bag of supplies and set off through the trees.

Claire and Théophile walked towards them and there was a delighted reunion between mother and daughter. Turning back towards the château, Claire carried Pia and told them of their trip into Bordeaux.

"We will all have to go and explore." she told them. "It's a fabulous city. So old-fashioned, so solid, so elegant, so historic."

Just as they arrived at the outer moat, the convent van rattled up the driveway. Sisters Geneviève and Marie-Louise had brought more vegetables from the convent *potager*, homemade bread and a *tortière*. Pia was delighted to see Sister Geneviève, who kissed her heartily on both cheeks. Sister Marie-Louise was more circumspect, perhaps dreading some other uncomfortable revelation. Nonetheless she dutifully bent to kiss the child, as all adults must in France when greeting children. As she did, Pia took her hand and held it. The nun was caught. She turned nervously to look at Shaafia to see if there was something to be said.

"She is very happy to see you." And that's all there was.

As the supplies were carried into the château, Madame de Fortelle appeared. They all assembled in the kitchen and set about making lunch. Pia was propped on an armchair with cushions and she *coo-cooed* happily as the rest took up stations round the table to chop and slice. Sister Marie-Louise took charge of the stove and began heating olive oil.

Madame de Fortelle seemed quieter than usual and at one point she patted Sister Geneviève on the elbow and nodded to the back of the kitchen. The sister put down her knife and went out with her. The minute they did, Pia began to crow with loud "*ha*" calls. Everyone turned to look at her. Claire put down her chopping knife and wiped away her onion tears.

"What's up with you?" she said to Pia. She knelt down next to the armchair to be at her daughter's height. Pia ran her fingers along her mother's cheeks where the tears had run.

Shaafia said "She is very happy that we are all here."

Claire stroked her daughter's face. "And so are we!"

Sister Marie-Louise, at the stove, asked Shaafia what had been said. In response to the translation, she came over to Pia. She looked to Shaafia to translate for her. "I wish to say…" Marie-Louise began and her lip quivered as she spoke. "I wish to say, that I thank you for your words to me. I do not know who you are, but you knew what to say to me. Your words broke the chains of my tormented soul. God speaks through you. You must know that I have been in hell and you have opened the door. You have…" And she could say no more. She turned back to the big frying pan on the stove to hide her tears.

The silence that followed had the same electricity they had experienced at the convent. Claire remained beside Pia and now hugged her close. Kate and Shaafia looked at each other across the table. Théophile had quietly worked away at his pile of carrots at the end of the table, head down. No one wanted to speak.

Into this silence sailed Sister Geneviève. "I have some wonderful news!" she said and completely broke the stillness. "We, the sisters of Le Nid des Oiseaux Sérenes are invited to go to Lourdes for the Ascension of Our Lady. All of us will go. And we are allowed to invite guests. We would like you all to come with us. I have discussed this with Thérèse. She likes the idea but of course you must all decide."

Her enthusiasm lit up the room. Once Théophile had translated, Kate asked him

"What are we invited for? I didn't get it."

"Lourdes?"

"Any of it."

Théophile deferred to Sister Geneviève, whose eyes widened. "You do not know of Lourdes and the apparition of Our Lady?" He was much happier to translate than to tell the story. "Oh I am very happy to tell you about this." Sister Geneviève lowered her broad posterior onto a wooden chair at the table, and beckoned Madame de Fortelle to sit next to her. Then she looked around the table as if she was about to share a special secret.

"First let me tell you that Lourdes is a town in the Pyrénées. It is very beautiful there. A fast river, La Garve, tumbles in twists and turns through the town, with icy blue water from the snow. All around the town you see the white peaks of the mountains and you see eagles flying high above. But you must know that Lourdes is most famous because of Bernadette Soubirou. She is Saint Bernadette because many miracles took place through her intercession. When she was just a girl, just fourteen years old, she was a shepherdess, minding her flock. This was in the nineteenth century. She was a simple girl, not so clever. In fact she could barely read or write. But," the nun paused and looked around the table, "she had a heart so full of love that God gave her a priceless gift."

Pia began to laugh, which broke the train of the narrative. Sister Geneviève however was delighted by the sound of it and she turned to her. "Yes, my little angel I am sure you know what I am saying." Everyone looked to Shaafia to see if there was anything to be said. She looked at Pia, who gave her a laughing *coo-coo*, and then she said "Pia likes this story."

"But of course" beamed Sister Geneviève. "It's about love." She said this in French and as she said the word "*amour*", Pia suddenly said it back. It was clear and unmistakable, her lips coming out to make the 'moue' at the end.

Everyone was stunned. Madame de Fortelle cried out "*Ecoute!*

She speaks!" Sister Geneviève nodded. "It's the most beautiful word in the French language, so why not."

Pia began to murmur it to herself. "*Amour, amour, amour.*"

Claire had kept her place next to Pia and joined in with her. Then everyone joined it and it became a chant around the table. And even Sister Marie-Louise joined in at the stove. Finally Pia broke it up by laughing so much she began to cough. Kate came round to her, patted her on the back, then reached into her supply bag for a bottle and gave her some drops which helped her to get her breath back.

Everyone took a breath. Sister Geneviève looked around the table. "So now I will continue with the story of the Apparition of our Lady. *D'accord?*" Everyone agreed and Pia said "*Amour*".

"So, when Bernadette was in the valley of what was, at that time, the little town of Lourdes, she was close to the river with her flock of sheep."

Kate asked Théophile, on the side, "When was this?" He repeated the question for the nun.

"It was in the year of our Lord 1858. It was in February, so it was very cold. To protect her flock, she took them into the shelter of a grotto, a cave, and it was there, that Our Lady, the Virgin Mary appeared to her"

Kate asked "Do you mean she saw a vision?"

"A vision? Many will say that Our Lady herself appeared. And what is more Our Lady told Bernadette that if she made a hole in the earth of that grotto, there would be a spring. That water, she promised, would heal the sick and the afflicted."

Sister Marie-Louise spoke from beside the stove. "That water is holy and has cured many people. The son of the Emperor Napoleon was cured of a deadly disease."

"And many other people." agreed Sister Geneviève. "Now there are beautiful churches there and there are places where you can bathe in the holy water. You can see the statue of Our Lady right where Saint Bernadette saw her. It is a wonderful place."

Claire said "It sounds fascinating. I have to say that I have not had much experience with miracles and all that." Then she looked at her daughter's tiny hand, which was waving in the air. "Except perhaps this one. "

"Ah yes", said Sister Geneviève. "My heart fills with excitement when I think of our little Pia going to Lourdes. Who knows what miraculous things could happen."

Suddenly Pia jumped as if she had been surprised by something and Shaafia spoke in French. "Pia says the lady in blue and white says to drink the water is to overcome the disease of wrong thinking." Then she repeated it in English. To the Australians it meant nothing but to the nuns it was very significant.

With emotion in her voice Sister Geneviève asked "My child, can you see her?" Pia fixed her good eye on the nun and grinned. "*Amour*", she said.

Sister Geneviève sat still nodding her head and looking with so much love at the small misshapen person at the end of the table propped up on a cushion in an armchair. Then she turned to the rest of the table to explain. "It is so", she said. "Our Lady is dressed in blue and white in the statue of Lourdes. The statue was made according to the description given by Bernadette Soubirou."

"So, when do we go?" asked Claire.

"The Ascension of Our Lady is August the 15th."

"We would love to go. Don't you think so?" Claire stroked her daughter's face. Pia gave her a sweet "*ha*" and Claire turned to Kate. "Will you come?"

"It sounds amazing. Sure, I'd love to come."

Suddenly the table was alive with discussing the details of their trip. As it was still only late June there was plenty of time. They would all go with the nuns in a big bus and be housed at Cité Saint Pierre above the town where the nuns always stayed.

As they talked, the ingredients of lunch came together and they sat to eat. Sister Marie-Louise brought her big pot of chicken and vegetables to the table and served generous helpings.

Sister Geneviève said the grace, which did not get translated. There was no need.

Throughout the lunch preparations, Théophile had been aware of his own inner churning. He had come from his morning with Claire, which had carried all kinds of promise and portents, into this kitchen scene that was something else again. The words that Shaafia spoke from Pia struck Théophile and he kept going back to them: "the disease of wrong thinking." What was that? The *Samhita* basically said the same thing, and he hadn't understood it in that context either. He wrestled with this koan, trying to put some kind of order to his thoughts, as he ate his chicken.

Around him, the conversation was mostly about Lourdes. Although his mother had gone many times, almost always with the nuns, Théophile had never been to Lourdes. The two nuns told of miracle stories of cripples throwing away their crutches, blind men seeing and bankrupts finding gold bars in the streets. At least that's how it all sounded to Théophile. He had never been a believer in miracles. He was like Claire. Or was it that he wanted to be like Claire so that Claire would like to be with him. Ah see how the mind works. That must be wrong thinking, *sans doubt*.

Across from him but far down the table Pia was being fed, spoonful by spoonful by her mother. Now she looked up and yelled a "*Ha*" at

Théophile, fixing him with her good eye and he knew what was coming. Now she would shame him for his wrong thinking.

Sure enough, Shaafia looked at him too. She said "Pia wants you to know that the little book says everything." He nodded because of course she would know about the little book. She, or was it he, had written it. "She says that you are the king. You live in the château, like a king lives in his castle. She says the true king knows that he is not really the king. He is just wearing the clothes of the king."

All this had been said in French, so neither Kate nor Claire had followed. Pia then turned to her mother and was looking for another mouthful of chicken. Sitting next to Théophile, Kate asked him what had been said. He repeated what Shaafia had said, but it made no sense to her.

"Does it mean anything to you?"

"Oh yes." He wondered how much to tell. As surely as he had been sent to this place at this particular time, it was no accident that Kate was here too. Around them other conversations had begun again and so he leaned towards her and told her about Padmananda and the *Ashtavakra Samhita*. It was difficult to tell his story so that it was both simple and made sense. Even as he searched for the right words to describe this chapter of his life, it sounded incongruous to his own ears. Kate, however, leaned in close to him and listened carefully.

"So I have been studying this book every day." he said. "And you know I still don't truly comprehend what it is trying to tell me."

Kate was wide-eyed and now spoke almost in a whisper. "And you really think that Pia is that boy saint, the cripple? Like in a new body?"

"I don't know. Padmananda told me he was reincarnated in my house and I was to go back. I came back and there was no new baby or anything. How could there be, in this place? And then almost as soon as I get here, here is Pia and she knows about the book. What else could it be?"

Kate nodded. And in her turn she whispered to him about the birth of "her" spirit child as predicted by the aboriginal elder in the desert beyond Meekatharra. "The minute I saw Pia, I knew she was the one and she knew me."

They looked at each other. There was now a bond between them. They both turned to look down the table and Pia looked up. Her hand waved in the air, narrowly missing the next spoonful of vegetables, and she grinned in their direction. "*Amour*", she said.

XX

In the following days the idea of renovation took hold and everyone had opinions. Sister Geneviève had spoken very highly of the three brothers of Sister Albertine, the Costauds. Their family had lived in the village just beyond the convent for generations, artisans in the father-to-son tradition. Sister Geneviève's description of the work they had done on the convent over the years was enough to fill Claire with a certainty that the renovations were going to happen and they were going to be very good. Madame de Fortelle was both pleased and embarrassed. On the one hand at last her home might become as she had always wanted it to be, but on the other it was not to be her doing. Claire sensed her unease and was careful to ask her mother-in-law to describe what she would like to see done. At first Madame de Fortelle was diffident and said they should just fix all the things that are broken. That list in itself was vast. As the discussions went on, however, the older woman let herself begin to think about modernising, just a little. Getting electricity into all the rooms? Getting hot water to all the bathrooms? Maybe even heating? Would that be too much? Claire's bright enthusiasm carried her along and Théophile began to realise that his mother was as happy as he had ever seen her.

The Costauds came in their three white Jumpys. They came in a line, up the driveway and parked the identical Citröen vans, side by side. The three drivers were almost as look-alike as their vehicles. All three wore blue overalls, all three had moustaches and a bald spot, and all three had potbellies.

They had been summoned by Sister Geneviève and she was there to introduce them. Gregoire was the artisan mason, Eric did plumbing and electrics and Serge was the *charpentier,* the master of wood. Together, they said, they could renovate any château from dungeon to turret. They were quite familiar with Château des Mésanges. Gregoire told them that when he was an apprentice, he had worked with his father for the father of Monsieur de Fortelle. They had rebuilt some of the outer walls where the mortar had begun to crumble. He pointed to one side where the ground dropped away into a dip. Narcissus grew in profusion now but in the winter, Monsieur Costaud said, it would fill with water. "You can be certain", he said with unsmiling conviction, "the outer walls are still in perfect condition."

They spoke no English, so Théophile was kept very busy. Shaafia hovered in the background to see if she was needed, but her knowledge of building materials and the words employed in the building industry were no better than her knowledge of wine. Théophile wasn't much better but he managed. Often one would translate while the other dived into the battered family English-French dictionary.

They spent the morning peering into every nook and cranny, from the waterlogged dungeon, through the many floors that the Capricorn beetles had rendered dangerously porous, up into the attic rooms where the roof holes were noted. Each of the Costauds carried a notebook. They also seemed to be able to speak to each other in code, so that no one understood what they said to each other.

As they went, Kate and Claire took turns carrying Pia. She seemed very happy, even giving the Costaud brothers a *coo-coo* when she was first introduced. None of them came forward to kiss her however.

Every now and then Madame de Fortelle wanted Théophile to remind Claire how grateful she was, how wonderful that it was all happening and that it was her good fortune that her son had been so fortunate—fortunate to have chosen such a good wife and fortunate to have made enough money to fix his ancestral home. Claire put up with it, smiling benignly.

On the side, she quietly said to Théophile. "I wish she wouldn't keep saying that."

He shrugged. "This is all so much for her to grasp. You must give her some time to get used to it."

By the end of the tour, the Costauds had amassed pages of notes and were nodding sagely to each other and muttering incomprehensibly.

Sister Marie-Louise had made coffee for all and laid it out in the parlour. Since her little speech to Pia, she seemed to have almost moved into the château and, whenever she could, she would station herself so that she could see Pia. She seemed frightened to come too close but she wanted to be near her as much as she could.

Returning from the tour, now seated around the kitchen table, the party drank their coffee and took slices of the *tortière* that had been made by Sister Hortensia. It had a wonderfully crusty top, folded over the pie like a crispy coral reef, and the pie was filled with apple compote and soaked in Armagnac.

Sister Geneviève naturally assumed the role of chairperson for the meeting. "Perhaps the best question to ask our dear brothers is now that you have inspected the state of the château, what do you think? Is this a project you can accomplish."

Gregoire, as the oldest, was obviously the "*porte-parole*" for his team. "It is a project worthy of our skills. As this sister will attest, we have done this work on many occasions and you can go to some châteaux to see. The Sheik of, what was that place Eric?" There was a pause while the brothers conferred. "We do not remember, but he bought a château in a terrible state and it took us three years to complete. It is not far from Bergerac, overlooking the Dordogne. We had to rebuild one whole wing and the *donjons* were full of water." His two brothers nodded in unison.

He paused to see what effect his *discours* had had. Everyone else nodded and he felt justified in continuing. "We will have to make *devis* for all of the different aspects and we will need to have others to help with the work. The question is, to be honest and direct, do you have a budget and do you have a time scale?"

Claire frowned and was not sure what kind of answer to give. She glanced at Madame de Fortelle. Her hesitation gave her mother-in-law an opening to at last be of use. "We will discuss this of course, Monsieur Costaud." she said with an imperiousness that she obviously enjoyed. "We will await your *devis*. You must give us your best estimation of what will be required, according to what we have asked you so far. Is this agreeable to you?"

He looked to his brothers and they nodded. "It is", he said.

What then followed was a long and confused discussion about details and the three notebooks came back out for further notation. Dictionary pages flew and Théophile's head was beginning to swim as he valiantly tried to keep up with the two-way flow.

Luckily the three brothers had another appointment to go to and, in unison, they rose to their feet and wished the assemblage a good morning, shook hands around the table, except for Pia, and trooped out.

"So," said Sister Geneviève as the sound of the three Jumpys faded down the driveway, "This has been a very successful *rencontre* has it not?"

Madame de Fortelle sat beside the nun with something of a flushed complexion. "Oh!" she said, "you cannot imagine how my heart is filled with gratitude. That our château, can be once again a magnificent domain. My husband, who I usually do not speak of, would be amazed to see what has come to our family."

Pia said "*Amour!*" and swatted Shaafia's elbow.

Shaafia looked pained and took a moment to speak. "Pia says that he is dead."

Instantly the atmosphere in the kitchen took on an almost electrical charge, feeling as if the current of it had connected every person round the table. Madame de Fortelle went as white as a sheet, and Théophile felt a jolt that made him jump. He had been at pains to keep his father out of his consciousness, but now a torrent of conflicted emotions coursed through him, bringing a rush of nausea. All that was clear to him was that there was an innate truth to the statement. He was certain that whatever Pia decided to communicate carried a truth.

Sister Geneviève asked Pia. "Are we to take this literally? Or does it mean something else?"

Pia rocked in her cushioned armchair and murmured something incoherent.

Shaafia said, very quietly in French, as if afraid to be the bearer of such news, "She says that his heart, which was full of guilt, has broken." She then repeated it in English.

Sister Geneviève's comforting voice soothed the atmosphere. "If it is so, then we will hold a mass for him."

A powerful sob erupted from Madame de Fortelle, and Théophile instinctively went to her and put his arms around her. Neither of them had been physically demonstrative with the other and it surprised him that without a thought he would do such a thing. He held her, as she sobbed and he thought he heard, inside himself, Pia's voice saying

"Amour." He glanced up at her, but she had her head back and seemed to be looking at the ceiling. Her left hand idly caressed Shaafia's elbow.

Meanwhile Sister Geneviève, who had stood up, was taking charge. She told Marie-Louise that they would return to the convent and they would organise a mass to be held the following morning. As they were preparing to leave, Madame de Fortelle managed to still her sobbing enough to say "I wish to go to the chapel now. I must make peace with his soul."

"Perhaps we should all go." Sister Geneviève said. "What do you think?"

This had all happened rather fast for the Australians and they were at a loss as to how to respond. Claire was ambivalent. "Maybe we should stay here." But instantly her daughter let out a huge *"Nah!"* and that was that.

In a very short time they were off down the drive in the Citröen, following the convent van. Once again Madame de Fortelle rode with the nuns.

As Théophile drove, Claire quietly asked him "How do you feel?"

He shook his head. "I don't know." He glanced at her and felt grateful that he could speak with her. "I was not close to my father, as I told you. I despised what he did but I don't think I hated him. Maybe I even felt a bit sorry for him."

"Do you think your mother loved him?"

"Who knows! I couldn't really say, but he was, for good or bad, her husband and she had the old-fashioned attitudes to marriage and what is correct. Her world is the Catholic Church world, where you must honour your husband, no matter what."

They drove on in silence.

Théophile said: "I feel sorry that I could not say to him that I did not hate him. I regret that I did not reply to his letters. I think his life was a sad sequence of *faux pas,* missteps."

"Your mother wishes to make peace with his soul, isn't that what she said?"

"Yes."

"Do you think you can do that?"

Théophile thought about it as he turned the Citröen into the driveway of the convent under the leafy canopy of the platane trees. "Not in the same way as my mother, but yes."

By the time the Citröen passengers reached the chapel, Madame de Fortelle had already gone in. Théophile went after her, while Claire helped Kate and Shaafia with Pia. They had not brought the wheelchair, so Kate carried the child.

Sitting in the back of the Citröen, Kate had cuddled close to Pia, who was crooning away to herself. She had said "Where are you, Possum? What are you thinking?"

Pia's good eye swiveled towards her and she said "*Haay.*"

Kate gave her a squeeze and looked at Shaafia to see if there was anything to add. It was becoming so natural to think of Shaafia as the means by which Pia spoke.

Shaafia smiled and said: "Most of the time, she is very quiet inside. Right now she is giving her love to her grandmother." And Pia added her own "*amour*".

Once Pia was out of the car, they all went into the chapel.

There Madame de Fortelle had prostrated herself in the front and lay facedown, as Shaafia had seen her do once before. The two nuns sat in the front row side by side in prayer. The others came in and sat also at the front. Théophile looked at the prone solid bulk of his mother lying before him. He felt powerless and conflicted. To have Claire sitting next to him added yet another dimension to his inner unrest.

Kate held Pia on her lap and Shaafia sat on the other side. After a moment, she got up and went forward, kneeling down beside Madame de Fortelle as she had done the previous time. She rubbed the woman's back as the body shook. Shaafia looked up at the now familiar statue of the Christ and repeated her Koranic verse.

Into this tableau came the other nuns in time for their noon observance. They quietly took their places and after a while the swelling notes of the organ began and the nuns launched into their noon chant. The resonance of the music, rising and echoing in the domed chapel brought harmony and quietude, the voices of the nuns eddying into every corner.

XXI

The phone call came the following morning. Luckily it was Théophile who answered. Monsieur Malherbe, the family *notaire*, who had his office in Creon, handled all the family's legal affairs, as his father had done before him.

He was relieved when he realised that it was Théophile, since the man was not looking forward to the reaction of Madame de Fortelle, who to tell the truth, rather frightened him. He informed Théophile of the death of his father in Ushuai, the southern-most town in Argentina.

Diplomatically, Théophile said that it was not unexpected. Monsieur Malherbe had steeled himself for the family's reaction to his news and Théophile's calm was reassuring. He passed straight to the details. He had been notified by Le Département des Affaires Etrangers that Monsieur de Fortelle had died of a *crise cadiac* several weeks ago, but it was some time before the authorities had been notified. It seemed that Monsieur de Fortelle had lived in a small apartment by himself and his death had not been discovered for some time. Théophile asked about the woman who, he had assumed, was still with his father. The *notaire* had no information about that.

"So," Théophile said, dreading what was to come, "what do we have to do?"

"In effect it is up to you. I understand that he had no possessions to speak of. And I am sorry to say that, as his landlord had not been paid for sometime, he had the body taken away and it was given a pauper's burial. I have a copy of his will, but as there seems to be nothing of value, it is simply necessary to sign some papers. As his sole surviving child, you should be the one to sign."

That was led to a technical discussion that Théophile followed with half his mind. French inheritance laws leave everything to the children unless otherwise stated. The will, what little it contained, had not deviated from standard practice. The papers would be ready in a few days if he would come into the Creon office.

"Do you think," the *notaire* was hesitant to ask, "you will want to repatriate the body?"

"I will have to ask *Maman*."

"Of course." And there followed the expected platitudes of condolence before the *notaire* was gone.

Instead of looking for his mother, Théophile went to Claire. It was a sunny morning and all the others were out in the courtyard sitting on the benches along the walls facing the open space above the inner moat. Pia sat on her mother's lap while Kate and Shaafia sat side by side. Their morning coffees were on a little green wooden table with three out of four good legs.

Kate was telling them about living in the desert and how difficult it had been to get beyond her upbringing and her prejudices.

"And you would eat a snake?" asked Shaafia whose eyes were wide with amazement.

Théophile approached them with a warm feeling of friendship. What he had just dealt with was so much easier with all of them in the château. If it had just been his mother and himself? He shuddered to imagine the scene.

They looked round as he came out and Pia crowed a greeting.

He gave her a little bow, saying "*Bonjour, Mademoiselle*" and he bent to kiss her on each cheek. She stroked his cheek and said "*Amour*".

Then he settled on the bench beside them, poured himself a coffee from the *cafetière* and told them about the phone call. When he had finished, they sat in silence with their coffees.

Finally he said, "Have you seen Maman?"

Nobody had, but Shaafia said "Pia says she is getting rid of his shadow." This was said in French and was followed by a short discussion about how to translate *eliminer son ombre*.

"Then I know where to look for her." Théophile said, drained his coffee and went upstairs.

In the room to which she had banished all her husband's belongings, his mother was now huffing loudly as she pulled bags and piles of clothes from broad ceiling-high wardrobes. She had her back to the door and did not hear him approach.

He watched her and then said "*Maman?*" She turned her flushed and sweaty face towards him. He told her of the *notaire's* phone call and she nodded. Then she put down the gabardine coat she had draped over her arm and sat on the unmattressed single bed frame, the only other furniture in the room. There she breathed heavily for a moment, as if recovering from a marathon, before she looked up.

"*D'accord, d'accord.* It was to be expected. Did you ever have any doubt we would receive such a call?" He shook his head. "Do you have any doubt that this child has knowledge that is not normal."

"No, *Maman.* She has shown us what is she capable of."

"Then it is not a surprise. And do you know, I can now say, without shame, I have lost my husband. I am a widow."

"There is no shame in being a widow."

"No. But there was a deep shame in being a woman whose husband did not wish…" She let it go.

He came and sat next to her on the bed frame. It squeaked under his added weight. "We are asked to consider bringing the body to France."

She sighed deeply. "Of what use is his body to us?"

"It was just a question Monsieur Malherbe was required to ask."

"Do you wish it?" His mother turned to look at him, and he shook his head. "Then we will leave it at the bottom of the world where he put it. We will say the mass as we planned."

He gave her a hug and got up. He knew she would doggedly continue. "When you are ready," he said. "We can give all this stuff to the Croix Rouge."

She remained seated on the bed frame. "You do not wish to have anything of his? This coat is very good quality. It is English." She flipped back the collar to show the lable. "*Chez* Marks and Spencers."

He stood in the doorway. "No *Maman.* Thank you." Then he turned and left her to her memories and the last vestiges of her husband. Théophile called the *notaire* and passed on the message. He was told there would be formalities, in the fullness of time. The *notaire* wanted to give them time to grieve.

As Théophile went out into the sun he checked in with himself and felt no onset of grieving at all. He recognised that his father had long since ceased to play any significant role in Théophile's universe. What was buried would stay buried. The sun on his face and the company of his new family warmed him perfectly.

XXII

The mass was simple and free from emotion. There were flowers from the château, the nuns made up most of the congregation with a few people from the village. Now in identical suits the three Costauds were present, escorting three very dissimilar spouses. Father Lefait officiated. Madame de Fortelle had dressed as a widow but did not wear a veil. She had applied her make-up and carried herself almost regally. The others had put on the most respectful clothes they had.

At the end of the mass, for the communion, Théophile accompanied his mother, which always pleased her. As they stood at the chapel's rail with the nuns accepting the body and the blood of Christ, there was a small commotion behind and they turned to see Shaafia bringing Pia forward to join them. Shaafia said to Sister Geneviève. "She wishes that we should all do…this." She was not sure what to call it.

Sister Geneviève looked pained. "It is not possible., she said, looking to the priest for confirmation. "It is for Catholics who are confirmed in the church. I am sorry."

Claire and Kate had hastily stood up but now hung back feeling awkward. Claire saw the troubled look on Shaafia's face and Pia let out a huge cry, not exactly a scream but an animal sound of perhaps rage, perhaps anguish. Claire rushed to her and took her from Shaafia.

"What is it?" She held her daughter tight. Pia was breathing rapidly and still made loud sounds. Claire took her away from the group of nuns, and Shaafia followed as she hurried with Kate from the chapel. The nuns had all turned to face them and watched in stunned silence.

The communion continued once the door had closed, but with a palpable tension in the air. As soon as Théophile had received communion, he hurried out.

He found them on the lawn, sitting on a bench in the generous shade of a maple. They looked up as he approached. Claire held Pia and rocked her with the other two on either side. As he approached, Shaafia said. "I explained what she wanted. She is very upset that she could not be with them in the love of God."

He nodded and squatted down in front of Pia. He rubbed her back as she lay against her mother's chest. In English, he said "There is a difference, I think, between love for God and the rituals of the church." Then he waited to see if she would respond.

Slowly she pulled back and her good eye focused on his face. "*Amour*" she said and let herself fall backwards so that he had to catch her. Then she wriggled round so that she could put her arms around his neck and she held onto him as best she could. It moved him deeply. He was still holding her when his mother came out of the chapel.

He watched her come across the lawn trying to gauge what she felt. Her step was purposeful and steady. When she reached the maple, she looked at her son holding her granddaughter.

"I wish to say," she began, as if she had been rehearsing as she walked across the lawn, "I do not understand this daughter of my son. But I wish to ask her, please, that she forgive us for our…" She searched for the right word, the *mot juste*. ". . . Our old ways, our stubborn and rigid adherence to the rules." Madame de Fortelle paused frowning. "That is all I wish to say." Théophile translated it into English and there was a silence. Pia continued to hold Théophile and she quietly crooned "*Amour*."

After a moment Shaafi said: "Pia says, it is not necessary to forgive. This moment of love was lost. There will be others."

Madame de Fortelle nodded. Then she took her seat next to Kate on the bench and they all sat in silence.

When Sister Geneviève came to join them, no one had spoken. She had anticipated upset but sensed the air of peace in their silence, and she said nothing.

Then Sister Marie-Louise called from near the chapel. "Are you coming?"

Sister Geneviève told the family party that the nuns wanted to invite them for morning refreshments. They had prepared something in honour of the mass. Together they got up and began walking towards the convent. As they walked, Shaafia repeated to the Geneviève what Pia had said. She nodded. Then she looked over at Pia. "I would wish to share what you have said with my sisters, if you will permit." Shaafia repeated it in English.

Pia pushed back from Théophile's chest so that she could see the nun clearly. She said "*Hah!*" and dropped back again.

Once they had gathered in the parlour and had their tea, coffee, fruit juice and the usual petit fours, Sister Geneviève tapped her teaspoon against her cup for silence.

"I have something I wish to tell you all." She looked around the room at the assembled nuns, Father Lefait and the family. "You all know our dear Thérèse of course. Many of you will have met her son Théophile. We offer them both our condolences for yet another loss in their family." The sister paused to let her words sink in. Then she went on: "For those who have not yet done so I wish to introduce the wife of her late son Hugues. This is Claire." She looked at Claire who was getting the translation from Shaafia. Not sure what to do, she awkwardly got to her feet and bowed to the nuns. Then she sat again.

"This is her daughter, Pia" Sister Geneviève rested a gentle hand on the child's head as she lay in Théophile's arms. Around the room the nuns leaned forward to look at the child

"This is a very special child. I wish to explain to you what happened in the chapel. She felt our love for God, and she wished to join us in that moment of communion. I want to say to you all that it was a moment of great beauty that I did not have the grace to recognise. I take this moment now to tell her, before you all, that I will try not to ever miss the God-given instances of beauty again." She looked at the assembled nuns who seemed to be enthralled by what she had said.

From behind the coffee pot Sister Marie-Louise spoke. It took them all by surprise, as she was not known as much of a speaker in public. Her voice was a bit gruff and embarrassed as she spoke, but the force of what she said, stunned the room.

"This child is a saint. She is a saint sent by God. God has given her gifts of his grace. She has shown me her powers of grace, and I know beyond all doubt, she is divinely inspired."

The other nuns stared at Marie-Louise in stupefaction, both at what she had said and the fact that she was the one who said it. Hortensia turned to Sister Geneviève and asked "What's our sister saying?"

Sister Geneviève put down her coffee cup. "There is some truth to what Marie-Louise has said." She looked around the room, rather regretting that the priest was still present. She chose her words carefully. "Since Pia has arrived, I have been privileged to see that she does in fact seem to be a very specially gifted young person. She has shown me that we can be too hasty to judge the appearance of others. She may have physical handicaps but, as our dear sister has said, in so many other ways she has been graced."

Hortensia had been frowning at this. "But Marie-Louise believes she is a saint?"

The priest felt called upon to add his opinion. "To be a saint, one must surely lead a life of sanctity as exemplified by the many saints of our church, One must demonstrate a devotion to God, a manifest faith, a tangible proof in the form of miracles." Father Lefait looked around, now enjoying the full focus of the room. Shaafia was trying valiantly to translate for the two Australians.

"She has done that!" Marie-Louise was vehement. "I have seen it with my own eyes. She has the divine gifts of God." The nun was flushed and belligerent.

"I think," said Sister Geneviève, keen to regain some control, "That we must discuss this calmly. I will say that I too have seen that Pia has some, shall we say, unique abilities."

"She told us of my husband's death before we heard the news", Madame de Fortelle said. This sent a ripple of response through the nuns. They all stared at Pia, lying back passively against her uncle. She appeared to be taking no interest in the conversation at all.

Hortensia seemed to have become the spokesperson for the rest of the nuns. "But does she speak?" She looked at Claire, who waited for Shaafia to fill her in. Sister Geneviève pre-empted her.

"She does not speak in the way you and I speak, no. But she has shown us that she is perfectly capable of communicating what she wishes to be understood."

"If I were to ask her a question would she give me an answer?" asked Sister Agnés leaning forward in her chair. "And how would she do that if she does not speak as you and I speak?"

Geneviève weighed her response before she said. "I cannot promise you that she would answer your question but I will say this. She has found a unique way to convey what she wishes to say. She speaks through our friend Shaafia."

Again there was a frisson of excitement rippling through the group, and Shaafia found herself uncomfortably under scrutiny. She blushed and looked down at her feet.

Father Lefait felt he needed to be in a position of some authority. He cleared his throat noisily and the nuns quietened.

"This is all very conjectural,» he said and allowed the gravity of his words to sink in. «And, I must say, perhaps not an appropriate or suitable discussion in a religious institution such as ours. We are after all, devoted to a certain spiritual ethic, which does not allow us to become infatuated with the trappings of what we might call the new age." He paused again to allow his words to be appreciated. "This is clearly a child who is not like others and I can imagine it is perhaps easy to be convinced, out of compassion for her obvious deformities, that she has somehow been given a compensating ability of some kind." He smiled at Claire, conveying his compassion. Then he turned back to the assembled nuns. " However, I find it highly improbable that this very small child, who cannot speak in the usual way, can use what we could term telepathy to communicate. And I do not think such a claim should be made."

And then Pia came to life. She lifted up and back from Théophile's chest and started to laugh. It was a trumpeting laugh, high and full. Louder than anything Claire had ever heard from her. It shook the room and stunned the priest. Father Lefait flushed and inadvertently straightened his robes as if she might be laughing at his appearance. Within seconds several of the nuns began to laugh too, almost embarrassed but inexorably pulled into the sound. Claire, Kate and Shaafia were laughing; Théophile and his mother were laughing. And although she tried to stop herself, Sister Geneviéve seemed to be laughing more uproariously than anyone with tears rolling down her cheeks. Marie-Louise, her face radiant, came across the room and threw herself in front of Théophile to stroke the feet of her now beloved Pia.

Father Lefait, the only person in the room not laughing, retreated to his chair. He frowned at the hysteria in the room and started to speak several times but stopped himself, aware that no one was paying attention. He took up his coffee cup and hid behind it.

At last the laughter died down and Claire used a towel to wipe the saliva from her daughter's front. Marie-Louise stayed right where she was. The last titters faded and into this quiet Shaafia spoke.

"Pia would like to say: to be a saint is to bring God's love into the world. Everyone has that possibility. To be a saint is be a body of love, a body in many different shapes and sizes, but a body of love."

Sister Agnès said "Oh how beautiful." She looked at Shaafia as she said this. Then she added "Is that what they say in your tradition?"

Shaafia shook her head. "It is not I who speaks. This is what Pia wishes you to know."

Sister Agnès was puzzled. "My child, how can you be sure of this?"

Shaafia shrugged, uncomfortable to be cross-examined in front of so many people. "She speaks to me inside and I repeat what she says."

Sister Catherine joined in. "How does she speak, as you say?"

"I hear her. I hear her inside."

Hortensia was leaning forward in her chair frowning. "But how can you be so certain it is her? Are you not worried it is some kind of delusion—the devil, dare I say?"

Marie-Louise jumped to her feet. "I will prove it to you." She stood defiantly and although Sister Geneviève sent her warning frowns, she told them the story of her childhood and what Pia had said to her through Shaafia. "No one in this convent knew about what I had done, except Geneviève, no one." There was an absolute and electrified silence when she concluded. She turned away from them and resumed her position at Pia's feet.

"I too have received a communication about something that no one else could know", Geneviève said into the silence. "I am now convinced this child has the ability to see what others cannot. I can testify to it. This child has made a new advent in my own devotions, that I marvel at, and for which I am most deeply grateful."

The sisters sat there is a state of wonder. Sister Albertine asked "Would she be willing to say something to us?" They looked at Pia, now lying once again against the chest of her uncle. She coughed a little and her mother leant over and wiped her mouth. Then she put her hand up to Théophile's face above her head and stroked his cheek, murmuring *"Amour."*

Sister Albertine turned to Shaafia. "That is all she says?"

Shaafia waited for a moment and then spoke: "Pia says that there is nothing more important than love."

The child continued to murmur. Shaafia spoke again. "She wants you all to know, although you have given your life to God, it does not mean anything if you have not given your heart to God." The nuns were suddenly alert and intent. They stared at Shaafia and kept looking to the small figure resting against her uncle's chest. Shaafia looked at them all and said. "If you sit in the chapel with your heart closed, then God will not hear you. If you kneel to pray before the sun rises but the windows of your heart are not open, then nothing can fly out."

The nuns were struck by the power of what was said. Only Sister Marie-Louise responded. At Pia's feet she said, in a voice redolent with emotion. "Amen! Amen!" The others sat in silence, several with their eyes now closed.

At last Sister Geneviève's soothing voice eased into the silence. "What Pia has to tell us is very appropriate; it is at the core of our vocation and I thank her for it." Théophile translated her words and the child on his lap murmured.

Then Sister Geneviève got to her feet "We have much to learn even from the smallest and humblest of our sisters. I thank our dear Shaafia for being the voice for such wisdom."

This all seemed to be the signal that morning tea was concluded. The nuns got to their feet. Several of them spoke briefly to Shaafia, Catherine, Hortensia, Agnés, Albertine. Their kind and gentle words relieved her tension. It was hard for her to have had so many eyes on her. The priest was in intense whispered conversation with Sister Geneviève, his hands and face muscles working furiously. Father Lefait was obviously not pleased with what had happened. Then he turned to leave, saying goodbye to Madame De Fortelle but ignoring the rest of the family. As he reached the door, Shaafia turned to Sister Geneviève, with an alarmed look on her face.

"Pia wants to say something to him but I am afraid of him. Can you please come with me?"

"Come." said the sister and took her hand to follow the priest. He strode towards the chapel and they did not catch up with him until he was crossing the driveway. "Father." called the nun, and he paused to wait for her. His eyes passed over the girl beside her with a frown.

"I am sorry to detain you, but there is message for you."

"Is it more of this nonsense that we have been hearing in there?" He gestured at the parlour.

"I would ask you to hear what she has to say and you may judge for yourself." She put a comforting hand on Shaafia's shoulder. Shaafia took a breath and then said: "Pia wishes you to know that she understands your anger. She asks you not to close yourself to the gifts that God wishes to give you. She says that God is pleased with you."

He was obviously very uncomfortable with this. He shuffled his feet in the gravel. "Very well." he said, hoping this was all there was.

But there was more. "Pia says that God is pleased with the discipline that you have shown." Father Lefait's eyes narrowed and his hands went to his crucifix. Shaafia took a breath, then plunged on: "The beautiful boy in Alsace, who you did not touch, although the desire was so strong…"

This struck him like a thunderbolt. His hand went from his crucifix to his mouth and he stifled a cry. Then he turned and fled into the chapel.

The two women stood together in the morning sun.

At last Sister Geneviève gave Shaafia a brief hug. "It is a difficult task that God has given you.

You must be a strong. I believe that God has chosen you."

XXIII

As they travelled back in convoy, Madame de Fortelle once again with the nuns, Théophile felt himself at peace. He had laid his father to rest, he had held his guru in his arms, he was driving his new family home to the château that he believed would no longer house ghosts of any kind. He felt he was beginning a new life. His heart was as light and as open as he had ever experienced. He dared to sense that maybe, maybe he was beginning to discover just a little of what Ashtavakra was alluding to.

Claire looked at his face as he drove and again lightly rested her hand on his knee. "It was very beautiful what happened."

He glanced sideways at her. How beautiful she looked. "Very beautiful." he said and knew to what he was referring. Then smiling to himself, he looked up into the rear vision mirror to see if Pia was aware, but she had her eyes closed.

And then the Citröen died. It coughed and bucked, and the engine gave up. Théophile attempted to re-engage the engine as the car rolled along in silence, but there was nothing. He checked the fuel gauge and there seemed to be plenty of diesel left. He let the car roll into the driveway of the next vineyard and pulled on the brake, as the convent van barrelled off ahead.

As the old girl sagged down onto her tired haunches, perhaps for the last time, he grinned at Claire. "Another death. Perhaps we will need another mass."

She smiled back at him. "Do you think it's something serious?"

Shaking his head, he said "I have no mechanical skills at all so I cannot say." He turned to the back seat. "I am sorry to announce that our chariot has no horses." Then he took out his cell phone and dialled the convent's number.

The van reappeared and soon everyone was back at the château, preparing for lunch. Madame de Fortelle, clearly upset that her faithful carrier was stranded in an unfamiliar driveway, phoned her *garagiste* in Créon, who promised to retrieve the aging dowager during the afternoon.

At lunch Claire brought up the subject. "I think perhaps we must invest in a new car. It is very old isn't it?"

"Nearly as old as me", grinned Théophile.

"*Mais non!*" protested his mother, "It is a Citrôen and therefore will be good for many years. This is something simple I am sure."

"I was thinking about it even before this happened." said Claire. "We are going to need something big enough for all of us to fit in." She smiled warmly at her mother-in-law. "We're a big family now."

Thérèse had to smile in response. "It is true, but a new car, *mon Dieu,* it is very expensive."

"*Maman.*" cautioned Théophile.

"We should have a vehicle like the nuns, big enough for everyone to fit in." said Claire. "I would like to buy one as soon possible."

Sister Génevieve leaned back in her chair. "I believe we are seeing a renovation on many levels, Thérèse." Including the whole table in her look, the nun went on. "You have offered your faithful service to Our Lord and he has seen fit to reward your offering. Now, my dear Thérèse, you must learn to accept what is graciously given."

At the end of the afternoon the *garagiste* called with the sad news that the dowager Citröen, the "*Déesse*", had suffered its own *crise cardiac*. It would cost more than the car was worth to try to repair it. Madame de Fortelle had been forewarned, and having accepted the wise counsel of the nun, she accepted his opinion with resignation. She told him that if the Citröen was of any value to him for parts, he could keep it. She mentioned the need for something larger and he immediately undertook to find her just the right thing. "Never fear, Madame", he promised. "I have taken care of your family's vehicles since my own father retired, as you must know. You can be sure I will find exactly what you require."

Claire seemed a little sceptical about this arrangement, sniffing for a mechanic on the make, until Sister Geneviève reassured her by saying that Monsieur Culasse was a great friend of the convent and could be trusted implicitly. True to his word, the *garagiste* appeared two days later with a slate grey Mercedes Benz passenger van with all the bells and whistles the Germans are renowned for. He was a genial man with a thick moustache and thick eyebrows to match. His eyes twinkled with a mischievous look, but when he alighted from the new van he was suitably serious with Madame de Fortelle. No doubt having Sister

Geneviève's supervision in mind, he was on his best behaviour. Everyone inspected the van, tested the seats, checked the space for Pia's wheelchair and tried all the buttons on the dashboard. The van, which he assured them was a very good price, *un prix exceptionnel,* was approved by all and the deal was approved. Monsieur Culasse promised to speed the paper work along. "I have very good connections at the *prefecture."* he said with an exaggerated wink. He shook hands with all concerned and was driven away by one of his apprentices in the tiniest tow-truck Claire had ever seen.

In the meantime Claire had been busy with her finances and had spent quite some hours on the phone with Alan and Vito, organising the transfers of what would be needed, both for the renovations and for their unfolding life in France. She had described her project with such enthusiasm that they both wanted to come and visit. What a romantic project, the restoration of a genuine French château! She was equally encouraged by their support and told them she loved them both. They gave her a glowing report of their own business in which she was an equal one-third partner, and she promised them they would have their own beautifully restored rooms when they came to visit Château des Mésanges. «Come soon! You wont believe it till you see it!»

At the French end, Jeremy at Barclays Bank had been very eager to help, not altogether altruistically, Théophile thought, as the sums of money involved were not small. Théophile took Claire into Bordeaux several times in a rattle-prone Fiat Pinto, loaned by the *garagiste,* while the Mercedes van was acquiring its *carte grise.*

The bank seemed to require endless papers, the norm of the French bureaucracy for all fiscal matters, and one by one they were duly signed. Claire found herself in possession of a French chequebook. The French have total trust in chequebooks, Jeremy assured her. "You can even use it in the supermarket!"

Theophile made sure that each visit to the bank included an excursion to one or other of Bordeaux's attractions. He showed Claire the Roman ruins of the amphitheatre at Palais Gallien on a sunny summer's day when not one other tourist was in sight. "Why don't people come to see this?" she asked him. "It's incredible, two thousand years old and so solid."

He shrugged in reply. "Perhaps it is because, you must understand, in so many places all over France you will find such vestiges. For us it is normal—as it is maybe for you to see kangaroos."

«There are no two thousand year old kangaroos.» she smiled mischeviously

On another day he walked her through the Arab quarter of the city, down narrow angular streets on which tiny shops selling Moroccan spices and cheap phone cards to the Maghreb mingled with African braid salons and kebab vendors. They drank mint tea in a single-fronted dark café where everyone but them spoke Arabic. "I feel like I am in Africa." she whispered.

The streets of the Arab quarter opened out at the Basilica of Saint Michel with its big square facing the church, which like many in France had a detatched steeple. The square hosted a thriving flea market where stall-holders of all shapes and ethnicities were selling secondhand clothes and *objet's d'art*. Claire laughed when she saw how many of the sellers looked like hippies. "They are like refugees from Woodstock or somewhere in the 70's."

He smiled at her, loving her wide-eyed enjoyment of everything she saw. "In France we call them *baba-cool.*"

"Really?"

"It is French for the hippies."

Théophile's favourite day was when he took her on a river trip. The Garonne is wide, browny-green and tidal as it sweeps round its half-moon-shaped division of the city, the elegant formality of the Bourse, and the refurbished warehouses of the Quai that lead to the port. He pointed out the German U-boat base still intact from World War Two, its concrete defences so thick no one had found a way to destroy it. "Now it is an art gallery", he told her. "It is always dark inside, no windows, so each work of art must have its own light. One day I will take you there."

Downstream, the Garonne absorbs its junior partner, the serpentine Dordogne and together they become the Estuaire de la Gironde. The tourist boat hugged the right side of the river, past its industrial banks, but once the two rivers came together, the confluence flowed past hills bearing vineyards, with small waterside villages and equally small fishing fleets at their docks. Théophile stood with Claire in the prow of the boat translating the tourist guide's patter from the loudspeaker. The sea air blew her hair back from her face and Théophile found himself watching her rather than the passing river bank. Occasionally she would turn and smile at him but she was preoccupied.

For Claire, coming back to the smell of the sea was a mixed experience. The air of the estuary did not smell like the surf of Barrenjoey, it did not look like the dark still Pittwater, or carry the tangy air of eucalyptus, but it was the sea. It was the sea that had taken her men and thrown them back at her feet. Now she rode into it, loving the breeze and the sounds of the water passing beneath the boat, but still aching with the tearing loss of those she loved.

The boat terminated at Blaye, where they climbed the ramparts to explore the medieval fortifications, La Citadelle, built on Roman foundations. So many battles had been fought on and below these massive stone walls, so many different regimes had defended or attacked. Théophile dug deep into his unreliable memory of the history of Burdegala, as Bordeaux had been known in Roman times. Luckily ubiquitous tourist plaques helped to fill the gaps, dating the battles and naming the conquerers.

The two of them had lunch in a restaurant built into the solid officers' quarters of La Citadelle and he introduced her to the tradition of *brandade de morue*, the blend of cod and potato that for centuries had been peasant food for the commoners but is now considered one of Bordeaux's culinary specialities. They finished with a local cognac, created just kilometers away in the hinterland of the Charente Maritime. Reluctantly, he let her pay, knowing that in fact he could not have done so. Recognising his discomfort, she leaned across the table and held his hands. "This is so good for me" she said. "You are bringing the joyful part of me back to life."

As the boat headed back up river in the early afternoon, a strong sea breeze sprang up and Théophile put his arm around her to keep her warm. She melted into

his protection and leaned against him as the boat gently rocked on the incoming tide. He breathed in her scent and longed to hold her more closely. By the time the boat had passed under the Pont d'Aquitaine on the return journey, their bodies warmed each other and his happiness seemed to reach up into another impossible level.

XXIV

In the days following the funeral mass, while they were restricted to using only the tiny Fiat, everybody else stayed at the château. However the family was never left alone, as more and more nuns put in an appearance. Since the revelations in the parlour, the scepticism of a few of the nuns had been swept away by the rest of the convent's full-hearted embrace of the presence of their own private saint. One by one the sisters had found some excuse to come to the château to help with something. Hortensia offered to help with the rose garden. Agnés volunteered to help restore the tiny chapel, which had not been used, as far as anyone could remember, for more than a hundred years. Albertine sensed that someone with oenological expertise could help with the relations between the de Fortelles and the vigneron who leased their vineyard. Others fabricated almost ridiculous excuses for coming, but in general Sister Geneviève's attitude was one of benign indulgence. Secretly it pleased her deeply to watch her sisters become excited and even a little fearful of what might be revealed. Her own meditations having been wonderfully refreshed, she was filled with a renewed devotion. She saw the nuns' enthusiasm not only as innocent but also as a stimulus in refreshing their vocations. She had total faith in Pia and she supported her wholeheartedly.

Father Lafait, on the other hand, was not seen at the château .

In all this, Pia seemed to float along in her own world. Shaafia was her constant companion and Kate always stayed close. From time to time, Kate attempted to draw Pia into saying more, sometimes asking directly, and while the hugs and the one-syllable responses that came were always welcome, she yearned for more. Whenever she asked Shaafia if there was anything that Pia wanted to tell her, the message was always the same: trust in her love. Kate had to be content with that.

Théophile was torn between the intoxicating joy of accompanying his sister-in-law to the city and the mysterious company of his guru, her daughter. In the quiet of his bedroom, he studied the *Samhita* and told himself that he was understanding it better. The best moments came when he read a little, quieted his mind and sat in meditation. No great revelation arose, but he always got up feeling calmer and at peace. Often after a meditation, Pia would greet him with open arms and require a good long hug. It was confirmation enough.

There were some less than dignified attempts by the nuns to get to be with Pia and Shaafia on their own, hoping for some private revelations, but Pia mostly chose to remain silent with them, other than her gentle murmuring of "*amour*" which had become her almost constant mantra. She would *coocoo* when she felt like it and often explode into laughter for no apparent reason. Her most treasured offerings were her hugs. When she chose to hug any of the nuns, they would melt under the sweet influence of the love that poured from her narrow chest and her fragile limbs. Wherever she was, they covertly watched Pia, hoping for a cuddle or some word. They were becoming very devoted to her.

Marie-Louise had gone one step further and, with Geneviève's blessing, she had moved into a small room at the end of the outer courtyard. She was now the official cook, on loan from the convent. The other nuns took their cue from this and vied to be her assistant whenever they could.

When Sister Agnés proposed to work on the tiny chapel at one end of the ground floor of the château, tucked into a corner behind the main parlour, the other nuns all readily volunteered to join her. It had been so neglected that the door was permanently jammed partly open. The chapel had been so ignored for so long, that in the first tour of the château, Madame de Fortelle hadn't even bothered to mention it. It was if it had ceased to exist. Now anyone brave enough to try entering this former place of worship had to squeeze through the narrow crack. After Agnés had brought it up, Sister Geneviève had to be content with popping her head in, as the rest of her generous proportions did not allow her to pass. She surveyed the darkened small room, filled with dust, ruined furniture and intricate cobwebs, and whose two small arch-shaped windows, veiled by filthy torn discoloured curtains, were covered in ivy from outside. She decided it would make a good project for the nuns. She gave her permission and Sister Marie-Louise was summoned to open the door. She arrived with an iron bar and proceeded to lever the door to full openness.

Standing tentatively at the now fully open portal, Sister Agnés doubted the wisdom of her project. She was not alone in that assessment, as everyone who looked at the chapel was struck by just how impossibly dirty it was.

Why the family had neglected the chapel was a mystery. Claire broached the subject with Théophile and he shrugged that it had always been like that. He could not remember a time when either he or Hugues had gone in there. When he decided to ask his mother, she said that it was not appropriate for them to have a church in their house. She would say no more about it and he sensed it was not wise to push. Sister Geneviève had no idea of its history when he asked her, and he decided to let it be a mystery.

And that it was, until Pia changed everything.

On another sunny morning when everyone had gathered for Marie-Louise's coffee and a plate of *merveilles*, coated in sugar, they were discussing work on the chapel. Sister Agnès was of the opinion that the first cleaning should be the work of strong men in workclothes rather than nuns. Geneviève's gentle mockery of her reluctance had made Agnès defensive, and she was protesting that once the heavy dirt was removed, then the nuns could really clean it and make it into a proper place of worship. Shaafia was translating this into English for Claire, when suddenly she stopped. She glanced down at Pia who had sugar all over her face and was making a poor job of trying to angle half a *merveille* into her mouth. Pia said "*Ha*" and the pastry fell onto the flagstones in a shower of white flakes.

"Pia says", began Shaafia and the group was instantly alert. "…in the little church, the ghost of the baby is lost in the dark." She then repeated it in English. The group was stunned.

"What does it mean?" asked Sister Agnés, looking to Shaafia for more information, but Shaafia shook her head. Agnés turned to Sister Geneviève. She in turn shook her head and added "I cannot say."

"It is the eldest child of Jean-Marie de Fortelle. A girl." Madame de Fortelle spoke as if she was giving confession. Her head was down and she was staring at the ruins of Pia's fallen *merveille* on the stones by her feet. There was a silence as the others waited to hear if there was more.

She looked up and turned to Théophile. He saw pleading in her eyes and added the only piece of information he had.

"Jean-Marie de Fortelle was the son of the two people whose portraits you see above the fireplace, Fernand de Fortelle and Odile Saint Sernin de Fortelle." Then he looked at his mother and gently lifted his shoulders. He had no more to add.

Madame de Fortelle sighed and looked around the group. "The child was to be baptised in the chapel, as all the children of the family de Fortelle had been for all those years. At the moment the mother passed the child to the priest to receive the baptism, he dropped the child and…" Her head tilted down and her next words were little more than a whisper. "Her head was fractured. They say…" She shook her head and looked up again. "It was just before the first world war and the chapel was never used again."

Pia broke the silence with a demanding "*Ha*", pointing to the plate of pastries. Kate absently lent forward, took one and broke it in half, before handing it over. Pia made a determined thrust and managed to get the pastry into her mouth, but then she breathed in some of the sugar and had to cough it out. Kate banged her on the back, broke off an even smaller piece and fed it to her. She chewed steadily, as the group watched her, expecting her to convey something more. Claire passed the juice and the straw and the *merveille* was successfully swallowed. Shaafia remained silent.

Finally it was Sister Geneviève's voice that drew their attention. "It would seem that our sisters have been given some divine insight into a work that must be done." She looked at Agnés. "You have been inspired. If indeed there is an unquiet spirit here in this chapel, then we will do what we can to bring the spirit of this poor child, as our dear Pia suggests, out of the dark."

There was a murmur of approval from the nuns while Théophile translated for the others.

Madame de Fortelle took her son's hand for support as she spoke. "The heavy hand of destiny lies upon us, the de Fortelle family. It is a burden we carry." She paused while Théophile translated. "And yet perhaps, we can no longer hide what it is that has embarrassed us and shamed us for so long. Here, as we sit, on the eve of a most magnificent restoration of our domain, I pray that we, who have lived in the shadows for all these years, may be restored in every way. If God wills."

"Amen" was the heartfelt and automatic response from the nuns.

An impulse surged up in Théophile's heart and he found himself speaking. "When I was in India, at the ashram of Swami Padmananda, she told me to return to the house of ghosts, where I was born. It meant nothing to me then, but now I understand. At least a little."

The group nodded and thought about what he had said, and then Shaafia spoke. "Pia says, she has no name. She wishes to have a name and that she be remembered. Then she will be at peace."

Madame de Fortelle let out a gasp as she heard this. "*Mais oui*! It is so." She turned to Sister Geneviève. "They were to name her at the baptism."

"Do you know what the name was to be?" the sister asked.

"It will be written, of that I am certain. I will find it." And she put down her coffee cup and clambered to her feet. "Come Théophile", she commanded imperiously and headed into the château. He shrugged and followed.

Now Sister Agnès had a completely renewed enthusiasm for her project. "We will begin immediately. We must clean out that terrible mess and we must clear the windows to let in the light and we must chant to bring in the light of God."

All coffee cups were put down and the nuns got up ready to attack the work.

Claire, Kate and Shaafia were left behind with Pia. They sat in the sun, each with her own thoughts. Finally Claire said "I feel like we are in some kind of dream, you know?" She frowned, trying to find the words. "It's like, it's like…It's almost too unreal."

Kate agreed. She had taken Pia into her arms and had cleaned her up with a damp cloth from the back of the wheelchair. "It's incredible." She looked up at the towering walls above them. "Thank God I am lucky enough to be here."

Shaafia, who in reality had said almost nothing in her own right for days on end, felt that she must add something. "It is as Madame has said just now. It is God's will. In Arabic we say *inche Allah,* which means exactly that. It is God's will."

At that moment, Madame de Fortelle came flying out of the château with Théophile close behind.

"The child's name was to be Lucia", she called excitedly. "Lucia, the light!"

XXV

Two days later, just a week after their inspection, the Costaud brothers brought their *devis,* a quote that covered the overview of what they expected the restoration of Château des Mesanges would cost.

The work of cleaning the chapel, which had become the fulltime intense focus of the nuns, had absorbed everyone. Claire and Kate had ventured into the chaos several times to help, and Théophile became the closest they had to male muscle when it was required. He rather thought Sister Marie-Louise had more to offer in that department than he did, but he did his best. After his efforts, a mound of nasty mouldy rotten furniture lay outside the barbican, waiting to be burned.

Shaafia stayed always close to Pia, who seemed to be at peace with the world and preferred to be outside, even in danger of her pale skin getting a little sunburnt. They would often be found sitting together, usually in silence. What passed between them was not shared, although everyone else wondered about it.

The afternoon of the Costaud's *devis* brought the chapel work to a halt and everyone took off their dirty work clothes and washed up in anticipation.

It was a sunny afternoon, and the Costauds marched into the inner courtyard, where everyone was already assembled to enjoy afternoon tea with Sister Hortensia's homemade *madeleines.* A large Italian umbrella had been spirited away from the convent and now sheltered a circle of mismatched chairs and the rickety three-legged table on which sat the teapot.

Gregoire stood before his two brothers and ceremonially presented Madame de Fortelle with his envelope. "I trust that you will find everything is to your satisfaction, Madame." he said. The three artisans were invited to sit with the others, the whole family plus four of the nuns. Gregoire placed himself next to his sister, Albertine. Madame de Fortelle held the envelope in her hands for a moment and looked around at the assembled faces.

"This is a moment of which I could only dream. It is a moment full of deep feeling. We have lost so much. Hugues, Antoine and my husband have all left us. Our château was falling into ruin over our heads. We have had a long history of tragedy, which threatened to consume us. And yet, here in my hand, I hold a *devis* for the restoration of the *domaine de la famille.* " (This last phrase challenged the two translators who could not find a good English expression for a such a precious concept, with its different levels of meaning).

It was a speech delivered with great emotion but with a formality that seemed like the inauguration of some important monument—and of course in many ways that is exactly what it was.

With a formal bow, Madame de Fortelle turned to Claire and gave her the unopened envelope. "I ask you, my daughter, to be the one who will open it."

Pia had been quiet throughout all this, drinking her juice from a straw held by Kate. Now she spat out the straw and began to call *"Amour, amour!"* and instantly the whole table, with the exception of the startled Costauds, joined in. The nuns were delighted with this, whenever it occurred and they sang it with the same gusto as they chanted in the chapel.

Then Pia began coughing, and Kate had to deal with it. As the sounds of *amour,* echoing from the stone walls of the château, faded away, Claire opened the envelope.

The *devis* consisted of several pages with various headings, subheadings and lists, all with estimates of costs beside them. On the final page, which, she turned to without studying the rest, Claire looked at the overall total. There was no change in her expression as she took it in. Then she folded the papers and reinserted them into the envelope.

"When will you begin the work?" she asked.

It was as if the entire gathering let out a sigh of satisfaction as she said it. Gregoire was a little surprised as her words were translated, but stood up and looked around the group. "It will be our pleasure to begin the work immediately. This project will be our priority and all other work shall be second to this." He looked at his two brothers. *"Vous êtes d'accord?"* At which the two brothers also stood up and gave the group a simultaneous bow. *"Nous sommes d'accord",* they said in perfect unison. And the group applauded.

Teacups were taken up, the Costauds were offered tea and *madeleines* and afternoon tea continued. Gregoire leaned in to speak to Sister Geneviève. "They do not wish to study the *devis*? » He seemed concerned.

She smiled at him. "My dear Monsieur Costaud. You can be sure that they will study the *devis*, but you must know that they are certain of your ability and your honesty. You are trusted."

"Then I am deeply honoured."

As the Costauds were preparing to make their *adieux*, Shaafia stood up. By now the nuns were very much aware of her and always expectant of something remarkable.

"Pia wishes to say" she began, speaking in French and immediately there was a powerful silence as everyone looked at her. Pia was chewing absently on her remnant of *madeleine*. "The soul of her father, the soul of her brother and the soul of the father of her father are happy." She paused. Far off a crow called and its voice bounced from the walls of the château.

Shaafia said "They wish you to know that they give their blessings."

There was a murmur of appreciation from the nuns, including Sister Agnés who said with a deep sigh of contentment "So beautiful."

Unsure of how to deal with this, the Costaud brothers stood as a group. Sister Geneviève came to their rescue. "With this blessing you must know that your work here will be splendid. You can be certain."

They bowed, backed away and returned to their three Jumpys.

Madame de Fortelle sat at the table with the envelope sitting next to her teacup. Her eyes shone and she looked at Claire with unbridled love. Then she opened the envelope, unfolded the pages and looked at the final figure.

"*Mon Dieu.*" she gasped, took off her glasses and closed her eyes.

XXVI

In less than two weeks, three huge red elevators appeared on the backs of semi-trailers with flashing orange lights. Each truck had *Convoi Exceptionel* written across the front and they elbowed their way up the driveway, destroying branches of the platanes on either side as they came. Gregoire Costaud stood in the middle of the wide circular area in front of the outer moat, regally conducting their arrival. Following them came two more large trucks loaded with scaffolding. The château began to look like the backdrop to a truck stop. In quick succession a number of other vehicles, mostly small white vans, bumped and rattled up the drive and parked themselves in whatever shade was on offer. They disgorged workers of all shapes, ages and complexions, carrying toolboxes and hard hats.

The residents of the château stood just outside the barbican and stared in amazement as they watched Gregoire shouting instructions at men running in all directions. The three huge elevators were rolled off their transports and positioned on the three sides of the château outside the inner courtyard. Their long extendable metal arms would reach all the way to the turrets. Once they were anchored with their hydraulic feet thrusting down into the earth, the residents of the château had to retreat inside as an army of workers penetrated the perimeter and began rigging scaffolding around the base of the inner defence of château, rapidly turning the sunny courtyard into a hard-hat zone where lengths of steel pipe were thrown up in ever-rising stages to form an industrial imitation of the centuries-old ivy that clung to the inner walls.

Théophile stood with Claire in the main room looking out of the window at the frenetic activity.

"It is as if we are witness to a siege of the castle and they have penetrated our defenses", he said.

She turned to smile at him. "We won't resist these invaders will we?»

«No, no. We surrender without a fight.»

They watched for a while and then she asked him «Are you happy to see all this?"

"You cannot believe what feelings this brings to me, after so long, when I was sure everything here would slowly collapse and end in complete ruin."

His mother was close behind and she asked what they were saying. He translated and she was pleased. "It is nothing more than a miracle." she said.

The week before, Gregoire and his two brothers had arrived for a planning meeting. Naturally Sister Albertine expected to be included, and as always Sister Geneviéve filled the role of president. Sister Marie-Louise had made two golden *gâteaux basques,* deluxe versions of the classic basque patisserie, filled with cherry compote. Sister Hortensia made herself indispensible in the serving of coffee. The front room was therefore quite full as they all assembled, every nun assuming she had a prefect right to be present and finding herself some kind of seat somewhere in the château. There was a parade of people appearing with a variety of chairs and stools from different rooms. The stairs had never creaked with such regularity.

Once the coffee had been served in all the mismatched cups the château could muster, the room hummed with quiet conversation until the mistress of ceremonies called them to order. Sister Geneviève had stationed herself on as solid a chair as she could find, in front of the empty fireplace and below the august and serious faces of the de Fortelle forebears. Now she tapped her spoon against her coffee cup and everyone looked up expectantly.

In her corner, tucked into her wheelchair, Pia sat between Shaafia and Kate with Sister Marie-Louise as close as she dared. Kate had peeled and sliced an apple and Pia was chewing contentedly and humming quietly. As the sound of the coffee spoon brought the room to silence, a piece of apple got stuck in her throat and she began to cough. Half the room jumped to their feet to help but Kate simply pounded her back, the offending lump of apple shot onto the carpet and everyone sat down again.

"*Mesdames et messieurs*", said Sister Geneviève and everyone paid strict attention. "We are here today so that our respected brothers, Monsieur Costaud, Monsieur Costaud and Monsieur Costaud", nodding at each one in turn, "can describe for us the strategy that they propose in order to renovate Château des Mésanges." At which point Pia, began to croon "*Amour*" and the others immediately joined her. Sister Geneviève let it run for a moment, amused by the stoic faces of the Costaud brothers, who were still very unsure of how to respond. Sister Albertine patted Eric on the knee and whispered, "It is our new tradition." He nodded absently and wiped his forehead.

Sister Geneviève beamed at the group "*Merci* Pia for your blessings" and the others murmured their appreciation. "Now I shall ask Monsieur Gregoire Costaud to explain the plan."

He stood and moved in front of the fireplace, looking almost, Théophile remarked to himself, like part of the family tree, a descendent of Fernand and Odile who towered above either shoulder. The stolid artisan however bore no ressemblance to any of the de Fortelles as he opened a folder in his hands and nervously cleared his throat to begin.

What followed was a long and detailed description of how the renovation would proceed. Théophile kept up as best he could with the translation, working as a team with Shaafia, who manned the dictionary.

The work would begin with the roof, Gregoire explained, as it was in urgent need of attention and the best weather was right now, but of course who can trust the weather? No one was sure if this was meant to be a joke, so he coughed and went on. They would replace whichever beams in the roof were unsafe and they would replace all defective terracotta tiles on the main roof and most of the slate on the two towers. "One must always begin with a good roof over our heads." He paused to let this be translated and absorbed. He had found, he went on, a very good team of roofers who he assured them were *top de top*. At least his sister got the joke this time and Sister Albertine chuckled generously. It took the others a moment to catch on and the translaters did not even try.

From the roof to the basement, everything was covered stage by stage, basic structural renovations to precede rewiring and replumbing for the entire building. Floors would be replaced, insulation added, the stairs would no longer creak or bannisters wobble. The finishing touches would include painting and carpets as required. It would take as much as twelve months, he said with finality, closing his folder definitively. He looked around the group to see if all were satisfied, then he bowed his head and took his seat.

Pia said "*Amour*" and the others echoed it.

And so the château became an ant's nest of activity. While roofers stripped back the broken tiles and threw them down into huge industrial bins with incredible noise, other workers were penetrating the different floors and wings, measuring and estimating. The Costauds were on hand all the time, if not all three together, at least always one. The air was filled with raised male voices, screaming electric tools, cigarette smoke and swirls of dust. The residents tried to keep themselves out of the way but it seemed that wherever they were, workmen needed to be as well. The nuns toiled away in the chapel, adding their accumulated rubbish to the huge industrial bins. Albertine had requisitioned a hard hat from the Costaud's so whenever a nun took took a load out, she wore the hard hat.

For the family, although they were all thrilled at what was taking place, it was not easy to be comfortable. Sister Marie-Louise kept the kitchen as clean as she could and so that became one of the best places to congregate. Of course this meant that Pia was there much of the time, which the nun adored. Marie-Louise would bring little titbits for her beloved Pia, although she never had the courage to feed Pia herself. In other parts of the château, Pia struggled with the air. She seemed to suffer from the slightest whiff of cigarette smoke and the dust made her cough continuously.

She did better when she was outside, where she would sit watching the workers from a safe distance. Whoever was with her would park the wheelchair under a shady tree and she would watch the big machines hoisting tiles and beams high into the air. The work seemed to fascinate her and Claire remarked on it.

"She likes all this activity." she said to Kate one day as they all sat under an oak across from the barbican. "I'm surprised because usually she doesn't like loud noises."

Kate stroked Pia's hair as they were talking. "You're turning into a construction fan, eh?" To which Pia responded with a "*Nah*" that could have been a sneer.

Shaafia was sitting at her feet and looked up.

"She doesn't like it, but she is making sure they are safe."

Claire smiled. "Are you sure?" she said, looking down at Shaafia, then getting down on her haunches, she looked at her daughter. "What do you mean?"

Pia's hand came out to her mother's face and she ran a bent finger across her cheek. Shaafia said: "She is aware that there is danger in this work. There are old spirits who are not happy. She can see them."

Claire stared into the face of her child, a face that she knew so intimately and yet she also knew that whoever was behind that face was utterly beyond her knowing.

Shaafia spoke again. "There is a boy who is working on the roof. He has not put his hat on. He must do it now."

Kate stood up to look at the workers. Then she saw him, a young thin blond boy in a white T-shirt unloading planks from an elevator. She pointed him out to Shaafia, who immediately got up and went to find one of the Costauds. The other three watched her as she approached Eric, who had just driven up in his Jumpy. He seemed startled at what she told him but came around to check. Then they heard him yell at the boy to come down. The boy swung effortlessly like a monkey from one level to the next on the scaffolding till he was on the ground, where Eric berated him for his carelessness. The boy wagged his unprotected head under the onslaught of the older man and obediently went to a small white van and put on a yellow hard hat. The group under the trees breathed a sigh of relief and Pia said "*Hu*".

The tile that fell from the roof ten minutes later hit him squarely on the helmet, stunned him and made him fall, but other than being a bit shocked, he was unharmed.

This event caused a stir not only with the nuns but with quite a few of the workers. The nuns were even more convinced of Pia's ability, and as they began to talk, some of the workers heard about the tiny bent figure watching them. Some made the effort to come across and say "*bonjour*".

Not everyone was convinced. Eric Costaud had at first thanked Shaafia until his sister Albertine had explained to him where the impulse came from. He shook his head as she sternly informed him that the small child in the wheelchair was a saint and he should thank her. Eric was a practical man, and although he dutifully attended church with his wife and daughters, he was not a deep believer in anything spiritually unorthodox. He withered however under the pressure of his conventual sibling, and under her direction, diffidently approached Claire. With Théophile's help he said that he wished to express his appreciation for the care that Pia was taking of their safety. He felt quite ridiculous saying this but his sister hovered at his shoulder. Claire accepted his appreciation on her daughter's behalf.

Pia however had another idea. Shaafia told Eric Costaud "She wishes to give you a hug". His tanned cheeks flushed a delightful shade of pink as she said this, and he glanced over his shoulder at his sister. She gave him a little push and he deferentially dropped to his knees and bent forward so he was at the right height. Pia tipped out of her chair and into his arms and he held her. Claire, Kate, Shaafia, Theophile and Sister Albertine stood around them and a small crowd of other workers gathered.

Eric turned as he sensed the audience. He said to them all "This is our own little guardian angel".

The final step in this play was the next day, when the young blond boy arrived with a bouquet of late spring flowers as a tribute. He shyly approached Pia under the oak tree and laid the bouquet in her lap, mumbling his thank you. Then he turned and hurried off to cover his embarrassment. Eric watched appreciatively from a distance.

XXVII

At the end of the first week of the restoration work, as the men prepared for their first weekend—no French worker ever works weekends—the château roof was draped in wide swathes of blue plastic tarpaulin, battened down with ropes against the possibility of rain. Gregoire mounted and descended on the platforms of the elevators inspecting every corner, tightening cords and making sure the structure was watertight. Once he was satisfied, the workers shook hands with each other and all the residents, offering an elbow if their hands were too dirty, the assorted vans made their convoyed dusty exits and a quiet relief descended on the château.

It was also the day on which the nuns completed their basic cleaning of the chapel. The bare wooden floor, although still presenting more than one dubious floorboard, was solid enough to walk on. The small stone altar to the right had a tiled surround, which, once it had been scrubbed, turned out to be elegant marble. The ivy had been removed from the windows, which had been washed for the first time in a hundred years. The afternoon light poured in through the diagonal squares, highlighting the textures of the dark oak floor and the flecks of reds and ochres in the marble around the altar. On the wall facing the altar, there was the faintest outline of a fresco. This had been discovered on the first day of cleaning and since then had been treated with great care and not cleaned too closely. All the other walls had been scrubbed and every scrap of furniture and the mouldy old curtains had been thrown out.

That evening a strong breeze billowed the huge blue sheets high on the roof, making the château sound like some great sailing ship. The nuns gathered to chant for the first time in the chapel. Candles were lit, chairs were carried in and a small crucifix was placed on the wall above the altar, which now held two huge vases of summer flowers from the garden. Red and yellow roses mixed with the more natural *fleurs des champs* and wild grasses. The rays from the westering sun threw golden splashes onto the fresco, clarifying it and revealing vague figures in robes in a pastoral scene with small birds. Madame de Fortelle supposed that they represented the *mésanges,* after which the château had been named.

Shaafia stared up at them the first time she saw them, so happy to see yet another symbol of the bird with crooked wings. Kate had quietly put her finger to the centre of her chest, although none of them looked like crows.

Now chairs were arrayed for the family before the altar and the nuns crowded around them. In the centre sat Pia on Claire's lap. Sister Agnés had brought a small portable harmonium from the convent and somehow most of the nuns had managed to find a way to be present.

Once everyone had squeezed in, Madame de Fortelle stood next to altar to welcome them. She asked Théophile to stand next to her for translation. As he looked around at the small, totally transformed room in which he had never spent a moment as child, he had a vision of the temple of Shree Durga Prasad Ashram. He could almost see the imperious statue of the Durga on her tiger on the altar. In some subtle way he transposed the two and he felt as if they merged, one absorbed in the other. He felt a tremor of emotion flicker along his spine and he wondered if he was about to weep. Then his mother spoke.

"My dear family and my dear friends, you are my spiritual family. What happiness, what good fortune it is, that we may be here at last to destroy the darkness that has inundated this little chapel. That we hid this chapel from the world for so long, that we removed it from the sight of God for so long, that we shamefully neglected the soul of the child lost herein, for all this, I ask forgiveness. May the long years of darkness now be replaced by the light of joy. Amen."

This had all come out in something of a rush and had allowed no space for the translation, so Théophile tried his best to replicate it, with a few gentle prompts from Shaafia.

In the silence that signalled that he had finished, Pia added her own touch, murmuring "*Amour, amour*", a call that everyone joined and that grew and swelled, echoing back from the walls and the high ceiling, and to which Sister Agnés added a one-note drone on her harmonium.

When the chorus had finally subsided, brought about by Pia coughing, Sister Geneviève stood up and said "We pray that the soul of the child Lucia Saint Sernin de Fortelle may now find peace and rest in the light of God". Then she looked down at Pia. Claire was wiping her face with a cloth, but when that was done, the child lay back against her mother's chest. "I would ask our beloved Pia if she has anything more to share with us."

The room waited, watching both Pia and Shaafia. The sound of the rising wind, lifting the blue tarpaulins on the roof, echoed around the courtyard outside.

At last Shaafia spoke, her small voice rising into the high ceiling, "Pia wishes to say that it is time for you to begin to know for yourselves whether or not you have done good work. You do not need someone else to tell you."

And that was all.

The nuns murmured "amen" and there was a reflective pause until Sister Agnés began to work the bellows on her harmonium and the nuns began to sing a hymn that invoked the name of Saint Lucia.

The last rays of the sun glowed a darker rose against the fresco and the flickering light from the two tall candles on the altar added its own warm aura. As the final cadences of the hymn died away, even as the last rays of the sun faded from the fresco wall, it did indeed feel to everyone there that the light had returned to the chapel.

XXVIII

The informal inauguration of the little chapel marked a turning point for everyone in the château, both residents and visitors. When the workers returned on Monday, the noise and dust of the renovations once again pervaded every corner, trucks and vans came, unloaded and rattled off again. Workers applied all manner of screeching and howling electrical tools, but despite all that, the chapel remained a sanctuary of peace. Flowers and candles were always on the altar and Sister Agnés had become the unofficial custodian. Little by little, various objects began to add their own character to the chapel. A larger crucifix was brought from the convent. A picture of Saint Lucia in a new gold frame found a place on the wall to the right of the crucifix, while to the left, Madame de Fortelle installed the photo of Hugues and Antoine with their surfboards. In a moment of personal commitment, Théophile brought his statue of the Durga and placed it on the altar. No one said anything and it stayed there.

In the same way, the chapel became a place for people to come for their own spiritual practices. It was the beginning of Ramadan, the fasting month for Muslims, and Shaafia explained that she would not eat or drink between sunrise and sunset. She told them this was a very important spiritual tradition for her and they respected that. Often while the others sat for lunch, she went into the chapel. There, Shaafia felt a strong presence of Adila, of Dada and of the Sharif as she sat quietly repeating her Koranic verse. She would often glance up and smile at the faded images of the *mésanges* on the wall.

Théophile's meditations were deeper in the chapel than anywhere else in the building and he would wave the candle to the altar when he was alone, as if he was back in the Indian temple. He developed the habit of coming early in the morning, bowing to the statue of the Durga and sitting on the floor on a cushion against the fresco wall.

Kate began to experience the same powerful thought-free state that she had previously associated with trees, the peace of it now descending naturally as she sat in the chapel on a cushion next to Théophile's with her back to the painted trees in the fresco.

The nuns happily made use of the chapel as well, their harmonium having taken up residence. Now whichever nuns were present would replicate the convent chapel schedule in the chapel of the château. Somehow everyone seemed to find their own time to be there without clashing, and even when more than one was there, the quiet practices seemed to be entirely complementary.

At the same time there was a turning point with Pia. Her statement in the chapel about self-responsibility had struck everyone and there were many conversations in corners about what was meant. The change in her was crystallised when Pia and Shaafia had their first argument.

It happened on a hot day when Théophile had driven Claire into Bordeaux to the bank. Pia was sitting on a rug with Shaafia in the shade of one of the massive oaks facing the château with a good view of the workers. The roof had been completely retiled, the towers seamlessly reslated and the workers had begun to replace rotten window frames and to fill and reinforce various wide cracks in the structural outer walls. All this necessitated endless trips up and down, the elevators carrying timber, cement and tools. No worker dared to be seen unprotected under Pia's eye.

Kate was just returning with a basket of juice and snacks from Sister Marie-Louise in the kitchen. As she approached, she saw Pia launch herself at Shaafia, and at first she thought it was the usual hug, but it was not. Pia was hitting Shaafia as best she could with her small hands and howling incoherently. Kate ran up to them and grabbed Pia from behind, lifting her into her arms.

"Hey, hey!" Kate said, as she held the angrily struggling body. "What's up with you?"

The closest Pia came to articulating anything was "*Nah! Nah! Nah!*"

Kate looked down at Shaafia who was in tears. "What happened?"

At first Shaafia would only shake her head but eventually she took a breath and said "I cannot do what she asks."

"What was it?"

"I do not wish to say." And this set Pia off again yelling and struggling. Then she began to cough. Kate tried patting her on the back but it only got worse. She dug into the bag of supplies looking for Pia's medication and poured some drops into her mouth, but this too did not help. Then suddenly she began to cough blood. Her saliva ran red and Kate wiped it away with a cloth. Kate was looking closely at Pia, trying to understand what was going on. She held Pia out from her so that they made eye contact. Pia's good eye, fierce and penetrating, seared into Kate and they stared at each other. Gradually her coughing died down. Kate said "You are being very cruel to Shaafia, aren't you?"

There was a long moment when their eyes continued to lock, Pia's breathing short and stertorous. Kate held her there looking into her eye, until at last Pia's tension began to soften, her breathing eased and her clenched limbs relaxed. Kate gave her some more drops and sat with her on the rug. She held her close, gently humming the melody she had learned in the desert. Pia hummed with her.

Shaafia had shrunk back into her self and had not seen what had happened between Kate and Pia. With her head down, she was still softly crying.

After a while Kate drew Pia away from her chest so she could look at her. She said "You threw this tantrum to frighten her, didn't you?" And Pia said "*Haay*"

"So whatever you asked her to do, it was too much."

Pia said quite clearly "*Nah.*"

Kate reached out a hand and gently stroked Shaafia's back, watching as the crying subsided. At last Shaafia looked up and wiped her eyes.

"I am sorry to be crying."

"It's okay", Kate said softly. She turned to Pia. "Do you want me to know what you are asking Shaafia to do?"

Pia ran her finger along Kate's cheek and murmured "*Amour*".

Shaafia whispered "I will say it". She sat up and looked at Pia. "She demands that I must ask for money."

"What for?"

"She says that it is because I work for her. But it is not so. I am not working for money. I would not ask. I cannot."

"Do you mean, as a translator, or because you can speak for Pia?"

Pia said, very strongly "*Haay*", which usually meant she agreed or she liked something.

"It is because I was asked to be a translator. It is also because. . ." She closed her eyes, willing herself to say what had to be said. "It is because

I have, I don't know the word in English exactly. I must give money. I must repay my brother-in-law and I must give to the mosque in my country, I must give *zakat*."

Pia's finger continued to stroke Kate's face.

"*Zakat*." Kate repeated the word. "What is it?"

"It is money that a good Muslim offers to God. It is for the good works of God."

"Do you have to do that?"

"No." Shaafia sounded tentative in her denial.

"But Pia says you have to, right?"

"It is something that I promised I would do."

"And Pia knows that?"

"Yes."

Kate thought about this for minute as she held Pia on her lap. The finger was slowly moving up and back along her face. Up on the scaffolding a worker yelled at another worker and all three of them turned to see what was happening. A bucket of freshly mixed cement ascended on a pulley and was retrieved high up on the wall and the young blond man, wearing his yellow hardhat, applied the cement to a wide trailing crack running diagonally down the wall.

They watched the deft strokes of the trowel as the cracks were filled and then Kate turned to Shaafia. "I will speak to Claire", she said.

"Please, no", Shaafia pleaded.

"Claire asked you to be our translator" insisted Kate. "And you have been wonderful. Pia is right. Of course you should be paid."

"But I cannot. . ."

"What you do with the money, that's up to you."

Shaafia was shaking her head, so Kate went on: "I am paid for what I do. I am paid very well. I would look after Pia for nothing, just like you, but Claire insists."

Pia added her own "*Haay*".

"See?" Kate grinned. "So of course you should be paid too. We are the same."

There was no more to be said and they sat quietly watching the cement bucket go up and down, until Shaafia noticed the bloodied cloth.

She frowned "What is that?"

Kate regretted that she had not put it away. "I don't think it's anything. Sometimes when she coughs, there is a little blood. I'm not worried about it."

"You don't think she must see a doctor?"

"No."

And Pia added her own muttered "*Nah*" to confirm it. At this moment something was communicated between Pia and Shaafia, and Shaafia lunged forward and held Pia tightly, which naturally included Kate. They rocked together as three interconnected bodies.

Finally, Kate spoke quietly. "What just happened?"

"She said she is sorry that she made me cry", said Shaafia whose face now radiated a new softness. "She is happy that you will speak to Claire."

"I was going to, whether she liked it or not", Kate said, making eye contact with Pia.

Pia said "*Haay*" and tapped her finger on Kate's chest.

"Yes I know you know about that. Are you getting rough with us now?"

"*Amour*" murmured Pia.

Shaafia said, "She says the time is not long." Looking at Kate, she frowned. "I do not know what is meant by this."

"You want to explain what you mean?" Asked Kate, engaging Pia's good eye. Pia merely jabbed her finger again and said "Nah".

They sat again in silence, until Shaafia said quietly "I will do as she says. I will pay the *zakat.*"

XXIX

The meeting with Jeremy Wheeler had been quick and business-like, verging on the incomprehensible for Théophile. They were discussing bank drafts, tax requirements, French fiscal policy and Australia's triumph in the rugby tri-nations. Not even Johnny Wilkinson could save the English from the brutal Wallabies. Théophile nodded and smiled, adding the occasional inconsequential monosyllable to pretend he was following.

Jeremy invited them for lunch and escorted them several blocks to a restaurant that Théophile was certain he would never have dared to enter under any other circumstances. He was aware that he was the only man in the room not wearing a suit, or at least designer jeans with Italian denim.

It was clear that Jeremy was a regular customer as he was treated with great deference. Once they were seated, Jeremy ordered a *Pineau de Charente* for their *aperitif* and then told Claire the story. He assumed that Théophile knew the story and asked him to add anything Jeremy missed. Théophile smiled politely, not willing to admit he had no idea about the history of Pineau.

The golden liquid was poured into tulip glasses as Jeremy explained how in 1589 a *vigneron* poured some grape must into a cognac barrel that he thought was clean. But it was not and two years later when he went to use the barrel, he discovered…voilà! Pineau. Always served cold, it is a blend of white wine and cognac. Claire was entranced, both with the sophisticated subtle flavour of the *aperitif* and Jeremy's enthusiastic narration. She laid a friendly hand on his arm. "I just love all these new sensations." Théophile was aware that her hand rested longer than he would have liked. "I feel so provincial sometimes" she said, and she laughed.

Jeremy smiled warmly. "I am delighted you like it." he said, leaning in to her and lightly resting his hand on top of hers.

The menus were brought and Théophile blinked at the prices. Even the "*formule*", the set menu was sixty euros and this was only lunch. The featured wine on the wine list was Saint Margaux from the Medoc, in what he assumed must have been a very good year. It was two thousand euros a bottle. He wondered how big an expense account Jeremy had at his disposal.

As it turned out, he ordered a fine classic Bordeaux from Côte de Bourg that was not all that expensive but was, Théophile had to admit, wonderful on the palate. It was, still, more than Théophile had ever paid for wine. As they tasted it, Jeremy asked Théophile: "So your family are *vignerons?*"

Allowing the mellow tones of the Côte de Bourg to lift to the back of his throat, Théophile considered the layers of potential response to the question. Claire watched him across the table.

"The wines of Château des Mésanges were, at one time, considered excellent." He felt slightly ridiculous saying this, almost hearing his mother speaking through him. "Now, it is not so."

"But you still produce wine?"

"Not now."

Suddenly Claire leaned forward and her eyes shone as she looked at him. "But you could", she said.

Her look struck him, his heart suddenly leaping up. It was not just that she was looking at him with her alluring enthusiasm but that her words seemed to have struck something deep inside him. The thought arose: "Could he? Could he somehow bring his family vineyard back?"

"I..." He took a sip of his wine. "It is possible, I suppose."

Jeremy smiled warmly. "Perhaps I am witness to the inauguration of a new vintage, the resurrection of the, what is it called?"

"Château des Mésanges." Claire said in a passable attempt at pronouncing it.

Jeremy lifted his glass. "Here's to the future Bordeaux Supérieur." They raised their glasses and Théophile met Claire's eyes. His heart was thumping in his chest and her smile rested long on his face.

Jeremy seemed unaware of the powerful energy that had just passed between them and enthusiastically described the menu options and what each dish was, very focussed on Claire so that Théophile felt less and less relevant to the occasion. His mind still swirled with the images of his family's vineyard.

Once they had ordered, the waiter brought tiny fluted glasses filled with different coloured layers. Jeremy explained that this was the *"amuse bouche"*, a small delicacy to "please the mouth" and wake up the taste buds. It was an exotic blend of green avocado, pink salmon, white jerusalem artichokes (*"topinambour"* Jeremy said in his best French accent*)* and red sundried tomatoes, marinated in lime juice. "It's on the house." He smiled and said *"Bon appetit"*.

"My *bouche* is amused." Claire said as the flavours sang on her palate. Jeremy sat back in his chair and laughed, and Théophile had to smile, despite his discomfort. The *amuse bouche* was superb.

For their entrée, Jeremy challenged Claire to be courageous and try the *boulots*, the sea snails, and she accepted the challenge, diving into them with the elegant little forks designed for the purpose. Then for her *plat principal,* she chose her first ever *pintade farci,* the little guinea fowl, packed with *cépes* mushrooms and *échalottes*. Théophile's *Dorade Royale* was as delicately sauced and perfectly cooked a fish as he had ever tasted, so he almost forgave Jeremy's chair moving a little closer to Claire's and his constant inclination to touch her as he spoke.

Jeremy had to laugh again when it came for dessert and Claire could not resist the idea of *pain perdu,* the "lost bread". "Oh I love this!" she exclaimed when she took her first bite. "It's eggy bread, like my Mum used to make, but so-o-o-o much better!"

Jeremy smiled "My American friends have the same reaction. They call it French toast."

Over coffee, as the restaurant emptied and businessmen and women filed out, Jeremy nodded for *"la note"*. Théophile tried to imagine the total but his head was not that arithmetically inclined. He mustered up his best friendly smile as he thanked Jeremy, and watched as Claire reached up to kiss him on both cheeks. Surely it was not necessary for an Australian to do that to an Englishman, he thought.

As they walked Jeremy back to his office, Claire promised he would soon be invited to come out to Château des Mésanges to see the progress of the restoration. The two men shook hands and Claire kissed her banker again.

Driving back, now in the comfort of the new big Mercedes van, Claire was expansive in her enjoyment of their outing, oblivious to the inner glower of her chauffeur. "He is such an English gentleman, don't you think? He has such good manners. I wonder if he is married."

Théophile had nothing to say about that and concentrated on the road. His mind was consumed with two contrasting waves of preoccupation. On the one hand he could not push away the references to resurrecting the vineyard, bringing his family back from their penury, contributing something tangible. There was a vineyard and it could be made to be profitable again. But could Théophile really do that? The family had let it go and he had learned nothing about it from his own father.

On the other hand he kept seeing the way Claire looked at Jeremy, and he burned. He saw in his mind the casual, easy sophistication of the English banker sweeping his sister-in-law into its world, while he, just a French nobody, a drop-out brother-in-law who was not much more use than a chauffeur.

He had to make two attempts to negotiate the driveway, as they met a massive orange cement truck coming out and they had to back out to the road to let it pass. Finally he parked the van amongst the various white vans of the workers and turned off the ignition.

Claire turned to him. "Thank you for another wonderful day. I just love being squired around." Then oblivious to her esquire's mood, she opened her door and was gone. He sat for a moment trying to calm his inner turmoil. If nothing else, he did not want to be near Pia with his thoughts in any state other than quiet. He invoked the presence of Padmananda and imagined bowing at her feet, sitting silently in her courtyard. His breathing deepened and he felt the calm that he sought begin to descend. He opened his door and went to follow Claire. She had stopped in the inner courtyard and was looking up when he joined her. Gregoire Costaud was high up on the scaffolding, yelling at several workers.

"What is he saying?" she asked as Théophile walked up.

He listened for a moment and said "He is not happy with the mixture, maybe you say thickness in English, of the cement."

"Oh." She nodded. "That's good." She turned a sunny smile towards him. "It so exciting to see them all taking this château back to what it should be, don't you think?"

"It is."

Théophile agreed but he could not match her exuberance, and she caught it. "Are you alright? You seem a bit subdued?"

He shrugged and felt the beginnings of colour rise to his cheeks. "Maybe after such a lunch, I need to rest.."

"No." she said. "You can't fool me. What's up?"

Now he really was blushing. "It is nothing."

"Have I said something?" she asked putting her hand on his arm.

"No, no. Please it is nothing."

"You would tell me if I did, wouldn't you?" she said, searching his face. "I mean we are all family now, you know." She gave him a friendly smile, patted his arm and went into the château to find her daughter.

"All family?" he repeated to himself, "What does that mean?"

Not finding Pia in her room, Claire went into the kitchen where Sister Marie-Louise was chopping vegetables. "Pia?" asked Claire and the nun pointed. "*Au dehors.*" she said waving in the general direction of the barbican..

Claire found them under the oak. The afternoon had turned very warm and Pia was asleep between the two girls. Kate was studying a "learn to speak French" book and Shaafia was sitting with her eyes closed and her lips moving.

Claire quietly approached and the two girls both looked up. She joined them on the rug and whispered: "Everything okay?"

"*Oui.*" Kate spoke with a smile, glancing down at her text book. "*Il fait beau aujourd'hui.*"

Shaafia said "Your accent is quite nice."

Pia came to life. "*Coo-coo*", she said as she saw her mother, and Claire gathered her up into her arms.

"Did you have a good morning?" she asked and received a nod. "The boys behaved themselves, did they?" pointing up to the scaffolding. She loved the idea that Pia was making sure everyone was safe. It seemed so incongruous, that such a tiny person, with such handicaps, would think like that.

Kate said. "We had an interesting discussion this morning." She glanced at Shaafia, who looked embarrassed, knowing what was about to be said.

"Oh yes?" Claire was rubbing Pia's back and the child was humming to herself.

"Well, Pia and Shaafia had a bit of an argument."

"No, no, it was not…" Shaafia, however, could not decide what it was, so she stopped.

"What about?" Claire looked down at her daughter who seemed not to be following. "Pia, my darling what have you been up to?"

"*Amour.*" was Pia's response and she tilted herself sideways towards Shaafia's lap. Shaafia caught her and held her close.

Kate said "Pia wanted Shaafia to ask for her salary, and Shaafia wouldn't do it."

"Oh my God!" said Claire, turning to face Shaafia. "I am so sorry. You know with everything else going on, I completely forgot. Pia is quite right. I will do it right now."

"No, please." pleaded Shaafia. "It is not necessary, it is not urgent."

At which Pia turned on her and hit her with her small hand. It was not much of a blow but the intent behind it was obvious.

Claire said "Pia agrees with me." Then she frowned. "What is the best way to pay you? Can I give you a cheque?"

"Oh" Shaafia looked confused. "I don't think so."

"So cash would be better?"

Shaafia lowered her eyes. "Thank you."

Instead of getting up, Claire sat still. Then she leaned over and took her daughter back from Shaafia.

"Thank you for reminding me of my duties." She rubbed the child's back and held her. For a while they watched the workers without speaking, and then Claire picked Pia up and walked back towards the château. Shaafia began to stand but Kate shook her head, and she sat down again.

"See?" said Kate. "That wasn't so hard, was it?"

"No, you are right. I wish to thank you."

"Oh, don't thank me" she said. "Thank the little saint."

"Yes. It is as you say." But Shaafia still felt inspired to give Kate a kiss on the cheek.

Claire found Théophile in the kitchen, talking with his mother and Sister Marie-Louise. When there was a break in the conversation, that she could not follow at all, she asked Théophile: "Can you help me with something?" He excused himself and walked out with her.

"Can you please call Sister Geneviève for me?"

"Of course."

"Can you ask her how much I should pay for Shaafia?" When Théophile looked puzzled, she explained. "It is terrible to admit this, but I have not remembered to pay her all this time."

His first reaction was to wonder why she did not ask him. Maybe she did not trust his opinion in such matters. Probably she was right. What did he know? Nonetheless he nodded, aware of Pia in her mother's arms and the possibility that she knew exactly what he was thinking. He was relieved that Shaafia was not there. Pia was humming to herself and seemed not to be following what they were saying. They walked together into the room his mother used as an office which had the only working phone in the château. There would be phones in every room soon.

The ever-practical Sister Geneviève had an immediate answer, which Théophile conveyed and then she added that it would be best to give it to her as cash in hand. "It is not strictly legal but it avoids so many complications."

Now Pia came back into focus. She watched as Sister Geneviève's message was conveyed and Théophile became aware of her good eye studying him. He dreaded to think what she was reading in him and was aware that sooner or later it would come to light.

XXX

That evening Théophile's relationship with Pia changed completely. Sister Marie-Louise had set up a table in the courtyard under the Italian umbrella. All the workers had gone for the day, their tools and equipment stacked around the walls, leaving just enough space for chairs and the table. The heat still radiated from the stone walls facing west so everyone was dressed in T-shirts, except of course the nuns, but even they were in the lightest materials their order permitted.

A big pot of chilled *gazpacho aux corgettes* dominated the table. Sisters Hortensia and Agnés had stayed for the meal and everyone arranged themselves, waiting for Madame de Fortelle to say grace. However before she could open her mouth, Pia let out a very strong "Nah". Madame de Fortelle peered through her glasses at her granddaughter and then glanced at Shaafia.

Shaafia said "Pia would like for the king to welcome God to the table." This was then repeated in English and everyone looked puzzled. Théophile knew what she meant.

"I will say the grace." he said, standing up and making a small bow to Pia.

"*Amour.*" she replied and waved at him.

He took a moment to gather his thoughts. All day he had been conscious of how his mind was so often out of his control, constantly making him afraid of being discovered. He remembered being in the courtyard in India and experiencing the same fear in facing Padmananda. Now here he was before the one who was his guru. He knew he could no longer be afraid of being discovered. He knew she was homing in on him and he was both relieved and terrified. He let himself become as still as he could and then inwardly he asked : Ashtvakra, please give me the right words. And from there words began to flow. He spoke in English.

"There is a great power that has created the universe and everything in it." He looked at Shaafia and she translated. "This power we call God. It is our desire to be become united with this power that makes us search. We wish to be freed from our not knowing. Therefore, as we come to this table, we thank that power that invites us to rejoin him."

The nuns and his mother responded with an enthusiastic "Amen"

His mother leant over to him with admiration in her eyes. "Never has one heard such beautiful words of grace. My son, you fill me with joy."

As they sipped the cool soup, everyone talked about the grace. The nuns and Madame de Fortelle were parsing what had been said, and Hortensia said she was going to write it down.

Kate was next to Théophile and she asked him where he learned it. They had enjoyed many quiet conversations about their respective searches and her question was one he wanted to answer.

"She gave it to me, just now." he said.

Her eyes widened. "You mean you can hear her too?"

"I don't know." he whispered. "It has only happened just this one time."

They both turned to look at Pia who was being fed by her mother. She seemed to be totally absorbed in the movement of the spoon. Shaafia noticed their shift of attention, and she smiled and put her fingers up to her lips. Kate and Théophile both nodded, knowing that after dinner there would be something interesting to find out.

The evening was still hot so the group went for a walk in the oak woods, where the air was much cooler. Claire carried Pia across the ground that was too uneven for the wheelchair. As they walked, Pia sang "*Coo-coo!*" every now and then as if she was talking to the trees. Théophile wondered if she was seeing something they couldn't see.

They came to the small stream, now reduced by the summer heat to a trickle. They all took their shoes off and dipped their toes in the narrow runnels of water, still cold enough to make them squeal. Claire put Pia's feet into the water but she didn't like it, yelling "Nah!" Then they all sat on the grassy bank and gazed up into the massive oaks and elms that towered overhead.

After a moment Shaafia said "Pia says we are arriving at the centre."

This took everyone by surprise. Claire who was holding her daughter, tilted her back so they could make eye contact.

"Would you care to say a bit more about that?"

The small fingers caressed her mother's face and she purred "*Amour.*"

"She says" went on Shaafia, "we have come from the outside, and now we approach the middle."

Théophile found his heart pumping, streams of thoughts and images were coursing through his mind. Were they from her or was it just his imagination getting out of hand? Then he was sure of the source and it began to flow out of him. "We were all wandering," he said, "lost somewhere and we all wanted to find the heart. Pia is the one who can show us."

"*Amour.*"

"The heart" continued Théophile, allowing what was flowing through him to come out without hindrance. "The heart is the centre. We each wish to know the heart, to live in the heart, to become the heart."

"*Amour.*"

Shaafia, whose face was radiant as she bathed in the relief and the comfort of no longer being the sole transmitter, added "Pia is very happy that the king can hear her voice at last."

Claire was staring at him. "You can hear her too?"

He nodded.

Then she looked down at Pia. "Why won't you speak to me?"

"*Amour.*"

"Or me?" asked Kate and she had tears in her eyes.

"*Amour.*"

Shaafia said "The mothers do not need to hear the words. The words enter their hearts without words."

"Mmm." said Claire and held her daughter close.

Théophile closed his eyes, listening to the trickles of the water at his feet and he had a vision. He was indeed the king. He was Janaka, he was surrounded by courtiers who were bowing to him. And then he saw the entrance of Ashtavakra, bent and misshapen, barely able to walk. He saw the courtiers laughing in derision, but he, King Janaka, did not. He bowed reverently before his Guru.

When Théophile opened his eyes, Pia was watching him. His love for her pounded through him. His heart was on fire.

She whispered "*Amour*", and he said it back, with all his heart.

XXXI

By the first week of August, the air was hot and dry, and all work had ceased on the château. The workers had gone off for *les vacances* with their families, heading to the coast with their caravans and tents to whichever resort was their family tradition. Although France is a secular state, the doctrine of the summer vacation is universally and religiously observed.

The scaffolding had been dismantled, the elevators had been trucked out and all the exterior work had been completed. Before they left, the three Costauds had come to say *"Au revoir et bons vacances"* to everyone. Their families were going to live in a rambling house owned by the Costauds for generations. The house was near Saint-Georges-de-Didonne, where the Charente Maritime looks out to the Atlantic and across to the northern-most tip of the Medoc at Le-Verdon-sur-mer. As Sister Albertine explained, obviously quite happy not to be going, the extended Costaud family had been gathering there every summer since she was born, the lot of them jammed into the old *maison bourgeois,* filling the house with children and dogs playing and fighting, mothers yelling, smells of fresh fish cooking and endless sand being ground into the wooden floors.

Now a quiet descended on the château that was as delicious as the cool within the stone walls. Everyone pitched in to clean away as much of the dust and workers' mess as they could,. Nonetheless the dust still bothered Pia, and she seemed to be coughing more and more. This cough began to concern Claire, and she talked about it with Kate. Kate was not so worried, but she admitted that there had been more blood appearing when Pia coughed. Claire was at the point of deciding to find an English-speaking paediatrician when Pia herself intervened.

It happened on a day when Shaafia had gone with Sister Geneviève to organise the transfer of money that she wished to give as her *zakat.* This was another opportunity to speak with her family on a telephone call organised by the nun. As always Shaafia was shy about accepting the generosity of others, and as always the nun brushed her reluctance aside. So the phone call had been made and Shaafia had told her father that she would be sending money to repay her brother-in-law Ahmed and also her *zakat,* her debt promised to God. Her father solemnly told her that she had chosen the perfect time. In just one week it would be *Eid Il Fitr,* the end of Ramadan and the most auspicious day of the whole year to give *zakat.*

In a flood of memory Shaafia saw the wrinkled face of the healer when she had been so young. "One day…" she had said. And now here it was. She could barely contain her emotion as her father blessed her in his formal way, and she silently shed tears as he spoke. Then he was gone.

She went into the convent chapel to sit quietly and it was there that Pia came to her. *There is no value in this body.* The words seemed to echo from the walls of the chapel, caught in the dust whorls of the summer light, glinting blue from the stained glass windows. Shaafia looked up at the tortured body of the Jesus on his cross. It too was thin and angular, just like Pia.

This body is in service to love. Pia's voice was clear and yet it seemed linked to the body above the altar. Two powerful thoughts arose in Shaafia's mind. Now she understood perhaps why Christians worshipped that statue. And she also understood that Pia did not wish that anything be done about the condition of her own body.

When she returned to the château and heard Claire discussing how to find a paediatrician, Shaafia said: "Pia does not want that you find a doctor. It is not useful."

Claire was surprised. She looked at Kate who shrugged and said "Better ask her."

Théophile had taken Pia into the chapel and was showing her the statue of the Durga. He sat with her on his lap and she held the statue. He kept his hands close in case she dropped it. He was talking to her in English, but not as he would have to a child. It was like speaking to an adult, to someone he knew understood totally. She lay back against his chest holding the statue firmly and caressing the tiger.

"Her eyes stared at me when I went into that temple." he was saying. "She knew who I was, she knew what I had done, she knew I had wasted my life."

"*Naah*", said Pia, dragging out the one syllable.

He hugged her. "Oh yes, I know. It wasn't really the statue, it was me. It was me, as her, looking at me. Like me looking in the mirror."

She continued to stroke the tiger. "*Amour.*" she purred.

Claire, Kate and Shaaifa came in together. "Are we interrupting something?" Claire asked, obviously joking.

"Not at all." Théophile said. "Just the king and his teacher talking about tigers."

"Well, Your Majesty," Claire came and sat next to Théophile, "we have a question for Pia."

"*Nah!*" said Pia and very nearly dropped the statue. Théophile grabbed it as it slipped from her grasp.

"What do you mean, my darling?" Claire said, looking Pia in the eye.

Shaafia and Théophile spoke in unison: "Pia says…" Then they stopped and laughed. Pia laughed with them, and neither Claire nor Kate could suppress their smiles.

"So now you can talk in stereo!" Kate said as the laughter faded.

"*Haay.*" said Pia and leant over towards Kate for a hug. As Kate picked her up Théophile glanced at Shaafia who nodded. Then he said "Pia asks that we not take her to a doctor. It is not what she wishes."

"That's clear enough", Claire said. "But not even for a check-up?"

"*Nah!*" was the response, low and guttural.

Shaafia added "She says the doctor would see only what is physical. Doctors are trapped in the world of the body."

Kate smiled, thinking of all the doctors she had known.

Claire said "Okay, you win."

XXXII

On the thirteenth of August, they packed bags for the trip to Lourdes and drove *en famille* in the Mercedes van to the convent. Towering over the fountain with the small stone birds was a massive red and gold coach with its underside doors open, where Sister Marie-Louise was stowing the bags of the nuns. The driver of the coach, who rightly should have been doing the work, had obviously been told to back off, so he lounged in the shade of a liquid amber tree and smoked.

As Théophile and Kate helped to load the family's bags and Pia's chair, the nuns greeted them all excitedly. Madame de Fortelle was glad to see Father Lefait, who throughout the summer had been largely absent. She told him how happy she was, to be going once again to Lourdes and this time bringing her family. Her granddaughter, she told him, was a wonderful child and maybe, by God's grace and the intercession of Our Lady, something miraculous could happen. "It is possible, don't you think?" she said, smiling warmly at him.

The priest held himself erect and inclined his head. "*Tout est possible.*" Then he excused himself and went into the chapel to avoid any further contact with the rest of the family. Shaafia noticed and so did Sister Geneviève. The nun smiled at her.

"I believe we will have a most beautiful visit to Our Lady." she said quietly to Shaafia, "I believe that all of us will achieve many things there. I am certain that in the company of our dear Pia, this will be a journey to remember."

In celebration of their midsummer outing, every nun was wearing sunglasses, as if they had added a new requirement to their habits. As Claire carried Pia into the bus, the nuns made a rather undignified scramble for the seats closest to her. This meant that Kate, Shaafia and Théophile ended up in the back of the bus with Madame de Fortelle and the priest. Father Lefait had hurried past Pia and had sunk low into his seat opening his briefcase and taking out a newspaper. The driver climbed into his seat, smelling nastily of whatever he had just smoked, and closed the doors. He glanced up into his huge rear vision mirror ready to go, but Sister Geneviève stood up at the front.

"Let us take a moment to ask our blessings for this journey." she said, having to raise her voice as the driver uncharitably gunned the engine. "*Monsieur.*" She turned on him. "*S'il vous plait.*" He was no match for her severity and he meekly turned the engine off.

Father Lefait looked up as if he thought he was expected to lead the blessing but into the silence Pia's little voice wafted through the bus.

"*Amour.*"

Instantly the entire bus, except for the priest and the driver, picked it up and the choral intonations gathered in strength until Sister Geneviève judged they had taken its course.

"*Merci* Pia." the nun said. "Our journey is surely blessed." and Sister Geneviève nodded to the driver and he restarted the engine.

The coach swept down the driveway under the shade of the platanes, brushing the branches on either side and out onto the narrow road beyond. The coach was so wide any vehicle coming the other way had to move off to the side.

Soon it was on the freeway, which would take them directly to Lourdes. It was a brand new freeway that had just been opened from Langon to Tarbes and was remarkably empty. The big coach powered along at maximum speed and its passengers were soon lulled into the somnolence of long distance road travel. There was not much to see as the freeway traversed the vast pine forests of les Landes and skirted the towns of Mont de Marsan and Pau, before turning off just before Tarbes. As the bus passed through the tollgate, *le péage*, the nuns became animated.

Sister Agnés who had been a little slow in mounting the bus and was therefore sitting towards the back, leaned over to Shaafia. "We are very close now. Soon you will see the snow of the Pyrenees. In twenty minutes we will be there."

Shaafia passed the message to the others and they all looked eagerly out of the windows for their first glances of the snow. And soon enough there they were, hidden in the haze of the hot August sun but visible. The Pyrenees make up the youngest mountain range in the world and are therefore sharply pointed.

For Kate and for Shaafia, it was the first time they had ever seen snow. "Oh my God!" Kate exclaimed. "This is so beautiful."

The big coach took a detour round the narrow streets of Lourdes itself, until it reached the far side and began to climb away from the town up a perilously narrow winding road until it turned into a wide gateway, which presaged a park-like setting with long white buildings sheltered under broad oaks.

Holding firmly to the seat beside her, as the coach moved up the driveway, Sister Geneviève stood up and faced the back of the bus. "*Voici la cité de Saint Pierre. Bienvenu.*"

Pia had slept the entire three hours of the journey. Now she came to life, as the nuns began to stand up and gather their belongings. Many of them stopped as they passed her, to say "*Bienvenu à Lourdes.*" Pia responded with her "*Coo-coo*", and they were delighted.

Her chair was retrieved from under the coach and Sister Geneviève led them, trailing their baggage, into the reception area. A jolly woman with a Spanish accent introduced herself as Adoracion and welcomed them all. The business of key allocation and the scrutiny of maps of the retreat site took a while to be sorted out, but pair by pair, the new arrivals headed for their rooms. Claire had been given a double room with Pia. When she saw this, she dropped down to be at the same height as her daughter in the wheelchair. "Can I sleep with you?" she asked.

Pia's good eye came to rest on her mother. "*Ha.*" she said and her mother kissed her.

Kate and Shaafia were to share a room and they set off together using their map to find it. As they walked, Kate looked up to the towering peaks above them.

"This is incredible." she said. "They are so high and so, I don't know, massive. It makes you feel small doesn't it?"

Shaafia smiled. "In my country, we have mountains with snow but I have never been there. It is amazing that it is so hot here but there is snow up there."

They stood together gazing upwards. Some of peaks had concrete bunkers on them.

Kate said "What do you think those are?" Just then Sisters Hortensia and Catherine walked past trailing their little carry-on suitcases, and Shaafia asked them.

"Ah." Catherine said, propping her suitcase up, "I will explain. They are facing south and they were built in a time when that was the direction the enemy might come. They have big guns in them."

"South?" Kate asked. "Who were they pointing at?"

"Spain."

"Do you mean Spain was the enemy?"

"For us in France, at one time or another, everyone has been the enemy."

Sister Hortensia added "It is why we are always cautious with strangers". Then she smiled. "But we always warmly welcome our friends, no matter where they come from."

Once they had stowed away their belongings, everyone gathered in the big dining hall for lunch, Sister Geneviève, quietly alerting Shaafia to the chips of *lardon,* pig fat, in the rice dish. Shaafia thanked her warmly. "Today is *Eid Il Fitr* in our tradition." she said "It is the day of eating. Ramadan has concluded."

Grace was offered by the priest, who came in at the last minute and placed himself as far from Pia as he could.

Once lunch was over, topped off with a massive *créme caramèl* passed from table to table, so everyone could help themselves, Sister Geneviève stood to announce that they would walk down the hill to the town for their first visit to the holy sites. Everyone scattered to find hats and sunglasses and then amassed under the mighty elm that shaded the reception centre.

A gentle breeze drifted down from the peaks, which had become veiled by the afternoon haze. It was as if, having impressed the new arrivals, they had withdrawn to their higher realms.

The company was soon strung out along the narrow winding road above the town, Sister Marie-Louise begging to be the one who pushed Pia's chair. As they walked, the nuns pointed out the most important features. Hidden in the clouds was Le Pic de Jers, with its century-old funicular railway climbing to a restaurant on the top. After the feast of the Ascension of Our Lady, they promised, they would ascend themselves and go to that restaurant. To the right of the town was the old grey-stone fortress, over which battles had been fought in the middle ages. Perched on top of a rocky outcrop above the river Gave, it had resisted even Simon de Montfort in the year 1216. To the left could be seen the steeple of the Basilica built in honour of the apparition and in between was a mass of buildings jammed into the cleft of the valley. "More than two hundred hotels." said Sister Agnés, walking beside Shaafia. "And not one good enough to stay in." Sister Hortensia said with a mild sneer, walking behind. "They boast four stars but none of them is worth more than two."

Certainly as they entered the town, it was clear that every building seemed to house a hotel, boasting plaques with names like "Hotel des Pyrenees" or "Hotel de la Vision Sublime". Each hotel consisted only of an entrance, because the front of every building was occupied by endless souvenir shops, restaurants or the offices of a plethora of Catholic institutions. The narrow curving streets dropping steeply down towards the river offered infinite opportunities to purchase candles, statues, rosaries, framed pictures and holy water bottles in the shape of the Virgin, where you could screw her hat off to fill them.

The nuns were familiar with all this and took not much notice, but to Kate, Claire and Shaafia everything was exotic and begging to be explored. The whole party stopped often, blocking the entire street while one of them looked at an intriguingly sculpted candle or the garishly coloured portrait of some saint or other. Pia seemed indrawn and bounced along in her chair over the cobbled streets without giving any outward signs of interest. When the party stopped again, while Kate and Claire were drawn to a huge showy picture of Jesus with coloured lights flashing round it, Father Lefait, who had been hovering at the outskirts of the group, made a decision. He motioned to Sister Geneviève and she made her way through the group to stand next to him.

"I wish to ask you something." He took a step away from the group and she followed him. "Our sisters are very attentive to this poor child and it is very touching. I do not wish to question what she has said, including, as you know, what she has said to me."

Sister Geneviève's face was a carefully composed study of diplomatic neutrality.

"I have the impulse" the priest continued in an undertone, "to intercede on her behalf. I am sure that Our Lady will look favourably upon her. I would like to purchase a candle for the child so that she may pray to Our Lady for her mercy and her grace."

"It is a wonderful impulse, Father."

"You do not think it too unorthodox?" He was frowning as he thought about this. "She is, after all, not a Catholic."

Managing to control her desire to smile, Sister Geneviève said "I believe it would be a very generous gesture."

"Then it shall be so." With that, he walked into a souvenir shop and bought a tall white candle. When he returned to the group, he stood in front of Pia's chair.

"I wish to offer zis candle." the priest said in his awkward English and bowed to Pia. Her good eye focussed and she said "Nah!" very forcefully so that the group spun round to see what she was doing. The priest found himself in the centre of the group holding his candle. Shaafia edged closer to the chair so she could speak to him. She was still wary of him but she took courage from the big group of nuns around her.

"Pia asks that you keep the candle." She saw a frown darken his face but she pressed on. "It is because your brother is burning, and he waiting for you on his knees. You must give it to him."

This made no sense at all and the priest looked flustered. "I do not understand."

Pia said "*Amour*" and Shaafia added "She asks you to carry it for her and she will show you".

Father Lefait stared down at Pia, then he bowed his head. "*D'accord.*" he said. As the group continued down the hill, he felt compelled to walk beside her, holding the candle like a crucifix and feeling decidedly ridiculous.

Crossing the rushing blue snow-fed waters of the Gave, and threading through one more lane of creperies and statuettes, they came to the entrance of the holy site.

Here groups of people were funnelling in through the wide iron gates and descending the last slope to arrive at the enormous open space in front of the Basilica. Théophile was struck by the irony of seeing so many Indians. He had gone to India to find his spiritual inspiration, and here were Indians coming to France to find theirs.

The nuns formed a wide phalanx behind Sister Marie-Louise pushing Pia's chair with the priest striding beside it, joining several other parties following their own wheelchairs. Some carried children, others held older people a few of whom were decidedly cadaverous. Other pilgrims made their way on crutches and several inert patients were wheeled on gurneys.

The nuns were keen to take Pia to the grotto where the sighting of the Virgin had taken place, so they pushed through the crowd in front of the Basilica, round various stalls selling different sized candles of the kind that the priest had bought for Pia. Beyond the Basilica, which stood on the edge of a cliff, the space opened out again into a wide sun-drenched plaza, where on one side the river Gave had looped back and on the other the cliff-face under the Basilica sheltered a row of taps where people were lining up to fill their bottles with holy water. At the centre of the cliff was *La Grotte de Massabielle*, the Cave of the Apparition.

"Voilà!" said Sister Geneviève drawing closer to Pia's chair. Pia jerked in her chair as if surprised, but it was nothing to do with Sister Geneviève's invitation. Instead she was pointing to the centre of the plaza, where, on his knees, the sweat pouring from his forehead, a priest in black vestments knelt. His bare head, showing the beginnings of sunburn, was bowed in prayer, his hands clasped in front of him.

The group around Pia stopped and looked at Shaafia expectantly.

"This is the brother, the one who has need of the candle." Shaafia said, willing herself to look at the priest with his candle. "Pia says you should kneel with him and tell him you know his pain."

With all eyes on him, the priest bowed to Pia again.

His voice husky with emotion, Father Lefait said "I will do as she asks." They watched him as he approached the kneeling supplicant. He knelt next to him, holding the candle. The group stood around them at a discrete distance, forming a kind of human amphitheatre. The sweating priest did not open his eyes or waver in his concentration.

Pia said "*Amour*" and then "*Ha!*"

Shaafia said in quite a loud voice, "Pia says we should not stare at them. They are talking to God."

Obediently the group moved on towards the Grotte, leaving the two men on their knees in the sun.

There was a very long line of people waiting to go into the shallow cave, where they could walk past the spot where the Virgin had instructed Saint Bernadette to dig the hole for water, now protected by a chain and a security guard. Once past that, they could then kiss the rock under the statue, which stood on the ledge where the Virgin had appeared. The line was mostly in the sun and Sister Geneviève decided it was not a good time to join it.

"We can see her from here", she said leading the group closer to the Grotte, where banks of chairs were placed so people could sit in prayer before the statue. That too was in the sun. They all stood behind the chains guarding the outer edge of the Grotte and many of the nuns closed their eyes in prayer.

Kate knelt down next to Pia and asked "Does she look like this when you see her?"

Pia tipped her head sideways and said "*Nah!*"

Théophile, who was on the other side, said "Pia says she sees her as light, not as a body. The body has no value."

Pia said "*Amour*" and began coughing powerfully. Kate gave her some drops and wiped her sweating face and the coughing subsided. Claire thought perhaps the sun was too strong for her. The group then moved away from the Grotte and gathered under the shadow of the cliff-face farther down.

Many of the nuns had brought water bottles with them and they decided this was the moment to fill them. So while the family rested, the nuns went off to the lines at the taps. Sister Geneviève and Sister Marie-Louise stayed behind.

"We are great believers in the healing power of this water", Sister Geneviève said. "Many are the stories of miracles that have taken place with just one sip. It is my belief that Pia's cough will go away when she drinks some of it."

"I hope so", Claire said. "She worries me."

<h1 style="text-align:center">XXXIII</h1>

As the afternoon cooled and the shadows lengthened, the family sipped the holy water that the nuns had collected and a peace descended on the group. They sat in the shade of the cliff-face, not far from the statue of the Virgin, watching the crowds of pilgrims pass by, chattering in a dozen different languages, the Italians louder than anyone else. Lourdes had drawn pilgrims from around the world, many of them carrying candles to burn in the pavilions set up for that purpose.

Claire found a straw and inserted it into a bottle of the holy water and gave it to Pia, who sipped a little then stroked her mother's face. Shaafia was close by and said quietly "Pia says, you have been the perfect mother."

Claire smiled and took her daughter's tiny hand in her own. "You amaze me." she said. "You are truly amazing."

Pia purred *"Amour"*, losing the straw, and then she made an effort to find it and and sucked on it. After a moment she looked up again, the straw still in her mouth, and said "Haay!"

Kate responded. "What's up?"

"Amour." said Pia and leaned over towards her. Kate knelt down and gave her a hug. She rested in Kate's embrace for a moment then pulled back and sucked on her straw.

The crowds of nuns and brothers, families with children, nurses pushing gurneys and wheelchairs flowed by and through the throng came Father Lefait. He had brought the other priest with him. They were both sweating profusely, and the priest who had been kneeling in the sun was now bright red in the face. He carried the candle out in front of him as if he was leading a procession.

As they approached Pia, everyone turned to watch.

"I wish to introduce you my bruzzer." said Father Lefait, looking down at Pia in her wheelchair. "He is from America."

"I…er, I…" The priest seemed unable to get his tongue to work.

"Zis is Fazzer Benedict from Cincinnati." Father Lefait felt called upon to render assistance. "As you see, 'e 'as ze candle."

"Um, yes." Father Benedict made a concerted effort. "Thank you very much. I am very moved by, by…" He licked his lips and Sister Agnés passed him a bottle of holy water. He poured a little into his hand and wiped his face with it.

"Thank you." he said bowing his head to the nun.

Pia was lying back in her chair, sipping water through her straw. Now she spat it out and leaned out. "*Coo-coo.*" she said towards the American.

He smiled at her and said "Hi".

Théophile spoke. "This is Pia and she would like to tell you something."

"Oh yes?" The priest came forward and leaned, expecting Pia to speak.

Théophile took a step, bringing himself to the priest's side, and squatted down. He was at the same level as Pia and looking up at the American. "Pia tells you that this priest", gesturing toward Father Lefait, "he must tell you of his own pain. It is the same as yours."

The priest looked confused, looking from Théophile to Pia. "Sorry," he said. "I don't get it."

Théophile said "Pia says this to you."

"This little girl?"

"It is what she wishes you to know. She says God has heard you calling to him."

The priest looked at Théophile. "What does it mean?"

"She knows what you are praying for."

The sweat flowed down the man's face and he found a handkerchief to wipe it.

Father Lefait moved forward to stand beside his brother priest. "Listen to 'er." he said quietly.

Théophile said "Pia tells you to burn this candle and the sin that was not in fact a sin, the one that fills you with guilt, it will be burnt away."

As the American priest stared down at the small girl with one eye wandering in its socket, surrounded by a company of silent nuns, something opened in him and he sank to his knees. There was an audible sigh from the circle that had formed around him and everything became still.

And then Pia began to cough blood, a lot of blood, and people leapt up. Kate had the cloth out and Claire was ready with the bottle of drops but the blood kept flowing. Sister Marie-Louise turned and ran. Sister Agnés came behind Pia and gently sprinkled drops of the holy water on her head. Several of the nuns went down on their knees and began to pray aloud. Others quickly picked it up. The two priests, backing away from the wheelchair to give her some space, kneeled with the nuns and joined in the prayer. Sister Geneviève stood with Madame de Fortelle who was looking panic stricken. The big nun took her hand and held it as they prayed together.

Théophile and Shaafia looked at each other with horrified faces and they both moved to be behind Pia so that everyone could see them.

"Pia asks you to listen carefully." Théophile spoke as loudly as he dared, to make sure they all heard him.

The murmured prayers ceased and the circle focussed inward.

Shaafia said "Pia tells you, do not be afraid."

"The lady in blue and white is here." said Théophile. A ripple of excitement radiated from the group. Théophile went on "She has said to Pia: Now you are free to go."

The electricity pulsing in and through the group was palpable, but it was as if they were in an enclosed, secluded, impenetrable sphere. The crowds of pilgrims moved back and forth across the plaza, passing the group, seemingly unaware.

Sister Marie-Louise reappeared, running with a man in a white coat carrying a white box with a red cross on it. She burst into the group but was struck by the power of the silence that greeted her. The doctor nearly crashed into her and she grabbed his arm to hold him.

At the centre of the sphere, the front of her T-shirt soaked in blood, sat Pia, now upright in her chair. Her good eye moved from one to another in the circle searching for them, one after the other. She seemed to be full of light radiating out towards each one. Her other eye became still, then it turned down and became focussed.

There was a collective in-breath of astonishment in the circle around her.

Théophile felt an enormous rush of energy fill his body and he called out *"Le corps humain est un fardeau lourd."*

Suddenly the small body erupted out of the chair. There was a moment when she stood somehow upright, free standing, her two eyes, now in intense focus, swept around the circle, searing into one after another of those gazing at her. The nuns, the priests, Shaafia, Théophile, Kate and then Claire, each was held in the powerful lock of her gaze

Then her eyes rolled upward and she crashed to the stone plaza.

A collective wail rose from the circle, a cry of grief and loss.

The crumpled tiny, thin, empty body lay in a pool of blood.

PIA

I t is done.

Now at last I have let go of this body. This blood-soaked rag. I am its prisoner no more. I am free to fly back to those beings in whose love I was so sweetly cradled.

This poor body, these angular limbs, the brittle bones, what little flesh it bore, falls away. It will become the unidentifiable scattered fragments of its completed incarnation. Dead leaves in the wind.

I am grateful to this body, fragile as it was. It was the chosen vehicle; not my choice, but it was the way it had to be. I have struggled to accept it, to triumph over its limitations, to reach out through it and beyond it. It was the body I had to have. When other people looked at this body, they saw it as being handicapped, unfortunate.

Now I look at it lying there, in its bloody pool. It is not me. It was never really me. Here where I can float, here where I am at last in the presence of Antoine, my dear Antoine, and my Daddy, here there is no handicap.

I can ascend now, unembodied, as they were, as they are now, in that ethereal body that carries no weight. I will glide with them effortlessly in the realms of air and light. The lady in blue and white beckons to me. We, she and I, will ascend together.

The work is done. The ones who looked for me, they have found me, each in their own way and I am happy. I see each one, even now, though they will miss me, their light is shining out of them. They don't need me now and they can go wherever they are supposed to go and they can share that light. My blessings go with them. Because of them, now I can go. They have given me my freedom. And I have given them theirs.

I will speak no more.
The message of love has been passed on.
We are all free to go.
I was Pia and I came for Love.

Author's Notes

Novels that focus on the spiritual search present a delicate challenge: how much description of an acutely personal spiritual experience is readable and credible? Belief systems are endless and idiosyncratic, so a novel in which different credos intersect allows at least the possibility that somewhere in there the reader will find something to identify with. Of course at the deepest level, there is no difference, all paths ultimately lead to the same ineffable conclusion, of which no description can do justice.

The two inspiring spiritual seekers to whom this book is dedicated have been wonderful role models of how we each must discover our own unique unfolding path to the heart. Thank you Khadija and Lorie for your unwavering faith in your own journeys, the love you both embody and light you both bring to those around you.

Quotations from the *Ashtavakra Samhita* are my own renderings drawn from the generous translation by John Richards, which he has offered to the public domain with his affection. As he says, the work has been a constant inspiration in his life for many years. He offers it in the hope that it "May be so for many others". His version is accessible via www.realization.org .

All descriptions of women's aboriginal spiritual practices are entirely fictional, created to suit the trajectory of the narration and in no way does any of it pretend to be knowingly accurate of the rituals that still take place today and for which I have the utmost respect.

Descriptions of the ashram in Goa are also entirely imaginary and are not intended to relate to any known ashram. Having travelled widely in India, it's an amalgam of many I have seen, but no one in particular.

I welcome input from readers via email rudra.sharp@laposte.net or through my website www.alastairsharp.com

Finally thank you, you who hold this book in your hand. May the deep pleasure the unfoldment of this story has brought to me, be transferable, no matter what spiritual inclination you find yourself pursuing. May you reach your goal. May your journey to the heart be achieved. And if in some small way, reading this book has been an inspiration, well so much the better!

And then, if the impetus is there, a sequel awaits you. « Spreading Wings » came as a surprise to me. When I reached the conclusion that you have just read, I felt that was the conclusion but not so. Pia has a lot more to do. A lot more.

Alastair Sharp
Bordeaux
2020

www.ingramcontent.com/pod-product-compliance
Lightning Source LLC
Chambersburg PA
CBHW071144100726
47908CB00002B/246